DUDLEY PUBLIC LIBRARIES

The loan of this book may be renewed if not required by other readers, by contacting the library from which it was borrowed.

CP/494

D0419996

A Cinderella Story

COLLECTION

A Modern Cinderella

TRISH WYLIE

KATE HARDY

BARBARA WALLACE

MIX
Paper from
responsible sources
FSC
FSC C007454

This book is produced from independently certified FSC™ paper
to ensure responsible forest management.

For more information visit: www.harpercollins.co.uk/green

Printed and bound in Spain
by CPI, Barcelona

MILLS & BOON

First Published in Great Britain 2020
By Mills & Boon, an imprint of HarperCollins*Publishers*
1 London Bridge Street, London, SE1 9GF

A MODERN CINDERELLA © 2020 Harlequin Books S.A.

His L.A. Cinderella © 2009 Trish Wylie
His Shy Cinderella © 2017 Pamela Brooks
A Millionaire for Cinderella © 2015 Barbara Wallace

ISBN: 978-0-263-28066-1

HIS L.A. CINDERELLA

TRISH WYLIE

For my new friend Lisa from Warner Bros.
Studios for the behind the scenes tour.

CHAPTER ONE

THERE he was: the infamous Will Ryan.

Pathetically, her palms felt clammy. Though that could just have been the horrible cold she'd picked up on her way to California, she supposed…

But, truthfully, Cassidy Malone couldn't remember the last time she'd felt so nervous or self-conscious. Or so completely incapable of fooling people into thinking she was more self-confident than she actually was. She really needed the latter if she was going to stand a chance of pulling off the deception of a lifetime. And if she couldn't do it in the land of make-believe, then where could she? If she just didn't have this stupid cold to add to everything else. Who flew halfway across the planet to a place twenty degrees warmer than home and ended up with a cold? She felt awful. So much for the theory that she would feel more confident away from home, where nobody knew her…

But therein lay her immediate problem. Because the man making his way across the beautiful lobby of the Beverly Wilshire knew her all too well. A decade ago he'd known every inch of her body intimately, and had held her heart in the palm of his large hand—the same heart that now jumped in joyous recognition and then twisted in regret at how comfortable *he* looked in their surroundings.

Cassidy was incredibly jealous of that.

Will didn't so much as bat an eyelid at the white marble, the large chandelier, the carved wooden elevator doors or the polished brass and black accents. *I belong here*, his confident stride said silently. But then Cassidy couldn't remember a time when there'd ever been a place he *hadn't* had that air of self-assurance. He'd always had a way of carrying himself that practically dared people to say he was somewhere he didn't belong.

That confidence, and the hint of potential danger if pushed, had added to his potent sexuality from the very beginning as far as Cassidy was concerned. Add boyish good-looks and a smile that could genuinely melt female knees… He'd been the flame and she the moth. But to see him so at home in a place where she felt so very lost… Well, it just widened the already cavernous gap between them, didn't it?

Ridiculously, it hurt. When it really shouldn't have. Not after so long…

His bright green gaze sought her out and brushed non-chalantly from her head to her toes and back up again, forcing her to suck in her stomach and silently pray that he couldn't see any sign of the foundation underwear she'd struggled her way into. Like every woman Cassidy knew, every inch counted in times of crisis—even though she had absolutely no idea where those missing inches had been re-located *to*. With any luck Will would keep their meetings to places where there was air-conditioning, so she stood a better chance of not passing out in the California heat and the thin air of Los Angeles. Restricted circulation plus bunged-up nose didn't exactly give her a head start…

Mentally she crossed her fingers.

'Cass.'

He held out a ridiculously large hand when he got to her, and for a second Cassidy looked down at it with an arched brow, as if confused by what she was supposed to do with it. They were *shaking hands*? Like complete strangers? *Really?*

Okay, then.

Surreptitiously swiping a clammy palm on her hip, she placed it in his; the heat of long fingers curled around her cooler ones, sending another jolt of recognition through her veins to her heart. Good to know her body hadn't forgotten him either. She tried to think professional thoughts. It wasn't easy. But she had to *work* with this man.

Will let go of her hand somewhat abruptly. 'Recovered from your flight?'

'Yes. Thank you. I think it's easier this way than going back.'

'Happy with the hotel?'

'How could I not be?' She glanced around, but couldn't stop her gaze from shifting back to study him. Still boyish. He hadn't aged a day. How was that fair?

Will nodded, and glanced around him the way she had. 'It has a history firmly tied up in Hollywood. Dashiell Hammet wrote *The Thin Man* here. Elvis lived here while making movies at Paramount, and they've had everyone from members of the British royal family to the Dalai Lama stay at one time or another.'

'That's nice.' Inwardly she rolled her eyes as the words slipped off the tip of her tongue. Eloquent, Cassidy. Way to go. But, however foolish she felt, it was nothing in comparison to how stunned she was by his coolness. It was like talking to a tour guide. An uninvolved, unattached and in fairness disgustingly good-looking tour guide. But nevertheless...

'I thought you might appreciate it.'

Cassidy lifted a brow again. Meaning what? That she should be thanking her lucky stars she was here in the first place? True. But she didn't need to be made to feel as if she'd been invited to Tinsel Town by some miraculous accident. Some *timely* miraculous accident, she corrected. Because she couldn't have needed a break more if she'd tried.

He was right, though. She'd been as thrilled by the hotel as she had by her first glimpse of the Hollywood sign on the hill. Located only a few steps away from the glittering shops of Rodeo Drive, she knew the famous hotel's ornate European façade, with its distinctly rounded awnings and rows of sculpted trees, was straight out of the pages of Hollywood history—not to mention being the site of one of her favourite films of all time. It was just a shame she wasn't going to be there at Christmas, when they reportedly did an outstanding job of decorating, transforming its exterior into a dazzling display of twinkling lights.

By then she'd probably have been discovered as a fraud and sent home with her tail between her legs—back to eating rice and pasta like she had in her student days, while she'd waited for her grant money to arrive. Only this time she'd be waiting for meager pay-cheques that couldn't support the debts she had after caring for her father before he died. Well, now, *there* was something to look forward to.

'Ready?'

She nodded as Will swung a long arm in invitation and allowed her to step ahead of him. Squinting at the bright light outside, she took her sunglasses off the top of her head moments after Will donned his. A California necessity, she'd discovered since she'd landed. And as much of a status symbol as everything else, judging by the designer wear everyone but her had shading their eyes.

Silently, they turned right—Will matching his longer stride to hers—then right again at a major light, until they approached a strip of nice-looking semi-casual restaurants. Will's choice was an ivy-covered courtyard, where the *maître d'* greeted him by name and held out chairs for them before unfurling linen napkins onto their laps and handing them leather-bound menus with a flourish and a small bow.

Cassidy fought the need to giggle like a schoolgirl. At the grand old age of thirty, she should be more mature. 'Well, this beats cheese sandwiches in the park.'

Thick dark lashes flickered upwards from their study of the menu. They brushed his deeply tanned skin once, twice, and then he quirked his brows a minuscule amount and continued reading. 'That was a long time ago.'

Seeing him again, it felt like yesterday to her. But she didn't say that. Instead she allowed herself a moment to surreptitiously examine him while he made a decision on what to eat. Had he got sexier as he'd got older? Yes, she decided, he had. Darn it. Men were known to do that. Wasn't the fact he was more successful than her, richer than her and plainly more confident than her enough? At least one of them had got it right. Small consolation, though.

It was tough not to be as mesmerised by the sight of him as she had been at twenty. And twenty-one. And twenty-two. From the thick dark hair that curled disobediently outwards at his nape, all the way down the lean six foot three of his body, he was one of those guys blessed with the ability to mesmerise woman. Who could have blamed her for the crush she'd had from a distance for over a year? Or for how shy she'd been when he'd first talked to her during a group project in their screenwriting class? Or how…?

'Do you know what you want?' Will asked, in a low rumble that sent a sudden shiver up her spine.

The spine she straightened a little in her chair. Because, yes, actually—she did know what she wanted. She had a list, as it happened. High up on it was the ability to make the most of an opportunity when it came e-mailing her way, without blowing it by drooling all over the man who had long since left her behind. So now he'd given her an opening, it seemed as good a time as any to ask:

'A better idea of what the studio expects from me would be nice.' She even managed to tack on a smile when he looked at her again. See—she could do confident if she tried.

Will took a breath and closed the menu, calmly setting it down on his side-plate as he glanced around at the lunchtime crowd. 'They expect what they paid us that hefty advance for back in the day. We both knew what we were doing when we signed on the dotted line.'

Did *we?* If she'd known the heartache signing that contract would bring her way she wasn't so sure she would go back in time and sign it again. But Cassidy let it slide. 'So, after all this time they suddenly want script three? Just like that? When movie number two pretty much fell flat on its face…'

'At the box office. But thanks to a rabid internet fan base

it made money on long-term residuals. You'd know that from the fact we still get royalty cheques. This time we have the opportunity to be one of those sleepers that might well prove an accidental tent pole, with a good script and the right budget.'

Cassidy blinked at him for a moment, and then confessed, 'I have no idea what you just said.'

He almost smiled. 'Hollywood speak.'

'Is there a dictionary?'

'Not that I'm aware of.'

'Pity.' She tried another smile to see if it had any effect. 'You'll have to translate for me, then.'

'Bottom line?'

Oh, please, yes. 'That might help.'

Something resembling amusement glittered across his amazing eyes. 'They want a script yesterday, and as you and I own the rights jointly to the original copyright we've both got to do it. We're joined at the hip till it's done and they're happy…'

'No pressure, then.'

The wide shoulders beneath his expensive dark jacket lifted and fell in a brief nonchalant shrug. 'We did it before, Cass. We can do it again.'

The tiny word 'we' seemed to tug on a ragged corner of her heart every time he said it in his deep rumble of a voice. Not that it meant anything any more. He probably didn't feel the pressure she did. Why would he? He'd been writing scripts ever since he left—had success after success to his name: award nominations, contracts and his own production company. Whereas she, his former writing partner…?

Well, she had a knack for getting seven-year-olds to

stay quiet, but that was about it. The closest she'd got to writing was putting her lessons on a blackboard…

Automatically she reached for iced water the second a waiter poured it, swallowing a large gulp to dampen her dry mouth. A cold dew of perspiration broke out on her skin while she wondered when was a good time to confess how long it had been since she last written a single original word. Maybe just as well she hadn't unpacked properly yet.

The waiter smiled at her as if he felt her pain. So she smiled back.

Will's voice deepened. 'Have you done much writing?'

Oh, come on! How could he still read her mind when it had been so long since he'd seen her? It was the perfect opening for honesty; yes. But since she already had a shovel in her hand it seemed a shame not to use it.

'Not much scriptwriting. I've dabbled with other stuff.' In that she'd read instructional books—lots of them—to no avail. 'You know how it is. Use it or—'

'Lose it.' He nodded, the corners of his wide mouth tugging in a way that suggested he was fighting off one of the smiles that would addle her thoughts. 'This shouldn't take long, then. If you were rusty it might have taken a while to get you back up to speed.'

Cassidy swallowed more water to stop a confession from slipping free. Had it got warmer all of a sudden? She suddenly felt a little light-headed.

Out of nowhere he added, 'We made a good team once.'

She almost choked, her eyes watering a little as she looked at him and he finally let *that* smile loose. Oh, that was just unfair. She instantly hated him for it. With the white-hot intensity of a million burning suns she hated him for the fact *that* smile could still knock her on her ear. But even more than that she hated him because she'd been *waiting* for it to appear and knock her on her ear. She'd *known*! Had known from the second his name appeared in her In-box that he would have the capability to do damage to her self-control all over again.

But then being attracted to him had never been a problem. It had been his complete lack of availability to commit that had. She wasn't ending up the fool twice. She darn well *wasn't*!

Lifting her chin an inch, she set her glass safely on the white tablecloth and dampened her lips in preparation for saying the right words to make it plain to him it was strictly business between them this time round. After all, if she wanted to be made to look a fool she could do it all by herself. She didn't actually *need* any help.

But her resolve faltered in the sight of *that* smile. Light twinkled in his eyes, fine laughter lines fanned out from their edges, the grooves in his cheeks deepened, and his lips slid back over even teeth that looked even whiter than she remembered when contrasted with the golden hue of his Californian tan.

Put all those things together and it was infectious. Cassidy could even feel the reciprocal upward tug of her own mouth. No, no, *no*—she mustn't smile back. That was how it had started last time.

Will's deep voice added words husky with appreciation. 'You look beautiful—as always…'

The woman inside her so lacking in self-confidence blossomed under the simple, if unfounded praise. She

could feel her skin warming, could feel her heart racing—
could feel her smile breaking loose…

Then a sultry female voice sounded above her head. 'As
always flattery will get you everywhere, Irish boy…'

Whipping her head round, Cassidy found herself staring
up at a face she recognised from movie billboards and TV
screens. The woman wasn't just beautiful, she was perfection. Even without airbrushing.

When Will pushed his chair back, the actress stepped over
to him and kissed each of his cheeks, European-style. 'I
heard you got a green light for your pet project. Bravo, you!'

'You know what I had for breakfast this morning too?'

'Not in a long time.' She aimed a wink at Cassidy, who
smiled weakly in return. 'Not that you haven't been invited
often enough…'

Will remembered his manners. 'Angie—this is Cassidy
Malone. Cass, this is—'

'Angelique Warden. Yes, I know.' Cassidy made the smile
more genuine as she stood up and stretched a hand across
the table. 'It's nice to meet you. I loved your last movie.'

'Shame the box office didn't feel the same way. But
thank you.' Her eyes narrowed momentarily. 'Wait a second.
You're not Cassidy Malone as in *Ryan* and Malone?'

Cassidy's gaze slid briefly to Will and then back. 'A
long time ago…'

'Then the rumour is true? They picked up the option?'

Will nodded, and glanced around him as if it was a state
secret. He even lowered his voice. 'It's not been announced yet, so—'

'Oh, you don't have to tell me, you idiot. *How exciting!*'

Suddenly Cassidy was much more interesting to her than

before, and a matching set of European cheek kisses were bestowed on her before Cassidy could warn her of her cold.

'So nice to meet you. Make him bring you to dinner. I have a million and one questions to ask about the Ryan and Malone years. Will thinks being enigmatic makes him more interesting.'

'Not everyone likes their every move reported in the dailies.'

Still blinking in stunned amazement at having been kissed by one of the highest paid actresses on the globe, Cassidy found her attention caught by the drawl of Will's newfound American twang. The words made her scowl in recrimination. He'd been many things back in the day, but cruel had never been one of them. The famous Angelique Warden had hardly had an easy time with the press in the last year.

But Angelique laughed huskily and batted his upper arm with her designer purse, pouting and rolling her eyes. 'Yes, but it's such a joy for the rest of us. Dinner. Saturday. Bring your partner. I'm going to learn all your darkest secrets.'

'No, you're not.'

'I'll ply her with alcohol if I have to.' She winked at Cassidy for the second time and Cassidy was immediately charmed by her.

In fairness, if she plied the only Irish native on the planet who couldn't hold her drink with alcohol then she would get everything she'd probably never wanted to hear. Half a glass of wine and Cassidy's tongue tended to take on a life of its own.

'No, you won't. I need her lucid for the next few weeks.'

'Was he always so serious?'

Cassidy looked at Will, found him staring at her with a

disconcertingly unreadable expression, and her answer kind of popped out. 'No. He wasn't.'

He stared at her until she could feel her toes curling in her shoes.

So she bravely lifted her chin in challenge.

After what felt like a very long time, Angelique laughed musically. 'Okay, then. Well, you two kids have fun. I can highly recommend the scallops. Saturday, Irish boy—you hear me?'

'I hear you.'

He waved an arm to indicate Cassidy should sit back down, and she was glad of it. She really was starting to feel light-headed. Maybe she should have dragged herself out of bed for breakfast after all?

'I'll call on Saturday and tell her we can't make it.' He re-opened his menu. 'I think we should start brain-storming tomorrow and get something down on paper over the weekend.'

That fast? Great. Now she felt nauseous as well.

Hiding partially behind her auburn hair as she lowered her chin to scan the menu, she cleared her throat and asked, 'You have any ideas?'

'A few.'

It was like pulling teeth. 'Any you'd care to share?'

When she glanced at him she saw the slight upward pull on the corners of his mouth before he answered. 'Not here, no.'

Cassidy's gaze moved from side to side and she lowered her voice to a stage whisper. 'Are they watching?'

'They?' His gaze rose, curiosity lifting his brows.

'The script gremlins…'

There was a second of silence, and then a brief rumble of low laughter broke free. 'Haven't changed, have you?'

Oh, how little he knew.

They managed small talk after that. The latest movies Will's company had produced, the differences in living in California compared to Ireland… They even segued from there to the *weather*. But she couldn't help missing the ease they'd once had with each other. Angelique was right—Will *had* got serious with age. It made Cassidy feel like even more of an idiot. She couldn't seem to manage a conversation without a wisecrack or teasing him the way she'd used to, and it added to her feeling of awkwardness. Then she hit rock bottom in the embarrassment stakes when he walked her back to the hotel.

The air really was thinner in California. And it really was incredibly warm. Food hadn't got rid of her lightheadedness. Her nose felt more blocked than ever, her throat hurt, and her voice was beginning to fade…

Then, back in the foyer of the beautiful hotel, surrounded by beautiful people in expensive clothes, Will turned to say goodbye and the world began to spin. The edges of her vision blurred—she swayed. And, as she had figuratively speaking so many years ago, Cassidy fell at his feet.

She came to with her head resting against Will's hard chest, his warmth surrounding her. He must have sat her up. He had his arm around her. Blinking the world into focus, her eyes immediately sought his.

He was frowning. 'What happened?'

'If I had to guess, I'd say I fell down,' she informed him dryly.

'Are you sick?'

'Bit of a cold. I spent the morning in bed.'

His mouth narrowed into a thin line as he held a glass of water to her lips. 'You should have said something.'

Allowing the water to wash the dryness from her mouth and throat, she glanced around at the sea of interested by-standers and immediately felt colour rising in her cheeks. Great. The never-ending humiliation continued. It re-minded her of that time in high school, before she'd had laser surgery, when she'd forgotten her glasses and got into the wrong car outside the school gates. She'd held a five-minute conversation with a complete stranger before she'd realised what she'd done…

Irritation sounding in her voice, she tried to push up on to her feet. 'I'm good now, Will. Thanks. Let me up.'

But he held her in place. 'Give it a minute.'

When he held the glass back to her mouth, her sense of mortification was raised several notches. She pushed his hand away. 'Stop that. I can do it. I don't need a minute.'

Taking the glass from him, she struggled anything but gracefully to her feet, splashing water onto her hand and the floor. Once she was upright, she swayed precariously. Will stepped forward—one hand removing the glass, one arm circling her waist as he calmly informed her, 'That went well.'

Cassidy scowled at the grumbled words as he handed the glass to a hovering concierge before demanding, 'Key card.'

'What?'

'Give me your key card.' Lifting his free hand in front of her body, he waggled long fingers. 'Hand it over. You're going back to bed.'

'I don't think—'

'Good. Run with that. *Key card.*'

While her brain tried to think up an argument against the new and not necessarily improved attitude he seemed to have acquired with age, her traitorous hand reached into her bag for the card. Apparently the best she could come up with in reply was, 'I don't remember you being this bossy.'

'Comes with the territory in my job.' His fingers closed around the card.

'Can we get anything for the lady?'

Will nodded at the concierge's question. 'You could send up some chilled orange juice to room…?'

When he lifted his brows at Cassidy, she sighed. 'Ten-twenty-eight.'

'And send out to the nearest pharmacy for cold medicine of some kind.'

The concierge nodded. 'Of course, sir.'

Completely out of nowhere, Will did the last thing she'd expected and bent at the waist, scooping her into his arms like some kind of caped superhero. The man would put his back out! She was a good twenty pounds over the weight she'd been the last time he'd pulled that stunt.

A part of her curled up and died even as her arm automatically circled his neck. 'Put me down, Will. I can walk.'

As she whispered the words her gaze met that of several fascinated observers, and a couple of women who looked distinctly as if they were swooning. Now her cheeks were on fire. 'Will, I'm serious! I'm too heavy.'

'No, you're not. Shut up, Cass.'

She wriggled, and felt her lunch rearrange itself inside her stomach, drawing a low moan from her lips. If she threw up in public she was taking the next plane home. It would serve Will Ryan right if she threw up over *him!*

He walked through the remainder of the foyer as if she weighed nothing, and then turned to hit the elevator button with his elbow. Adding even further to her nightmare, he then moved the hand at her waist and dropped his chin to frown at her body. 'What *are* you wearing under that blouse?'

Oh. Dear. *God.*

'I think you'll find we're eight years too late for a conversation about my underwear.'

When he looked at her, she summoned a smirk.

His green gaze travelling over her face, he took in her flushed cheeks and the way she was chewing on her lower lip before he looked back into her eyes. 'Wearing something so tight that it restricts your breathing is hardly going to help any, is it?'

'It's not like I *planned* on falling at your feet.' Oh, she just didn't know when to stop, did she?

Amusement danced across his eyes. Before he could say anything the elevator doors opened, so he turned sideways and guided her inside. 'Push the button, Cass.'

She did. Then Will took a step back and lifted his chin to watch the numbers as they lit up above the doors.

'You can put me down now. Seriously.'

'That's not happening.'

Cassidy sighed heavily. His stubborn streak, she remembered. When Will had dug his heels in over something he'd been an immovable object. It had led to more than one heated debate when they were writing, but back then they'd had one heck of a good time making up afterwards. Naturally now she'd thought about *that* her body reacted.

So she tried to think of the names of all of the seven dwarfs to distract herself—there was always one she couldn't remember; now, which one was it? Scrunching her nose up while she concentrated didn't help. Nope still couldn't get him. Elusive seventh dwarf! She sighed again.

'Huff all you want, Cass. I'm not putting you down.'

The elevator pinged and the doors slid open while she informed him, 'You'll have to put me down eventually. It'll make it a tad difficult to do the basics, lugging me around like a sack of spuds all day.'

When he turned from side to side to search for the plates on the wall that would indicate where her room was, she waved a limp arm. 'That way.'

'Why didn't you call and say you weren't feeling well?'

Because a part of her had been looking forward to seeing him again, that was why. Her curiosity had been getting the better of her ever since his e-mail had arrived. Only natural considering their history, she'd told herself. What girl *wasn't* fascinated by how her first love looked years after the last time she saw him? It was one of those things that never completely went away. Along with the associated paranoia of wondering whether time had built her memories of him into some kind of magical figure he couldn't possibly live up to, or whether he would have aged much better than she had.

In the face of further humiliation, she lied, 'I felt better when I got up.'

'Liar.'

Cassidy sighed louder than before. 'I *hate* that you can still do that. Fine, then—I wanted to know why I was here.'

'Yes, obviously. Because I didn't explain it in the e-mails I sent you…'

Was he fishing? She lifted her chin and frowned up at his profile at the exact moment he chose to lower his dense lashes and look down at her. It made her breath catch in her lungs. One man should *not* look that good! It took every ounce of strength she had not to drop her gaze to his mouth. Then she had to dig deeper to make herself breathe normally again.

She should never have made the trip over. 'It wasn't like you picked up a phone to discuss it.'

Broad shoulders shrugged before he slotted her key card into the door. 'Different time zones. And my schedule has been crazy.'

Cassidy lifted a brow. 'Liar.'

'Nope.' He shouldered the door open. 'You're seven hours behind over there. I've been dealing with a movie that's running over budget every second. Any time I had to call you would have been during school hours your end. Plus, if you were worried about making the trip and *wanted* me to call you, you'd have said so in your e-mails— wouldn't you?'

She hated it when he used reasoning on her. And when she couldn't read him the way he did her. Back in the good old days the former had been useful mid-debate, and the latter had been endearing as heck—especially when he'd told her what she was thinking in a husky voice, with his mouth hovering above hers. But now? Now it just kept on making her feel like even more of an idiot than she already did for not realising the physical attraction she'd had for him would be as uncontrollable as it had been before. There was no fighting chemistry. When the pheromones said it worked, it worked. It was up to the brain to list the reasons why it couldn't.

Setting her gently on her feet by the giant bed, he leaned over to drag the covers back before standing tall and letting a small smile loose. 'Take it off.'

'Excuse me?'

He jerked his chin. 'That industrial-strength whatever-it-is you're wearing. What is it with women and those boned things, anyway?'

A squeak of outrage sounded in the base of her sore throat. 'You're unbelievable. Go away.'

'I'll go when you're all tucked up in bed. Anything happens to you within twenty-four hours of hitting L.A. I might feel guilty for bringing you here…'

Somewhere in the growing red mist of her anger came a question that temporarily made her gape at him. *'You* brought me here? I thought the studio brought me here? Are you telling me *you* paid for all of this—the flights and the limo pick-up and the fancy room and everything?'

Say no!

'Yes.'

Uh-oh. Room swaying again. But when his hands grasped her elbows she tugged them away and managed to turn round before she flumped down onto the mattress. Automatically toeing her shoes off her feet, she shook her head and blinked into the middle distance. 'I thought the studio paid for it.'

'They paid for a script. We took the money. Now we have to deliver.'

What had she got herself into? She couldn't be beholden to him. It wasn't as if she had the money to pay him back—not until they were paid the balance of their advance for the last script. Even then. Every cent was precious. There was no guarantee she could start writing again without Will and make money at it. Not that she'd tried the last time…

A crooked forefinger arrived under her chin and lifted it to force her gaze upwards. Then he examined her eyes for the most maddening amount of time while she held her breath. 'You need to sleep. I'll come back later and check up on how you're feeling.'

'You don't have to.'

'Go take that ridiculous thing off while I'm here—in case you pass out again.'

'I won't pass—'

'Humour me.'

Pursing her lips, she reached for her pyjamas from under the soft pillows, pushed to her feet and scowled at him on her way to the bathroom, 'I don't know that I can work with this new bossy Will.' She lifted her chin. 'I don't like him.'

Closing the door with a satisfyingly loud click, she took a second to lean against the wood until the world stopped spinning again. For a long time she'd told herself her life was a mess, but it was a glorious kind of mess. Now she felt very much like dropping the 'glorious' part…

She had to sit on the edge of the bathtub to struggle her way out of everything without another dizzy spell. Then she hid the offending underwear under a pile of towels, in case he decided to use the bathroom before he left. Stupid cold! That was what she got for working in a room full of children—she must have incubated the germs on the plane. So much for being considerate and taking the time to see the children through the last term, postponing her trip by a couple of weeks until the summer holidays. They'd repaid her in germs. Bless them.

'You okay in there?' He sounded as if he was standing right by the door.

When she yanked it open, he was.

'You can go away now.'

Will blocked her exit and took his sweet time looking her over from head to toe and back up again, for the second time in as many hours. Only this time it left her skin tingling with more than the cold sweat from her cold. Just one comment about her two-sizes-too-big pyjamas and he was a dead man.

Then his gaze clashed with hers and her eyes widened. What was *that*?

He stepped back. 'Bed.'

Cassidy made a big deal about making sure she patted the covers down the full length of her legs when she was between the cool cotton sheets. The room was wonderfully cool too. Had he turned on the air-conditioning for her? Then she saw the glass of water on the bedside table, alongside the remote control for the television, a box of tissues and the large folder with all the hotel's numbers in it. He'd thought of everything. It was amazingly considerate, actually. It tempered the sharpness brought on by her humiliation, and her voice was calmer as she snuggled down against the large pile of cushions.

'There. Happy now?'

When she chanced another look at him he had the edges of his dark jacket pushed back and his large hands deep in the pockets of his jeans. He seemed so much larger than she remembered—as if he filled the room. And yet still with those boyishly devastating good looks and that thick head of dark hair, with its upward curls at his nape, and the sharply intelligent eyes that studied her so intensely she felt a need to run and hide…

Half of her silently pleaded with him to go away.

The other half probably wished he'd never left to begin with.

'I'll be back later.'

'You don't need to. Call in the morning if you like. I'll sleep.'

The green of his eyes flashed with determination. 'I'll be back later.'

The balance of power within Cassidy swayed towards 'go away'. 'I won't open the door Will.'

'I know.' He took his hands out of his pockets and backed towards the door, his long legs making the journey in three steps. Then he lifted a hand and casually turned something over between his long fingers like a baton, 'That's why I'm keeping your key card.'

Cassidy could have growled at him. But instead she rolled her eyes as she turned away and punched the pillows into shape, hearing the door click quietly shut behind her. After counting to ten, just to be sure, she fought the need to cry. Oh, how much easier it would be if she could hate him…

He was way out of her league now. *Way out.*

She wanted to go home.

CHAPTER TWO

THE dream was feverish. In the no man's land between deep sleep and consciousness came vivid images that were a mixture of the past, the present and some imaginary point in time real only in her mind. The sheets knotted around her legs felt cumbersome, still heavy, even though she'd long since kicked the blanket to one side and damp strands of her auburn hair were stuck to her cheeks and her forehead.

She felt awful.

But she was old enough and wise enough to know she was at the sweating-it-out stage. She just had to let it run its course and her body would fight it off. It might mean she was looking at a few days holed up in the hotel room, but it wasn't as if it was the worst hotel in the world, was it?

The low light from her bedside lamp shone irritatingly through the backs of her eyelids, and voices sounded from the television she had on low volume to help lull her to sleep. She'd never been particularly good with silence. But then neither was she accustomed to the noises of a busy American hotel. So keeping the TV on had seemed like a plan—especially when she'd discovered a channel that showed the familiar programmes she was used to watching at home. That was why it took a moment for her to drag her mind out of its half-slumber into a cognitive state. The door had to have been knocked on several times by then, she figured—with increasing levels of volume…

'Cass?' It was Will.

She groaned and croaked back at him. 'Go away, Will.'

Please go away. Don't make it worse. Let me die in peace. Then if he wanted to he could come and take her body away and donate it to medical science. She was beyond caring any more.

'I'm coming in.'

The man had no idea when to take a hint! The next thing she knew the door was open and he was walking in, with a large paper bag in his hand. So she did the mature thing and grabbed a pillow to hold over her face with both hands. Maybe she could suffocate herself…

'How's the patient?'

'Not in the mood for company,' she mumbled from under the pillow.

'You have a pillow over your face, so I couldn't quite hear that. Here, let me help you.' He pried her fingers loose and removed the pillow. Then he waited for her to squint up at him through narrowed eyes. 'Hello there.'

Cassidy silently called him a really bad name. 'Please go away Will.'

Setting the pillow on the other side of her head, he laid the backs of his fingers against her forehead and frowned. 'When's the last time you took tablets?'

'I don't know—half an hour after you left…maybe…'

'Time for more.'

Struggling her way into a sitting position, she accepted

the tablets he dropped into her palm and washed them down with what was left of the glass of juice on her side table. Then she set the glass back down and lifted her heavy arms to try and tidy her hair before looking up at him from under her lashes.

'I appreciate what you're doing, Will. I do. *And* whatever it is you've brought me in the paper bag. But I just need to sleep it out. It'll be some kind of freaky twenty-four-hour thing, that's all. I've taken my tablets and had some juice, and now I'm going back to sleep. If you leave a number I'll call you when I wake up. I'm not that bad. Really.'

She then ruined the effect by sneezing with enough force to make it feel as if she'd just blown the top off her aching head. She moaned. Someone should just shoot her.

Will calmly handed her a tissue.

She decided to disgust him to get him to leave, blowing her nose loud enough to alert all shipping routes of an incoming fog.

Will had the gall to look vaguely amused. 'You need to eat something. I brought you chicken noodle soup.'

How *could* he? As he reached a large hand into the bag memory slammed into her frontal lobe and ricocheted down her closing throat, wrapping around her heart so tight it made it difficult to breathe. Because he'd done this before, hadn't he? Only she'd had flu that time. They'd been in the tiny bedsit they'd shared for a while instead of living in halls of residence. As well as bringing her everything she'd needed to feel better, and heating endless pans of chicken noodle soup, he had sat up with her, watched television with her, held her in his arms, smoothed her hair until she fell asleep...

It wasn't that she'd forgotten. It was just that the memory hadn't been so vivid in a long time. There had been so many different memories to overshadow it. Heartbreak had a tendency to do that—taking the best of memories and tingeing them with a hint of painful regret for the fact there wouldn't be more memories made in the future. But right now he *was* adding a new one. One that was surrounded in bittersweetness because it wasn't one she could hold onto the same way as the first.

It hurt.

Removing the lid of the soup carton, he wrapped it in a napkin and handed it to her along with a plastic spoon. 'Here…'

Dampening her lips, she hesitated briefly before reaching for the carton. She had no choice but to slide her fingers over his during the exchange, and a jolt of electricity shot up her arm. Her chest was aching when he slid his fingers away. It would have been easier if he'd just set the carton down. Darn it.

Purposefully she took the spoon from him by grasping the opposite end from his fingers, croaking a low, 'Thank you.'

'You're welcome.' He inclined his head.

When she blew too hard on the soup, and splattered just enough hot liquid on the back of her hand to make her frown, she glanced up at him and found amusement dancing in his eyes again. He truly was the most irritating man in the world.

Then he sat on the edge of the bed and turned towards her. 'If you're not better tomorrow I'll get a doctor to come see you.'

'I don't need a doctor; it's a cold—not bubonic plague.'

'And they say *men* make lousy patients…'

Cassidy shook her head. Then leaned in and blew more gently on her soup to cool it. When she looked up, Will was studying her intently—almost as if he'd never seen her before. It made her sigh for the hundredth time that day. 'What now?'

'You changed your hair.'

The words surprised her, but as usual her sarcasm kicked in. 'Yeah. Women tend to do that a couple of times in eight years. We're fickle that way.'

'Still have a smart mouth, though.'

Which apparently gave him leave to drop his gaze and look at it as she formed another pouting 'O' to blow air on the soup. She immediately pursed her lips in response. When his thick lashes lifted she scowled at him. 'Your good deed is done for the day now. You can go and do whatever it is you normally do at this time of night. Wherever you do it and with whomever you do it.'

'Whomever?' The corners of his mouth tugged again. 'Nice use of the English language. Fishing for details, Cass?'

Cassidy had never wanted to scream so much in all her born days. 'Writers are supposed to have a good grasp of the language. Not that you'd understand that. I spent half our time together correcting your spelling mistakes…'

She really had. It wasn't that he couldn't spell, it was just that sometimes his mind worked faster than his typing fingers.

Then she addressed his cockiness. 'And I'm not fishing. It's none of my business.'

'You could try asking me.'

'I'm sorry. Wasn't "it's none of my business" clear enough?'

'Not the littlest bit curious?'

'Why would I be?'

The beginning of one of *those* smiles started in his eyes. And if it started in his eyes first it was devastating when it made it to his mouth. She *knew*. So she stopped it happening by throwing out somewhat desperate words. 'Even if you're free as a bird it doesn't make any difference. You and me? We're workmates. Business partners, if you like. Barely platonic ones. We're like two people stranded on a desert island who have to make the best of it till the next rescue boat arrives—as good as strangers. You don't know any more about who I am now than I know about—'

'You're babbling. You always babble when you're nervous. Why are you nervous, Cass?'

Screwing up her face, she set the soup carton onto the side table and slid down under the covers, lifting them and tucking them over her head. 'I hate you. Would you *go away*? I'm not up to this. You're still the most annoying man I've ever known.'

'Makes me memorable…'

Cassidy growled, and promptly ended up coughing when the vibration hurt her raw throat. Somewhere mid-cough she heard what sounded like a low chuckle of laughter. She peeked over the edge of the covers ready to scowl at him and found him lifting his brows in a question, a completely unreadable expression on his face. It made her narrow her eyes.

'You know we need to get on better than this to work together, don't you?'

She did, and immediately felt like a fool again. 'Can we try and get on better when I don't feel like the hotel fell on me?'

'When you're weak is probably the best time to talk this through.'

'That's evil.'

Will had more difficulty stifling his smile than he had so far. 'True.'

He wasn't apologising for it, though, was he? The rat. Cassidy tried hard not to be charmed by it; she did. But a small sparkle-eyed smile was apparently nearly as effective as a killer one, and before she knew it she was smiling back at him. Then she shook her head. 'I hate you.'

'Mmm.' He leaned forward, his large body distractingly close to hers and his familiar scent somehow making it through her blocked nose. 'You said.'

When he lifted the soup carton Cassidy lifted her gaze to his hair. He had great hair. The colour of dark chocolate, thick enough to tempt a woman's fingertips, and distinctly male to the touch when she touched it, but soft enough to encourage her to slide her fingers deep... She wished she didn't remember so much...

Will leaned back. 'You need to eat.'

'Bossing me again, Ryan?'

'Necessary, Malone.'

Without comment she went ahead and sipped at the soup, her gaze flickering to his often enough for her to know he was still watching her. Not that she needed to look to confirm it. She'd always known when Will was looking at her. In the same way she could feel the newfound tension lying between them.

Thick lashes blinked lazily at even intervals, and then he asked, 'Good?'

'Mmm-hmm.' She nodded. *'Good.'*

Looking around the room for a moment, Will folded his dark brows in thought before he took a deep breath and focused on her again. 'I think you should stay at my place while you're in L.A.'

Cassidy almost choked on her soup. He had a knack of doing that to her. But he couldn't be serious! There was no way she could go and stay at his place—be under the same roof with him twenty-four-seven. They were barely managing to make civil conversation between his short sentences and her loose tongue. And now he wanted them somewhere they couldn't escape from each other? Oh, yeah. That would help.

Then she thought about the fact he was paying for the hotel room she was in and felt guilty. Maybe if she found a computer and checked her meager bank account she could discover somewhere cheap and cheerful to stay? It didn't need to be fancy: a bed, a door that locked, a shower, a minimal number of cockroaches...

Will continued while she blinked at him, 'We need to spitball ideas and get to work. And we never used to stick to a nine to five, so if we're working through the night it makes sense to be somewhere we can do that. I'll come get you in the morning.'

Cassidy wondered if there was ever going to be a point where she got to make decisions on her own. 'Don't you have an office?'

'I have one we can work in at home, yes.'

Not what she'd meant, and he knew it. 'In the city. You can't run an entire production company from home.'

'I probably could. But, yes, I do have offices in the city. Still the same problem there—this makes more sense.'

It didn't matter if it made sense. Surely he remembered that about her? But before she could even string together a thought, never mind form the words to argue it out, he was pushing to his feet. 'While you're not feeling well you can take a break to sleep any time you need to. I'll come get you at nine.'

Cassidy watched him get halfway to the door before she managed to open her mouth. 'I'm not comfortable with the idea of living in your house—or apartment—or whatever it is you have.'

'You'll forget that when you've been there a few days.'

'Damn it, Will!' She frowned at him when he turned round. 'You can't keep riding roughshod over me like this. If I don't want to stay in your house I don't have to. And if it's because you're paying for this hotel then I can find somewhere—'

Lowering his chin, he lifted his brows with amused disbelief. 'You think paying for this room is a problem for me?'

'That's not the point. Whether or not you can afford—'

Will shook his head, smiling incredulously. 'It's got nothing to do with money. It's got to do with practicality. *Man.* I'd forgotten how stubborn you can be.'

Swallowing down another pang of hurt that he'd forgotten *anything* about her when she remembered everything about him, Cassidy arched a brow. 'Pot, meet kettle. Regardless of whether or not you can afford to pay for this room, the simple fact is you shouldn't be. I'll pay you back whatever you've already forked out. I don't want to owe you anything. This is business and we both know it. Whatever we once had doesn't matter any more. We're not even friends now.'

'And blunt. That part I hadn't forgotten.' He lifted his chin and frowned at a random point in the air while taking a deep breath that expanded his wide chest. Then he dropped his chin and looked her straight in the eye. 'You're right. It *is* business. You have a job back home. I have a job here. So the sooner we get this done the sooner we can get back to work. If we dig in, and eat, drink and sleep this script for the next few weeks, we can nail it.'

It was all about the script; of course it was.

Will quirked his brows. 'Well?'

'It's business.'

'Exactly.'

'Right.' She didn't have the energy to keep fighting with him. 'Fine, then.'

With his mouth drawn into a thin line and a frown darkening his face, Will swung round and tugged on the door. 'Nine o'clock.'

When the door closed behind him Cassidy blinked at it. For a brief second he'd almost looked angry. How on earth were they supposed to communicate well enough to write a script if they couldn't even hold a conversation? She flumped further down on the pillows and put what was left of her soup on the nightstand before tugging the covers up over her shoulders. She felt cold again, she was shivery— and suddenly she had an incredible sense of loneliness to add to her feeling homesick.

Her first trip to Hollywood should be a fairytale experience. It was a dream she'd had since childhood, when the magic of movies had sucked her into the kind of imaginary worlds that had enthralled her for most of her life. Everything about it had fascinated her as she got older: the sets, the effects, the lighting, the locations, where the words the actors and actresses spoke came from. The latter had then become something she wanted to do—she wanted to put those words there. To watch a movie on a big screen and hear words she had written on a flat page spoken by an actor or actress who could add depths and nuances she might never even have thought of.

When she'd got her dream the world had become the most amazing place to her. And she'd got to share that magic with the man she loved. It had been perfect. She had been so happy.

But there was no such thing as perfect happiness. Life had taught her that. Failure had taken the sparkly-eyed wonder from her eyes. Then she'd had to give up her dreams, her confidence shattered, her heart broken, because Will had gone and she'd had no choice but to watch him walk away. The last time she had seen him was indelibly imprinted on her brain, and in the empty part of her heart that had died that day…

Cassidy had felt as if all the magic had been sucked out of her life. And she'd never got it back. Just small pockets of happiness ever since. But then that was everyone's life, she had told herself. She just needed to get on with it. One day after another.

Even if for a very, very brief moment on her flight over she'd allowed herself to dream again. Not so much of Will, but of the other great love she'd lost. She'd foolishly allowed herself to think about what might happen if she rediscovered her muse and decided to take a chance in Hollywood for a while. But this script was simply something to get out of the way. Then she would go home. End of story. No pun intended.

Then she would have to decide what she wanted to do with the rest of her life.

At nine she'd been in the foyer for ten minutes, glad of the concierge to help her with her bags and glad at how easy checking out proved to be. Still a little light headed, she found a plump cushioned chair and waited…

Will was outside at the stroke of nine. Something else that was new about him. He'd once been the worst time-keeper she'd ever known.

'You'll be late for your own funeral,' she would tell him.

'Ah, now, that's the one time I can guarantee I'll be on time,' he would tease back with a smile.

Cassidy missed that Will.

The new Will was frowning behind his designer sun-glasses the second he got out of his lowslung silver sports car. He said something to the uniformed man in charge of valet parking as he slipped him a folded bill, then pushed through the doors and removed his sunglasses before seeking her out. Four steps later he had his hand on the handle of her case.

'Did you check out?'

'Yes.'

'Any problems?'

'No. They said it was taken care of.'

With a nod he stepped back, watching her rise. 'Feeling any better?'

It was said with just enough softness in his deep voice to make it sound as if he cared, which made Cassidy feel the need to sigh again. Instead she managed a small smile as she stood. 'Yes. Thank you.'

Somewhere in the wee small hours of the night she had decided the best way not to be so physically aware of Will's presence was to avoid looking at him whenever possible. So she didn't make eye contact as she waited for him to load her case into the boot of his car. Instead she smiled at the liveried valet as he opened the passenger door for her—though she did almost embarrass herself again by trying to get in the wrong side of the car...

When Will got into the driver's seat and buckled up she looked out of the side window to watch Rodeo Drive starting to think about coming to life. But they had barely pulled away from the hotel before he took advantage of the fact she was trapped.

'Want to tell me what's *really* bothering you about staying at my place?'

Not so much. No. She puffed her cheeks out for a second and controlled her errant tongue before answering. 'We don't know each other that well any more. It's going be like spending time in a stranger's house.'

There was a brief silence, then; 'I disagree.'

Well, now, there was a surprise. They worked their way through intersections and filtered into traffic while Cassidy noticed all the differences that indicated she was in a different country from home. Larger cars, palm trees, billboards advertising things she'd never heard of before, different shaped traffic lights...

Will kept going. 'We're not strangers. People don't change that much.'

She begged to differ. And if she hadn't had living proof

in herself then she had it in the man sitting so close to her in the confined space of what she now knew was a Mustang something-or-other—she'd seen a little tag somewhere. Not that she was going to turn her head to look for it again, if it meant she might end up catching a glimpse of him from her peripheral vision. Just being so close to him, so aware of every breath he took and every movement of his large hands or long legs, was enough for her to deal with, thanks very much.

'Yes, they do. Life changes them. Experiences change them…' She had a sudden brainwave. 'It's exactly the kind of problem Nick and Rachel will have when they meet again.'

The mention of their fictional characters momentarily silenced Will. Then she heard him take a breath and let it out. 'That's true.'

So it was true for their fictional characters but not for them? How did *that* work? It was enough to make her turn her head and aim a suspicious sideways glance at his general gorgeousness. 'It's not like they're going to trust each other either.'

'Well, she did steal the artifact from him.'

'No—she took it to give it back to its rightful owners. There's a difference. He'd have sold it on the open market for whatever he could get.'

'She lived off the money they made doing the same thing in the past. You can't use that as an argument against him.'

'Oh? Now we're saying there has to be moral equivalency?'

Will shot her a quick yet intense gaze as they waited in traffic, his deep voice somehow more intense within the car's interior. 'It's not the best plan to alienate everyone to the hero and heroine before we even get started, is it? There are always two sides to every story. You want to make him into a bad boy then you have to make the audience understand why his morals are lower than hers.'

'Bad heroes sell. You can't tell me they don't. Bad heroines are universally hated.' Cassidy lifted her chin, but she could feel the smile forming on her face. It was like one of their debates of old. 'Unless you're thinking of turning her evil—which, incidentally, you'll do over my dead body. The audience needs to empathise with her. That'll sell.'

'Actually, I can tell you exactly what sells these days. Right now its superheroes and family-friendly.' His long fingers flexed against the steering wheel. 'The real money can be found in family-oriented movies, where good is good and bad is bad. It's black and white. Moral equivalency needn't apply. Last year seven films with a G or PG rating earned more than one hundred million at the domestic box office, and three PG-rated films were among the year's top ten earners. Only one R-rated film was in the ten top grossing films—and there was no moral equivalency in that movie, I can assure you.'

The smile on her face faded and was replaced with blinking surprise as he recited it all in an even tone, negotiating increasing traffic at the same time. It seemed everyone in Los Angeles had a car.

He knew his stuff, didn't he? Who was she to argue? Not that it stopped her. 'Correct me if I'm wrong, but haven't you just proved my point on moral equivalency?'

Silence. Then to her utter astonishment a burst of laughter—deep, rumbling, oh-so-very-male laughter—

then a wry smile and a shake of his head. 'It's been a long time since anyone spoke to me the way you do.'

Cassidy blinked some more. 'Maybe people should do it more often.'

'If they did they'd get fired more often.'

The corners of her mouth tugged upwards. 'Wow. Who knew you were a tyrant in the making, back in the day?'

'I'm not a tyrant.' He seemed surprised she thought he was.

'No?' Turning a little more towards him, she leaned her back against the passenger door and angled her head in question. 'What are you, then?'

'The boss.'

'So no one can correct you when you're wrong?'

'They can put forward a different point of view, if that's what you mean.' He was forced to break eye contact with her to concentrate on where they were going. 'No one ever does it the way you do, though.'

Cassidy couldn't help but allow the chuckle of laugher forming in her chest to widen her smile. 'So no one actually looks you in the eye and tells you you're wrong?'

'Not in so many words, no.'

No wonder he'd got so arrogant over the years. If no one ever stood up to him, or gave as good as they got, it would be a breeding ground for arrogance. Irrationally, it made her feel sorry for him. Everyone needed someone who cared enough about them to be brutally honest when it was needed. No one was ever right one hundred percent of the time, after all. Being blunt on the odd occasion to demonstrate another point of view showed you cared enough about them to try and save them from the kind of mistakes arrogance might make. To Cassidy,

knowing no one did that for Will made him seem very…
alone…

'She'll probably feel awkward when she sees him again.'

Huh? Oh, he meant Rachel, didn't he? Right—script
stuff. Stay with the flow of conversation, Cassidy. 'I doubt
she'd have sought him out voluntarily.'

'So we need something that brings them together.'

Cassidy arched a brow. 'You're going to want him to
rescue her, aren't you?'

The one corner of his full mouth she could see hitched
upwards. 'Who doesn't like it when the hero swoops in to
rescue the heroine?'

'*Sexist.* Why can't the heroine rescue the hero? Or
rescue herself? Or just be in the same place as him searching for something when they *both* get in trouble and have
to work *together* to get out of it…?'

Will shot a brief, sparkle eyed glance her way. 'Okay,
then. He has to rescue her from something when they end
up in the same place hunting for something.'

Cassidy rolled her eyes. 'Fine. But I'm fighting for a
later scene when *she* has to rescue *him* right back.'

'We're not making Nick look weak.'

'Vulnerable—not weak. Women find vulnerability sexy
in a strong male. You should try it some time. Might get
you a girlfriend…' The reappearance of her errant tongue
made her groan inwardly and avoid his gaze when he
looked her way again.

'You don't know I don't have a girlfriend.'

'I told you, it's none of my—'

'I don't have one right now. But all you had to do was ask.'

Oh, for crying out loud. Not only had she just caused a

self-inflicted wound at the idea of him with another woman, but now he'd managed to slip that little piece of unwanted information into the conversation it was only a matter of time before—

'What about you?'

Yep. There it was. Well, if he thought for one single, solitary second she was discussing the disastrous attempts she had eventually made at having a love life—long, *long* after he'd left—then he had another think coming. Not that it would be a long conversation.

Lifting her chin, she smiled sweetly. 'I don't have a girlfriend either.'

Will chuckled for the second time.

The sound was ridiculously distracting to her. How did it do that? It wasn't as if she hadn't heard him laugh before; she'd heard him chuckle, laugh softly, laugh out loud—had felt the rumble in his chest and been in his arms when his body had shaken with the reverberations. She knew how the light would dance in his eyes, how he would smile the amazingly infectious smile that gave everyone around him no choice but to smile along with him. For a long time Cassidy had believed she'd fallen for his laughter first. Yes, his boyish looks, height, gorgeous hair, etc., etc. might have been what had initially caught her eye. But it had been the sound of his laughter and the first glimpse of *that* smile that had drawn her heart to him.

Since she'd got to Los Angeles she'd wondered if she'd imagined the effect his laughter had on her. As if her memories were tangled up on some mythical pedestal she might have elevated him to over the years. But it was having exactly the same effect on her as before: skin tingling, chest warming—as if the sound had somehow reached out and physically touched her...

Forcing her gaze away, she turned forward in the seat to look out through the windscreen, and was surprised to see the ocean beside them. 'Where are we?'

'Pacific Coast Highway. It's the equivalent of Malibu's main street.'

'Malibu?'

'It's where I live.'

It was? Malibu? Where the rich and famous lived? She knew he'd done well since he came to California, but that he'd done well enough to be able to afford—

'It was originally part of the territory of the Chumash Nation of Native Americans. They called it Humaliwo— or "the surf sounds loudly". The current name derives from that. but the "Hu" syllable isn't stressed...' When she gaped at him he looked away from the highway long enough to raise his brows at her. 'What?'

'Who *are* you?'

The question was out before she could stop it, her words low and filled with incredulity. It was just the more he said the less she felt she knew him; it was as if he had somehow morphed into a completely different person when he'd moved halfway across the planet—and it was just so at odds with the many things that were familiar to her that it left her feeling a little...*lost*...

Will checked the road again, then looked back at her. 'You know me, Cass.'

His saying it in a low rumble that made goosebumps break out on her skin and her heart do a kind of weird twisting move in her chest only made her study him even more intently. 'How do you know all this stuff?'

'About Malibu?'

'It's like you've swallowed an encyclopaedia since you got here. Hollywood-speak, movie industry stats, local history…'

What looked almost like confusion flickered across the green of his eyes before he turned his head to watch the road again. 'Hollywood speak is everyday language here. Movie stats I study as part of my job, and Malibu I just happen to like—it's why I moved here the minute I could afford it. I hate the city.'

Actually, the last part she understood. Home of Disneyland and movie stars, Beverly Hills and Hollywood, she knew Los Angeles had long lured people into its glittering fantasy world, with its endless sunshine, palm trees, shopping malls and beautiful people. The city was like no place she'd ever been before. But after so many years dreaming about it, she'd known in less than twenty-four hours that she couldn't live there. Not in the city anyway. Too many people, too many cars, too much smog. No one saying hello to their fellow human beings in the street unless they were dressed as iconic movie figures and demanding money in exchange for a photograph with them. Cassidy had taken one afternoon to wander along Hollywood Boulevard, and as fascinating as it had been, reading the iconic stars beneath her feet, it hadn't made her feel at home. And now she'd discovered Will possibly felt that way too…

Well, it gave them some common ground, didn't it? A stretch maybe, but she would take what she could get…

Despite the danger, Cassidy wanted to know more. Her dilemma became whether or not to actually *ask* any more. If she did she would be getting a window into his life—

would have new Will Ryan memories to add to the cornu-
copia of old ones she already carried around with her. If
somewhere along the way the new version of him proved as
addictive as the old? Well, then she was in big, *big* trouble…

Who was she kidding? Cassidy had always been one of
those people that needed to know. Christmas presents—she
shook them. Books—she read the last pages before she got
halfway through them. Favourite TV shows—she trawled
the internet looking for spoilers for a new series before the
episodes made it to the screen. There was about as much
chance of her not asking as—

'So tell me more about Malibu.'

'What do you want to know?'

'Whatever you decide to tell me…'

She looked out through the windscreen at the glittering
aquamarine blue of the Pacific Ocean, the thrill of seeing
it for the first time bringing a soft smile to her mouth. She
had always loved the ocean. Not surprising, really, when
she lived on a tiny island surrounded by it. But there was
just something about the ebb and flow of the tide…as if it
was the subliminal heartbeat of the planet. Every time she
saw the sea it made her smile. Seeing the Pacific for the
first time was like meeting a new friend.

'That's the Pacific. Beautiful, isn't she?'

'She is.' Cassidy allowed herself to wonder why
anything associated with the sea was always a 'she'.
Probably something to do with moods and unpredictabil-
ity and seduction, she supposed. From that point of view
it was easy to see why seafaring men of old would have
chosen the feminine to describe her.

'Malibu hugs the Pacific north of Santa Monica. It

has over twenty miles of coastline. Surfing is the big thing, obviously—endless opportunities for catching the perfect wave…'

The smile she could hear in his voice made her turn to look at his strong profile; the flicker of his thick dark lashes as he watched the traffic was unbelievably hypnotic to her. 'You surf?'

The corner of his mouth tugged. 'Used to. Don't have as much time now…'

A sudden visual image of Will walking out of the surf, glistening with water and shaking his head to loosen silvery droplets from his thick hair while he smiled *that* smile, did all sorts of delicious things to Cassidy's libido and left her mouth unbearably dry. There were times her active imagination took on a life of its own—useful in writerly terms, but not so useful when she was supposed to be thinking in terms of Will as a business partner. There could be no thinking of him bare-chested. Or towelling his hair for him. Or lying down on a large blanket beside him on warm sand.

Goodness, it was hot all of a sudden…

'It's part of the reason I bought a house on the beach.'

Suddenly staying at his house was looking more attractive to her. But… 'You bought a house on the beach so you could surf more, and then quit surfing? That makes perfect sense.'

He shrugged. 'Just the way it worked out.'

The house they pulled up in front of looked small and cosy. The sound of the ocean filled her ears as she stepped outside into warm salty air that made her breathe deep and appreciate the difference in air quality after the lack of oxygen in Los Angeles. But when Will unlocked the front door and stepped back to allow her to go ahead of him her eyes widened. Okay, it wasn't small and cosy. Will's house was… Well, it was amazing…

The deceptive frontage on the road made it look like it was just the one storey, and not all that big, when in fact it was split level and stretched for miles, with its lower level suspended above golden sands outside so that the huge picture windows made it look as if the entire house was floating above the waves. Open-plan, rich wooden floors, sparse furniture that didn't take anything from the views. It was very male, very modern, but stunningly beautiful.

It yelled *money* from every corner.

When Cassidy hovered at the top of the stairs, Will closed the front door and stepped over beside her. 'The view sold it.'

'Well, it would, wouldn't it?'

'Kitchen, living room, gym, home cinema and office are all on the lower level. Your room is over here to the left.' He took her case in that direction while she continued staring out of the windows.

Now she knew why Lizzie had fallen for Pemberley before she fell for Darcy. Because the part of Cassidy's soul that loved the ocean could live happily ever after in a house like Will's. Give or take a few feminine touches. If *she* lived there she would have bright comfy cushions on the large sofas, flowers in vases, books on the almost empty shelves where pieces of modern art were displayed. She could picture it in her mind's eye. She could practically hear music playing from an invisible stereo, laughter echoing off the walls, and the sound of small, running bare feet coming in from the beach. It made her heart hurt. How dared he have the house of her dreams? It was as if he'd purposely gone out and stolen every dream she'd ever had and held it from her, to add to breaking her heart the way he had.

She genuinely hated him for that.

With a deep breath she turned on her heel and followed Will along the hall that skirted the floor below, rolling her eyes when she got to the open doorway and looked in at the bedroom she would be staying in. Of course it had the same ocean view. And naturally Will was sliding open the glass windows so the sea breeze caught the light curtains. Was there ever any doubt it would have its own balcony, with comfy lounge chairs just waiting to be occupied so she could watch the sunset at the end of the day?

Stepping into a little corner of heaven, she plunked down on the end of the large bed and allowed herself to bounce just once on the deep mattress while she fought the need to cry. It really wasn't fair. How *could* he? What had she ever done to him to deserve this kind of torture?

Will turned from the windows and pushed his hands deep into the pockets of his dark jeans as he studied her. 'Tired?'

Weary would have been a better word, she felt. 'A little. Coffee would probably help. And I should take some tablets again, just in case.'

'Okay.' He nodded. 'Did you have breakfast?'

'No.'

'Yeah, that'll help you get better. Will bagels and lox do?'

'Depends.' Cassidy lifted her chin, stifled a wry smile and arched a brow. 'What is lox, exactly?'

His eyes sparkled. 'It's smoked salmon. Bagels with cream cheese and smoked salmon.'

'Ahh.'

'Is that "Yes, Will"?'

A more genuine smile broke free as she inclined her head. 'Yes, Will. Thank you. Bagels and lox sounds lovely.'

As if to emphasise her approval her stomach growled softly, making Will's mouth twitch as he left the room. 'Come down when you're ready. Feed a cold and all that…'

She wished he would stop being nice. Annoying Will her heart could cope with. But if he started adding Nice Will to the house she'd fallen in love with at first sight she would be in even bigger trouble than she had been twenty-four hours ago.

Lying back on the bed, she turned her head and closed her eyes, breathing as deep as her aching chest would allow while she compared Will's life to the one she had. It wasn't hard to see who had fared better. If her self-confidence had been low before she'd stepped on the plane in Dublin, it was pretty much sitting at the bottom of a dark pit of despair now. She really needed to do something that would make her feel like herself again. But that was just it. Since Will, she'd never really discovered who Cassidy Malone was without him. Maybe it was time to find out?

After all, she was in the house of her dreams in California, a stone's throw away from the industry she still found completely absorbing—even from the periphery, as a viewer of the art form. It was a step in the right direction, wasn't it? Nothing ventured, nothing gained?

She slapped her palms against the cool covers and sat upright, reaching into her bag for her tablets and taking them with her as she left the room. Coffee, bagels and lox, tablets—and then she was going to start work and see if she still remembered how to write. That was somewhere to start…

CHAPTER THREE

'THAT'S the most ridiculous thing I've ever heard.'

'How is it?'

'How is it *not*?' She blinked incredulously at him, then continued looking around the large glass desk for the pen she knew she'd had five minutes ago. 'You want them to find a hidden nuclear warhead in the middle of an archaeological dig?'

Will allowed a pen to twirl between his thumb and forefinger, as if teasing her with it because she couldn't find her own. 'We need explosions.'

'A nuclear warhead is a little more than a simple explosion. And how on earth did the terrorist group get the thing down there, when we've already said that no one has discovered the site after centuries of searching?' Cassidy shook her head, lifting discarded scene cards in her search.

'We can change that. It's one line.' His pen stilled and his deep voice informed her, 'Behind your ear.'

'What?' She scowled at him, her pulse hitching when she realised how intensely he was staring at her as he lounged in his chair and swung it from side to side. That chair had been driving her crazy. It had a squeak. She'd have thought a man of Will's means could afford a can of oil to fix something that irritating, but *no*. He just kept swinging and squeaking, and swinging and squeaking, until she thought she might have to kill him.

He jerked his chin at her. 'Your pen. It's behind your ear.'

When she reached up her hand she sighed; of course it was.

Retrieving the pen from behind her ear, she reached for the last card he'd scrawled notes on and scribbled through half of it forcefully. 'Rachel wouldn't be seen dead wearing *that* either. You're turning her into a sex object.'

The chair squeaked back and forth. 'Bad boy hero, sexy heroine, explosions, treasure hunt, hint of romance—all the ingredients of a blockbuster, trust me…'

'The box office is all that matters to you, is it?' Cassidy began rhythmically tapping the end of her pen on the glass tabletop. 'Forget telling a story, or little things such as character arc and continuity.'

'We're still at the brainstorming stage. We're miles away from character arc and continuity. This is the fun part.'

Really? Because Cassidy hadn't noticed the 'fun part' so much. It was almost as if Will was determined to get her to argue with him. Surely a man with his experience in the business knew better than to fall into the usual traps of cliché and plot device? If she didn't know better she might say he was playing with her on purpose…

While she considered the possibility of that with narrowed eyes, she tapped her pen harder and faster against the glass. Will continued to add to the ambient noise with the squeaking of his chair.

Then his mouth twitched and he nodded at her pen. 'That could get irritating after a while…'

'You think?' She lifted her brows and tapped the pen harder. 'Like the squeaking of your chair, perhaps?'

When she pouted there was a split second of silence as the tapping and the squeaking stopped. Then, out of nowhere, they both laughed at the same time. Cassidy tossed the pen down, running her palms over her face as she groaned loudly. The man was making her *insane*!

Residual laughter sounded in the deep rumble of Will's voice. 'Time for a break.'

It only occurred to her that his voice sounded closer when warm hands closed over hers to lift them from her face, and she found herself tilting her chin up to look into the green of his gaze. He was gorgeous. Take-a-girl's-breath-away gorgeous. Her heart thundered against her breastbone loud enough for her to hear it in her ears as he smiled a small smile that darkened his eyes a shade, then lowered her hands before stepping back and gently tugging her upright.

'I need food.'

'Again? We ate less than an hour ago.' There had been sandwiches. Cassidy definitely remembered there being sandwiches.

'Five hours ago.'

It was? She looked out of the windows as Will turned, keeping hold of one of her wrists to draw her towards the door. Sure enough, outside the light was changing, the tide was turning and people were beginning to—

Hang on a minute. *Why* did Will still have hold of her wrist?

Turning her head, she dropped her chin and frowned down at the human handcuff. Long fingers were lightly hooked over her pulse-point, but they were hooked never-theless, and he was walking them through the living area towards the kitchen. She couldn't take a chance on him re-alising what he did to her pulse. So she gently twisted her wrist and reclaimed it, frowning all the harder at the fact her skin still tingled where he had touched.

Will glanced briefly over his shoulder, then walked to the giant refrigerator and looked inside. 'Steaks okay with you? We can flame-grill them on the deck.'

'Sounds more than fine with me.' She stopped at the end of the narrow breakfast bar and rested her palms on the granite surface. 'What can I do to help?'

'Chop some salad, if you like. Use whatever you fancy out of the fridge.'

Cassidy forgot herself and smiled as he reappeared, tossed the steaks down on the counter and reached into a drawer for barbecue utensils. 'You have the weirdest ac-cent now, you know. Tang of American, but still using Irish phrases.'

A brief sideways glance of sparkle-eyed amusement was aimed her way. 'You can take the boy out of Ireland...'

She rolled her eyes.

Will jerked his dark brows as he unwrapped the steaks. 'Everyone does it. You spend time in a certain environ-ment, surrounded by people who talk a certain way, and you absorb some of it. It's probably a subliminal need for acceptance.'

The idea that a man like Will would feel the need for acceptance anywhere momentarily baffled Cassidy. Maybe she was reading too much into it? She was known to do that. A lot of women were. She stepped towards the fridge to have a poke around for salad ingredients. 'Was it weird at first? Living here, I mean?'

'In Malibu or in California?'

When he reached past her for a bottle of sauce Cassidy's breathing hitched. He'd bent his upper body over hers, had reached his arm over her shoulder and brushed his fingertips against her hair on the way past, surrounding her for a fleeting moment with an intensely male body heat that contrasted so very sharply with the cold air from the refrigerator's interior. It had an immediate visceral reaction on her. Goosebumps broke out on her skin, her abdomen tensed, her breasts grew heavy. She even had to swallow hard to dampen her dry mouth and close her eyes to stifle a low moan.

For crying out loud—she knew it had been a long time since she'd last made love, but it was really no excuse for the compulsive need she suddenly felt to turn round and launch herself at him, so they could spend several hours seeing if they still remembered how to play each other's bodies like fine instruments…

One, two, three breaths of cool, refrigerated air—then she reappeared from behind the door with an iceberg lettuce, tomatoes, a cucumber, and two different bottles of salad dressing. When she chanced a sideways glance at Will she found him on the other side of the breakfast bar, studying her intently.

'Malibu or California?'

'What?'

'You asked was it weird living here. I asked Malibu or California.'

Oh, yes, that was right. She had done that. 'California.'

'Yes.'

She set her things on the counter and lifted a brow. 'Malibu?'

'No.'

When light danced across his eyes she knew he was messing with her, so she shook her head. 'A bowl for this stuff?'

'Second cupboard on the left, underneath you.'

'So why was California weird?' She opened the cupboard and hunched down to look inside.

'Why don't you hit me with *your* first impressions and I'll tell you if I felt the same way when I got here…' The sound of doors sliding told her he had moved towards the deck.

By the time she came back up, with a large wooden bowl in hand, he was firing up the outdoor grill. So she found a knife and a chopping board all on her own, while raising her voice to continue the conversation. 'Way more people, nobody smiles and says hello the way they do at home, hotter, brighter—drier. Nothing as green as you'd see in Ireland. Food's different, television is different, the cars people drive are different… Some things are familiar, but the vast majority of differences outshadow them…'

Will was smiling yet another small smile as he came back in, the sea breeze outside having created unruly waves in his dark hair that made him look even more boyish than he already did in his simple white T-shirt and blue jeans combo. No one would ever look at the man and put him in his early thirties. Good genetics, Cassidy supposed. His kids would inherit that anti-ageing gene, and the boys would all look like him, wouldn't they? With dark hair that even when tamed would rebel, with that outward flick at the nape, and green eyes that sparkled with amusement, and the charm of the devil when they wanted something, and—

Cassidy couldn't believe she was standing in his beautiful house and picturing dozens of mini-Wills standing between them. She'd be naming them next. Maybe her biological clock was kicking in?

'In other words weird…'

She smiled as she chopped. 'Okay. Point taken. So why is Malibu different?'

'It's not so crowded here. The air's better.' He shrugged his shoulders as he turned bottles of wine on a rack to read the labels. 'Quieter. More private. I'd lived in California long enough by the time I bought this place that it wasn't so alien to me any more. But this was the first place I felt I could call home.'

'You don't see Ireland as home any more?'

'I see it as where I come from, and a part of who I am, but I have my life in California now.'

Cassidy had known that for a long time. But hearing him say it didn't make it any easier. It was another thing that highlighted how different they were. Somehow she knew she would always see Ireland as home. She had thirty years' worth of memories there—not all of them good, granted. But it was the good and the bad that made her who she was—for better or worse. A part of her would always ache for the green, green grass of home if she left it behind. The fact Will had left *everything* behind without any apparent sense of poignancy made her wonder if he remembered their time together the same way she did. Or remembered that he had said he loved her.

Maybe the harsh truth was he hadn't. Not the way she had loved him. If he had he would never have left her, would he?

The sound of a cork popping brought her gaze back to him as he set a bottle of red wine on the counter to breathe. But when he reached for deep bowled glasses and she opened her mouth to remind him of the dangers of her errant tongue and alcohol, he surprised her.

'Why teaching?' he asked.

She frowned in confusion. 'What?'

'Why teaching?' He turned around and leaned back against the counter, folding his arms across his chest and studying her with hooded eyes. 'I don't remember you ever showing an interest in it when I knew you before.'

Well, no, because when he'd known her she'd still had dreams that felt as if they were within her grasp. Then she'd been given a harsh reality check. She shrugged and tossed the chopped-up salad ingredients in the bowl. 'Necessity to start with, I guess. I needed a job with a regular wage. If I was going to spend a good portion of my life working, it made sense to me to be doing something I might enjoy…'

'Do you?'

'Do I what?'

'Enjoy it?'

'I'd enjoy it more if I was better paid.' She shot him a brief smile, then concentrated on reading the labels on the salad dressings. 'I like little kids. They think in straight lines. They still believe in magic. Adults get the magic knocked out of them with age. Every day when I spend time with a classroom full of kids, and they do or say or discover something that makes me smile, I get a little of that magic back for a minute.'

When he remained silent, curiosity made her turn her head so she could try and read his expression. He was still staring at her, thick lashes still at half-mast so she couldn't see his eyes properly. It was disconcerting.

Then he tugged on a ragged corner of her heart with a low, rumbled comment. 'You used to believe in magic more than anyone I'd ever met…'

Cassidy felt a hard lump forming in her throat, and immediately felt the need to turn her face away, dropping her chin and hiding behind a strand of hair that had escaped from her up-do as she tried to open the lid of the salad dressing. 'Like I said. It gets knocked out of you with age.'

Was this lid cemented on? She pursed her lips and felt the cap digging into her palm as she tried twisting it with a little more force, shifting her shoulder so she was literally putting her back into it, while forcing words out through tight lips at the same time.

'Just part—of life—that's all. Nobody's fault. Or any—'

A large hand settled lightly over her fingers and Cassidy's chin snapped up. He gently removed the bottle from her hand and opened it with one deft twist of his wrist. Then he held it out for her, warmth shining from his eyes and the corners of his mouth tugging upwards. 'Borderline babbling again, Malone.'

Sighing heavily, she reached for the bottle. 'You're the one in charge of the magic these days—industry of dreams and all that. Maybe I handed on the baton.'

Will's head lowered closer to hers, his voice dropping an octave. 'You're saying I couldn't make magic back in the day?' Apparently it was enough to bring one of *those* smiles her way. 'I think my ego might be bruised.'

That wasn't the kind of magic she'd meant. But before she could form a coherent sentence he turned away, lifting the steaks from the counter-top and walking out onto the deck. Leaving Cassidy staring through the glass at him and feeling distinctly confused. Her inability to read him was really starting to bug her.

Once the steaks were on the fancy stainless steel grill he had on the deck, Will closed the lid and came back to the open door, leaning on the frame and studying her before he took a deep breath and asked, 'How are you feeling?'

'Better.' She smiled before turning to put away everything she hadn't used. 'I've stayed upright for more than twenty-four hours now—go me.'

'How do you feel about a trip tomorrow?'

Cassidy's eyes narrowed with suspicion. 'Where to?'

'Magic land…'

Leaning forward in her seat on the golf cart, Cassidy couldn't help but grin like an idiot at her surroundings. It was better than Christmas as far as she was concerned.

'You want to stop and take a look around?'

Yes! She turned to nod enthusiastically at Will. *'Please.'*

It might have seemed like an ordinary street to some people, but to Cassidy it really was magic land. From the second they'd pulled up at the studio's parking lot it had been nigh on impossible to keep the smile off her face. She'd dreamed about places like this for most of her life— but to actually be there…

To Will, visiting the back lots of a studio was probably like taking a busman's holiday, but there wasn't a single thing that Cassidy didn't find fascinating, with an almost child-like glee. Every large warehouse structure they passed was the cover of a storybook waiting to be opened; every extra in full costume was someone she wanted to talk to; every truck full of props was an adventure playground. And the streets of the back lot, with houses and storefronts and windows and open doorways, were just calling out for fictional characters to live there and tell their stories. Cassidy could practically *see* them walking around, hear their voices as they spoke.

She even found her imagination filling in the words...

With her short lap belt undone, she turned in her seat and found Will standing beside the open-sided cart. He held out a large hand to help her down, and in her excitement Cassidy forgot all the reasons why she shouldn't let him hold on to the hand she slipped into his as he led her down the deserted pseudo-New York street.

After a few steps he asked, 'You want to see inside?'

Nodding, she threw another smile his way.

So Will took them to the nearest open doorway and stepped back, setting her hand free to allow her to go ahead of him. 'Some have a room like this they can dress to be any kind of store they want, but most of the buildings only go back a couple of feet from the frontage.'

Cassidy turned a circle in the empty space, tilting her head back to look up at the skeletal structure of wood and ladders. Her nostrils were filled with the scent of that same wood warmed by the Californian heat outside, and it was all too easy to see why there were so many fire extinguishers around. The danger of fire would always be a worry for a studio. The whole place would go up like a tinderbox, wouldn't it?

'When they dress the room they put in a false ceiling and leave space to hang the lighting. If you look outside you'll see there aren't any door handles or streetlights; they get changed by the props department according to the era of the shoot…'

Drinking in every word, she felt her chest fill with what felt distinctly like joy. It had been such a long time since she'd felt that way. She could have wept with how wonderful everything was. To some it might have seemed false and empty, a charade—but not to her. To her it was a world full of possibilities…

Will's deep voice lowered until it was barely above a whisper, making Cassidy wonder for a moment if he'd even realised he'd spoken out loud. 'Yeah, I had a feeling you'd love this.'

Lowering her chin, she caught her breath when she realised how close he was to her. There was the beginning of a smile in the green of his eyes, and the accompanying warmth she could see seemed to reach out and wrap around her like a blanket on a winter's night. Then his gaze studied each of her eyes in turn, thick lashes flickering.

The intensity forced Cassidy to silently clear her throat before she could speak. 'I do. It's amazing. Thank you for bringing me here.'

Will studied her for another long moment that made her feel as if time stood still. Then he took a breath and looked around, shrugging wide shoulders beneath the pale blue shirt he wore loose over his jeans. 'Sometimes seeing where movies are made can help with the writing process. Anything that can be filmed on a back lot or on a stage saves money on the budget. Studios like that.'

It all came down to business for him, didn't it? He saw everything in terms of the bottom dollar. Another thing that was different. Yes, Cassidy knew it was part of his job—but it was yet another reminder that he wasn't the same Will Ryan she had known. In the last twenty-four hours she had actually convinced herself she'd seen brief glimpses of the old Will she had loved. But every time she thought she saw something in him that might help rebuild the merest shadow of the relationship they once had—and would therefore make it easier to remember how well they could work together—it was as if a switch flipped inside him. Then the Will she didn't know and couldn't read was back.

It was both disconcerting and frustrating. For a second she even wanted to grasp hold of his wide shoulders and shake him, demand that he let out the Will she knew from behind the impenetrable wall he seemed to have built around himself.

'I guess you have to worry more about that kind of stuff these days?'

'I do.' He wandered around the empty room, glancing briefly out through the windows clouded almost opaque with dust. 'It's one thing letting your imagination run riot in a script, but it's another producing something all the way through onto the screen.'

Cassidy nodded, her gaze following him around the room. He was practically prowling. Almost restless, silently alert, his steps taking him in a wide circle around her. His gaze slid unerringly to tangle with hers at regular intervals, and it felt as if he was assessing her, trying to decide what to say and what not to. It felt vaguely predatory to her. But that was ridiculous…

Finding her mouth dry again, she swallowed, and then dampened her lips before asking, 'So tell me what your company does.'

Pushing his hands into his pockets—a move Cassidy noticed he made a lot—Will continued circling her. 'We're responsible for the development and physical production of films and television shows. Sometimes we're directly responsible for the raising of funding for a production—sometimes we do it through an intermediary. Then we sell the end product to the big studios when it's done.'

'You script some of them yourself?'

'Some, yes.'

'Is it easier to sell your scripts if you can produce them?'

'Not always.' The corners of his mouth tugged wryly.

He was so guarded. Had Hollywood taught him to be that way? she wondered. It was a tough industry, after all. The fact he'd been successful in it meant he'd had to learn to play hard ball at some point. But then Will had always been driven. He'd had a rougher upbringing than most. To go from fostercare kid, handed from home to home, to end up rich and successful in Hollywood was one heck of an achievement. Surely he knew that?

As jealous as she was of his success, in practically every corner of his life in comparison to how very ordinarily hers had turned out, Cassidy was incredibly proud of him. She just wished she could tell him. Not that he wanted or needed to hear it.

'One of our productions is filming on one of the sound stages here. You want to go watch for a while?'

It was enough to put the smile back on her face. 'Can we?'

Will looked amused by her enthusiasm. 'Wouldn't have offered if we couldn't, would I?'

Oh, he could try and make her feel like a child for being so excited by everything he was showing her, but it wasn't going to stop her feeling that way. She rushed to the door and yanked it open to walk into the bright sunshine, jerking her head and grinning at him. 'Hurry up, then. We might miss some of the good stuff.'

An hour later she was sitting on a high folding chair, with her hands over the headphones on her ears, watching the small screen in front of her and listening to the dialogue from the actors mere feet from her. She wasn't even distracted by the fact Will was in a similar chair close beside her—or that every time she glanced at him he was watching her with silent amusement glowing in his eyes. In fact the only thing that took some of the excitement away was when she foolishly allowed reality to seep in around the edges of the experience.

It was a one-off experience for her—and no matter how much joy she felt, it was tainted by the fact it was another fleeting glance of what could have been. Had she been brave enough or selfish enough to leave Ireland behind her, follow the man she loved to California, her life could have been as wrapped up in the world of make-believe as Will's was. With luck, hard work and Will by her side, maybe she'd have made a go of it too. She could have been so happy. Maybe there would even have been a couple of those miniature Wills she kept seeing in her mind's eye running around that beachfront house of his by now...

The thought made her heart twist painfully in her chest. When the director yelled 'Cut!' she removed the headphones and swallowed away the lump in her throat as she handed them back to the sound engineer. 'Thank you.'

'No problem.' He smiled at her before moving away.

Will's low voice rumbled at her shoulder. 'What's wrong?'

'Nothing's wrong. Thanks again for this, Will—it's been amazing.' She flashed him a smile.

But he could still read her too well, and his eyes narrowed almost imperceptibly. 'Feeling sick again?'

Actually, she'd pretty much forgotten the tail-end of her cold as the day progressed, so she could answer that one with conviction. 'No. I'm feeling much better, as it happens—haven't even needed tablets.'

He continued studying her eyes. 'Then what is it?'

If she lied and said she was tired there was the chance he might suggest they leave—if he didn't see right through her the way he usually did when she lied—and she wasn't ready to leave yet. It wasn't as if she could tell him the truth, was it? How was she supposed to look him in the eye and tell him her active imagination had painted a picture of a life that wasn't hers so vividly that it made her feel the loss of it like a bereavement?

So she avoided his gaze and changed the subject. 'Is this a new show?'

'End of the first season. It's done well in the ratings. Already been renewed.' He waited for her to glance at him again before he added, 'We'll go take a look at the editing department next. Special effects are done somewhere else.'

Cassidy found herself mesmerised by the softness in his deep voice. And her errant tongue couldn't help but ask, 'Why are you doing this?'

Dark brows lifted in question.

'I thought you were mad keen to get the script done.'

He shrugged. 'Thought it might help.'

When he continued looking her straight in the eye, Cassidy had a moment of fear that he might know how much of a fraud she was. Was that what this whole behind-the-scenes day trip was? A way to try and get her creative juices flowing again? In fairness, it was a pretty great plan if that *had* been his aim. But if it had how, exactly, had he known? Had she been so transparent? Had the scenes she'd worked on with him been so dreadful in Hollywood terms? If they had, why hadn't he said so? If he knew what a phoney she was why hadn't he said something? Bringing her all the way across the world to allow her to make a fool of herself when in all probability he could more than likely have just bought her out of the contract…

'You were always as fascinated by this stuff as I was.' He stared into her eyes for another long moment, then looked away, turning his profile to her as he got to his feet. 'Seeing it should keep it real in your mind while we work on the script. And if we can cut a few corners by filming some scenes here instead of on location then we can free up some of the budget for better effects.'

Ah. Right. *Business.* That made more sense to her than him doing it because he knew how much she would love it. It put her mind at ease that he hadn't seen right through her charade. She didn't feel any better, though—it would have been nice if he'd cared enough to do it just because he knew the pleasure she would get from it.

But then Will Ryan had long since ceased to think of

Cassidy in terms of anything remotely resembling the word 'pleasure'—physically or otherwise…

She nodded firmly and edged off the seat. 'Editing department it is, then.'

CHAPTER FOUR

THEY'D spent most of the day at the studio, so it meant they had to spend the next few days digging in. To Cassidy's amazement it was going pretty well, all things considered.

Will's guided tour had indeed given her an extra dimension of insight to the logistics of each scene they came up with, and—even though she knew he hadn't intended it— it had also got her creative juices flowing. When they started getting words down on paper she felt as if she was getting a part of herself back again. It was exhilarating, and it boosted her self-confidence no end. Heck, she was even starting to have *fun*.

That would be the reason she would cite later for not having seen the danger coming her way before it arrived. Because if she'd been paying more attention…

When they couldn't agree on what should happen at the end of an action scene, Will came up with the idea that they read the lines aloud. Nothing unusual about that, she had thought at the time. It wasn't anything new, after all. When they had worked on the first of Nick Fortune's adventures they'd often acted out a scene before they'd even put words down, and sometimes they'd become so absorbed in the roles they were playing that it had added a dimension to the fictional characters they might never have thought of otherwise.

But back then they'd had a very different relationship. And it never occurred to Cassidy to take that into consideration when they got to their feet with their matching sheets of script in hand, hot from the printer.

Nick and Rachel had got themselves into trouble, and had been arguing about whose fault it was they were in the mess they were. They were minutes away from being tossed off the edge of a cliff by armed terrorists...

"'I suppose you're going to kill us now?" *That's* what you asked them? Why didn't you just offer to shoot us too?' said Will as Nick.

'Oooohhh,' laughed Cassidy as Rachel. 'Believe me if I had a gun right now I'd be more than happy to shoot you!'

She grinned when Will changed his voice to read one of the terrorists' lines. 'Would you two shut up? You've got about five minutes to make your peace.' He threw her an all too brief smile before jerking his chin at her to indicate it was her line.

Cassidy lifted her sheet and tried to find where they were. 'Just make sure *he* goes first. He's the one that got us into this mess.'

'*Me*? I'm not the one who screamed and gave away our position!'

'That spider was the size of Moby Dick!' Cassidy couldn't help but laugh again at the line. She *loved* that line. It was her line; she'd thought of it. She was *back*! What had made her think she couldn't do this again?

Will became Will again. 'Which brings us to the part under debate...'

The original idea had been to have Nick and Rachel fight their way out of the situation by distracting the terrorists with increased arguing. Cassidy had wanted it to be Rachel's idea; funnily enough Will had wanted it to be Nick's. Will suggested Nick should wink at Rachel, to let her know what he was doing. Cassidy said Rachel was too mad at him to play along with anything he came up with.

Suddenly Will looked at her, with a gaze that made her heart jump out of rhythm.

'What?' she asked a little breathlessly.

'I have an idea.' He stepped closer. 'Play along.'

Cassidy turned her head and eyed him with suspicion. 'What are you doing?'

'They get to the edge of the cliff. They're still arguing. Guns at their backs.'

'Uh-huh… And then…?'

Something dangerous shimmered across Will's eyes as he closed the gap between them, his deep voice lowering to a husky-edged rumble. 'Then, just before they're pushed over the edge, Nick asks for a last request for a dying man…'

'And that request would be…?'

Will smiled *that* smile and knocked her on her ear again. 'He asks to kiss Rachel.'

Cassidy's eyes widened. 'He *what*?'

'Just for the record, her face looks exactly like yours does right now…'

Somewhere in the foggy haze of her completely distracted brain Cassidy knew it would ramp up the scene to a new level, but that wasn't what made her heart thunder loudly in her ears and her body temperature rise. *No*. It was the fact that Will was staring down at her with a darkening gaze.

He wasn't seriously going to—?

Thick dark lashes lowered slowly as he took the last step to bring his body within inches of hers. And as she swayed a little on her feet he angled his head, his gaze lowering to focus on her mouth. Oh, God. *He was*. But why? He couldn't—

Cassidy's lips reached for his of their own volition when he was less than an inch away, like a flower lifting towards the sun. His mouth was full and firm and hotter than she remembered from the hundreds of times she'd kissed him before, but no less familiar. When his large hands framed her face, she took a deep breath through her nose. When he leaned into her she exhaled against his lips, her heavy eyelids closing…

If anyone had told her a month ago that some time in the very near future Will Ryan would be kissing her again, and she would be feeling it in every cell in her body, she'd have laughed out loud at the ridiculousness of the notion. But he was—and she did.

It was surreal. And at the same time it was like coming home.

Long fingers slid down her cheeks, around her neck and into her hair. The taste of him was on her lips and the heady scent of clean laundry and pure Will was surrounding her. Cassidy forgot about the script, forgot about the fact they were playing the part of Nick and Rachel, forgot about the danger in what they were doing. She forgot all those things.

Instead she dropped her sheet of paper and reached for handfuls of the shirt above his lean waist, while he slipped a hand up to cradle the back of her head, his fingers threading into her hair as Cassidy drowned in the sensations flooding her body.

She'd missed kissing him. *How she'd missed it.* It was as if her body had been asleep like Snow White's, and only now, with the right man, was she being kissed back into life. But then no one had ever kissed her like Will kissed her. He could make the world tilt on its axis beneath her feet. *Always.* From the very first time he'd kissed her. He'd caught her similarly off-guard as they'd walked over the O'Connell Street Bridge in Dublin, after taking photographs of possible locations for a short film they'd been working on for their class. With no warning he had taken her hand, tugged her to him and kissed her. *Because he had to*, he had told her afterwards. As if it had been as vital to him as breathing or drinking water, or any of the other things a person had to do to survive...

When he slowly drew his lips from hers, her mouth followed his back for the inch she'd closed, her eyes opening wide and searching his with a combination of wonder and fear.

After a brief moment of studying her with a dark unreadable gaze, Will rested his cheek against hers, whispering into her ear in a husky voice, 'Then Nick says, "You take the one on the left".'

Cassidy's heart plummeted to the soles of her feet.

Will released her and stepped back, turning abruptly and informing her in a flat, businesslike voice, 'That works better. So, we'll add that in and jump straight to the fight and the chase scene...'

'Right.' Cassidy nodded dumbly while she tried to get her breathing under control. The script. Nick and Rachel. Not Will and Cassidy. That was what the kiss had been about. He hadn't kissed her because he'd wanted to. He'd just forgotten they didn't have the same relationship now they'd had before when they would have played out similar Nick and Rachel scenes—*apparently*.

Bending down to retrieve the sheets of paper on the floor, she took a deep breath and puffed out her cheeks as she exhaled. She could only pray he wasn't planning on acting out the love scene they had planned for Scene Three…

She didn't think she could survive Will Ryan breaking her heart twice in one lifetime. She wasn't entirely sure she'd got over the first time.

The kiss changed things. At least it did for Cassidy. She tried not to let it, but she couldn't stop it—partly because she couldn't seem to get it out of her head…

What she needed to do was focus on what they were doing. Heck, at this point she would even take a stab at re-building some kind of platonic friendship with Will. After all, she had to work across a desk from him every day. How was she supposed to do any of those things if every time she looked at him she was thinking about how it had felt to be kissed by him and to kiss him back? Why was she so obsessed by it anyway? It wasn't as if she'd kissed him back because she'd wanted to—at least she told herself it wasn't. She'd been playing a part, the same way he had, thinking on her feet, reacting to what he'd done—that was all. It didn't *mean* anything.

Darn it, he was looking at her again. She could *feel it*. Every time he did it the hair on the back of her neck tingled.

'Stir crazy?'

She kept pacing around the room, the same way she had for most of the two days since they'd kissed. 'I'm fine.'

'Well, I'm not,' his voice rumbled back. 'All that pacing is making *me* crazy.' Will sighed heavily. 'You're not used to sharing space with someone these days, are you? I never pictured you as that much of a loner…'

Cassidy stopped dead in her tracks and angled her head. 'Excuse me?'

'Lived with someone else after me, did you?'

Her jaw dropped. What business was it of his who she had or hadn't lived with? She could have lived with twenty men. Not that she *had* lived with anyone else, barring the time she'd lived in her father's house while he was ill. But that wasn't the point.

A few times over the years she'd considered advertising for a flatmate, but by then she'd got used to having her own space. Living on her own, she didn't have to worry about someone else's opinions on things like what TV channel to watch, or how loud she could play music, or any of a dozen other compromises a person made when they shared living space.

'Compromises…'

Cassidy frowned when he said the very thing she'd just thought—as if he'd somehow stepped inside her head. 'What?'

'I said living with someone involves compromises.'

'It does.' She nodded. 'And forced intimacy…'

'Shared responsibilities…'

When he looked up at her she turned away and began pacing again, the words quietly slipping off the tip of her tongue. 'Never being alone.'

She frowned sideways at him when she said it, confusion clouding her vision as he studied her with a curious expression that almost said he suspected why she'd been so uneasy with him of late. She hoped he didn't! But while he continued staring at her there was an inexplicably heavy tension in the room.

Her chin lifted. 'Okay. Fine. You're right—all are things I suck royally at. Barring the last one. I excel at being alone these days—it's what I do best.'

'Cass…' He kept his voice low. 'Living with someone is nothing like what we're doing now. You know that. And being alone isn't—'

'Of course it's nothing like this. This is artificial. And temporary.' Cassidy tried to figure out why that felt so bad and couldn't seem to find an answer. Maybe being alone for so long had affected her more than she'd realized? She started pacing again. 'This isn't sharing space. It's temporary. A charade.'

'A charade?' he repeated dryly.

She glanced sideways at him again as she changed direction. 'Oh, come on. It's miraculous enough that we've managed to work together this last while…'

'We shared space before and it was never this much of a problem…' Will reached for his mug and frowned when he discovered it was empty. 'You want coffee?'

He didn't wait for an answer, reaching across the large desk for her empty mug and pushing his squeaky chair back. 'I don't think this has anything to do with sharing space with me. I think trying to keep me at arm's length is starting to take its toll on you.'

When he left the room her feet immediately followed him. 'And what exactly is *that* supposed to mean?'

'I think you know what it means.'

How dared he assume he knew her every thought? Just because nine times out of ten he was in the ballpark area, it didn't mean he could read her damn mind.

She followed him across the living room. 'So if I'm not throwing myself at you it means I'm fighting some inner battle, does it? How do you get that head of yours through doors?'

Setting their mugs down on the breakfast bar, Will went about refilling the coffee-maker, replacing the filter and spooning in coffee granules. 'Doesn't have anything to do with throwing yourself at me. You're determined not to allow yourself to even be friends with me again. It's childish, frankly. We're both adults.'

Placing her hands on her hips, she stopped dead at one end of the breakfast bar, speechless.

With the coffee set to percolate, Will turned around, leaning nonchalantly against the counter-top on the opposite side of the kitchen from her and calmly folding his arms across the studio logo on his T-shirt. 'You're different. The Cass I met in the Beverly Wilshire just over a week ago isn't the girl I knew in Dublin. The girl I knew in Dublin was open-minded and honest to the point of bluntness, and she would never have let something brood in her the way you have since you got here. So let's just clear the air and get it over with, shall we?'

Cassidy opened her mouth to tell him to go straight to—

But he looked her in the eye and knocked the air out of her lungs by saying, 'You blame me for our break-up, don't you?'

He wasn't done, either. Not content with opening the can of worms, he then twisted the knife she felt she had in her chest by adding, 'Maybe you should just take a minute and remember who it was that did the breaking up before I left…'

The sharp gasp of air hurt her already raw throat.

Then a muted doorbell sounded, and the door at the top of the stairs was flung open. 'Hello? Anybody home? Time to put down the keyboard!'

Cassidy had a brief glimpse of the frown on Will's face before she snapped her head around to watch with wide eyes as Angelique appeared. If it wasn't surprise enough finding out that the woman had a key to Will's house, there was then a thundering of footsteps and a small blonde-haired ball of energy ran down the stairs, across the wooden floor, and launched itself into Will's waiting arms.

'Uncle Will!'

Uncle Will? Cassidy couldn't help it; her jaw dropped. Not just at the sight of the little girl throwing her small arms around the column of his neck. What really amazed her was Will's expression as he held her. He was transformed. Gone was the intense, unreadable, pain-in-the-rear Will, and in his place was a man who looked as if he'd just shed five years. Light danced in his eyes, he grinned broadly, and there was the sound of deep, rumbling, happy laughter before he made an exaggerated groan and leaned his head back to look down at her.

'Hey, munchkin.'

'We brought a picnic!'

'Did you, now?' He lifted his dark brows as he looked in Angelique's direction, 'Did I know we were having a picnic?'

'It's a surprise, silly!' the little girl informed him.

'Indeed it is,' he answered dryly.

Angelique had made it to Cassidy's side. 'This is what

happens when you two stand me up for dinner. Script or no script, you still have to eat.'

Will looked up as he bent to set the child on her feet. 'We have managed to feed ourselves on our own. Ever hear of a little thing called a phone, Angie?'

'Ah, but if we'd phoned ahead it wouldn't be a surprise, would it?'

'Remind me to ask for my key back some time.'

Cassidy was rapidly putting two and two together. She even found her gaze sliding across to the little girl who was tugging on Will's jeans to see if she could see any similarities between them. Having had such vivid images of miniature Wills in her mind since she'd arrived in his gorgeous house, she felt the ragged edges of her heart grate painfully at the thought of finding any. She didn't *want* Will to have any children she might be forced to look at. The thought of him having them with any woman who wasn't her was apparently painful enough.

Which made no sense whatsoever, considering how much she currently disliked him and how close they had been to a major argument not five minutes earlier.

'Uncle Will?'

He hunched down to look the little girl in the eye; the thoughtfulness of the simple act made Cassidy's heart hurt all over again. 'Yes, munchkin, what can I do for you?'

'The picnic's for the beach.'

'Is it indeed?'

She nodded enthusiastically. 'And I brought my swimsuit and my bodyboard.'

'Ah.' Will pursed his mouth into a thin line and frowned almost comically at her, before taking a deep breath through his nose. 'We'd better go check the sea is still there, then, hadn't we?'

The little girl giggled, and Cassidy found herself smiling at them as Angelique linked their arms at the elbow and lowered her voice conspiratorially. 'Sometimes I wonder who has who wrapped around their little finger. I hope you've brought a bikini with you?'

The thought of publicly displaying her body on a Malibu beach next to the goddess that was Angelique Warden made Cassidy want to curl up in a ball and die. That was not happening in this lifetime. Not that she owned a bikini to begin with, but still…

'Will could give you a surfing lesson while he's helping Lily bodyboard.'

Cassidy's gaze shifted sharply and crashed into Will's as he stood to his full height. Then her troublesome imagination revisited the image she'd had of him emerging from the surf and she swallowed hard. For a moment she even thought she could hear herself making a gulping noise.

Thick lashes blinked while he stared at her. The intensity returning to his gaze was even fiercer than before. Oh, please, *please* don't let now be one of the times when he can read my mind, she silently pleaded. There was only so much humiliation she could take.

Then he nodded. 'You'll need sunscreen. Beach towels are in the laundry room. Angie knows where everything is.'

Before Cassidy could protest, he turned his attention to Lily. 'Right, then. While Cass and I get changed, you and your mom can go get this picnic we've been promised. Are there cookies?'

'*Duh*, Uncle Will.'

* * *

Despite many, many, *many* carefully worded protests, Cassidy found herself on the beach—thankfully in a swimsuit rather than a bikini. Even that was covered by a thigh-length light shirt. Smothered in the highest factor sunscreen she'd packed, she also had the large-brimmed straw hat Angelique had left behind on her last visit to Will's house on her head. She had the prerequisite sunglasses on, and had bent one knee as artfully as she could manage as she sat on the large blanket beside the bikini-clad Angelique. If people squinted Cassidy reckoned they might look like nineteen-fifties movie star next to modern-day goddess. Hopefully. After all, women had been adored for their hourglass figures back then—which meant, as always, her timing was severely off. Not that it made her feel any more comfortable in her own skin.

Watching Will playing in the surf with Lily was the worst form of water torture she'd ever been submitted to. It was just plain *wrong* to be drooling at the sight of him in long swim shorts—bare chest, toned, tanned, gorgeous enough to die for—while he played with a small child. Especially if he was that small child's father, and she was sitting chatting to the woman he'd made that child with. Cassidy had never had a worse case of the green-eyed monster in all her life.

'Lily adores him.' Angelique was smiling at them when Cassidy looked her way. 'He'll make a great father some day.'

Cassidy exhaled with relief as quietly as she could manage it. 'She's gorgeous.'

'Obviously I think so. But then I'm a tad biased. Do you have kids, Cass?'

'Thirty of them.' She smiled at Angelique's expression. 'I'm a schoolteacher.'

'Ahh. You scared me for a minute.'

Despite a lingering modicum of jealousy over her relationship with Will, Cassidy found herself warming to Angie. She wasn't at all the way the tabloids portrayed her. And seeing her obvious love for her daughter humanised her.

Turning onto her stomach, Angie swung her feet back and forth in the air and studied Cassidy from behind her sunglasses. 'Did you and Will ever talk about having kids when you were together?'

It was a very personal question, but by asking it she'd already shown she knew there had been more to their relationship than being scriptwriting duo Ryan and Malone. The thing was, talking about their relationship with someone who might well be in, or have been in, a similar relationship with Will made Cassidy uncomfortable.

So she sought a simple answer. 'We were young.'

The fact she'd said it with a shrug of her shoulders didn't seem to fool Angie. 'Ever since I've known Will he's been reluctant to talk about you. It took us to get him drunk one night before he would even talk about growing up in Ireland…'

He'd talked about his childhood? Wow. Cassidy wondered if Angie knew what a big deal that was for Will. She'd been dating him for nearly a year before she'd got the full story—though in fairness she hadn't had to get him drunk.

But her brain had latched onto one seemingly insignificant word. *'Us?'*

Angie examined the perfectly manicured fingernails on one hand. 'Lily's father—my on-again off-again partner Eric—is one of Will's best friends. It's how I got to know Will. And why he's Lily's godfather.'

Immediately Cassidy's gaze sought them out again in the sea. Will was swinging the little girl round and round in circles, while she squealed in delight and he grinned boyishly at her. 'Oh.'

She'd got that one completely wrong, then, hadn't she?

There was a chuckle of laughter. 'Yes, I wondered if you'd thought that. You're delightfully easy to read, aren't you? I can't tell you how refreshing that is in Hollywood.'

Heat built on Cassidy's cheeks that had absolutely nothing to do with the sun.

'Can I ask you a question, Cass?'

A sense of dread made her cringe as she looked down at the woman she had a sneaking suspicion was about to ask the one question she didn't want to answer. 'Depends on what it is.'

Angelique smiled. 'I've wondered why Will didn't bring you with him.'

'When he moved here from Ireland?'

'Yes. You were quite the writing team, on top of the re-lationship you had.'

Okay, not the question she'd been waiting for. Maybe that was why she answered it honestly, her chin dropping and her voice lowering even though there wasn't any chance he could hear her from where he was. 'I couldn't leave.'

'So he did ask?'

'Yes.' It was a simplistic answer to a situation that had been very complicated.

There was a moment of silence, then, 'Do you regret it?'

Cassidy smiled sadly. 'That's not an easy one to answer. It's not a case of regretting; it's more of a case of what was right and what was wrong at the time, and what was meant to be and what wasn't. And I have *no idea* why I'm telling you this…'

'Maybe you need a friend?' Angelique waited until Cassidy looked at her, and then she nodded sharply and beamed. 'I've decided I like you, Cass. I think we'll be great friends. You don't treat me like a movie star, and that's a huge bonus.'

Cassidy lowered her voice to a conspiratorial whisper. 'You *are* a movie star.'

Angie lowered her voice to a similar level, 'Shh. Somebody might hear you.'

They were laughing when the sun was suddenly blocked out, forcing Cassidy to shade her eyes with a hand as she looked up at the dark silhouette surrounded by bright light.

'Ready for your surfing lesson?'

CHAPTER FIVE

'I DON'T actually want a surfing lesson. Honestly.'

'Don't knock it till you've tried it.' Will turned round and took the two steps required to get to where she'd been dragging her heels. Reaching out, he captured her wrist in long fingers and tugged her along behind him. 'You might like it.'

'I'll sink like a whale,' she grumbled.

'Whales don't sink; they swim. So will you.' He threw a frown over his shoulder as he continued tugging her along the sand, 'Stop being paranoid about your weight, Cass. Women are supposed to curve. I'm sick to death of being surrounded by stick-thin women counting the calories in a bottle of water.'

Trying to free her wrist was getting her nowhere. 'Bullying me again, Ryan?'

'Nope. Forcing you to have a good time. It's for your own good. You seem to have forgotten how.'

'Said by the man who doesn't have time to go surfing, having bought a house by the ocean for that very purpose? I think you'll find that falls into the category of *I will when you will*,' she retorted.

He stopped so suddenly she careened into the wall of

his back, and grunted in a very unladylike manner before scowling up at his face.

The sight of his face leaning closer to hers made her eyes widen. That was before he lowered his voice and rumbled a meaningful, 'Oh, I know how to have *fun*, Cass. Don't you worry…'

Judging by the glint in his eyes, he wasn't talking about surfing fun either.

Standing back a little, he frowned at her body. 'That's got to go.'

When he released her wrist, she lifted both hands to grip hold of her shirt as if he might try to remove it at any second. 'The shirt *stays*.'

Will folded his arms across the sculpted chest she was trying very hard not to look at. 'You *do* know it's going to be transparent in the water, don't you?'

Actually, that thought hadn't occurred to her. But now he'd pointed it out she was even less likely to participate in a surfing lesson than she had been sixty seconds ago…

She started backing away. 'Well, I don't know about you, but I'm famished. I've heard a rumour there's a picnic on the go, so I think we should just—'

There was a short chuckle of deep male laughter, and then he leaned over and captured her wrist again, shaking his head as he tugged her forward. 'Down on your stomach on the board…'

Huh? Her gaze dropped and discovered a surfboard on the sand. She scowled at his words. 'On my stomach? On the board?'

He ducked down a little to get her attention, his nose mere inches from hers. 'Surfing lesson—remember?'

'I thought it would be in the water.' How was she supposed to think straight when he was so close?

Will's gaze dropped briefly to her mouth when she dampened her lips, then lifted to tangle with hers for equally as brief a moment before he leaned back and looked down at the board. 'Basics on dry land. *Then* we go in the water.'

Well, how was she supposed to know that? Okay, on her stomach—with Will standing over her, looking down at her rear. Cassidy silently prayed for a tidal wave…

'Why am I getting on my stomach?'

'Because that's what you do to paddle the board out far enough to catch an incoming wave…'

Right. Except that statement presupposed she actually *wanted* to catch a wave—which frankly she didn't. Waves shouldn't be caught. Cassidy believed they should be allowed to roam the earth in freedom, with all their other wave friends. She might even start a campaign of some kind: *Save the Wave*. Catchy, she thought.

She sighed heavily, focused her mind on another method of stalling Will, and came up with, 'Maybe you should demonstrate first?'

With a shake of his head that indicated he was fully aware of what she was doing, Will dropped onto the board, leaving her staring down at him in the same way she'd feared he would stare at her. Somehow she had the feeling her view was much better than his would be. Then he started to move his arms, and she became fascinated with the play of muscles on his tanned back. Was he working out nowadays? She didn't remember him being so…*toned*…

'Paddle evenly with both arms, and then turn and watch

for a wave. Try to time it so you jump to your feet as it hits your board.' He demonstrated by jumping lithely to his feet and reaching his arms out to his sides for balance. 'Then use your feet to steer the board. If you shift your weight to your toes you'll go one way; rock back onto your heels and you go the other.'

He made it sound so easy. But his description of brain surgery would probably consist of *Pop skull open, move jelly stuff around and put lid back on*. Whereas Cassidy suspected *her* version of surfing would involve less of the standing up and more of the getting wet and spluttering as she tried to get salt water out of her lungs.

'Your turn.' Will stepped off the board and quirked his brows when she hesitated, his voice lowering and his eyes sparkling. '*Chicken*. Whatever happened to the hunger to learn and the spirit of adventure you used to have?'

Cassidy threw another scowl at him, pursed her lips and lowered herself cautiously onto the board. 'I really do hate you, you know.'

'No, you don't.' He hunched down beside her.

When she was on her stomach, she looked up at him in time to see his gaze rise from studying her body. It made her laugh. 'Oh, yes, I do.'

The first time she attempted jumping up to her feet she fell over, but managed to get a hand on the hot sand to help right herself. Will encouraged her with a low, 'Try again.'

The second time she fell on her rear, and frowned hard at his obvious amusement. He cleared his throat and held out a hand to help her up. 'Again.'

Cassidy growled at him. 'When does it start to be fun, exactly?'

The third time was the charm. She not only fell over, she fell on Will, and toppled him backwards onto the sand, creating a tangle of legs and forcing him to wrap her body in his arms. Yup—her run of incredible luck had continued. Because when she puffed air at the loose strand of hair that had got in her eyes and looked down her face was inches away from his. And he was smiling one of *those* smiles.

Someone, somewhere really had it in for her.

The heat from his bare chest seeped through the thin material of her shirt and made every cell of her body unbearably aware of where she was fitted against him. It was like being set on fire. She felt the lack of oxygen to her brain making her dizzy, felt the ache of physical awareness so keenly it almost snapped her in two. Then one large hand lifted, and impossibly gentle fingertips brushed her hair back and tucked the strand behind her ear.

Cassidy felt her heart beating so hard against her sensitised breasts that she was certain Will must feel the erratic rhythm too. She needed to say something funny to break the tension—needed to move as far away from him as possible before he realised how damn turned on she was—needed—

She saw his throat convulse before he took a deep breath that crushed her breasts tighter to the wall of his chest. 'We should try again.'

What? Her eyes widened at the words. He couldn't possibly mean—

Will studied her eyes, then rolled her to the side. 'You need to pick a point in front of you to focus on as you jump onto your feet. That'll make it easier to balance…'

Struggling awkwardly to her feet while she felt her cheeks burning, Cassidy avoided his gaze and frowned at her foolishness—or her wishful thinking, or whatever it was that had made her heart leap the way it had. 'If I can't do this on dry land I don't see how I stand a bat's chance of doing it on moving water.'

While she bent over to swipe the sand off her legs, Will's deep voice sounded above her head. 'Don't give up so easy, Cass. Some things are worth the effort.'

Her gaze shot up to tangle with his and he shrugged. 'You love the ocean. Always did. Makes sense that anything that allows you to appreciate it more you'll end up enjoying.'

Several hours later she discovered he was right. The fact he'd been just the right degree of persuasive, determined and patient at varying stages to get her to that point had not gone unnoticed either. Any more than she'd failed to notice when he saw his theory on the transparency of her shirt when wet had been right too.

It was her last attempt. She managed to stay upright long enough to ride the wave for several feet, and the exhilaration of achievement burst forth from her lips in joyous laughter at the same time as Will let out a victory yell. When she inevitably fell off and surfaced from the water, lifting her hands to smooth her wet hair back from her face as she grinned like an idiot, she looked up—and her grin faltered. He had hold of the board as he waded towards her, waist deep in water the same way she was. But then he lifted his chin, his gaze travelling across the foaming surface and sliding up her body oh-so-very-slowly.

When he looked into her eyes the heat she could see both robbed her of her ability to breathe and slammed into her midriff with such force that the next wave almost made her lose her footing in the shifting sands.

For the longest time they stared at each other. The ebb and flow of the tide dragging her abdomen back and forth was all too evocative, considering the ferocity of her physical desire, and eliciting a low moan from the base of her throat that the wind thankfully dragged away. Then Will frowned—hard—turning his head and looking out to sea so that Cassidy caught sight of a muscle moving in his clenched jaw.

Almost in slow motion she saw him exerting control over himself. It was heartbreaking. Especially considering the fact that she was faced with the very image of him she'd conjured in her imagination when he had first told her he surfed. Standing there, with silvery rivulets of water running off his body, shining silvery in the bright sunshine, droplets of the same shimmering water falling from wet tendrils of the dark hair that clung to his forehead and the column of his neck. *He was glorious.* More than that, even. He was the most sensationally sexy man she had ever laid eyes on. And she had never wanted him as much as she did at that moment—while he'd taken a deep breath and got his self-control back in the blink of an eye.

When he looked at her again the small smile on his full mouth didn't make it all the way up into his eyes. 'Told you you'd get it. Well done.'

But Cassidy couldn't let it go that easily. And the very fact he had so obviously been affected by her gave her enough of a subliminal confidence boost to take a step towards him. 'Will—'

His eyes narrowed at the husky edge of her voice. 'I'm going to catch a few waves of my own. Be back in a while.'

With that he turned away, got on the board, paddled further out to sea—and the moment was gone. He'd made it plain that whatever moment of remembered desire from the past he'd just experienced could be dismissed in a heartbeat. Men were supposed to think about sex at ridiculously regular intervals, so they said. Cassidy was merely a woman in the nearest equivalent of a wet T-shirt. She got that.

But the rejection hurt. It hurt *bad*.

Setting a sheet of the first draft of their script to one side after she'd proofread it, Cassidy reached for another. Even though they worked in silence for the following fifteen minutes, she could still feel him studying her. He'd been doing it for days. And it was getting to her big-time.

'What, Will?'

'I'm just thinking of going to the kitchen to get a knife.'

'To do what?' She didn't look at him. He might have been studying her like some kind of bug under a microscope, but since the beach she'd been able to look at him for no longer than a few seconds before she had to avert her gaze. Apparently his rejection still hurt. And looking at him made it worse.

'To cut the atmosphere in this room…'

She sighed heavily. 'Will—'

'Right.' He pushed to his feet and lifted the sheets from her hand, setting them to one side. Then he grabbed hold of her hands and tugged. 'Time for a change of scenery. And lunch.'

It was beginning to feel as if she'd been trapped in the house with Will for years on end. People didn't get jail sentences as long. Every hour felt as if it was dragging. Plus, if Will kept feeding her the way he was she was going to go home weighing more than when she'd arrived.

The second she was on her feet he let go of her hands, turned, and headed into the next room. Cassidy automatically fell into step behind him, somehow unable to drag her disobedient gaze from the errant curls of dark hair brushing the collar of his cream shirt. It was easier looking at him when he didn't know she was, she supposed...

'We'll eat on the deck,' he announced as he glanced over his shoulder. 'The ocean is supposed to have a calming effect.'

Cass shook her head at his dry wit as they moved into the kitchen. 'You want me to take anything out?'

'Juice and glasses would be good.'

She opened a cupboard for glasses and the fridge for juice, feeling a pang of sadness at how they moved around each other as if they'd been doing it for years. It was like a choreographed dance. He reached an arm up to the cupboard door; she ducked under it. She turned for the fridge; he circled around her in one fluent step. She opened the refrigerator door to put away the juice; he reached inside for mayo and ham before he closed it again...

Cassidy had watched her parents doing a similar dance hundreds of times over the years during her childhood, and had never appreciated how much it demonstrated their ease with each other. But then they'd had decades to learn the moves; Cassidy and Will hadn't had all that long even when they were together.

Without thinking she casually handed him a chopping board on her way to opening the sliding doors. When he looked sideways at her, he frowned for a second before taking it.

'It's always beautiful out here,' she said from the doorway.

'I know,' Will answered, with a smile in his deep voice.

Stepping on to the deck, she set the glasses down on a small table and then moved towards the railing, where she breathed deep and smiled. It was the kind of place she would have allowed herself to relax and just 'be', under better circumstances. She wondered if Will ever felt that way. Pleasure in the simple things had never been the young Will's thing—not that he hadn't appreciated them; he'd just always been ambitious for more. But Cassidy had learned how precious and fragile life could be. It was important to take pleasure in the simple things, she felt.

But, looking at the ocean, she found her thoughts wandering inevitably to the same things. For the hundredth time since it had happened she found herself revisiting what had happened the day he'd taught her to surf—which in turn led her to revisiting the kiss during their 'rehearsal'. She had no idea why she was so obsessed by that kiss. Okay, admittedly the mature version of Will was oh-so-sexy—she would have to be blind not to have noticed. Under tall, dark and handsome in the dictionary it probably said *see Will Ryan*.

The sound of a plate being set on the table behind her gave her enough warning to get her thoughts under control before he appeared in her peripheral vision. Then they stood there for a while, side-by-side in silence, before Cassidy chanced a sideways glance at him just as Will turned his head to look at her.

He smiled a more genuine smile than he had in days, and she felt another shiver of awareness as he asked in his deliciously deep voice, 'Better?'

'I shook the cold a week ago.'

'That wasn't what I meant.'

Yes, she knew it wasn't what he'd meant. Since stalling never seemed to work with him any better than lying did, she took a deep breath and admitted, 'I'm sorry. I guess being cooped up in that room is starting to get to me…'

Will nodded his head, as if he'd already known the answer, his gaze shifting back to the ocean. After a few moments he said, 'Thank you.'

'For what?'

Turning around, he reached out and lifted a glass before smiling at her with a light sparkling in the green of his eyes. 'For helping with lunch.'

Cass smiled back at him. *Liar.* But she didn't call him on it; she appreciated that he hadn't pushed her any further on why she was feeling the way she was. Apparently a little honesty really did go a long way. Anyway, she had a sneaking suspicion he already knew, and was letting her off the hook by not saying it out loud. She should really thank him in return for that. But she didn't, because that would be bringing it up all over again. Instead she turned away from the railing and sat down in one of the comfortably padded wicker chairs on the deck, reaching for a sandwich as Will did the same and sank into a matching chair beside her.

They managed a whole ten minutes of companionable silence, but then he casually ruined it by asking, 'So… you want to tell me what else has been bugging you?'

The half-eaten sandwich froze halfway to her mouth, her appetite waning. Then she took a deep breath and went right ahead and took a bite, filling one side of her cheek as she chewed.

'Okay, then.' Will lifted another sandwich. 'I'll just ask

every half hour from here on in until you yell it at me in the middle of an argument. That usually works.'

Then he glanced at her from the corner of his eye and had the gall to add a wink. She forced herself to speak. 'Still got that pitbull quality to your personality, don't you?'

'Mmm-hmm.' He took a large bite of sandwich and grinned at her as he chewed.

'That wasn't actually meant as a compliment…'

He spoke with the food still in his mouth. 'I prefer to think of it as a dogged determination to get to the root of an issue before it becomes a bigger problem than it needs to be.' Ridiculously thick lashes brushed against his skin a couple of times while he considered her and swallowed his food. 'If my memory serves right—letting you work things through in your head for too long before you talk about them does that.'

'I've been stuck under a roof with someone I can barely hold a conversation with for two weeks. How is that *not* supposed to get to me? Maybe I have a *right* to be moody for a while under those circumstances?'

'No, you don't. Not if talking about it is all it takes to fix it.' He frowned, 'Who *likes* being moody anyway?'

Shrugging her shoulders, Cassidy focused her attention on her sandwich, mumbling under her breath, 'In my experience cute guys who think it adds to their feeble attempts at seeming mysterious…'

There was a very noticeable silence that drew her gaze back to his face, where a stunned expression was warring with amusement. She scowled at him. 'What now?'

'You think I'm *cute*?'

'I didn't say that.' Well, not on purpose she hadn't.

'It's okay. I'm fine with you thinking I'm cute. Though I should probably tell you it has a slightly different meaning over here than it does in Ireland...'

'I know what it means over here, and for the record it's not all that different to what it means back home. And I *don't* think that about you.'

Very visibly having to control his smile, Will leaned back and nodded. 'See, I was going to tell you what I really think is making you feel cooped up...and how I feel about the same thing... But now...? Now I think I'm just going to let you come to your own conclusions. That way I get to be both cute *and* mysterious...'

'That's not what I—' She fought the need to throw her sandwich at him as she felt heat rising on her neck. 'Don't edit my lines outside the office, Ryan.'

'You know,' he sighed dramatically, and let loose a killer one of *those* smiles, 'suddenly I'm in a much better mood than I was twenty minutes ago.'

Will had the gall to chuckle, looking at her from the corner of his sparkling eyes. Darn it. He was gloating, wasn't he? What had happened to the supposedly professional relationship they'd agreed to have? Flirting with her, using a combination of random winks, sparkling eyes and *that* smile, could hardly be considered *professional*.

Cassidy felt distinctly as if she was constantly waging a battle of some kind with him and...heaven help her...he was *winning*.

He was showing her that he could read her better than anyone ever had—get under her skin and bug her more than anyone ever had—get her hormones to scatter all rational thought to the wind and make her laugh when she really didn't want to by lifting his eyebrows ridiculously at her like he currently was…

With a shake of her head she dragged her gaze away from him, to look for some of the peace the ocean had briefly brought her way. 'You are still the most annoying man on the planet, you know.'

'Ahh…but I'm also *cute*.' He inhaled deeply through his nose, smug satisfaction oozing from the rumble of his voice. 'And *mysterious*…'

When she glanced sideways she saw him take another bite of his sandwich. Instead of saying anything smart in return she did the same thing. They sat for another ten minutes in what could almost have been misconstrued as a companionable silence, eating and looking out over the ocean. It was nice. Under further scrutiny Cassidy realised to her complete and utter astonishment it was better than nice. She almost felt…*content*…and it had been a long time since she'd felt that way…

'Do you think she'll ever forgive him?' Will asked.

Cassidy turned her head to look at his face. 'Rachel?'

He nodded, studying her eyes with the silent intensity she was now almost used to. 'She can be pretty bloody-minded when she digs her heels in.'

Cassidy shrugged one shoulder. 'It's self-preservation. Look where being up-front with him got her last time.'

'She knew how Nick felt about her.'

'No. She *thought* she knew how Nick felt about her. Then she convinced herself she was wrong…' A memory from real life wrapped itself around Cassidy's memories of their last script, making her turn her gaze away and frown at the ocean. 'The last argument they had was pretty heated.'

'Lots of things can get said in the heat of an argument that might not have been meant the way they sounded…'

'They can.'

'Maybe we should have them talk it through?'

Cassidy grimaced, then looked sideways at him. 'I think Rachel would rather have needles poked in her eyes.'

'So would Nick. *Hot ones.*'

It made her smile. 'They both need a smack upside the head.'

To her amazement, Will smiled back. 'That would make for a short script.'

'True.'

Dark lashes flickered as he searched her eyes, then Will nodded firmly—just the once—as if he'd made some kind of momentous decision. Swiping a palm against his thigh, he reached his large hand towards her. 'Will Ryan.'

Cassidy arched a brow, her smile still in place. 'What are you doing, you idiot?'

'Starting over.' He jerked his chin at his hand. 'The idea is that you now put your hand in mine and introduce yourself the way I just did. Give it a try. Take a deep breath if you need to. Go on. You can do it.'

'Uh-huh.' The smile grew. 'Patronising me is really going to help your cause.'

Will shook his head. 'Count to ten and swallow down the sarcasm. Otherwise it's going to get to the point where—when we're done with the script—only one of us is coming out of that room alive…'

'You were the one who suggested getting a knife.'

'*Malone.* Don't make me turn on the charm.'

It wasn't an empty threat. If Cassidy hadn't known that

from experience she'd have known it from the way his eyes darkened several shades and his voice lowered an octave to a deep grumble that spoke of tangled sheets and early morning pillow talk. The thought made her smile falter.

Dropping her chin so she could study his outstretched hand with caution, she weighed up the danger of keeping her distance versus taking a chance and ending up friends with him again without her heart wanting more. It was risky.

Long fingers waggled in the air between them, and his voice lowered another octave, sending a shimmer of sensual feminine awareness of nearby hot male across her body. 'Come on, Cass…'

She wondered how he managed to sound like temptation itself—and scary at the same time. Did he even know he was doing it? Or how dangerous a decision it was? Because, despite the intimation, they had never actually been 'friends' at any point of their relationship—there had always been something more.

Taking a deep breath, she swallowed hard and lifted her arm, her hand hesitating mere inches from his. It was Will who closed the gap this time, circling his fingers around hers and holding on—allowing the warmth of his touch to seep through her skin and travel into her veins, where it rushed up her arm towards her racing heart. He clasped more firmly and shook their joined hands up and down.

Then he repeated, in a voice laced with determination, 'Will Ryan. Known to be the most annoying man on the planet at times. Tendency towards occasional arrogance that I'm never going to learn to control. Strange obsession with peanut butter and jelly sandwiches at two in the morning…'

Cassidy smiled as her gaze travelled up his arm, past the

lock of errantly curled hair below his ear to the sparkling green of his eyes. Then she shook her head and swallowed down the need to giggle like a shy schoolgirl. 'Cassidy Malone. Known to be the woman with a natural knack for public humiliation. Tendency to over-think things to the point of complete randomness. Strong belief that peanut butter and jelly anywhere in the vicinity of a slice of bread is just *wrong*…'

'Hello, Cassidy Malone—can I call you Cass?'

'Somehow I doubt I'll be able to stop you.'

Will smiled *that* smile, then cocked his head as he ran the pad of his thumb back and forth over her knuckles. 'We could use this for Nick and Rachel, you know…'

Cassidy rolled her eyes and attempted to quietly extricate her hand from his. 'Just no escaping those two, is there?'

'You want to?' He held onto her hand.

'Do I want to what?'

'Escape them for a while?' The thumb kept brushing over her skin, distracting her from looking away from his mesmerising eyes.

It meant it took a second or two longer than normal for her to focus on what he'd said. 'Will, we can't keep taking breaks if you want to get this thing done. It's counter-productive. You know that.'

He studied her intently. 'You're hating every minute of this, aren't you?'

Not *every* minute, no. She loved rediscovering her muse, she loved it when their scenes started coming together, she loved staying in Will's beautiful house by the ocean, she'd even loved spending time with Angie and Lily on the beach—and she agreed that, given the chance, she probably could end up good friends with a world-famous actress…

But she couldn't allow herself to enjoy those moments. Not properly. Not when she was living in a fantasy world on borrowed time. One day soon she would have to walk away from Will's life and try to find one of her own. One more fulfilling than the one she'd been living. Because if she'd been happy in the life she had she wouldn't have been so quick to leave it behind, would she?

'Cass?' The thumb stilled, and the impossibly gentle use of her name made her realise she'd dropped her gaze to the beating pulse at the base of his neck.

She looked back up. 'Sorry. Drifted off for a minute. I've got a tendency to do that too.'

'I remember.' He said it with just enough softness in his voice to suggest he remembered it with a degree of affection. Darn it.

When she made another attempt at freeing her hand he let her. So she folded her fingers into her palm and let her arm drop to her side as he leaned back, his expression changing to the unreadable blankness she hated so much,

'It's okay, I've got my answer.' Lifting a glass of juice, he pushed to his feet and turned towards the open door. 'We'd better get back to it then.'

CHAPTER SIX

WITHOUT any idea why she felt compelled to correct his assumption, Cassidy found herself on her feet, matching glass in hand, and following him into the kitchen. 'Wait, Will. You're wrong. You didn't get an answer.'

Turning in the middle of the room, he lifted his chin and looked at her with hooded eyes.

Which left her squirming inwardly as she tried to find the words to explain it to him without giving too much away.

'I'm not… That is it's not that I'm not…' She puffed her cheeks out in exasperation, and avoided his gaze by glancing at random points around the room. 'I guess I just—' A deep breath and a grimace, and then she silently said to heck with it and took a run at it. 'I feel a bit—lost, I suppose. You and me? We're not the same. This living together under the same roof—' One of her hands flailed in the air in front of her body, towards him. 'Well, we're not the *same*…'

'You already said that.'

Cassidy scowled at his calm tone, and the fact that her gaze shifted to meet his and discovered what looked like a glint of amusement only made her feel more stupid than she already did.

She sighed heavily. 'This is your life, Will, not mine. I'm just a visitor here. But this script…it's important…it means a lot. I don't want to mess it up.'

When there was silence it drew her gaze back to him again, then he took a shallow breath and asked, 'Why is it so important?'

Now, there was a question with a loaded answer.

Her hesitation brought him a step closer, his hand reaching out to set his glass on the nearest counter top. 'I get the not wanting to mess up part. Everyone feels that way when they work on a script. Or on any kind of a project that means something to them. There was a time you wanted to succeed in this business as much as I did…'

Cassidy smiled wryly. 'Apparently not *quite* as much as you did…'

The low words were enough to tug on the edges of his mouth. 'Okay. Fair enough. We had different motivations but the same goal—at least I thought we did. Maybe I was wrong about that?'

If she had, she'd have left everything behind to go with him to California. That was what he was intimating, wasn't it? Yes, Will had been driven for different reasons from Cassidy. But the goal *had* been a dream they'd shared. What had broken them apart had been Cassidy's starry-eyed romanticism over the life they would have together weighed against Will's need to be successful enough to prove to all those people who had thought him worthless that they'd been spectacularly wrong in their assessment. Cassidy had believed they would achieve their dreams together. Will had left her behind and done it on his own. But she'd let him go, hadn't she?

Will took another step closer. 'Why is it so important, Cass?'

She took a deep breath, while warily watching to see how close he planned on getting. 'We bombed last time, Will. You remember how bad that felt as well as I do…'

'Oh, sweetheart, I've bombed a few times since then—trust me. It's par for the course out here.'

The use of the drawled 'sweetheart' made her cock a recriminating brow at him, but she let it slide when she saw the light in his eyes. 'But you're a success, Will. Look around you—this house, your company, the awards you've won—you've made it. I'm a *schoolteacher*. Not that there's anything wrong with that—it's one of the most honourable professions on the planet—but it wasn't something I'd planned on doing for the rest of my life.' Any more than living on her own had been. 'The last script I cowrote with you is the only thing I have on my movie-writing CV. The script for a movie that bombed at the box office and gave movie reviewers globally the excuse to ramp the venom volume up to high—remember? I ended on a failure. A very public failure. I don't want another one. Seriously, I don't think I could take it…and… And I'm babbling again, aren't I?'

'Like a brook.' He smiled indulgently.

Another step forward brought him to within reaching distance. But instead of offering her the kind of comforting hug she desperately needed and dreaded at the same time, he lifted his hands and pushed them deep into the pockets of his jeans—meaning the only way a hug would happen was if *she* reached for *him*.

But that wasn't going to happen, was it? No matter how much she sorely needed to be held—just held—for long enough not to feel as if she had somehow detached herself from her fellow human beings. Now that she thought about it, it was probably the same fear that brought tears of emotion to her eyes when small arms would hug so tightly around her neck on the last day of term…

'It was a success in the long haul, Cass. Or we wouldn't be here. You need to remember that. Sometimes the road to success has its twists and turns. That's all.'

She managed a somewhat shaky smile and a roll of her eyes at her continuing inability to listen to reason or appreciate thoughtfulness without the need to cry. 'I'd just rather skip the hobnailed boots stomping all over my self-confidence this time round, if that's all right with you.'

The green of Will's eyes softened and warmed. 'Welcome to Hollywood.'

Cassidy laughed softly, then stared at him in wonder. 'How do you do it?'

'Thick skin.' He shrugged.

'Is there a store nearby where I can pick one of those up?'

''Fraid not. It's something you acquire over time. Wouldn't suit you, anyway.'

Sighing heavily, she nodded. 'I'd be willing to try it out for a while.'

Whether it was something he saw in her eyes, or something he knew instinctively she needed—as he so often had once upon a time—Will pulled his hands out of his pockets and closed the gap between them. He reached for her with a rumbled, 'Come here, Malone.'

Oh, great. Now she was welling up the way she did with the kids. Only this time it was bittersweet for different reasons. Even as Will drew her close to the wall of his chest and circled her with his arms, she felt the deep-seated sensation of coming home after a long, long time in exile. She hadn't realised how homesick she'd been for him until he was holding her and she had her arms around his lean waist. The scent of clean laundry and pure Will surrounded her, but she breathed it deeper anyway. When one of the large hands on her back gently rubbed to soothe her she had to fight the need to sob uncontrollably. But not just because it was a hug when she so desperately needed a hug. It was because it was *Will*. The Will she'd missed so very much that even while she was being held in his arms the fact she knew it might never happen again was enough to break another corner off her ragged-edged heart.

'You're doing great, Cass. Don't be so hard on yourself. There are days in that room I forget it's been so long since we worked together.'

She *had* been feeling better about her scriptwriting abilities, but hearing him say it meant a lot to her. 'Thank you.'

'You're welcome.' The smile sounded in his voice.

It made her smile too, as she tilted her head back to rest her chin on his shoulder. Then she took another deep breath and forced herself to step away from him. 'I guess I can stand to be cooped up in that room for another few hours if you can.'

'Good.' A devilish smile was backed up by another wink. 'We can talk about Rachel wearing that harem girl outfit again.'

Cassidy laughed. 'No. we can't. She's not doing the Dance of the Seven Veils for Nick…'

'She'd be very sexy doing it.'

'She'd feel like a complete idiot doing it.'

Will retrieved his glass and headed back towards the office. 'Okay, then. We'll play out the scene and see how it goes.'

Cassidy chuckled; he could go right ahead and hold his breath for that one. But she suddenly felt a lot better going back into his office with him. *Much better.*

Ryan and Malone were on top form when they pitched their script for the first time—even if it was technically just a trial run.

Will had driven them into Los Angeles, to his plush, if chaotic offices. making small talk on the journey that Cassidy knew was meant to distract her from her nervousness. It was yet another thoughtful gesture she both needed and feared at the same time. Between his thoughtfulness, his ability to read what she needed—sometimes before she realised it herself—and the amount of mild flirting he'd been doing since the day of their partial truce she was already walking a fine line. If she made the mistake of falling for him again…

Once they were in the conference room with selected members of Will's team, and they began the read-through, something clicked. Maybe it was because she let herself get lost in what they were doing. Maybe it was because, for the guts of an hour, reality was shut out. Maybe it was because they became Nick and Rachel again. Maybe it was the fact their audience laughed and sat forward in their seats with rapt expressions at the right times. Heck, maybe it was a combination of all those things. But whatever it was, it was magical. For the first time since she'd come to California it felt as if the old Will was completely back.

He laughed more, he smiled *that* smile at her when she

blushed as she skirted over any kisses or love scenes in the script, he even danced with her and dipped her the way the script directed—to the obvious amusement of their captive audience. He took her hand so they could both take a bow when that same audience applauded at the end...

Then they spent another hour talking with the team about special effects and storyboarding and locations—and Cassidy forgot she was with a group of complete strangers who worked for Will, and debated with him the way she usually did when they were alone.

After handing out work assignments, Will watched her shake the last hand at the open doorway, then leaned casually against the doorframe. 'Trying to start a revolution inside my production company, Malone?'

'Meaning?'

'You didn't see some of their faces when you debated with me?'

She had—and she might have been worried he was angry about it if she hadn't seen the sparkle of amusement in his eyes. 'I noticed the look on their faces when you conceded anything. I get the impression that doesn't happen too often...'

'It's rare.' He shrugged and cast a glance over the open-plan work area outside the conference room like some ruler surveying his kingdom. 'But not unheard-of.'

'Hmm.' Cassidy leaned against the other side of the frame, pursed her lips and then smiled when he looked at her. 'Might do you good if it happened more often, Ryan. Who knows what creativity you have here, hidden under too many layers of fear to speak up in front of the boss. You should thank me.'

'Or hire you.'

Her jaw dropped. But before she could figure out if he was being serious, he pushed off the door frame and jerked his head. 'Come on. I have something I want you to see while we're here…'

Of all the things she had expected to be shown—fancy office, great views over Los Angeles, other productions he might be working on—a room the size of a large stationery cupboard, filled with piles of paper and sacks of letters pretty much came at the bottom of the list. So when he turned the lights on and closed the door behind them, she turned round and lifted a brow.

'A mailroom? That's what you wanted to show me?' Her voice was flat.

Will blinked lazily at her. 'Pick a letter.'

She was obviously missing something. Frowning, she turned her head and examined the room more closely. Nope—it still looked like a mailroom to her. Not a particularly well-organised one either.

'Pick a letter. Or an e-mail—doesn't matter.' He stepped closer to her. 'Any one you want.'

Okay, she'd play. Glancing at him from the corner of her eye, she made a big deal out of waving her hand in circles before closing her eyes and feeling around for a random selection—not helping with any invisible filing system he might have.

When she opened her eyes and held it up in front of her face, the corners of Will's mouth were tugging upward. 'Read it.'

Dragging her gaze from his, she slipped the letter from the opened envelope and began to read, her eyes widening when she realized what it was. Lifting her chin, she stared at the rest of the papers—then at Will.

The green of his eyes radiated warmth, and his deep voice lowered as he told her, 'Pick another one.'

She did—and got an e-mail that made her throat tighten.

Will's voice was lower and closer when he spoke again. 'Keep going.'

'All of them?' Cassidy lifted her chin and silently cleared her throat, so her voice didn't sound so strangled. 'This whole room is fan mail for our movie?'

'Yes. The studio forwarded it here to begin with, but when it started increasing we changed the address on the website. We get mail from all over the world.' He searched her eyes and smiled. 'They call themselves the Fortune Hunters.'

For the first time in her life Cassidy was at a complete loss for words.

So Will kept going, his gaze locked on hers. 'It started with message boards. Then they launched their own site and it grew from there. There are role-playing games, conspiracy theories—some of them have all the lines memorised so when they have a screening they can join in. They even dress up as the characters at conventions…'

With her emotions threatening to overwhelm her, Cassidy forcibly dragged her gaze from his and reached for another letter. 'What's this one?'

Will held an edge so he could read it. 'California's Fortune Hunters. There are chapters all over the place now, but California was the first. They organise a yearly charity screening of the movie, and let us know when it is so we can send memorabilia to auction on the night.'

'I had no idea.'

'I didn't think you did.' He waited for her to look at him before he told her. 'The movie may have tanked at the box office, Cass, but it's been successful in ways no one could ever have predicted. It's brought people together—it's even been the catalyst for a few weddings. There's a community of amazing people out there who are making a difference to other people's lives with their charitable causes through it. Does that sound like a failure to you?'

Cassidy shook her head.

'No.' Will smiled one of *those* smiles as he reached up and tucked a strand of hair behind her ear. 'If you didn't get enough of a self-confidence boost from the reaction to the pitch we just did, then maybe this will do it.'

She still couldn't speak.

When Will's gaze dropped briefly to her mouth she held her breath, her heart thundering against her breastbone as she waited to see if he was going to kiss her...

But he dropped his hand and stepped back. 'Read through some of them while I make a few calls, if you like. There's a coffee machine down the hall. Then I'll come back and drive us home, so we can work on the changes we agreed in the meeting.'

She nodded. Then watched as he turned round and opened the door. The first tear slipped onto her lower lashes after he'd disappeared. It wasn't just because of what he'd shown her and told her, or the fact he had known how much she'd needed to see it. It was because he'd used the word 'home'.

As if it was *her* home too...

The thing was, somewhere along the way, his house *had* started to feel more like home than the one she had in Ireland. It would take strength to leave and close the door on their relationship for once and for all. She knew she'd be leaving even more of herself behind than he'd taken with him the first time.

They didn't go straight to work on the script revisions when they got back to Will's house. Cassidy couldn't allow herself to think of it as 'home'. She'd already allowed herself to get too comfortable in her surroundings as it was.

Unusually—since she'd arrived anyway—it was raining outside: hot, heavy, humid rain. So they had a take-away Moroccan dinner inside—plates of a half-dozen dishes she'd never tried before spread out on a coffee table in front of them while they sat on one of Will's large sofas.

'I'm curious about your life,' he said.

'Why?'

'I can't ask you a simple question?'

'Maybe I'm *curious* why you need to know.' Cassidy was fully aware of the verbal game of poker they were playing over dessert, but she wasn't backing down.

'I thought we'd decided we're friends again?'

She avoided his gaze, playing with the ice cream in her tub. 'Okay, we're friends.'

'Friends talk about stuff. Try me.'

It took a long while for her to make a decision, and Cassidy couldn't help but smile when he lifted dark brows in challenge. She knew *he* knew the reason she was reluctant to talk about her life was because it involved emotion. She knew *he* knew that *she knew* Will didn't talk about emotion. End of story. He'd rather chew off his own arm. So it was, therefore, a case of what was sauce for the goose…

But this change for the better in their relationship had allowed them to start getting to know each other again, and she was reluctant to put a dampener on that. Especially when they were both smiling more, and working together had got easier, and he'd been so thoughtful of late…

The ice cream took several violent digs before she sighed heavily. 'One hint of anything resembling sympathy, Will Ryan…'

When she glanced up he was continuing to smile his patented humouring smile at her.

She frowned. 'You're doing it already.'

'I'm not.' He pasted a serious expression on his face, folding his arms and jerking his chin at her. 'Go on. I'm listening.'

'I hate this. I tell you about my life and it's just going to sound pathetically ordinary compared to yours.'

'Not necessarily. Most of my life is more ordinary than people might think.'

Cassidy snorted softly in disbelief. 'Like what, for instance? Hanging out with movie stars? Working in the motion picture industry? The fact you attend the Oscars every year? The millionaire's beach house you live in?'

It took a second, then one of *those* smiles broke free, the green in his eyes glittering hypnotically. He shook his head before looking at a point over her left shoulder as he considered his answer. 'It's hard to find words.'

'Will, you work with words every day.' She kept her voice purposefully soft. 'Can't spell them—but you know how to use them…'

'Very funny.'

'Try. One ordinary thing about your life.'

'Just the one and you'll tell me about *your* life.' He looked as if he doubted that.

'Make it a truly mundane one and I'll fill in the blanks.' She lifted her spoon and made a cross in the air above her breasts. 'Cross my heart.'

The move apparently gave him an open invitation to drop his gaze and watch the increased rise and fall of her breasts as he looked at them. Then his thick lashes lifted and he chuckled at her look of accusation before informing her, 'I don't have a housekeeper. So I do all my own cleaning.'

'Oh, no—your obsession with neatness doesn't count.' It was something that had never ceased to astound her, but he'd always seemed to get pleasure from an organised environment. Whereas Cassidy had always lived in the kind of chaos that was reflective of her life in general. In the end she'd put his borderline obsession down to control—the same kind of control that he'd exerted over so many areas of his life.

Only in the bedroom had he ever fully lost that precious self-control. When he'd made love to her she'd never had any doubts about how he felt. But then neither had he about how *she* felt. They'd been stripped naked—emotionally as well as physically. Something Cassidy had never allowed herself to come close to experiencing with anyone else. Not that he would ever know that.

Will shrugged and stole a spoonful of her ice cream. 'Still counts as ordinary. Everyone does housework. It's a universal equaliser.'

Cassidy laughed. 'I've made a valiant effort to avoid it wherever possible, believe me.'

The corners of his mouth quirked. 'I believe you. Now I've lived up to my end of the bargain it's your turn. Tell me about this ordinary life of yours.'

It was on the tip of her tongue to ask again why he wanted to know, but instead she dropped her chin and played some more with the ice cream. 'I teach, so I work according to the school terms. In the summer I usually manage to find work at camps, or at places where working parents can leave their kids while they do their nine to fives. I have a flat. I have teacher friends I meet for lunches or coffees or whatever. I used to have a cat—'

'What happened to it?'

'It must have been about a hundred years old when I got it from the shelter, so it didn't last long.'

'Didn't get another one?'

'Nope.' She smiled wryly at her ice cream. 'Apparently I wasn't ready to deal with another loss after my dad. I cried for weeks over that dumb cat.'

When Will didn't say anything she stole an upward glance at him from underneath a wave of lose hair. He was studying her again. But instead of asking *What?* that way she usually did, she took the opportunity to say, 'Thank you. For the card and the flowers you sent.'

He knew she didn't mean after the cat had died. 'I got your note. You don't have to thank me again.'

Cassidy dampened her lips and took a breath. 'It meant

a lot. I didn't put that in the note. And I should have. That time is kind of a blur to me now.'

'Grief can be like that.' His gaze shifted to her loose hair, and Cassidy wondered if he was thinking of tucking it away again. 'You had a lot to do to wrap everything up as well. At least you had your family to help you.'

'I did.' Unlike the eight-year-old Will, who'd had no one when his mother had passed away; it still killed Cassidy that he'd been left so alone.

'You could have called me if you'd needed anything— you know that.'

She did. Even if he hadn't written it in the card he had sent. 'Wasn't that easy.'

Taking a deep breath, he reached forward for the remote control of his ridiculously large widescreen TV and handed it to her. 'I've decided we're taking the night off. Pick a movie.'

Cassidy blinked in surprise. 'I thought you wanted to get this thing done?'

'It'll wait.' He waved the remote in the air. 'Pick a movie.'

Setting the ice cream tub between her knees, Cassidy took the remote with one hand, leaning forward and resting the back of her other hand against his forehead. 'Are you feeling sick? Do you have a temperature? Maybe you caught my cold…'

He removed her hand. 'You can't spend an evening just sitting doing nothing with me, can you?'

'Yes, I can.' But she could feel her cheeks warming at the 'doing nothing with me' part. Because in the past sitting on a sofa watching a movie with him would have led to kissing. Kissing would have led to touching. Then—

'Prove it. Pick a movie.'

With an arched brow she lifted her chin and curled her legs underneath her, glaring sideways at him as she pointed the remote at the TV. 'You'll regret this.'

Will toed off his shoes and lifted his feet to rest them on the coffee table, settling back into the large cushions. 'No, I'm not.'

'Oh, yes you are.' She smirked as the screen jumped to life and she flicked through the channels to find what she was looking for. There it was. That would do, 'Because it is now officially chick-flick night…'

When the credits played at the end of the movie, Cassidy turned her head against the back of the sofa and found Will fast asleep, his face turned towards her. He was gorgeous. Strands of dark hair falling across his forehead, cheeks flushed with sleep, full lips parted as he breathed deep, even breaths. For a long while she just looked at him, drinking in the sight and memorising every detail. Then she gave in to temptation and brushed a single strand of rich hair off his forehead with her fingertips. Her voice was a whisper, as if she was reluctant to lose the stolen moment. 'Will?'

He didn't react, so she smiled and tried again with a slightly stronger voice. 'Will.'

'Hmm…?'

Still smiling, she watched as he slowly made his way into consciousness. How many times had she watched him waking up? Probably hundreds. Yet apparently, even after so many years, it was still one of her favourite things to do.

Will blinked her into focus with heavy lashes. 'Cass?'

Though obviously still caught between sleeping and

waking, he lifted a hand and gently brushed her hair back from her cheek. *'Cass…'*

Cassidy froze when he leaned towards her. What was he—?

Oh, no—no, no, no, no, *no!* This wasn't happening! Why had he—? What did he think he was—? Was he seriously—? He was *kissing her*! *Unscripted*! No, wait—it was worse than that. He was kissing her, and it was…it was—well, it was…

Oh, wow.

At first she was stunned at how fast her body responded. The heat built like a flashfire in dry scrubland, even though the kiss was soft and sweet and so tender it shredded yet another edge off Cassidy's already ragged heart. It seemed endless, as if the world turned more slowly, while her heart pounded heavily against her breasts. Nothing had *ever* felt as right in her entire life—not one single thing—and knowing that scared her to death. She *could not* fall in love with this man again. Oh, *please*. But what if she'd never fallen *out of love* with him?

Oh. God.

Now she was kissing him back. Stupid, *stupid* girl! What was she doing? It was Will Ryan—the man who broke her heart and changed her life for ever, ruining her for any other man who ever showed the vaguest little interest in her! What was she doing kissing him back? Had she lost her mind?

When the moan formed low in her chest she had the fight of her life to keep it there. She couldn't let the sound out. If she let it out he'd know. He'd know he was making her toes curl. He would know how little it would take to get her horizontal again. Who did that after eight years apart? What was it about him? Was she really so needy that she—?

Oh, it was *good*. She never wanted it to end.

But it had to. *It. Had. To.* So she dragged her mouth from his—then stared at him as she fought to control her breathing, while his eyes opened and his warm breath washed over her flushed cheeks. He stared back. Then frowned and opened his mouth…

CHAPTER SEVEN

SHE couldn't have him say anything. Not when she still felt as if she was drowning in sensation. From somewhere she found the strength to beat him to it.

'You fell asleep.'

Will looked at her as if she had two heads.

'That must have been one hell of a dream I interrupted…' It was the only thing that made any sense to her.

'It was,' he said with a husky-edged voice.

Oh, thank you, god. As much as it hurt, at least it was a way out. 'Thought so.'

Her half-hearted attempt at a smile was met with a narrowed, searching gaze. But before he could say anything else Cassidy pushed to her feet and gathered together their plates. 'I'll clear up down here. You should go and grab more sleep. Maybe you can pick up that dream where you left off?'

There was silence from the sofa as she walked across the room, then; 'What's going on, Cass?'

'I'm clearing up. I already told you that.'

She'd made it all the way into the kitchen, and had set the plates on the drainer, when two large hands settled on her shoulders and turned her around.

'You're the one who avoids housework, remember? So what's going on?' Will moved one hand, the backs of his fingertips tracing along her jawline and pushing into the hair at her nape. Then he unfurled his fingers and curled his palm around her neck—his thumb smoothing against her cheek.

If he kissed her again…

Dampening her lips, and almost moaning out loud when his gaze followed the movement, she lifted her hand to quietly remove his. 'If you kiss me I won't be able to think straight.'

Oh, dear! That tongue of hers just didn't know when to stop, did it?

The brief glow in his eyes told her how much the confession meant to him. But he dropped his arms and then shook his head.

'I know you're scared,' he said, in a low voice that made her stomach cramp.

Cassidy lifted her chin. 'I'm not scared.'

'No?'

'No.' She quirked her brows in warning, and then angled her head and answered his slow smile with one of her own. 'I'm…wary…'

When she purposefully took her time enunciating the word his smile grew. 'Wary is a good word.'

'I have more.'

'I don't doubt that.'

She nodded, letting her gaze examine a thick strand of his dark hair. 'Cautious would be another good one.'

'It would. Even if means the same thing as wary.'

'Forewarned, then…'

'Can't say I'm happy with that one…'

Drawing her lower lip between her teeth, she made the

mistake of glancing at his eyes and found him watching the movement. His gaze rose, locked with hers, and coherent thought left her brain at speed. How did he still *do* that to her?

His next words removed her ability to breathe. 'I'm wary too.'

In the absence of thinking or breathing, she asked him a silent question. And he must have read it in her face, the way he was so very good at, because he nodded, the warmth in his stunning green eyes sending her temperature up a notch.

'I knew what I was doing when I kissed you.'

Cassidy stared at him with wide eyes. He really was so much braver than she was. And because he'd laid it so tenderly on the line for her, she met him halfway, her voice one octave above a whisper as she asked, 'You did?'

'I did. I've been thinking about it ever since the day we rehearsed that scene.'

When he'd kissed her as Nick?

Will took a breath. 'But this was never the part we had a problem with—was it, Cass?'

Swallowing to dampen her dry mouth and take the sandpaper edge off her throat, Cassidy shook her head. 'No. It wasn't.'

Will laid his palms on the counter either side of her body, effectively boxing her in as he took a step closer. 'You kissed me back.'

'I know I did.' She was about thirty seconds away from having a heart attack, judging by her rapid heartbeat and her continued inability to breathe.

'I bet I can make you kiss me again.'

'Probably. But there wouldn't be any point to it—and you know that as well as I do.' She silently prayed he did.

'Why wouldn't there?'

'Because… Well, because it's not as if we're going to end up… Well…*you know*…'

His eyes sparkled dangerously. 'Aren't we? We always did before.'

'Well, we're not this time!' When she wriggled away from him it had the opposite effect she'd been aiming for. Instead it made her all too aware of everywhere his body had touched hers. While she was still catching her breath from that realisation he made his move—he had her hands in his and tugged her forward—then rearranged her hands behind her back so that he had both of them trapped at the wrists in one of his.

'What do you think you're doing?' she gasped.

With a glint in his eyes, and a killer one of *those* smiles, Will leaned her back over the counter. 'I'm not going to kiss you. Don't worry. I'm checking to see how your body feels about me touching you…'

Cassidy gasped, her eyes wide. 'Don't you *dare*—'

As he let his fingers skate across her midriff he watched the reaction in her eyes. 'Tell me you don't want me, Cass.'

'I don't want you.'

'*Liar.*'

She didn't want him to stop. And now his hand was moving higher…

When she trembled, he studied her eyes again. Then his gaze dropped to the rapid rise and fall of her breasts. But just when Cassidy was about to take the safer option and cave in to kissing him, his thumb moved. An involuntary giggle escaped.

'Ticklish…' He leaned into her, his voice a husky rumble above her ear. 'I remember that…'

'*No.*' Now her knees were giving out on her.

Will moved his thumb to prove his point, and chuckled above her ear when she squirmed. 'When are you going to learn you can't lie to me, Cass? You never could.'

He was killing her!

'You want me. And I want you.' He pressed a soft kiss to her throat—on the sensitive skin below her ear—before whispering, 'I remember what we were like together. How good we were. How many weekends we spent in bed…'

When he kissed his way to her collarbone Cassidy's head automatically dropped back to make room for him, while she gasped short, sharp breaths of air that tasted of Will's familiar scent.

He lifted his head, placed his cheek against hers and told her, 'But I'm not going to seduce you, Cass. You're going to come to *me*. That way I won't take the blame this time…'

When it fell apart—that was the part he left out. But that was what he meant. Meaning he didn't see it as anything lasting? Meaning this time it would be an affair? Cassidy wasn't sure she could do that. Not with Will.

Releasing her hands, he stepped back and looked down at her wide eyes, studying them each in turn. 'Think it over if you need to. But this isn't going away, Cass. You know that just as well as I do.'

She did. But it didn't make it any easier a decision.

There was an edge of warning to his deep voice when she continued staring at him. 'You need to go upstairs now.'

Or he would kiss her until she made her decision? Was that what he was saying?

'*Cass.*'

Practically running from the room, she made short work

of the stairs and of walking along the hall—only glancing back down at him when she had her hand on the door to her bedroom. He stood with his back to her, looking out at the reflection of the moon on the rolling ocean, tension radiating from every pore of his large body.

It would be so very easy to give in to how much she wanted him. *Too easy.* But, with a strength that surprised her, she pushed open the door and turned away. Shredding yet another edge off her heart along the way…

He was officially making her crazy. *Again.*

Her disobedient gaze flickered across to look at him for the twenty-eighth time that morning. Like the other twenty-seven times, he looked at her at the same time and smiled knowingly. It was infuriating. And Cassidy was deeply resentful that Will was so in control. She hadn't managed a single night's sleep in three.

She forced her gaze back to her screen and pursed her lips, narrowing her eyes and willing herself to read an entire sentence and get all the way to the end of it knowing what she'd read!

Her peripheral vision caught him moving a second before his chair began to squeak. That was another thing that was making her crazy. 'The *chair.*'

'Hmm?' He looked at her when she looked at him. 'Sorry?'

'Your chair. Don't you have a can of oil somewhere?'

'Oil?' He blinked at her.

Nice try, Mr Butter-Wouldn't-Melt. Her eyes narrowed.

He pushed his chair back and got up. Something else he'd been doing a lot of was leaving the room at regular intervals. But she didn't say anything. She just smiled sweetly when he glanced her way before turning to leave—and could tell from the small, incredibly satisfied frown on his face that he knew she'd been noticing the number of times he'd been wandering off during the day.

He was restless.

Will stopped, turned, and jerked a thumb over his shoulder. 'Thought I'd grab a sandwich. You hungry?'

'At eleven-thirty? Bit early for lunch, don't you think?'

Trying a new tactic, he smiled at her the way he'd taken to doing so much lately. 'I can't go and get something nice to surprise you with either, I suppose…?'

The word *'nice'* made her purse her lips again. If he did one more *'nice'* thing she thought she might scream. His campaign of *nice*—and thoughtful and considerate and caring and sweet and tender—was the worst form of torture she'd ever been subjected to in all her born days. Especially when coupled with his being effortlessly sexy. But, barring brushing her hair back from her face, and smiling *that* smile at her, he hadn't done one single thing to pick up where they'd left off in the kitchen the other day!

When she focused her gaze on his mouth she frowned harder, and felt her foot begin tapping in the air underneath the desk. 'I don't like surprises.'

'No—you don't like surprises you don't already know about. There's a difference. We discussed that many, many times in the past.' He stepped round to her side of the desk and rested one palm flat on the surface, while his other hand grasped the back of her chair and turned her to face him. 'So what do you want me to surprise you with?'

Cassidy's gaze shot upwards and locked with his.

Will smiled *that* smile in reply.

She scowled. 'Stop that.'

'Stop what?'

'*That.*' She felt a bubble of borderline manic laughter work its way up from the base of her throat as she pointed the tip of her pen at his face and made a circle. 'Don't think I don't know what you're doing, Ryan.'

'And what *am* I doing?'

'Trying to wear me down.' Leaning closer, she lowered her voice. 'So that if I say yes to you it'll seem like it's my decision. When in actuality *it's not*—you'll have backed me into a corner.'

'Oh, well, I'll stop, then—obviously.'

'This whole being nice to me thing can stop too. Nice *never* works on me. It just makes me suspicious. You *know* *that*.' She angled her head and lifted her chin.

Much to her annoyance, when he smiled again, she smiled back at him. How was this tactic *working on her*? In any relationship—including the one she'd been in *with him*—she couldn't remember there ever being the equivalent of a 'mating dance'. She hadn't a clue how it was supposed to work. It had her on tenterhooks. Her damn stomach even got butterflies when she woke up in the morning and knew she was going to see him! Then there was the whole smiling thing she was doing when he wasn't around…

At first she'd told herself every time he left her alone to go and tend to business elsewhere that she was glad of the break. Then she'd been annoyed with herself for noticing every time he was gone for more than five minutes—as if she was so addicted to the sight of him that she missed him when he wasn't within appreciation distance every time she needed a fix!

Which was pathetic—completely, totally and utterly *pathetic*.

When he left the room now she began tapping her pen and her foot again, only stilling when his voice yelled, 'We're getting low on provisions. Want to take a trip to the store with me? Or do you want to stay in there and spend the rest of the afternoon figuring out what dastardly plans I currently have on the go?'

She sighed heavily and tossed her pen down before yelling back, '*Store!*'

They were halfway around the giant supermarket when Will finally did what she'd wanted him to do for days— reached an arm out to hook it round her waist and pull her close so he could press a kiss to her lips.

Rocking forward onto the balls of her feet, Cassidy took a deep breath and looked up at him from beneath heavy lashes. 'What was that for?'

'You were pouting.'

'I was *not* pouting!'

'Kinda cute, actually…'

'Oh, my God.' She leaned back against his arm. 'Kill me now.'

Will chuckled as he released her and reached for avocados. 'See, when you called *me* cute I took it as a compliment…'

'Yes, but my head fits through doors…' When he looked at her she folded her arms. 'A woman ceases to be "cute" the second she leaves puberty and pigtails behind. Don't ever say I have a pretty face either—it means you think I'm fat.'

'I don't think you're fat,' he informed her dryly as he pushed their trolley down the aisle. 'And I don't remember you having this many body issues before.'

Well, *duh*. She'd been twenty pounds lighter before. Not that she hadn't noticed how Will's habit of feeding them little and often and disgustingly healthily had been having a positive effect on the tightness of her waistband, but even so…

Will stopped, waited for her to get to his side, and then asked, 'Is that why you're stalling the inevitable?'

'Excuse me?' Cassidy's eyes widened with disbelief. 'The *inevitable*?'

'Is it?'

'Inevitable? That ego of yours is the size of Europe.'

'That's not what I meant and you know it. It had better not be because of body issues, Cass. I'll be disappointed in you if it is.' He took a step closer that made her take a step back, but all it did was trap her between him and a large display of sweet potatoes. A fact that made his eyes sparkle with amusement. 'Just say the word and I'll show you exactly how far my appreciation for curves can go…'

She gaped at him. 'You're unbelievable.'

He stole another kiss before moving back. 'Takes two to flirt the way we have been of late—remember that.'

I-n-c-r-e-d-i-b-l-e. The man's arrogance knew no bounds. Angrily tossing sweet potatoes into a bag, she lifted a brow at him. 'And this is us flirting now, I suppose?'

'Nope.' He winked at her. 'This is our version of foreplay.'

Cassidy rolled her eyes.

But Will smiled, a hand lifting to brush her hair off her shoulder so he could set his fingertips against her neck—

the neck she immediately arched to the side, to allow him access. Despite her best efforts to fight it, he had a way of making her feel like the most sensual woman on the planet. The darkening of his eyes in reaction to her silent submission was as much an aphrodisiac as the feel of his fingertips on her sensitive skin.

Sliding those fingertips inside the collar of her blouse, he set his thumb against the beating pulse at the base of her neck and leaned his face closer to hers, lowering his voice to a husky rumble. 'Come to a film premiere with me on Friday. It's at the Chinese Theater.'

The words rocked her back on her heels, her eyes widening. 'A film premiere? You and me? Posh clothes, red carpet, movie stars, press photographers—all that stuff?'

He nodded firmly, moving back and releasing his hand to tangle their fingers and tug to get her to walk beside him. 'Yup. All that stuff.'

Oh, no. An affair was one thing—the equivalent of a date turned it into something else completely. Surely he knew that? What she was doing with him was already dangerous enough, never mind knocking her self-confidence again by demonstrating the fact she didn't fit in to the Hollywood set he mixed with.

'I don't have anything to wear.' It was an excuse as old as time itself. But it was the first thing that came to her mind under pressure.

'We can fix that.'

She glanced down at their joined hands and frowned at them. 'I don't think—'

Will stopped and reached past her for brie. 'Good. When you do think you have a tendency to make things more complicated than they need to be. We both know that. It's just another movie night, Cass—this time in a theatre, with fancy clothes.'

Quietly clearing her throat, Cassidy lifted her gaze to meet his. 'Oh, I think you'll find it's a little bit more than—'

'No, it's not. There's nothing to be nervous about.' He smiled almost affectionately at her. 'You'll have fun. Wait and see.'

But it didn't help. 'Will, taking me as your date to the equivalent of a Hollywood "see and be seen" is—well, it's ridiculous.'

'Why is it?'

'Because…' She floundered, giving him a wavering look that silently begged him to let her off the hook. When he stood firm she explained, 'We can't just go out in public…on a date…like normal Hollywood people…'

Will's brows rose. '*Normal* Hollywood people? There's no such thing.'

When he continued staring at her she chewed on her lower lip—and then the babbling began in earnest. 'It'll give the wrong impression. People might think…I mean, it's not like there won't be questions, is there? I know what happens with the pictures taken at these things…they end up beamed around the globe and on the internet and in magazines and… Well, it's not like we're a couple or this is anything permanent. And if anyone knows you they're going to ask who I am, and if they find out we were together before they're going to make assumptions—the *wrong kind* of assumptions. And then—'

'See? Over-thinking and making it more complicated—told you. No one will make assumptions. You're assuming

they'll be far more interested in my private life than they
actually are. I'm not a movie star—I'm a writer/producer.
I'm nowhere near interesting to the press unless I appear
somewhere with a movie star. The only time I've ever done
that was when she was someone in a movie I'd written and
produced. It was publicity for the movie. That's how
Hollywood has worked since the golden age.'

'Will—'

The use of his name as a plea for understanding made
him let go of her hand and frame her face in large warm
palms; his head lowered so he could look deep into her eyes
as he told her, 'Quit it, Cass. It's not that big a deal.' Her
eyes widened as he angled his head and lowered it even
further, his words a whisper over her lips. 'It's just a night
out. We're taking this slow and easy…'

It would be so very easy to give in to the heat between
them and forget everything else. But if she did then she'd
be in exactly the same vulnerable position she'd been
before. The very thought of it made her fight for control
all over again. Because a very primal part of her DNA
structure already knew he was indelibly printed on her
body. Nobody else's touch would ever have the same effect
on her. She was his, in that sense. Had been from the first
time he'd made love to her—when she'd given him something she could never give to another man ever again.

The fact she knew all that held her back. Slow and
steady, he'd said. But slow and steady suggested they
were working towards something more than an affair.
He'd never once mentioned the possibility of her staying
once the script was approved by the studio. A brief affair
was possibly a way of ending their relationship with the

kind of closure they'd plainly never had, and she felt they both deserved that. It was foolish to hope for anything more.

'We'll get you something to wear for Friday night. Angie can take you shopping. She'll love that.'

Cassidy sighed dramatically. 'I'll *think* about it…'

When he tangled their fingers again she took a deep breath and looked sideways at him as they started to walk. 'But it's a maybe. Not a yes. Going shopping isn't an actual guarantee of *finding* something to wear.'

Will chuckled. 'It is if you go shopping with Angie; Eric says she's never once come home with anything remotely resembling an empty car…'

Pursing her lips as she considered the kind of shopping budget Angelique Warden had compared to her own, Cassidy glanced sideways at him again. 'I'm glad we're giving me time to think this over and make up my own mind.'

The sight of Angelique rounding a corner as if on cue made Cassidy frown and attempt to tug her hand free.

Will simply tightened his fingers. 'Hey, Angie—excellent timing for a change. We need your help.'

'You do?' She glanced down at their joined hands, her finely arched brows rising in interest as she looked from one of them to the other.

Cassidy pursed her lips and tugged again. Will smiled and held on.

Angie looked thoroughly amused. 'Am I sensing a problem?'

'No.' Will's smile grew. 'Nothing the United Nations couldn't negotiate.'

Without warning Cassidy gasped and pointed her free

hand at the windows. 'Oh, my God. Is that someone doing something to your car, Will?'

Instantly both her companions swung round to look where she pointed, Will releasing her hand and stepping forward. He frowned. 'Where?'

There was a burst of melodic laughter from behind him. Turning in slow motion, he sighed heavily at her smug expression while Cassidy lifted her chin high, linked her arm with Angie's and stepped light-footed around him. 'I swear. You make it too easy for me sometimes…'

Angie laughed loudly as they rounded a corner. 'He should never have let you go, my friend—you're one in a million.'

Managing a small smile as she set her arm free, Cassidy took a deep breath and plunged into deep water with both feet. 'I need your help finding a dress for a film premiere Friday night. I wouldn't ask if—'

'Oooohhh—is Will taking you?'

'Yes.'

'Like, on a date?'

Cassidy grimaced. 'It's not as simple as that.'

While people stopped in the aisle to surreptitiously photograph Angelique with their cellphones, she took a step back and eyed Cassidy from head to toe, as if oblivious to her fans. 'I feel a make-over coming on. We'll use my usual hairdresser and make-up artist. Then I'll take you to see the hottest designer right now—I've worn enough of his dresses to premieres for him to owe me. Stilettoes for your feet— *naturally*—and we'll need to borrow something sparkly and worth millions from a big-name jeweler, of course…'

'*Oh, no.*' Cassidy's stomach dropped several feet. 'Angie, I didn't mean—'

The most famous eyebrow on the planet arched again. 'Do you want to knock Will on his ear or not?'

Actually, a little return of that particular favour wouldn't go amiss, but… *'Well…'*

'Exactly.' She linked their arms again. 'Rodeo Drive, here we come!'

A cellphone magically appeared, and with the tip of one manicured nail pressed to a single key—assumedly speed dial—appointments were made…

Cassidy was actually starting to feel a sense of optimism. Until they rounded an aisle and found Will talking to a stunning brunette who had her hand on his chest.

Cassidy froze. Will's gaze lifted and found hers. He didn't even flinch.

Then Angie came to her rescue again. 'I'm stealing Cass, Irish boy.'

'When are you planning on bringing her back?' The man seemed oblivious to the fact there was a woman attached to his side. One who *still* had her hand on his chest!

Angie shrugged. 'Whenever.'

Cassidy officially loved Angie—especially when she looked the other woman up and down with obvious disdain before smiling and waggling her fingers. 'Bye-bye, now.'

Turning swiftly on her heel, she leaned her head closer to Cassidy's and stage-whispered, 'You're about to get the make-over of your life.'

CHAPTER EIGHT

TRY as she might to put it to the back of her mind, curiosity was eating her up. Sighing heavily, Cassidy stretched to loosen the tension in her spine. It was her own stupid fault they were sat on the floor, checking the continuity in their rewrites; she was the one who'd insisted they get back to work the second she returned from a marathon of appointments to confirm other appointments. It wasn't as if she could casually grill him about his relationship with a certain touchy brunette, not without him knowing why, so work had seemed like a good idea at the time.

'Hungry?' He didn't look up from the sheet he was reading.

'Getting there…' She leaned over and pulled the sheet she was looking for from a pile. Then her errant tongue worked loose. 'Not all of us popped out for a nice long lunch…'

When his mouth twitched she wanted to kill him. 'We can eat any time you're ready, Cass. I'm easy.'

A burst of laughter escaped her lips. 'You said it.'

Will calmly set his sheet to one side. 'You got something you want to ask me?'

'Me? No-o.' She took a deep breath, inwardly cursing

the fact she *knew* she was about to wade in regardless. 'Why? Have you got something *you* want to tell *me?*'

'If you want to ask me about Diana, then go ahead. It's not like you to be so behind the door about it.'

She shrugged and fiddled with her papers. 'This is different.'

'Different how?'

Darn it—she wasn't answering that! He could whistle.

When she wasn't forthcoming, he pushed. 'Are you jealous?'

'What? No, I'm not jealous.' She scowled at him. 'Whatever you do in your own time is…'

'Yes?' His smile grew.

So she quirked her brows and reached for a sheet of paper she didn't actually need. '*Whatever you do.*'

In the blink of an eye she found her wrist captured by one large hand. She frowned at it and tugged. He held on. She looked up at him and glared in warning. He continued smiling and still held on.

Then his deep voice lowered. 'There's nothing going on with me and Diana. You don't need to worry.'

Worry? She wasn't *worried!* Although it didn't explain why she suddenly felt better.

'Your sex life is nothing to do with me.' Oh, terrific—now she'd mentioned the word sex. Her gaze snapped upwards and crashed into his. And the heat she could see there made her breath catch painfully in her chest.

When his thumb moved against the beating pulse in her wrist she felt her stomach clench, and the need to close her eyes and moan was so strong it almost flattened her. Oh this was bad. This was bad in global proportions.

Frowning even harder, she closed her eyes and tugged on her hand. 'Let go.'

'Cass, look at me.'

She didn't want to look at him. But she forced herself to—and immediately regretted it. 'I'm not jealous. You should be so lucky. Now, give me my hand back.'

'No.'

'What do you mean *no*?'

'I don't want to.'

He smiled the smile that did something all too familiar to her pulse-rate, his thumb brushing back and forth over her wrist in a hypnotic rhythm. She wasn't crossing that invisible line with him.

She shook her head. 'I've made my decision. This isn't going to happen.'

Will continued smiling.

'I'm serious, Will. It's not.'

He blinked lazily, his ridiculously thick lashes still the most fascinating thing in the world to her.

'All right—so maybe, somewhere very deep inside me, there is an eensy-weensy possibility I feel some sort of completely unwanted attraction to you...' His thumb moved down into her palm and started to draw a small circle. Cassidy heard a strangled noise in the base of her own throat. 'But I'm telling you—this is *not* going to happen. Not this time round.'

When his gaze lowered to her mouth she automatically dampened her lips with the tip of her tongue. As if she was preparing herself to be kissed. She saw his throat convulse as he swallowed. She saw his wide chest rise and fall faster than before, as if he was having as much difficulty breathing as she was. Then his gaze rose again, and she felt the force of wanting him slam into her midriff like a punch.

Fighting what she wanted was one thing. Fighting Will's wants was still another. Cassidy knew she wouldn't recover this time round. Not when the image of him with another woman had sat in her stomach like acid for the whole afternoon.

The fear must have shown in her eyes. Because Will let go of her hand. Cassidy immediately drew her arm back to her side, folding her fingers into her palm to hold onto the remnants of his touch while she floundered in a frantic search for words to put them back to where they should be.

When he spoke his voice was rough-edged, and deeper than she remembered it ever sounding before, telling her he was just as affected by what had had happened between them as she was. 'So, how was your shopping trip?'

'I don't think we should go out on Friday night either.'

'You'll find a dress, Cass.'

'It's got nothing to do with finding a dress. We found a dress.' The most beautiful dress she'd ever tried on or probably ever would again, as it happened. But even if the idea of never getting to wear it in public took some of the magic away from seeing herself in it for the first time, she knew she was making the right decision.

'Then what's the problem?'

Sighing heavily, she unfolded her legs so she could get to her feet. 'I'm not going out with you. Things have changed since this afternoon.'

While she swiped her clothes for any dust she might have picked up off the floor, Will lifted his chin to look at her. 'A lot of things have changed.'

Cassidy froze, staring down at him and feeling the same tension between them there had been when he'd held her wrist. She even had to swallow to make her throat work again.

'I know.' There was no avoiding it. They had. But even if they hadn't she couldn't let it change her decision. 'I'm going to put a fresh pot of coffee on…'

She was at the door when his voice sounded again. 'Cass?'

'Mmm-hmm?' She turned.

Will considered her for a long moment before he said, 'Diana has been chasing a part in one of my films for months now. I've never dated her.'

See, now, she didn't actually need to know that. 'If you say so. It's nothing to do with me. I've already said that.'

'Well, now you know.'

She'd turned away again when he added, 'And Cass?'

'What?' She swung round and frowned at him.

'Don't even *think* about cooking in my kitchen. We'll order pizza. Less chance of a fire that way…' He smiled a small smile at her.

Cassidy found herself smiling back. 'Cute. Go back to work, Ryan.'

The third time she made it all the way into the next room, then, 'Cass?'

Shaking her head and rolling her eyes, she spun on her heel and set her hands on the doorframe to lean back into the room. *'What?'*

The smile grew, his eyes sparkling. 'Nothing.'

Cassidy gaped at him, quirked her brows, and then ruined the effect by laughing. She continued laughing all the way into the kitchen, feeling irrationally light-hearted— until it hit her why she felt that way. Cold water was running over the back of her hand when she realised she was staring into nothing as it sank in. Then tears threatened. Spending time with Will was like riding a rollercoaster.

A part of her really wanted to knock him on his ear, the way he did her. And at some point during the afternoon she'd got sucked in to the possibility of being transformed into the kind of woman she wanted to be. The kind of woman a man like Will Ryan could look at and want for more than a fling. A woman he wouldn't want to leave behind. Regardless of her errant tongue, her chaotic life, her lack of cooking skills and her body issues…

Was one night of trying that woman on for size so much to ask for?

The next thing she knew she was back in the doorway, her hands pushed deep into the pockets of her sweat pants as she waited for him to notice she was there. 'About Friday night…'

Will lifted his brows, 'Yes?'

'I'll go, so long as it's understood it's not a date.'

'It's just a night at the movies in fancy clothes…'

Cassidy smiled somewhat half-heartedly. 'Like you said.'

'Exactly like I said…'

He wasn't going to make it easy for her, was he? As much as she wanted her one night, Cassidy didn't think she could bring herself to beg, so she shrugged as if it didn't matter to her one way or the other. 'Well, I have a dress now. So if—'

'I'll meet you in the bar at the Beverly Wilshire at seven.' He looked at her with his unreadable expression back in place. 'For our not-a-date-but-a-movie night.'

'Okay.' She smiled a more genuine smile.

Then he ruined the moment for her, by turning away and

adding, 'It'll be nice for you to get a glimpse of the glamorous side of Hollywood before you go home.'

He'd said it with a complete lack of emotion—confirming what she'd already known. An affair was all he was interested in. She didn't know that man—didn't want to either. The Will Ryan she'd loved would never have asked that of her.

Lifting her chin, she turned away from the door, determination straightening her spine. Come hell or high water she was going to knock him on his ear on Friday night. It would serve him right. Would show him what he was missing.

And then this time *she* would be the one to walk away.

How did Hollywood's elite ever get anything done when it took a full day to get ready for one night on the town?

That was the main question Cassidy had after almost eight hours of preparation. She'd been waxed, moisturised, filed, painted, plucked, tinted, washed, trimmed, highlighted, styled, blowdried, artfully curled, and polished to within an inch of her life. She had been scrutinised by enough critical eyes to make her feel abnormal, and had make-up applied with brushes so soft they'd almost lulled her to sleep. Then she'd had a lesson on how to walk—a skill she'd been fairly certain she'd mastered a few decades earlier—all while being steered away from anything resembling a mirror.

She really didn't think she had the patience for beauty if it took so much work.

By the time she was zipped into the beautiful emerald-green dress that slid against her ultra smooth skin like liquid, she was almost ready for a lie-down. It was only the butterflies in her stomach preceding Angie's big reveal that kept her from throwing in the towel in favour of pyjamas and a large tub of ice cream.

When she came out of the dressing room Angie and her team of stylists smiled at her like proud parents, while Cassidy wiped her palms together and fought the need to fidget. 'Tell me I don't look ridiculous. That's all I ask…'

'Oh, honey—you have no idea how far you are from ridiculous.'

'Closer to the sublime, actually,' the designer of her dress added in his thick Italian accent as he beamed at her.

Except in Cassidy's world the two words had a tendency to go together.

'Can I look now?' she asked, when she couldn't take it any more.

'After the final finishing touch,' Angie said as she stepped forward with a flat velvet case. 'Can't walk the carpet without the bling, darling…'

The 'bling' took her breath away, and her voice was barely above a squeak when the case was opened. 'I can't wear that! What if something happens to it?'

'That's what insurance is for. How do you think they ever sell jewellery this expensive without it regularly being draped on beautiful women?'

Bless her, but… 'Angie, I'm a realist. If you've managed to make me look even one step above pretty I'll love you for the rest of my days…'

'In that case put the jewellery on and prepare to love me into your next life too.'

With shaking fingers Cassidy carefully withdrew each strand of diamonds and placed them on her lobes, feeling the touch of their coolness against her neck as a matching pendant nestled between her breasts and enough money was attached to her wrist to make her feel the weight of every single cent.

'How much is this stuff worth?'

Angie shrugged. 'A little under a million, I believe. It's the teardrop the size of a small fist in your cleavage that's worth the most.'

Cassidy's jaw dropped.

Angie winked. 'Just a shame no one can take advantage of how good it would look on you when you're wearing nothing else…'

Before Cassidy could make a comment on that, her friend stepped back and studied her with a broad smile. 'You ready?'

'No.'

'Close your eyes.'

'You do know you've been watching entirely too many make-over shows…?'

'I never got the attraction of them till now.' She steered her towards a long mirror covered in a white sheet. 'Close your eyes.'

There was the whisper of a sheet the second she did. Then a pause that made her heart thunder loudly in her ears. 'Angie—you're killing me.'

'Open your eyes.'

The woman who walked through the foyer of the Beverly Wilshire was almost unrecognisable in comparison to the one who had passed out on its marble flooring a little less than a month before. Men followed her with their eyes, women looked at her with a mixture of open curiosity and envy—and Cassidy Malone knew they did, because she smiled at every single one of them.

She even laughed at the concierge who had brought her the cold medicine when he did a double-take. Stepping into a fantasy version of herself was an incredible feeling, and one she doubted she would ever forget.

Since she was living a fantasy, it seemed only fair she include her favourite movie in it too. So she headed straight for the tall stools at the bar and made herself comfortable. Then she ordered a martini while she waited for Will, who played his part to perfection by walking in wearing a dark tuxedo that—astonishingly—made him look even more gorgeous than he already did as he turned a slow circle and failed to find her…

With a deep breath, Cassidy turned her stool and waited for their gazes to lock. When they did the expression on his face was one she knew she would never forget as long as she lived. Looking in a mirror was one thing. Being told she was beautiful was another. But it took Will's reaction to make her truly *feel* that way.

With a confident lift of her chin she slid off the stool, walking towards him on heels that made her hips sway with each step so that the material of her floor-length skirt shimmered in the soft lighting.

Will dragged his gaze from hers long enough to sweep down her body and back up again as she approached him and smiled. 'Hi.'

'Hi…'

Cassidy's smile grew. 'Shall we go?'

'Mmm-hmm.' He nodded, but stayed exactly where he was—still staring at her.

'Are you okay?'

'There's a limo at the front door.'

'Okay.' She lifted her carefully shaped brows in amusement and stifled the need to laugh when the move made him frown and wave an arm out to his side in invitation. 'Are you sure you're all right?'

'I'm fine.' But it looked as if he was clenching his jaw as she stepped past him.

It was only when they were in the back of the stretch limousine that he seemed to snap to his senses; his gaze was openly explorative as he studied every soft curl artfully arranged on the crown of her head and brushing against her neck. 'They changed your hair colour.'

'Highlights.'

His gaze dropped to the strand of diamonds hanging from her ear. 'Who gave you the jewellery?'

'It's on loan.' In an uncharacteristic demonstration of self-confidence she turned towards him and lifted her breasts with a small arch of her back. 'The necklace is a doozy. Look.'

The move had the desired effect; his gaze dropped to the deep 'V' at the front of her dress, where the teardrop diamond nestled in the shadow between her breasts. The frown returned, darker than before. Then his gaze shifted sharply upwards.

What felt like his disapproval, combined with her errant tongue and a martini at the bar, brought the words into the open before she could stop them. 'Angie says it's just a shame no one will get to see me wearing it on its own. When I have nothing else on…'

Will sucked in a carefully controlled breath. 'You—

young lady—are playing a very dangerous game with me right now.'

Despite the immediate reaction of her body, Cassidy looked him straight in the eye. 'Am I?'

'Yes. And you know you are.' He leaned in closer and lowered his voice. 'So—unless you're planning on making love in the back of this limo—I suggest you tone it down some.'

Her eyes widened when she realised something. 'You're *angry*.'

'Drop it, Cass.'

'You are, aren't you? Want to tell me *why*?'

'You know me better than that.'

'Not any more I don't.' She studied each of his eyes in turn. 'What have I done?'

'It's not what you've done, Cass.' Will shook his head, looking at her with incredulity. 'It's what Angie let her team do.'

Just like that, the temporary confidence she'd had shattered. Oh, well, it had been nice while it lasted…

Turning her face away, she managed a low, 'I see.'

'Don't do that.' When he tried to reach his long fingers for her chin to turn her face towards him she moved her head back and looked sideways at him, forcing him to swear beneath his breath. 'You don't get it. Whatever paranoid thoughts you're thinking right now, you can forget it.'

The hurt was almost overtaking her. 'Then explain it to me,' she whispered.

Will looked as if the top of his head was ready to explode. Then he leaned forward and hit the intercom button. 'Stop the car.'

'Sir?'

'I said, *stop the car.*'

The second it pulled over to the side he was yanking open the door and practically flinging himself out. Leaving Cassidy with no choice but to scramble, as carefully as she could in her expensive dress, across the soft leather seats until she could swing her legs out and join him—where he was pacing up and down.

He shot her a dark glare as he ran the fingers of one hand through his hair, the jacket of his tuxedo flapping with his movements. 'Get back in the limo. I need a minute.'

'No.' She folded her arms across her breasts, trying to stop herself shaking. 'You're going to talk to me.'

'*No.* I'm going to take a minute, and then we're going to the theatre, or we'll be late.'

'You can go to the theatre if you want. I'm going home.' She lifted her chin another defensive notch as she inadvertently called his house 'home'. 'I'm not going to humiliate myself any further if I'm not dressed appropriately.'

It was a ridiculous claim. Even Cassidy knew that. If Angelique Warden and her team didn't know what they were doing then no one did—and Will knew that too, if his violent expletive was anything to go by.

'It's got nothing to do with how you're dressed!'

'Then what *is it*?' She took a step closer. 'I can't read your mind the way you read mine, Will. I never could. So you'll need to explain this to me.'

'You won't get it. You haven't been here long enough.'

'*Try*!'

Dropping his arms to his sides, he stopped pacing and stood in front of her, studying her for the longest time before he pressed his mouth into a thin line and she got a low, rumbled, 'You look incredibly beautiful, Cass. You know that. And if you didn't you'd sure as hell have known it from the way people were looking at you in the hotel. You're not stupid.'

It was the most back-handed compliment anyone had ever paid her. 'Well, if it's not the way I look, and it's not the way I'm dressed—'

'You didn't *need* highlights in your hair.' He clenched his jaw and continued staring into her eyes. 'Or to be draped in expensive jewels. Don't you *get* that?'

'What?'

Sighing heavily, Will started pacing again, his voice somewhat calmer than before. 'Obviously you don't…but then why would you? There are millions of people in this city who don't.'

After he'd made three more trips past her Cassidy had had enough; unfolding her arms, she reached out a hand to grasp his elbow and stop him in his tracks. When he looked at her she summoned a small smile of encouragement. 'Get *what*? You're not making any sense.'

He shook his head, his voice softer. 'Forget it.'

When he tried to remove her hand, she turned it and tangled her fingers with his, stepping closer. 'No. Talk to me.'

His words were the very last thing she'd expected to hear. 'You're beautiful without any help. You always were.'

'What?'

'Hollywood has no idea of what beauty is. It has nothing to do with highlights and expensive jewels. Those people who helped transform you were trying to put you into a box you'd never fit.' When she tried to free her hand he tightened his fingers around hers. 'You're unique—as individual as that giant walnut of a diamond hanging around your neck—and there was a time you knew that. If you were trying to remember by allowing those people to turn you into something you're not, then you're going about it the wrong way…'

Cassidy took a shaky breath and avoided the intensity of his gaze as she fought to control the emotions welling up inside her. When she'd blinked enough times to clear her vision, swallowed to loosen her vocal cords, and dampened her lips in preparation, she made another attempt at freeing her hand and was amazed when he set it free.

Then she looked at him. 'You're right. Partly. But I didn't let them make me over to fit into a stereotype, Will. I did it for me.' When her lower lip shook she bit down on it and lifted her shoulders towards her ears. 'I needed this. More than I can possibly make you understand. Because somewhere along the way I *did* forget who I am—and the kind of woman I always wanted to be. But when I looked in that mirror less than an hour ago…'

She had to stop and look away when emotion overwhelmed her again.

'Keep going…'

Shooting a brief frown his way, for the impossibly gentle tone of his deep voice, she took another shaky breath. 'I was proud of what I saw, Will. The woman in that mirror looked like she could do anything she wanted to do—be anyone she wanted to be. I know you probably think that's silly—'

'I don't think it's silly. I think it's sad you didn't know that already.' He waited until she looked at him before asking roughly, 'Did I do that to you, Cass?'

'No.' She smiled a wobbly smile as his face blurred behind tears she didn't want to shed. 'I let it happen to me. That's why I'm the only person who can fix it.'

'Did this fix it?'

'A lot of things are fixing it. Writing again—pitching successfully.' She laughed throatily. 'Debating back and forth with you even helped. I started to remember what it felt like to be *me* again. And I haven't felt that way in a very long time. Then today…looking in that mirror showed me another one of a hundred possibilities. It's why when I leave here I'll leave stronger than I was when I arrived. It's partly why I changed my mind about tonight too—about coming with you, I mean. If I can carry this image off on a red carpet, without falling flat on my face and making a fool of myself the way I have so many times before, then—'

Will reclaimed her hand. 'Come on. We're going to be late.'

'For movie night?'

'Best night of the week, sweetheart.'

Smiling, she let him turn her around and lead her back to the limo. 'Will there be popcorn?'

'If there isn't, I'll find you some. I promise.'

Cassidy had honestly never loved him more than she did in that moment. Not only had he talked to her, he'd listened—and he hadn't psychoanalysed her to death or made her feel foolish; he'd understood. And he'd said just enough to let her know he did.

But then she'd always been a sucker for popcorn too—so long as it was… 'Buttered, not—'

'Not salted.' He smiled one of *those* smiles at her as they got to the open door. 'I remember.'

Standing on her tiptoes, Cassidy placed a light kiss on his cleanshaven cheek, 'Thank you.'

Will looked momentarily confused. 'What for?'

'For the popcorn you're going to get me…'

CHAPTER NINE

IT WAS one of the most memorable nights of her life. Not for the famous foot and handprints outside the Chinese Theater. Not because she managed the red carpet without tripping over. Not because there was a group of California Fortune Hunters in the crowd to support Will's new film, who went crazy when he introduced her to them and demanded photographs and autographs that made her feel like one of the movie stars she was sharing the carpet with. And not just because Will found popcorn, handed her a handkerchief when she needed it at the end of the movie, or stayed by her side watching over her, but allowed her enough independence to stand on her own two feet...

It was no one thing on its own. It was everything.

By the time they were halfway home...no, back to *Will's house*, she mentally corrected herself as she slipped off her shoes and held them in one hand...she felt happier than she had in years.

'Tired?'

Turning her head on the buttery upholstery, she smiled at him. 'I was poked and preened for seven hours—so, yes, I'm tired. But it's a *good* kind of tired.'

'Okay.'

'Your movie was amazing, Will. I loved it.'

Leaning his head back, he turned his face towards her. 'Good.'

Impulsively she lightly punched his upper arm. 'For crying out loud, Ryan. Show a little enthusiasm, would you? The audience loved it too. They all laughed at all the right times, sat on the edge of their seats at the right times… Most of the women in the auditorium were handed a handkerchief at the end…'

'Yeah.' He pursed his lips and nodded firmly. 'You can keep that, by the way.'

'I only blew my nose once. And I did it delicately.' She pouted on purpose.

'The people in the row in front and behind us appreciated that, I'm sure. But the once was one time too many. It's all yours now.'

Now, see—*this* was the Will she'd missed the most. The Will whose eyes sparkled in the dim light; the Will with a loose bow tie and the top button of his shirt undone; the Will whose familiar boyish sexiness was lit up, then gone, then lit up, then gone in the headlights of passing cars…

When he reached for a loose curl and wrapped it around his forefinger Cassidy let her guard down for the first time since she'd arrived. 'Just in case I never get a chance to say it again, I'm proud of you, Will. You made it. You did everything we talked about and more…'

His hand stilled. Then, without answering, he turned his hand over and ran the backs of his fingers over the sensitive skin of her neck, watching the movement with one of his unreadable gazes. When he reached the hollow between her neck and shoulderblade he turned his hand again, tracing the very tips of his fingers towards the edge of her dress.

But when he began tracing that edge downwards... 'What are you doing?' It was a moot question, but she asked it anyway, her low voice thickly threaded with physical awareness.

'You know what I'm doing.' Changing direction, he caught the necklace between his thumb and forefinger and followed it down to the heavy pendant in her cleavage.

The touch of his knuckles against the curve of her breast made her squirm on the seat. 'Will—'

'Schools don't go back for another month.'

The rumble of his voice was seduction itself. But she still knew what he was offering her—even if he was trying a different angle. 'No, they don't. But—'

Cupping the diamond for a moment, he lifted his gaze so she could see the dark pools of his eyes. 'Checking your list of excuses?'

'What list?'

'The one you have to tell you why you can't get involved with me again.' Long fingers flexed away from the diamond and purposefully brushed her skin.

Cassidy felt the impact of it clean to the soles of her feet. 'I don't have a list of excuses.'

'Liar.'

'They're not excuses.'

'Liar.' The hint of a smile she saw on his face filtered through into his voice, and then he moved his fingers again. 'I can feel your heart beating...'

The heart that was causing such an ache in her chest again when he told her, 'Do you know how a lie detector works, Cass? I do. I had to research it for a script one time. It measures a person's breathing rate, their pulse, their blood pressure and perspiration levels. Right now I can read three out of four of those with you. So, while your head may be frantically searching that list for your next excuse, your body tells me something different. But then you never could lie to me, could you?'

No, she couldn't. Not that she'd ever been much of a liar to begin with. But he'd always been able to read her. It was why it had taken so much effort to hold stuff back from him since she'd come to California.

'They're not excuses, Will.' And that wasn't a lie, because they weren't. They were valid reasons. But then she couldn't tell him that either. Because by telling him she would be inviting him to ask what they were.

'Then why is your heart beating so fast?'

Cassidy reached up and closed her fingers around his hand on the pendant, tapping into a little of her newfound confidence as she lifted her chin. 'Stop it.'

When Will angled his head, her breath caught. But he didn't lean in to kiss her—instead he studied her face for the longest time, before coming to a realization. 'You're hiding something from me.'

Her soft laughter sounded nervous even to her own ears. 'Don't be ridiculous. Why would I need to hide something from you?'

He'd already got entirely more information from her than she'd ever planned on giving him. She'd talked about her doubts and fears and insecurities—granted, sometimes he'd guessed some of them, and *then* she'd talked about them, but it was still more than she'd planned. Heck, he'd even got details of how ordinary her life was when compared to his. Though, judging by his earlier reaction to her make-over, Hollywood maybe wasn't his idea of utopia…

'There is something, though.' His deep voice sounded almost hypnotic in the intimacy of the dimly lit limousine.

Working on prising his long fingers away from the pendant proved a mistake on her part, when Will simply released it and captured her hand in his, between her breasts. If he really could feel her heartbeat then he would know it was racing…

Her plea was barely above a whisper. 'Don't ruin tonight for me, Will. *Please*.'

While he weighed it up in his mind his face shadowed. The movement of the limo stopped. When Cass looked through the tinted windows she saw they were home.

She frowned. No, not *home*—they were at *Will's house*. She really needed to stop doing that.

Turning her attention back to the intense man beside her she twisted her wrist and tugged sharply. 'Let me go.'

For a moment she thought she heard the word 'no', but then her door opened and their driver stood back to let her out, leaving Will no choice but to set her hand free. Cassidy bolted for the door on her bare feet—only to sigh with frustration when she got there and remembered who had the key.

As the limo pulled away, briefly catching her in its head-lights, she saw Will's dark silhouette approaching. He took his own sweet time about it too. When he got to the door, instead of opening it he leaned on the frame, turned the key over in his long fingers and studied her beneath the lamp. Just long enough to make her squirm inwardly and feel the most basic of instincts that left her torn between fight or flight.

'Open the door, Will.'

Closing his fingers tighter around the key, he asked again, 'What are you hiding from me?'

'It's almost midnight. I'm tired. And I'm not hiding anything. Key, please.' She held out her palm and waggled her fingers for the key.

'Not till you tell me what it is.'

The calm tone to his voice did nothing to stop the frustration building inside her as she took a measured step closer to him. 'Do I have to come and get the key?'

'You could *try*.' His voice dropped an octave, sending a sharp spark of awareness through her body.

'Don't. Make. Me.'

Folding his arms across his chest, he angled his head a minute amount. 'Yeah. That's an empty threat, isn't it? All talk no action. That's your biggest problem, isn't it? You're afraid to step up to the plate.'

'What?'

'You heard me.' He rocked forward and dropped his chin, fighting hard to keep the smile off his face. 'You talk the talk, Malone. Always did. But the truth is you're a Tootsie Pop.'

Her eyes widened. '*Excuse me*?'

Will nodded. 'Yup. So I'll open the door when you tell me what you're hiding.'

Cassidy laughed, but it had an edge to it that weakened the tone she'd been aiming for. 'You—'

'I'm the most annoying man on the planet, you hate me—yada, yada. Yeah, you've said—several times…' His mouth curled into an almost cruel smile. 'What happened to all that talk back there about being the confident woman you always wanted to be? I happen to know a little about confident women, Cass…'

'Yeah, I'll just bet you do.' When he pretended to search the air above her head for an answer she scowled at him.

'Confident women have the guts to reach out for the things they want. They take chances. They lay it on the line. You used to be that woman, Cass…'

Cassidy's scowl became a frown when he looked at her again. 'Hadn't you heard? I'm now a *Tootsie Pop*.' Whatever a Tootsie Pop is…

'Yes. You are. But not a good one. You have to work too hard at it. You see, a Tootsie Pop is a lollipop that's hard on the outside and soft on the inside—'

'Oh, I get the analogy.' Her gaze lowered, looked pointedly from one of his hands to the other as if she was trying to remember which one he had the key in. 'What I don't get is when you decided bullying me again was the best way to get me to open up. Give me the key, Will.'

He waited for her gaze to rise, controlling his smile before he calmly challenged her. 'Come and get it.'

Her jaw dropped and a strangled squeak of outrage sounded low in her throat.

Will pushed away from the doorframe and took a step forward, his voice lowering. 'Or tell me what it is you're hiding from me.'

She worried her lower lip as she avoided his gaze, taking a deep breath as she aimed for a version of the truth that might get her out of trouble. 'I *am* attracted to you, Will.'

'But?'

'That was a confession, in case you missed it. Score one to you.'

'No, I got it. I'm just wondering what it's leading up to. Because there's more, isn't there?'

She scowled at him again. 'Do you *have* to do that?'

'Do what?'

'Play the *I can read you like a book* card?' She lifted a hand and tucked a curl behind her ear. 'It's incredibly irritating. And you don't know me anywhere near as well as you like to think you do. Not any more.'

'You might be surprised.'

'I don't *want* to be surprised. I *want* to be not standing outside your house.'

Unfolding his arms, he lifted his hand to tuck a matching curl behind her other ear. Her soft intake of breath made his fingers still for a second before he dropped his hand back to his side. 'Whatever it is you're hiding, it's getting in the way.'

Somewhere in the red haze clouding her vision Cassidy had a moment of clarity. 'You're *trying* to pick a fight with me.'

'Am I?'

A second clue slipped into her mind. 'Because everything else has failed.'

'Everything else?'

'This is what you do, isn't it? You deflect.'

Will clenched his teeth, and she could almost see the anger expand inside his chest. His tone was deathly calm. 'Like you are now?'

How could she have been so blind? Cassidy laughed at her own stupidity. 'You've made this all about *me*, haven't you? What is this? Your way of proving you can have me any time you want?'

'You're walking a very thin line now, Cass.'

'Am I?'

To her astonishment he slid the key into the lock, swung the door open and stepped inside. Walking away from her. *Again.* Well, not this time.

Slamming the door behind her, she raised her voice. 'Giving up so easy, Will?'

'Leave it be, Malone. I mean it.'

But she couldn't. She followed him down the hall, continuing to push. It was his own fault, she told herself. He'd pushed and prodded and tried every trick in his seduction handbook to get to her since she'd arrived. He couldn't even be content with the fact she still wanted him—oh, no, he had to push some more. While offering her some quick affair. To do what? Get it out of their systems?

Didn't he know it would cheapen everything they'd had before?

'But then walking away is what you do best, isn't it?'

'If I were you I'd quit now.' The deathly calm tone of his voice told her just how angry he was. And when Will was really angry, he placed it behind an impenetrable wall.

So Cassidy did what she'd always done. She pushed. 'Or what? You'll leave? A tad unlikely, seeing this is your house.'

He turned on his heel so fast she didn't have time to react. The next thing she knew he was striding back towards her, his eyes glinting dangerously as he finally lost control. 'You sent me away!'

'You didn't look back!'

There was sudden silence, both of them breathing hard, the combination of anger and pain palpable in the air between them. Then their mouths were fused together, lips slamming back against their teeth, forcing them to open up and tangle in a battle to take the upper hand. Cassidy didn't know who kissed who first, and she was still so angry she could see red behind her eyelids, but it didn't stop her from throwing her arms around his neck at the same time as he hauled her into his arms and crushed her to him. It wasn't soft or gentle or cautious or exploratory, because passion didn't know any of those things. All it knew was blinding need and desperate wanting and hungry desire and—

With a high-pitched moan of frustration she dragged her mouth from his and shifted her arms to push her palms against his wide chest. He let go. She stepped back. And slapped him.

She'd never slapped anyone before. As he flinched, and her palm stung, her eyes widened with the horror of it. She was opening her mouth to apologise profusely when Will's expression darkened, his mouth twisting wryly.

'*Finally*. Now we're actually getting somewhere.'

Cassidy cocked her head. '*Oh?* Getting me to slap you was part of your great plan too, was it?'

'I didn't *have* a plan! But if slapping me is what it takes for you to let out whatever it is you've been holding back, then *bring it on*!'

Everything in her rebelled against the idea of slapping him again; it had never been an option for her. Instead she grabbed two fistfuls of his tuxedo lapels and hauled him back again, picking up where they'd left off—only this time with duelling tongues. Will turned them, pushed her against the wall. She let go of his tuxedo and started undoing the buttons of his white shirt, reaching for heated skin.

'Slow down…' The words were muffled against her

mouth, and then he groaned and tried again, using his hands to set her back a little. 'Cass. *Wait.*'

Frowning in frustration as he lifted his head, she dropped her chin to focus on freeing the buttons faster while she demanded, '*Why?* This is what you wanted, isn't it?'

'*No.*' Frustration equal to her own sounded in the rumble of his rough voice as one hand landed on hers to still them. 'Not like this.'

'But this is what we do best.' She raised her chin and sought out his mouth again.

He ducked out of the way. 'What is *that* supposed to mean?'

'You said it. It's the one area we never had any problems.' She tugged on her hands in an attempt to free them, while pushing closer into his chest. 'I agree. You win. Congratulations.'

Will looked so stunned it was almost funny. Then he shook his head and his frown returned, impossibly darker than before. 'I *win*?'

'You wanted an affair. We'll have an affair.' She sought his mouth again.

He took a step back and placed her at arm's length; literally. 'I wanted *what*?'

'An affair! That's what all this is about, isn't it?' She frowned back up at him. 'Call it whatever you want to call it. It's purely physical. Nothing more. And, yes—I do remember what we were like together—so, yes—I do know how good it will be. We're both adults, right? And pretty soon I'll be gone again. So—hey—why not take advantage of it while I'm here?'

'You think that's what this is about?' Shaking his head, he

stared at her with a look of incredulity. 'At what point did you *ever* hear me suggest we had some kind of affair? It's *purely physical*? Are you even *listening* to what you're saying?'

When he let go of her and took a step back Cassidy frowned all the harder; the beginning of a major headache was forming at her temples. 'You know I have to go home—what else can it be?'

'I just asked you to stay in the limo—or did you miss that part?'

'You didn't ask me, Will.' She racked her brain to remember it clearly—just in case she'd misinterpreted it. But she hadn't. 'You don't ask. *You tell.*'

'We're having this whole argument because of semantics?'

Cassidy was rapidly losing the plot with him. Her voice was threaded with what almost sounded like hysteria. 'You've done nothing but bully me since I got here! At what point has *any* of this ever been my decision? A contract I signed almost a decade ago brought me here. A script we had to produce has kept me here. Not once—*not once* during the whole time, Will—have I been allowed to so much as choose what time I want to eat! Today was the first time I did something on my own—and look how well *that* went down with you.'

During her tirade she'd looked anywhere but directly at his face, swinging her arms at random points in the air while she fought the need to cry again as she let it all out. When her words were met with silence, she finally looked at him. What she saw stunned her. He looked as if she'd just completely knocked the wind out of him.

Even his voice was flatter than it had ever been before. 'Well. There it is. That'll be what you were hiding from me.'

No. It wasn't what she was hiding from him, darn it! How could he be so incredibly dense?

Taking a short breath, he nodded. 'You should have said something. I could have bought you out of the contract and then you would never have had to go through all that torture, would you?'

Oh, come *on*! What did she have to say to make him understand? It wasn't that it had been torture—well, not all of it. There had been times, yes, but it was the constant battle of trying to resist falling for him again that had been the real problem. Especially when he'd been so very hard to resist! And in actuality it had been a moot point, because—

Wait a minute. *He could have what?*

Pushing his hands into the pockets of his dress trousers, Will looked her in the eyes and told her, 'You're not a prisoner here, Cass. If you didn't want to make the trip you'd only to say so. One line in an e-mail would have done it, and you would never have had to see me again. If you don't want to see the script through to the end then fine; any minor rewrites from here on in shouldn't be that big a deal.'

He'd shut himself off again. The realisation made her throat close over. She didn't want them to end like this. She hadn't wanted them to end the way they had last time either.

'*Will*—' She stepped towards him.

But he stepped out of her reach, the small increase in distance as agonising to her as it had been to watch him walk away from her before. 'You can leave whenever you want. You always could.'

When he walked towards the door Cassidy followed him. 'Where are you going?'

'Out.'

'It's after midnight.'

'New York isn't the only city that never sleeps.' He yanked the door open, then stopped and looked over his shoulder. 'Let me know your flight times and I'll make sure you get to the airport.'

'Don't do this. Not again.'

The low plea was enough to get him to turn round, one hand holding onto the door as he looked her straight in the eye and told her, 'That's just it, Cass. I didn't do it last time either. You've made more choices along the way than you give yourself credit for.'

CHAPTER TEN

WILL had never considered himself a complicated man. He knew what he wanted and how to get it. He had worked long and hard to get where he was, and he had the life he'd always dreamed of—more or less. But then he'd never viewed Hollywood with the same rose-tinted glasses Cass had. She'd been the first person in his life outside of a movie screen to make him believe in magic.

When he'd first met her he'd found it amusing, her Tinkerbell-like enthusiasm for all things cinematic. But over time she'd smoothed off his rough edges and made him believe in things he never would have without her. He'd needed her more than she'd probably ever realised. Having her push him away had been the hardest thing he'd ever had to deal with. So what had possessed him to think it would be okay this time…?

Thing was, she'd only had to be back in his life for a matter of days and he'd known. He'd known he *still* needed her.

Taking a deep breath, he glanced upwards at the cloud-less sky. What was he doing? He'd spent the night on an uncomfortable sofa in his office when he had a perfectly good bed at home. *Home.* When was the last time he'd thought of somewhere that way? It was the answer to that question that had brought him looking for her.

But when he found her bags packed in her room he felt his anger rising. *Not this time*. She thought he'd never looked back? Well, she was wrong about that. And he wasn't spending the *next* eight years of his life looking back. This time they were getting it out in the open—whether she liked it or not.

The fact he couldn't find her anywhere in the house or see her on the beach turned his determination to panic. Then he thought of the night before and searched his jacket pocket for his cellphone,

'Angie? Will. Is Cass with you?'

'No. I had my PA pick up the dress and jewellery. Is something wrong?'

Will turned a circle in the living room and tried to think of where she might have gone. 'So you didn't speak to her?'

'No.' There was a brief pause, then, 'You had a fight, didn't you? I swear, Will, if you break that girl's heart—'

What was it with the universe suddenly deciding he was the bad guy? It made Will sigh heavily. 'How long have you known me now, Angie?'

'Five years. Why?'

'I'm the guy you're constantly accusing of never getting involved—remember?'

Another spell of silence, then Angie said, 'Never got over her, did you?'

'Let me know if she calls you.'

With her promise made, he considered going back upstairs to search her bags for her passport. But he wasn't going to go through her things. She wouldn't have flown home without them. So she had to be somewhere. He searched for a note—which was dumb. Because after their angry words why in hell would she leave him a note? It would be nice to think she would have if she'd got on a plane. But hadn't he said to let him know? He was pretty sure he had…

For a man who made his living from words, he apparently had a very poor grasp of them in real life. *Just physical*! Where had she got *that* from? He was going to ask her that. He was going to ask her a lot of things.

After pacing up and down for ten minutes he decided to try the beach again, tossing his jacket over the back of one of the sofas and rolling up the sleeves of the only shirt he'd had as a spare in his office as he slid the glass doors shut behind him and jogged down the wooden stairs onto the sand. Which way? If he was Cass, would he have gone left or right?

He shook his head—yeah, it had always been so easy to get inside that head of hers. If it wasn't for the fact she couldn't lie he would have spent half his life asking dumb questions like *What are you thinking?* But then he'd never had to do that back in the day, because she'd always been so open—something completely alien and fascinating to him at the same time. Discovering she'd got so guarded over the years had been quite a shock to his system.

Looking skywards again, he vowed if he had to fly halfway across the planet to talk to her then so be it. And then he lowered his chin and forgot to breathe. It couldn't be. For a split second he thought he was imagining what he was seeing. He told himself he wanted her to be there so badly that his heart must have somehow convinced his brain to tell his eyes she was there. But would his imagination have conjured up an image of her looking so sad? It never had before. Would he have seen her slumped shoulders or the slight hint of red to her nose that suggested she'd been in the sun for too long? Any time he'd ever pictured her it had been smiling and laughing, the way she had that day on the O'Connell Street Bridge in Dublin, when he'd *had* to kiss her. Not just needed to or wanted to but *had to*.

'*Cass…*' He said her name at the same time as she lifted her chin and saw him. If he'd conjured up the image of her then he didn't care; his feet were already carrying him to her, his voice as calm as he could manage to keep it. 'You're still here.'

Oh, yeah—that's great, Ryan. Let the woman think you want her to go.

He tried again. 'I saw your bags.'

She couldn't look him in the eye. Her shoulders lifted in a brief shrug as she took a shaky breath. 'I don't even know your address to call a cab. How pathetic is that?'

It wasn't pathetic. It was another example of what an inconsiderate oaf he was. Because she was right. He had been pretty controlling of their environment of late. He just hadn't realised it. 'Twenty-one-eighteen Shoreview.'

When she looked sideways at him he frowned. He was still giving her the impression he wanted her to leave, wasn't he?

'I said to call me and I'd make sure you got to the airport.' *Still* giving her the impression he wanted her to leave. He was a genius. He could do better than this. 'Do you want to go home?'

There. That was better. Now he was letting her make her own decision. Then he rethought that, and added a shrug. 'You could stay…'

'It's tempting.' She smiled out at the ocean. 'I've been out here walking for the last hour. It's beautiful. I can understand why you live here.'

Will glanced over at the house that had felt more like a home in the last month than it ever had before, then took a step closer to her and pushed his hands into his pockets so they wouldn't be tempted to reach for her. 'I knew the first time I saw it that it was somewhere you would love. You always had a thing for the sea...'

Long lashes flickered as her gaze travelled up to meet his, silent questions written across the chestnut depths of her eyes. She had amazing eyes: fathomless, soulful, bright with intelligence. They were especially amazing when she was laughing, or trying to hold laughter back. Will remembered how amazing they had looked the first time she'd told him she loved him.

Then she dropped her chin and hid her eyes from him. 'I've been thinking about some of the things you said last night.'

'Yeah. I've been doing some thinking too.' When her lashes lifted he tried a small smile on for size. 'We said a lot.'

She nodded. 'We did.'

'I never meant to make you feel trapped here. I genuinely did think it would make it easier to work on the script. And as for the food thing—you never eat when you're working; it was always me who had to remind you to take a break and eat something. I guess I fell back into old habits.'

Her finely arched brows rose. 'I never thought of it that way. You're right. That *is* the way we used to be when we were working. I still have erratic mealtimes, and I eat way too much junk. I've probably eaten healthier here than I have in years.'

Okay. This was good. So he took another step forward—then faltered when she frowned a little and looked away. Too much?

When she sighed he tried not to look down at the rise and fall of her breasts. He'd never been able to look at her without wanting her. How hadn't she *known* how beautiful she was? He would never understand that. Any more than he would forgive Angie for changing the hair he'd always loved so much. It had been bad enough seeing so much of it cut off since the last time he saw her. When he'd known her before it had been halfway down her back, and sometimes when she was lying on top of him they would kiss surrounded by a cocoon of flower-scented hair. Will wondered how long highlights lasted. Not that there was anything wrong with them *per se*, it was just that he preferred her hair the rich auburn of before. Then he thought about how she might take it if he told her how to have her hair… Okay…might not help him stay out of trouble.

'I guess the fact I'm still here shows how much braver you are than me…'

What? He frowned at her profile. What did *that* mean?

Before he could ask she elaborated. 'I always wondered how you did it. Walked away like that without looking back. I tried to do it this morning, but even if I had known the address to call for a cab I don't know that I could have. Not without clearing the air first.'

It was a 'give with one hand, take away with the other' situation. On the one hand she'd just told him she hadn't been able to leave without seeing him—which made his heart swell in his chest. But on the other she'd basically told him she still blamed him for their break-up, because *he* left. He was pretty sure that was what she meant—in a roundabout way, with a backhanded compliment about him being brave.

Will had something to say about that. 'I don't know what you remember about that day. But if you look back maybe you'll think about everything that went before it. No matter what I tried, you kept pushing me away. You—'

'I know. You're right. I *did* send you away.'

He wasn't expecting that one. It brought him forward another step. A step immediately counteracted by Cass, when she stiffened, turned, and waited for him to accept the silent invitation to walk and talk. So he did.

Waves fizzed against the hot sand, dragging back out to sea to be replaced by the next as Cass pushed her hands into the pockets of her light trousers and watched her bare feet as they walked side by side.

'I always knew one day I would have to take on the care of my parents. That's what happens when people wait till later in life to have a child. And my dad was never the same after Mum died. I just never knew that he would end up sick at the very time we had big decisions to make about *our* lives…'

Will walked silently at her side and let her talk it through. The fact they had time to do it was enough for him. She was still there. That was what mattered most.

Cass took a deep breath and lifted her gaze from her feet to stare down the endless beach. 'We shared the dream of coming out here and being a success. We came at it from different angles, but we knew that. I guess the movie knocked some of the wind out of my sails, but not you. You wouldn't give up. Braver than me.' She smiled briefly at him. 'Like I said.'

'We were supposed to do all this together.'

'I know.' The smile wavered and he saw her look skywards. 'I guess a part of me always took some small comfort from the fact one of us made it. I'm proud of you.'

She had no idea what it meant to hear her say she was proud of him. He wouldn't have cared had it been anyone else. From Cass it meant everything. She was the proud parent, the teacher who'd made a difference, the foster parents who'd got it right with him in his last home, and the first woman who had ever made him feel love all wrapped into one when she said those four simple words. With those words the last remnants of the boy who had never thought he would amount to anything had been laid to rest.

Will swallowed hard and battled with the need to hold her. He had to. But he couldn't. Not yet.

'In the end I had to choose between two people I loved.' She took a shaky breath, 'I knew you would make it without me, Will. I think a part of me always knew that. My dad needed me.'

'*I* needed you.' He'd always thought she'd understood that.

The next shaky breath she took caught on a sob. 'When I sent you away that last time I never thought you would go. I didn't want you to. But I couldn't make that decision for you either. It wouldn't have been fair.'

Just like always, her hurt became *his* hurt, making him frown hard at her profile as a lone tear streaked down her cheek and she rubbed it away. 'You made the decision for me. I would never have left if you hadn't.'

She smiled sadly. 'Maybe I knew that. Everything was

so mixed up. It hurt so badly—every time I look back on that time all I can see is hurt. Maybe it was easier to hate you for leaving than it was to face up to my part in it. I just…I never thought…'

When she stopped, placed her hands on her hips and dropped her head back to take several ragged breaths, Will took his hands out of his pockets in preparation.

'See.' It was half-sob, half self-recriminating laughter. 'This is exactly why I've avoided talking about this for so long. It *still* hurts.'

Will could barely breathe. His chest was too tight. He even had to clear his throat before he could speak. 'What was it you never thought, Cass?'

Sniffing, then swiping at her cheeks, she finally looked him in the eye. And smiled a smile that broke him in two. 'I never thought you would do it. And I've spent all morning trying to figure out if in some twisted way it was a test that I set up for you to fail. But I don't think it was. At least I hope it wasn't. I just never—even when I was sending you away and the words were coming out of my stupid mouth—I never for one second thought you wouldn't so much as look back. Or come back. I don't know what it was I expected you to do. All I know is I waited. I waited for a very long time. Maybe a part of me never stopped waiting. Then, when the e-mail came…'

Tears were streaming down her face as she got to the end and she let them flow, not trying to wipe them away or hide them. Will knew a babbling Cass was a nervous Cass—it was one of the quirks he'd always found the most endearing. But she wasn't babbling this time. She was clear and lucid between catches of breath and the odd break of her voice. So it wasn't babbling. It was her finally telling the secret she'd been hiding from him. All of them.

'I was so very in love with you. I don't even think I knew how much. Not until you were gone. Then it was too late.' She lifted her shoulders again, her voice smaller than before. 'Because you never looked back.'

Will tried to form a coherent sentence in his head before speaking. There was less chance of messing it up that way. He opened his mouth…

'No.' She held up a hand in front of her body. 'Don't say anything. That's not why I'm telling you all this. I'm telling you because we never had closure last time. And I can't do that to either one of us again.'

When he stayed silent she smiled in appreciation and nodded her head, wiping her cheeks dry before dropping her arm to her side and looking back out to sea again. 'I can't stay here and have an affair with you, Will. What we had before means too much to me to taint it with something less. So everything I said and did last night with regard to the whole physical thing— If you could try and forget about it, that would be great.'

'Can I speak now?'

Her gaze shifted to tangle with his, the first hint of amusement sparkling in her expressive eyes. 'You're asking for permission?'

Will pointed out the obvious. 'The "don't say anything" instruction you gave me might have something to do with that. So is it my turn to speak now?'

'Is there going to be sympathy in there anywhere. Because I'm not sure I could take it.'

It was her ability to exasperate, fascinate, amuse and

completely distract him from rational thought in equal measures that had first attracted Will to Cass, so he fell back into habits of old as his way of dealing with it. Reaching for her shoulder, he turned her round to face him, ignoring the fact the sea was washing over his shoes.

'Shut up, Cass. And listen. It's my turn.' When she cocked a brow at him he smiled at her. 'I tried being polite about it, but you took too long giving me permission to speak. All you did was remind me why I never ask for it…'

When he was sure he had her undivided attention, he let go of her shoulders and pushed his hands back into his pockets, frowning a little when her gaze dropped to watch the movement and she looked as if she might be figuring out why he did it.

'This whole I never looked back thing? It's rubbish.'

It brought her gaze back up to find his at speed. 'What?'

'You heard me. I've never stopped looking back. If you hadn't sent me away the way you did I would never have left. Or at the very least I'd have gone ahead of you and waited. All you had to do was say the word. I'd spent my whole life being sent away by people. You knew that. You were the very last person I expected to do it to me—technically I maybe should have been able to deal with it better after so much practice…'

The look on her face floored him.

'But, no, I didn't deal with it better. I don't think I've ever dealt with it.' He lifted his brows in question. 'Do you want to hazard a guess why that might have been?'

Her lower lip trembled. 'Because you loved me the way I loved you.'

Will nodded, his voice soft. 'Because I loved you more than I'd ever loved anyone. I didn't even know what love was until you.'

When more tears slipped free, his hands immediately came out of his pockets to frame her face and brush them away with his thumbs. 'Don't do that. I hate it when you do that. I loved you, Cass—I did. So you tell me how I could feel that much and never look back. No one could. There were dozens of times I tore it apart in my head to see what I could have done differently, but the simple fact was it was already done.'

'I know,' she sobbed.

Stepping in closer, he lowered his head at the same time as he used his thumbs to lift her chin. Then, when he was looking deep into her eyes, he took a deep breath. 'I knew when I sent you that first e-mail there was a chance we'd end up here again.'

'I felt the same way when I opened it.' She smiled tremulously.

'We're different people.'

'We are.'

'But we're the same too—if that makes sense…'

Cass nodded. 'It does.'

'It was when you hid under the pillow,' he told her.

It took a minute. Confusion clouded the bright light in her beautiful eyes until she got it. 'When I had the cold and you wouldn't go away?'

'Yes.' His thumbs brushed across her cheeks as he smiled. 'That's when I knew I was in trouble again.'

'It was?'

'Mmm-hmm. Then I tried every trick in the book to get

you to stop trying to hide from me. Have I ever mentioned you can be really hard work?'

She laughed, and the sound was musical and lighter than before. 'It's okay. I'm well aware of that fact, thank you.'

There was more to say, but it was no good. He had to kiss her. Using his thumbs, he tilted her head back a little more while he closed the last inch between their bodies. Then he searched her eyes, hesitating for a brief moment until she silently willed him not to stop. When he lowered his head she met him halfway. Her felt her hands gripping handfuls of his loose shirt at either side of his waist as his lips moved over hers. There was no doubt about it. This part was right. No arguing with chemistry.

Threading the fingers of one hand into her glorious windswept hair, he moved his other hand from her face, traced down her throat, over her shoulder, and then down her back so he could wrap an arm around her waist to draw her closer. Cassidy moved her hands and wrapped her arms around him to bring him closer still. And even the fact that the curves of her body seemed to fit perfectly into the dips and plains of his had always felt right to Will. Another sign that she was made to be there…

He lifted his head enough to mumble, 'Are you going to slap me again?'

She pulled back a little more and grimaced. 'I'm so sorry I did that.'

'And I shouldn't have lost my temper.'

It made her smile. 'Forget about it. I lose mine every…what?'

Will lifted a brow, his mouth twitching. 'Actually, you've improved with age. It used to be every three, four minutes…'

'Funny guy.'

He wasn't kidding. Chemistry like theirs combined with artistic temperaments and stubborn streaks? Oh, there had been fireworks, all right. But whoever it was who said not to play with fire had sure as hell never had as much fun with it as Will had.

'Now. About this supposed affair I suggested.' It took considerable effort not to chuckle when she grimaced again. 'Are we chalking that one down to the problem you have with over-thinking and letting it drop?'

Cass nodded enthusiastically. 'Please, yes.'

'Good—because that's not what I've been aiming for at all.' He flexed his fingers in her hair, cradling the back of her head and watching the reaction in her eyes. 'I was determined to take it slow with you this time—but to hell with it. I want you to stay. You had me with the pillow, Cass, but you knocked me on my ear last night with that dress. Do you have any idea how many guys were on my hit list before we even left the Beverly Wilshire last night? I'd have taken them on—you know that about me.'

In a heartbeat the Cass he'd fallen in love with a decade before was back, her smile lighting her up from inside. Right there, under unforgiving California sunshine, with her wind-blown hair and barely any make-up, and a slight sunburn on her nose and her lips swollen from his kisses, she had never, *ever* looked more beautiful to him. There wasn't a woman on the planet who was a patch on her, as far as he was concerned.

She lightly smacked his back. 'Now you know how it felt to find you with your complimentary female in the dried goods section of the supermarket.'

'You *were* jealous.' He grinned like a fool. 'I hoped you were.'

'No dastardly plans, huh?'

'Nope. I just want you to stay. I love you, Cass. I loved you before and I love you again. Maybe I never stopped.'

Sliding one arm free, she almost tentatively touched the very tips of her fingers to his cheek. He felt the slight tremor of her touch. The uncertainty was so at odds with the confident woman he knew she had in her that it felt as if she'd wrapped those same fingers around his heart and held it in the palm of her hand.

For most of his life he'd felt as if there was something missing in his life—he'd struggled and fought to find it, piece by tiny piece, each part of the puzzle hard-won but never quite enough to fill the void. For a long time he'd feared he was destined to live his life alone. But, despite how far he'd come and how much he'd learned along the way, he realised there and then that he'd never once felt whole the way he did when he held Cass in his arms.

Her eyes warmed to a darker shade of chestnut, and her voice was sure and even. 'I love you too. I never stopped. So, yes, I want to stay. I'm still here, aren't I?'

Will kissed her fiercely, with all the emotion he'd been holding so carefully in check, and then he held her tight and took a shuddering breath.

'You scared me last night.' He exhaled the rough words into her hair, and felt his heart kick against his ribs when she made a sound that was half-laughter, half-sob against his neck. 'I thought we'd got it wrong again.'

'Me too.'

He kept hold of her and closed his eyes as relief

washed over him. 'We'll get it right this time, Cass. I promise.'

The husky words brought her out of hiding, her head lifting so that when he looked at her he could see deep into her eyes. 'We'll get it right because we'll talk like we're talking now. We don't have to try and hide anything from each other any more. And this is worth fighting for—right?'

'Now who's the bossy one?'

'Right?'

'*Right.*' Will took a step back in water that was up to his ankles, setting her back a little before bending over and scooping her up off the ground. 'Now, we have eight years of making up to do.'

'*In one weekend?*'

'I was thinking more in terms of the rest of our lives…'

HIS SHY CINDERELLA

KATE HARDY

For Gerard, who answered a lot of very weird questions about motor racing with a great deal of patience (but I am still not going to a Grand Prix with you!) xxx

CHAPTER ONE

ANGEL FLICKED THROUGH the pile of mail on her desk.

Bills, bills, circulars and—just for a change—bills. Bills she really hoped she could pay without temporarily borrowing from the account she'd earmarked for paying the company's half-yearly tax liability.

And there was still no sign of the large envelope with an American postmark she'd been waiting for, containing the contract for supplying the new McKenzie Frost to feature in the next instalment of *Spyline*, a high-profile action movie series. Triffid Studios hadn't emailed to her it instead, either, because Angel had already checked her inbox and the spam box. Twice.

Maybe she'd send a polite enquiring email to their legal department tomorrow. There was a fine line between being enthusiastic about the project and coming across as desperate and needy.

Even though right now Angel felt desperate and needy. She couldn't let McKenzie's go under. Not on her watch. How could she live with herself if she lost the company her grandfather had started seventy years ago? The contract with Triffid would make all the difference. Seeing the McKenzie Frost in the film would remind people of just how wonderful McKenzie's cars were: hand-made, stylish, classic, and with full attention to every detail. And they were bang up to date: she intended to produce the Frost in an electric edition, too. Then their waiting list would be full again, with everyone wanting their own specially customised Frost, and she wouldn't have to lay anyone off at the factory.

Though she couldn't even talk about the deal yet. Not until she'd actually signed the contract—which she couldn't do until her lawyer had checked it over, and her lawyer couldn't do that until the contract actually arrived...

But there was no point in brooding over something she couldn't change. She'd just have to get on with things as best as she could, and hope that she didn't have to come up with plan B. And she didn't want to burden her parents with her worries. She knew they were enjoying their retirement, and the last thing she wanted was to drag them back from the extended vacation they'd been planning for years.

She'd grin and bear it, and if necessary she'd tell a white lie or two.

She went through the post, dealing with each piece as she opened it, and paused at the last envelope: cream vellum, with a handwritten address. Most people nowadays used computer-printed address labels, or if they did have to write something they'd simply grab the nearest ballpoint pen. This bold, flamboyant script looked as if it had been written with a proper fountain pen. Disappointingly, the letter itself was typewritten, but the signature at the bottom was in the same flamboyant handwriting as the envelope.

And her jaw dropped as she read the letter.

It was an offer to buy the company.

Selling up would be one way to solve McKenzie's financial problems. But selling McKenzie's to Brandon Stone? He seriously thought she would even consider it?

She knew the family history well enough. Her grandfather had set up in business with his best friend just after the Second World War, building quality cars that everyone could afford. Except then they'd both fallen in love with the same woman. Esther had chosen Jimmy McKenzie; in response, Barnaby Stone had dissolved their business partnership and left with all the equipment to go and start up another business, this time based on making factory-built cars. Jimmy McKenzie had started over, too, making his hand-built cars customisable—just as McKenzie's still built their cars today.

On the eve of the wedding, Barnaby Stone had come back and asked Esther to run away with him. She'd said no.

Since then, the two families had never spoken again.

Until now.

If you could call a letter speaking.

Angel could see it from Brandon's point of view. Buying McKenzie's would salve his sense of family honour because then, although the grandfather had lost the girl, the grandson had won the business. It would also be the end of everything McKenzie's did, because Stone's would definitely get rid of their hand-made and customised process. She knew that Stone's racing cars were all factory built, using robots and the newest technology; it was the total opposite of the hand-craftsmanship and personal experience at McKenzie's.

She'd heard on the grapevine that Stone's wanted to branch out into making roadsters, which would put them in direct competition with McKenzie's: and what better way to get rid of your competitor than to buy them out? No doubt he'd keep the name—McKenzie's was known for high quality, so the brand was definitely worth something. She'd overheard her parents discussing it during the last recession, when Larry Stone had offered to buy McKenzie's. According to her father, Barnaby Stone had been a ruthless businessman, and his sons and grandsons came from the same mould. She knew Max McKenzie was a good judge of character, so it was obvious that Brandon would asset-strip the business and make all her staff redundant.

No way.

She wouldn't sell her family business to Brandon Stone, not even if she was utterly desperate and he was the last person on earth.

And what did he really know about business, anyway? Driving race cars, yes: he'd won a few championships in his career, and had narrowly missed becoming the world champion a couple of times. But being good at driving a racing car wasn't the same as being good at running a business that made racing cars. As far as she knew, dating supermodels and quaffing magnums of champagne weren't requirements for running a successful business either. She was pretty sure that he was just the figurehead and someone else did the actual running of Stone's.

Regardless, she wasn't selling. Not to him.

She flicked into her email program. In his letter, Brandon Stone had said he looked forward to hearing from her at her earliest convenience. So she'd give him his answer right now.

Dear Mr Stone

No way is the McKenzie's logo going on the front of your factory-made identikit cars. I wouldn't sell my family business to you if you were the last person on earth. My grandfather would be turning in his grave even at the thought of it.

Then she took a deep breath and deleted the paragraph. Much as she'd like to send the email as it was, it sounded like a challenge. She wasn't looking for a fight; she was simply looking to shut down his attempts at buying her out.

What was it that all the experts said about saying no? Keep it short. No apologies, no explanations—just no.

Dear Mr Stone
Thank you for your letter. My company is not for sale.
Yours sincerely
Angel McKenzie

She couldn't make it much clearer than that.

When his computer pinged, Brandon flicked into his email program. Angel McKenzie was giving him an answer already? Good.

Then he read the email.

It was short, polite and definite.

And she was living in cloud cuckoo land.

She might not want to sell the business, but McKenzie's was definitely going under. He'd seen their published accounts for the last four years, and the balance sheet looked grimmer every year. The recession had bitten hard in their corner of the market. The way things were going, she couldn't afford not to sell the company.

Maybe he'd taken the wrong approach, writing to her. Maybe he should try shock tactics instead and be the first Stone to speak to a McKenzie for almost seven decades.

And, if he could talk her into selling the company to him, then finally he'd prove he was worthy of heading up Stone's. To his father, to his uncle, and to everyone else who thought that Brandon Stone was just an empty-headed playboy who was only bothered about driving fast cars. To those who were just waiting for the golden boy to fail.

He glanced at the photograph of his older brother on his desk. And maybe, if he could pull off the deal, it would be the one thing to help assuage the guilt he'd spent three years failing to get rid of. The knowledge that it should've been him in that car, the day of the race, not Sam. That if he hadn't gone skiing the week before the race and recklessly taken a diamond run, falling and breaking a rib in the process, he would've been fit to drive. Meaning that Sam wouldn't have been his backup driver, so he wouldn't have been in the crash; and Sam's baby daughter would've grown up knowing her father as more than just a photograph.

Brandon wasn't sure he'd ever be able to forgive himself for that.

But doing well by Stone's was one way to atone for what he'd done. He'd worked hard and learned fast, and the company was going from strength to strength. But it still wasn't enough to assuage the guilt.

'I'm sorry, Sammy,' he said quietly. 'I'm sorry I was such an immature, selfish brat. And I really wish you were still here.' For so many reasons. Sure, Brandon would still have been working in the family business by this point in his career—but Sam would've been at the helm of the company, where he belonged. Nobody would've doubted Sam's managerial abilities. And their uncle Eric wouldn't have been scrutinising Sam's every move, waiting for an opportunity to criticise.

He shook himself. Eric was just disappointed because he thought that he should be heading up the business. Brandon needed to find him a different role, one that would make him happy and feel that he had a say in things. If Brandon could bring McKenzie's into the fold, then maybe Eric could take charge there.

Getting Angel McKenzie to sell to him was definitely his priority now. Whatever the personal cost.

He rang her office to set up a meeting.

'I'm afraid Ms McKenzie's diary is full for the next

month,' the voice on the other end of the line informed him, with the clear implication that it would be 'full' for the month after, too, and the month after that.

Like hell it was.

Clearly Angel had anticipated his next move, and had briefed her PA to refuse to book any meetings with him.

'Maybe you could email her instead,' the PA suggested sweetly.

Any email would no doubt find its way straight into her trash box. 'I'll do that. Thank you,' Brandon said. Though he had no intention of sending an email. He'd try something else entirely. When he'd replaced the receiver, he went to talk to his own PA. 'Gina, I need everything you can find about Angel McKenzie, please,' he said. 'Her CV, what she likes doing, who she dates.'

'If you're interested in her, sweetie, shouldn't you be looking up that sort of thing for yourself?' Gina asked.

Oh, the joys of inheriting a PA who'd known you since you were a baby and was best friends with your mum, Brandon thought. 'I'm not interested in dating her,' he said. 'This is work. Angel McKenzie.' He emphasised the surname, in case she'd just blocked it out.

Gina winced. 'Ah. *Those* McKenzies.'

'I already know the business data,' he said. 'Now I need to know the personal stuff.'

'This sounds as if it's going to end in tears,' Gina warned.

'It's not. It's about knowing who you're doing business with and being prepared. And I'd prefer you not to mention any of this to Mum, Dad or Eric, please. OK?'

'Yes, Mr Bond. I'll keep it top secret,' Gina drawled.

Brandon groaned. 'Bond's PAs used to sigh with longing, flutter their eyelashes and do exactly what he asked.'

'Bond didn't have a PA. He flirted with everyone else's

PAs. And you can't flirt with someone who changed your nappy,' Gina retorted.

Brandon knew when he was beaten. 'I'll make the coffee. Skinny latte with half a spoonful of sweetener, right?'

She grinned. 'That's my boy.'

'You're supposed to respect your boss,' he grumbled, only half teasing.

'I do respect you, sweetie. But I also think you're about to do something stupid. And your mum—'

'Would never forgive you for letting me go right ahead,' Brandon finished. He'd heard that line from her quite a few times over the years. The worst thing was that she was usually right.

He made the coffee, then buried himself in paperwork.

Gina came in an hour later. 'One dossier, as requested,' she said, and put the buff-coloured folder on his desk.

She'd also printed a label for the folder, with the words *Top Sekrit!* typed in red ink and in a font that resembled a toddler's scrawled handwriting.

'You've made your point,' he said. She thought he was behaving like a three-year-old.

'Good. I hope you're listening.'

Given that Gina was one of the few people in the company who'd actually batted his corner when he'd first taken over from his father, he couldn't be angry with her. He knew she had his best interests at heart.

'There aren't going to be any tears at the end of this,' he said gently. 'I promise.'

'Good. Because I worry about you almost as much as your mum does.'

'I know. And I appreciate it.' He reached over to squeeze her hand, hoping he wasn't about to get the lecture regarding it being time he stopped playing the field and settled down. Because that didn't figure in his plans, either. How could he ever settle down and have a family, knowing he'd taken that opportunity away from his brother? He didn't deserve that kind of future. Which meant his focus was strictly on the business. 'Thanks, Gina.'

'I've emailed it to you as well,' she said. 'Don't do anything stupid.'

'I won't.'

The top of the file contained a photograph. Angel McKenzie looked like every other generic businesswoman, dressed in a well-cut dark suit teamed with a plain white shirt buttoned up to the neck, and her dark hair cut in a neat bob.

But her eyes were arresting.

Violet blue.

Brandon shook himself. An irrelevant detail. He wasn't intending to date her.

Her CV was impressive. A first-class degree in engineering from a top university, followed by an MA in automotive design from another top institution. And she hadn't gone in straight at the top of her family business, unlike himself: it looked as if she'd done a stint in every single department before becoming her father's second-in-command, and then Max McKenzie had stepped aside two years ago to let her take charge. Again, impressive: it meant she knew her business inside out.

But there was nothing in the dossier about her personal life. He had the distinct impression that she put the business first and spent all her time on it. Given the state of those balance sheets, he would've done the same.

But there was one small thing that he could use. Angel McKenzie went to the gym every morning before work. Even more helpfully, the gym she used belonged to the leisure club of a hotel near to her factory. All he had to do was book a room at the hotel, and he could use the leisure club and then accidentally-on-purpose bump into her.

Once they were face to face, she'd have to talk to him.

And it would all be done and dusted within a week.

At seven the next morning, Brandon walked into the leisure club's reception area and paused at the window. The badge on the woman's neat black polo shirt identified her as *Lorraine, Senior Trainer.*

'Good morning,' he said with a smile. 'I wonder if you can help me.'

She smiled back. 'Of course, sir. Are you a guest at the hotel?'

'I am.' He showed her his room key.

'And you'd like to use the facilities?'

'Sort of,' he said. 'I'm meeting Angel McKenzie here.'

'It's Thursday, so she'll be in the pool,' Lorraine told him. 'Would you like a towel?'

'Yes, please.' And he was glad he'd thought to bring swimming trunks as well as a T-shirt and sweatpants.

She handed him a thick cream-coloured towel. 'I just need you to sign in here, please.' She gestured to the book on the windowsill with its neatly ruled columns: name, room number, time in, time out. 'The changing rooms are through there on the left,' she said, indicating the door. 'The lockers take a pound coin, which will be returned to you when you open the locker. As a guest, you also have use of the sauna, steam room and spa pool. Just let us know if you need anything.' She gave him another smile.

'Thanks.' He signed in, went to change into his swimming gear, and followed the instructions on the wall to shower before using the pool.

The pool room itself was a little warm for his liking. Nobody was sitting in the spa pool, but there were three people using the small swimming pool: a middle-aged man and woman who were clearly there together, and a woman who was swimming length after length in a neat front crawl.

Angel McKenzie.

Brandon slid into the water in the lane next to hers and swam half a dozen lengths, enjoying the feel of slicing through the water.

Then he changed his course just enough that he accidentally bumped into her, knocking her very slightly off balance so she was forced to stand up in the pool.

He, too, halted and stood up. 'I'm so sorry.'

She looked at him. The first thing he noticed was how vivid her eyes were; the photograph had barely done her justice.

The second thing he noticed was that she was wearing earplugs, so she wouldn't have heard his apology.

'Sorry,' he said again, exaggerating the movement of his mouth.

She shrugged. 'It's OK.'

Clearly she planned to go straight back to swimming. Which wasn't what he wanted. 'No, it's not. Can I buy you a coffee?'

She took out one of the earplugs. 'I'm afraid I missed what you said.'

'Can I buy you a coffee to apologise?'

'There's no need.' She was starting to smile, but Brandon saw the exact moment that she recognised him, when her smile disappeared and those amazing violet eyes narrowed. 'Did you bump into me on purpose?'

He might as well be honest with her. 'Yes.'

'Why? And what are you doing here anyway?'

'I wanted to talk to you.'

'There's nothing to say.'

He rather thought there was. 'Hear me out?'

'We really have nothing to talk about, Mr Stone,' she repeated.

'I think we do, and your PA won't book a meeting with me.'

'So you stalked me?'

Put like that, it sounded bad. He spread his hands. 'Short of pitching up on your doorstep and refusing to budge, how else was I going to get you to speak to me other than by interrupting your morning workout?'

'My company isn't for sale. That isn't going to change.'

'That's not what I want to talk about.'

She frowned. 'Then why do you want to talk to me?'

'Have breakfast with me, and I'll tell you.'

She shook her head. 'I don't have time.'

'Lunch, then. Or dinner. Or breakfast tomorrow morning.' Brandon didn't usually have to work this hard with women, and it unsettled him slightly.

She folded her arms. 'You're persistent.'

'Persistence is a business asset,' he said. 'Have breakfast with me, Ms McKenzie. You have to eat before work, surely?'

'I…'

'Let's just have breakfast and a chat.' He summoned up his most charming smile. 'No strings.'

She said nothing while she thought about it; Brandon, sure that she was going to refuse, was planning his next argument to convince her when she said, 'All right. Breakfast and a chat. No strings.'

That was the first hurdle over. Good. He could work with this. 'Thank you. See you in the restaurant in—what, half an hour?'

'Fifteen minutes,' she corrected, and hauled herself out of the pool.

Brandon did the same, then showered and changed into his business suit and was sitting at a table in the hotel restaurant exactly fourteen minutes later.

One minute after that, Angel walked in, wearing a business suit, and he was glad that he'd second-guessed her and worn formal clothing rather than jeans. Though he also noticed that her hair was still wet and pulled back in a ponytail, her shoes were flat and she wasn't wearing any make-up. The women in his life would never have shown up for anything without perfect hair, high heels and full make-up; then again, they would also have made him wait for two hours while they finished getting ready. Angel McKenzie clearly valued time over her personal appearance, and he found that refreshing.

The other thing he noticed was that she was wearing a hearing aid in her left ear.

That hadn't been in his dossier. He was surprised that Gina had missed it, but it felt too awkward and intrusive to ask Angel about it.

Then she knocked him the tiniest bit off kilter by being the one to bring it up.

'Do you mind if we swap places? It's a bit noisy in here and it's easier for me to lip-read you if your face is in the light.'

'No problem,' he said, standing up immediately. 'And I'll ask if we can move tables to a quieter one.'

She gestured to the floor. 'It's wooden floor, so it's going to be noisy wherever we sit. Carpet dampens speech as well as footsteps.'

And there was a group of businessmen nearby; they were laughing heartily enough to drown out a conversation on the other side of the room. 'Or we could change the venue to my room, which really will be quieter,' Brandon said, 'but I don't want you to think I'm hitting on you.'

Though in other circumstances, he thought, I probably would, because she has the most amazing eyes.

He was shocked to realise how much he was attracted to Angel McKenzie. She was meant to be his business rival, from a family that was his own family's sworn enemy. He wasn't supposed to be attracted to her. Particularly as she was about six inches shorter and way less glamorous than the women he usually dated. She really wasn't his type.

'The restaurant's fine,' she said, and changed places with him. 'So what did you want to talk about? If it's your offer to buy McKenzie's, then it's going to be rather a short and pointless conversation, because the company isn't for sale.'

Before he could answer, the waitress came over. 'May I take your order?'

'Thank you.' Angel smiled at the waitress and ordered coffee, granola, fruit and yoghurt.

Brandon hadn't been expecting that smile, either.

It lit up her face, turning her from average to pretty; in all the photographs he'd seen, Angel had been serious and unsmiling.

And how weird was it that he wanted to be the one to make her smile like that?

Worse than that, focusing on her mouth had made him wonder what it would be like to kiss her. How crazy was that? He was supposed to be talking to her about business, not fantasising about her. She wasn't even his type.

He shook himself and glanced quickly through the menu.

'Sir?' the waitress asked.

'Coffee, please, and eggs Florentine on wholemeal toast—but without the hollandaise sauce, please.'

'Of course, sir.'

'I would've had you pegged as a full English man,' Angel said when the waitress had gone.

'Load up on fatty food and junk, and you're going to feel like a dog's breakfast by the end of a race,' he said with a grimace. 'Food's fuel. If you want to work effectively, you eat effectively. Lean protein, complex carbs, plenty of fruit and veg, and no added sugar.'

She inclined her head. 'Fair point.'

He needed to get this back on the rails. 'So. As I was saying, this discussion isn't about buying the company.'

She waited to let him explain more.

So that was her tactic in business. Say little and let the other party talk themselves into a hole. OK. He'd draw her out. 'I wanted to talk about research and development.'

She frowned. 'What about it?'

'I'm looking for someone to head up my R and D department.' He paused. 'I was considering headhunting you.'

She blinked. 'Yesterday you wanted to buy my company.'

He still did.

'And today you're offering me a job?'

'Yes.'

She looked wary. 'Why?'

'I heard you're a good designer. A first-class degree in engineering, followed by an MA in automotive design.'

'So you *have* been stalking me.'

'Doing research prior to headhunting you,' he corrected. 'You're a difficult woman to pin down, Ms McKenzie.' And he noticed that she still hadn't suggested that he used her first name. She was clearly keeping as many barriers between them as possible.

'Thank you for the job offer, Mr Stone,' she said. 'I'm flattered. But I rather like my current job.' She waited a beat to ram the point home. 'Running the company my grandfather started.'

'Together with my grandfather,' he pointed out.

'Who then dissolved the partnership and took all the equipment with him. McKenzie's has absolutely nothing to do with Barnaby Stone.'

'Not right now.' He held her gaze. 'But it could do.'

'I'm not selling to you, Mr Stone,' she said wearily. 'And I'm not working for you, either. So can you please just give up and stop wasting your time and mine?'

He applauded her loyalty to her family, but this was business and it was time for a reality check. 'I've seen your accounts for the last four years.'

She shrugged, seeming unbothered. 'They're on public record. As are yours.'

'And every year you're struggling more. You need an investor,' Brandon said.

Angel had been here before. The last man who'd wanted to invest in McKenzie's had assumed that it would give him rights over her as well. She'd put him very straight about that, and in response he'd withdrawn the offer.

No way would she let herself get in that situation again. She wasn't for sale, and neither was her business. 'I don't think so.'

'Hand-built cars are a luxury item. Yours are underpriced.'

'The idea was, and still is, to make hand-built customisable cars that anyone can afford,' she said. 'We have a waiting list.'

'Not a very long one.'

That was true; and it was worrying that he knew that. Did that mean she had a mole in the company—someone who might even scupper the deal with Triffid by talking about the McKenzie Frost too soon? No. Of course not. That was sheer paranoia. She'd known most of the staff since she was a small child, and had interviewed the newer members of staff herself. People didn't tend to leave McKenzie's unless they retired. And she trusted everyone on her team. 'Have you been spying on me?'

The waitress, who'd just arrived with their food and coffee, clearly overheard Angel's comment, because she looked a bit nervous and disappeared quickly.

'I think we just made our waitress feel a bit awkward,' Brandon said.

'You mean *you* did,' she said. 'Because you're the one who's been spying.'

'Making a very common-sense deduction, actually,' he countered. 'If you had a long waiting list, your balance sheet would look a lot healthier than it does.'

She knew that was true. 'So if we don't have a great balance sheet, why do you want to buy…?' She broke off. 'Hold on. You said you want a designer to head up your research and development team. Which means the rumours are true—Stone's really is looking at moving into the production of road cars.'

He said nothing and his expression was completely inscrutable, but she knew she was right.

So his plan was obvious: to buy McKenzie's, knocking out his closest competitor, and then use her to make his family's name in a different area.

No way.

She stared at him. His dark blond hair was just a little too long, making him look more like a rock star than a businessman; clearly it was a hangover from his days as the racing world's equivalent of a rock star. And he was obviously used to charming his way through life; he knew just how good-looking he was, and used that full-wattage smile and sensual grey eyes to make every female within a radius of a hundred metres feel as if her heart had just done a somersault. He was clearly well aware that men wanted to be him—a former star racing driver—and women wanted to be with him.

Well, he'd find out that she was immune to his charm. Yes, Brandon Stone was very easy on the eye; but she wasn't going to let any ridiculous attraction she felt towards him get in the way of her business. His family had been her family's rivals for seventy years. That wasn't about to change.

'So basically you want to buy McKenzie's so you can put our badge on the front of your roadsters?' She grimaced. 'That's tantamount to misleading the public—using a brand known for its handmade production and attention to detail to sell cars made in a factory.'

'Cars made using the latest technology to streamline the process,' he corrected. 'We still pay very close attention to detail.'

'It's not the same as a customer being able to meet and shake the hands of the actual people who built their car. McKenzie's has a unique selling point.'

'McKenzie's is in danger of going under.'

'That's not happening on my watch,' she said. 'And I'm not selling to you. To anyone,' she corrected herself swiftly.

But he picked up on her mistake. 'You're not selling to me because I'm a Stone.'

'Would you sell your company to me?' she countered.

'If my balance sheet was as bad as yours, you were going to keep on all my staff, and my family name was still going to be in the market place, then yes, I'd consider it—depending on the deal you were offering.'

'But that's the point. You won't keep my staff,' she said. 'You'll move production to your factory to take advantage of economies of scale. My staff might not want to move, for all kinds of reasons—their children might be in the middle of a crucial year at school, or they might have elderly parents they want to keep an eye on.' Her own parents were still both middle-aged and healthy, but she wouldn't want to move miles away from them in case that changed. If they needed her, she'd want to be there.

'Your staff would still have a job. I can guarantee that all their jobs will be safe when you sell to me.'

'Firstly, I'm not selling, however often you ask me. Secondly, they already have a job. With me.' She folded her arms. 'Whatever you think, McKenzie's isn't going under.'

'We could work together,' he said. 'It would be a win for both companies. Between us we could negotiate better discounts from our suppliers. You'd still be in charge of research and development.'

The thing she loved most. Instead of worrying about balance sheets and sales and PR, she could spend her days working on designing cars.

It was tempting.

But, even if they ignored the bad blood between their families, it couldn't work. Their management styles were too far apart. McKenzie's had always considered their teams to be part of the family, whereas Stone's was ruthless. Between them they had two completely opposing cultures—and there was no middle ground.

'I don't think so. And there's nothing more to say,' she said. 'Thank you for breakfast.' Even though she hadn't eaten her granola and had only drunk a couple of sips of coffee, she couldn't face any more. 'Goodbye, Mr Stone.' She gave him a tight smile, pushed her chair back and left.

CHAPTER TWO

'MISS MCKENZIE? THANK YOU for coming in.'

James Saunders gave her a very professional smile which did nothing to ease Angel's fears. When your bank asked you to come in to the branch for a meeting, it didn't usually mean good news. She'd been hoping all the way here that it was just a courtesy meeting for him to introduce himself as their new account manager, but she had a nasty feeling that it was nothing of the kind.

'My pleasure, Mr Saunders.' She gave him an equally professional smile. 'I'm assuming that today is simply to touch base, as you've just taken over from Miss Lennox?'

'I'm afraid it's a little more than that. May I offer you some coffee?'

Funny how that sounded more like, 'You're going to need a stiff gin.'

'Thanks, but I'm fine,' she said. 'So how can I help?'

'I've been going through your published accounts,' James said.

Uh-oh. She'd heard that from someone else, very recently. And that hadn't been a good meeting, either.

'I need to be frank with you, Miss McKenzie. We're really not happy with the way things are going. We're not sure you're going to be able to pay back your overdraft.'

'I can reassure you that I have a deal in the pipeline,'

she said. 'Obviously I'm telling you this in strictest business confidence, because you're my bank manager, but Triffid Studios is sending me a contract because they want to use our new design in their next *Spyline* film. Once the film comes out and people see the car, our waiting list will be full for at least the next year. We'll have to expand to meet demand.'

'And you've signed this contract?'

'I'm still waiting for them to send it. The film industry seems to drag its heels a bit where paperwork's concerned,' she admitted. 'But we've built the prototype, tweaked it and they're happy with it, so it's really just a formality.' She just wished they'd hurry up with the paperwork.

'I'd be much happier if I could see that signed contract,' James said.

So would she.

'Because,' he continued, 'I'm afraid I can't extend your overdraft any more.'

'You're calling it all back in? Right now?' Angel went cold. She had no idea where she'd get the money to pay back the overdraft. Even if she could negotiate a breathing space before it had to be paid back, and put her house on the market so it was priced to sell, she still wouldn't make that much money once she'd cleared the mortgage. Nowhere near enough to prop up McKenzie's. And, unlike her father in the last recession, she didn't have a valuable private car collection to sell.

So how else could she raise the money?

'I'll give you a month to get that contract signed,' James said. 'And then I'm afraid I'll have to call the majority of the overdraft in. In these times, banks have to be seen to lend responsibly.'

And businesses like hers that were going through temporary difficulties—despite being good clients for decades—ended up as the scapegoats. 'I see. Well, thank you for your frankness, Mr Saunders.'

'I'm sorry I can't give you better news.'

To his credit, he did look a little bit sorry. Or maybe that was how bank managers were trained nowadays, Angel thought. Though he didn't look quite old enough to manage a bank.

'I'll keep you posted on the contract development,' she said.

Her next stop was at her lawyer's, to see if they could get in contact with Triffid's lawyers and persuade them to firm up a date by when they'd have the contract.

She brooded all the way back to the factory. There had to be a way out of this. The last thing she wanted to do was worry her father or burden him with her problems. He'd trusted her to run the company, and she wasn't going to let him down.

If her parents rang in the next couple of days she'd either miss the call deliberately and blame it on her deafness—she'd been in the shower and hadn't heard the phone ring—or she'd distract her father by talking car design. It was the way she dealt with the shyness that had dogged her since childhood: switching the conversation to cars, engines or business, where she was confident in her abilities, meant she didn't have to worry about the personal stuff.

But she was really worried about this.

If the bank called in their loan before the contract was signed...

She'd just have to be more persuasive. She could put a presentation together quickly enough, with sales projections, based on the new Frost. Though she had a nasty feeling that only the signed contract would be enough to satisfy James Saunders.

The more she thought about it, the more she wondered

if she should've taken up Brandon Stone's offer after all. He'd said that every job at McKenzie's would be safe. He'd implied that they'd keep the McKenzie name on the road cars. He'd even offered her a job, heading up his research and development team, though it wasn't a part of the offer she could bring herself accept. Selling to him was probably the best thing she could do for everyone else.

But how could she live with herself if she threw away seventy years of her family's history and sold out to the company started by her grandfather's ex-best friend?

There had to be another way, beyond selling the company to Brandon Stone.

Plus there was something else she needed to address. Cambridge was a reasonably small city; if anyone had seen her with Brandon the other day and realised who he was, rumours could start circulating. The last thing she wanted was for her team to be unsettled. She needed everyone to pull together.

When she got back to the office, she called a team meeting on the factory floor. Everyone looked anxious, and she knew why. 'First of all,' she said, 'I want to reassure everyone that it's business as usual. Things are a bit slow, right now, but once that new contract's signed and the PR starts, it's going to pick up and the bank will be happy again.'

'Do you want us to go on short time?' Ravi, one of the engineers, asked.

It would be another solution, but Angel didn't think it was fair for her staff to bear the brunt of the company's problems. 'No. We'll manage,' she said firmly. 'The other thing is that Stone's has offered to buy us out.'

There was a general gasp. Ernie, the oldest member of her team, stood up. 'It might not be my place to say this, but I hope you said no. I worked for your grandfather. No way could I work for a Stone. They don't do things like we do.'

'I heard their staff's all on zero-hours contracts,' someone else said. 'I can't take that risk. I've got a mortgage and kids.'

'I can't comment on how they run their business,' Angel said, 'but I'm not selling. McKenzie's will continue to do things the way we always do things. The only change is that we'll be producing a new model, and I know I can trust you to keep everything under wraps.'

'What can we do to help?' Jane, one of the leather cutters, asked.

She smiled. 'Just keep doing what you do. Make our cars the best they can be—and leave the worrying to me. I just wanted you all to know what was going on and hear the truth from me. If anyone hears any rumours to the contrary, they're probably not true, so come and talk to me rather than panic, OK?'

'If things are tight,' Ernie said, 'you could always use our pension fund to plug the gap.'

'That's a nice offer,' she said, 'but using that money for anything except your pensions would get me slung straight into jail. And I'm not asking any of you to take any kind of risk.'

'I've got savings,' Jane said.

'Me, too,' Ravi said. 'We could invest in the company.'

It warmed Angel that her team trusted her that much. 'It's not going to come to that, but thank you for offering. It's good to know that my team believes in me. Well, you're not just my team. You're *family*.'

'Your grandad would be proud of you, lass,' Ernie said. 'Your dad, too. You're a McKenzie through and through.'

Tears pricked her eyelids. 'Thank you. All of you.' She

swallowed hard. 'So is anyone worried about anything else?'

Everyone shook their heads.

'OK, You know where I am if you think of anything later. And thank you all for being so supportive.'

Though after she'd left the team she found it hard to concentrate on her work. She just kept coming back to Brandon Stone and his offer to buy her out.

What really bothered her was that she couldn't get the man himself out of her head. The way he'd looked standing up in the swimming pool, with the water barely reaching his ribs: his shoulders had been broad and his chest and biceps firm. He'd looked just as good in the restaurant, clothed in a formal suit, shirt and tie. Those grey eyes had seemed to see everything. And that beautiful mouth…

Oh, for pity's sake.

She didn't do relationships. Her parents had pretty much wrapped her up in cotton wool after her deafness had been diagnosed, and as a result she'd been too shy to join in with parties when she'd gone to university. Once she'd finished her studies, her focus had been on working in the family business.

But when Brandon Stone had accidentally-on-purpose bumped into her in the pool, her skin had actually tingled where his touched hers. And, even though she was pretty sure that he turned that megawatt smile on anyone with an X chromosome, she had to admit that she was attracted to him—to the last man she should date.

Was he really the playboy she suspected he was?

She knew he had a dossier on her, so she had no compunction about looking up details about him.

He'd started heading up the family firm three years ago. Something about the date jogged a memory; she checked on a news archive site, and there it was. *Sam Stone killed in championship race.*

Brandon hadn't raced professionally since the crash. There had been no announcements about his retirement in the press; then again, there probably hadn't needed to be. Sam's death had clearly affected his younger brother badly. And the rest of his family, too, because Brandon's father had had a heart attack a couple of weeks after Sam's death—no doubt brought on by the stress of losing his oldest child. Poor man.

Angel continued to flick through the articles brought up by the search engine. Eric Stone—Brandon's uncle—had sideswiped him a few times in the press. Then again, Brandon had walked into the top job with no real experience; Eric probably thought he was the one who should be running Stone's and was making the point to anyone who'd listen.

Angel felt a twinge of sympathy for Brandon. Everyone at McKenzie's had supported her when she'd taken over from her father. Brandon had barely had time to settle in before his father had been taken ill and he'd taken over the reins, and it wouldn't be surprising if a few people resented him for it. She'd had the chance to get to know the business thoroughly before she'd taken over, whereas he'd had to hit the ground running. Despite what she'd thought earlier about his background not really qualifying him for the job, he'd done well in running the company, using the same concentration and focus on the business that he'd used to win races in his professional driving days. From the look of their published accounts, Stone's was going from strength to strength. They certainly had enough money to buy her out.

The rest of the newspaper stories she found made her wince. Even allowing for press exaggeration, Brandon

Stone seemed to be pictured with a different girl every couple of weeks. Most of them were supermodels and high-profile actresses, and none of the relationships seemed to last for more than three or four dates. His personal life was a complete disaster zone. He really wasn't the kind of guy she should even consider dating. She should be sensible about this and stop thinking about him as anything else other than a business rival.

Brandon scrubbed his hair in the shower on Sunday morning after his run, hoping to scrub some common sense back into his head.

This was ridiculous.

Why couldn't he stop thinking about Angel McKenzie and her violet eyes—and the smile that had made him practically want to sit up and beg? It had been three days since he'd met her, and he still kept wondering about her.

It threw him, because he'd never reacted to anyone like this before. Angel was nothing like the kind of women he normally dated: she was quiet and serious, and she probably didn't even own a pair of high heels. He wasn't even sure if she owned lipstick. Though he also had the feeling that, if they could put aside the family rivalry, he'd have a better conversation with her than he usually had with his girlfriends. She wouldn't glaze over if he talked about cars and engineering.

Oh, for pity's sake. Why was he even thinking like this? He didn't want to date anyone seriously. He really wasn't looking to settle down. Seeing the way that Maria, his sister-in-law, had fallen apart after Sam's death had cured him of ever wanting to get involved seriously with anyone; even though he didn't race now, he still didn't want to put anyone in Maria's position.

But he just couldn't get Angel McKenzie out of his head.

Or the crazy idea of dating her...

And then he smiled as he dried himself. Maybe that was the answer. If he dated her, it would get her out of his system; plus he'd be able to charm her into doing what he wanted and she'd sell the business to him. It was a win-win scenario.

So how was he going to ask her out?

Sending her a bouquet of red roses would be way too obvious. Too flashy. Too corny. Besides, did she even like flowers? Some women hated cut flowers, preferring to see them grow rather than withering in a vase. None of that information was in his dossier.

He could ring her PA and talk her into setting up a meeting, though he was pretty sure that Angel had given her strict instructions to do nothing of the kind.

Or he could try a slightly riskier option. He was pretty sure that Angel McKenzie spent all her energies on her business; so there was a very good chance that she'd work through her lunch break and eat a sandwich at her desk.

If he supplied the sandwich, she couldn't really refuse a lunch meeting with him on Monday, could she?

The more he thought about it all day, the more he liked the idea.

Gina's dossier didn't tell him whether Angel was vegetarian, hated fish or had any kind of food allergies. So at the supermarket on Monday morning he erred on the side of caution and bought good bread, good cheese, heritage tomatoes, a couple of deli salads and olives.

Though he had to be realistic: Angel could still say no and close the door in his face, so he needed a plan B to make sure she said yes. And there was one obvious thing. Something that, in her shoes, he wouldn't be able to resist.

He flicked the switch to trigger his car's voice-control audio system, connected it to his phone and called Gina as he drove home. 'I'm not going to be in the office today,' he said, 'and I won't be able to answer my phone, so can you text me if there's anything I need to deal with?'

'You're taking a day's holiday?' She sounded surprised: fair enough. He didn't take many days off, and he normally gave her a reasonable amount of notice.

'This is work,' he said. Of sorts.

'And it involves a girl,' Gina said dryly.

Yes, but not quite how she thought. And he could do without the lecture. 'I'll check in with you later,' he said.

Back at his house, he collected a couple of sharp knives, cutlery, glasses and plates from the kitchen, dug out a bottle of sparkling water, put the lot into a picnic basket and then headed out to his garage. He backed one of his cars into the driveway and took a photograph of it, then put the picnic basket in the back. If Angel refused to have lunch with him or even talk to him, he was pretty sure that the photograph would change her mind.

Angel's PA gave Brandon a rueful smile. 'I'm afraid you don't have an appointment, Mr Stone, and Ms McKenzie's diary is fully booked.'

Brandon glanced at the nameplate on her desk. 'If I didn't already have a fabulous PA who also happens to be my mother's best friend,' he said, 'I'd definitely think about poaching you, Stephanie, because I really admire your loyalty to Ms McKenzie.'

Stephanie went pink. 'Oh.'

'And, because I think you keep an eye on her,' he said, 'I'm pretty sure you're the one who actually makes her take a break at lunchtime, even if it's just five minutes for a sandwich at her desk.'

'Well—yes,' Stephanie admitted.

'So today I brought the sandwich instead of you having to do it,' he said, gesturing to the picnic basket he was carrying.

'I really can't—' she began.

'Stephie, is there a prob—?' Angel asked, walking out of her office. Then she stopped as she saw Brandon. 'Oh. You.'

'Yes. Me,' he agreed with a broad smile.

'What do you want?'

'I brought us some lunch.' He focused on charming her PA. 'Stephanie, if you'd like to join us, you're very welcome.'

'I, um…' Stephanie went even pinker.

'Don't try to use my PA as a pawn,' Angel said grimly. 'And I don't have time for lunch.'

'The same as your diary's allegedly fully booked, but there's nobody actually sitting in your office right now having a meeting with you?'

She frowned. 'You really are persistent, aren't you?'

'We've already discussed that. Persistence is a business asset.'

'Wasn't it Einstein who said the definition of insanity was doing the same thing over and over again and expecting different results?' she asked coolly.

'That's been attributed to quite a few other people, from ancient Chinese proverbs to Rita Mae Brown,' he said, enjoying himself. Sparring with someone with a mind like Angel McKenzie's was fun. 'Actually, I'm not doing the same thing over and over again. This is lunch, not breakfast.'

If Brandon had driven to Cambridgeshire from his family's factory near Oxford, that would've taken him at least a couple of hours if the traffic was good, Angel thought. He'd made an effort. Maybe she should make a little effort back. If she talked to him, maybe she might get him to understand that she was serious about not selling her company. 'Do you want some coffee?'

'Thank you. That would be lovely.'

And his smile wasn't in the least bit smug or triumphant. It was just…nice. And it made her spine tingle.

'I'll make it, if you like.'

Had her hearing system just gone wrong? The man was used to women hanging on his every word. He hadn't even been invited here and yet he'd walked in. And now… She blinked. 'You're offering to make coffee?'

'Is there something wrong with the idea of a man making coffee?'

Ouch. She'd just been sexist and he'd called her on it. Fairly. 'I guess not.'

'Don't make assumptions,' he said softly. 'Especially if you're basing them on what the press says about me.'

Was he telling her that he wasn't the playboy the press suggested he was? Or was he playing games? Brandon Stone flustered her. Big time. And she couldn't quite work out why. Was it just because he was so good-looking? Or did she see a tiny hint of vulnerability in his grey eyes, showing that there was more to him than just the cocky, confident racing champion? Or was that all just wishful thinking and he really was a shallow playboy?

What she did know was that he was her business rival. One who wanted to buy her out. She probably shouldn't even be talking to him.

On the other hand, if Triffid didn't get that contract to her and the bank carried out its threat of calling in her overdraft, she might be forced to eat humble pie and sell McKenzie's to him, no matter how much she'd hate it. Short of winning the lottery, right now she was all out of ideas.

'So where's the coffee machine?' he asked.

'The staff kitchen's next down the corridor on the left as you go out of the door,' Stephanie said. 'The mugs are in the cupboard and so are the coffee pods.'

'Thank you.' He smiled at her, and turned to Angel. 'Cappuccino, no sugar, right?'

She nodded. 'Thank you.'

'How do you like your coffee, Stephanie?' he asked.

His courtesy made Angel feel a little bit better about Plan C. If he treated junior staff well rather than ignoring them or being dismissive, that was a good sign for the future if he did end up taking over McKenzie's. Maybe he wasn't as ruthless as she feared, despite his family background. Or maybe he just wanted her to think that.

'I'm not drinking coffee at the moment,' Stephanie said, and rested her hand briefly on her stomach.

Angel could see from the change in Brandon's expression that he'd noticed the tiny gesture, too, and realised what it meant. Stephanie was pregnant. Was it her imagination, or did she see pain and regret flicker briefly over his expression? But why would a pregnancy make him react like that?

None of her business, she reminded herself.

'What can I get you, Stephanie?' Brandon asked.

'Fruit tea, please. There's some strawberry tea in the cupboard.'

He smiled. 'Got you. Is it OK to leave my basket here on your desk for a second?'

'Sure,' she said.

As he walked out, Stephanie mouthed to Angel, 'He's *nice.*'

Yeah. That was the problem. He wasn't just an arrogant playboy. There was another side to Brandon Stone—a side she could let herself like very, very much. Which made him dangerous to her peace of mind.

* * *

Brandon returned to Angel's office, carrying three mugs.
He put Stephanie's strawberry tea on her desk, then picked
up the picnic basket. 'Are you sure you don't want to join
us, Stephanie?'

She went very pink again. 'No, but thank you for asking.'

'Is it OK to put the coffee on your desk?' he asked when
he followed Angel through to her office.

'Sure.' She looked surprised that he'd asked. Did she
have a downer on all men? That would explain why Gina
hadn't been able to find any information about Angel dating anyone. But she was reportedly close to her father, so
maybe it wasn't *all* men. Maybe someone had hurt her
badly and she hadn't trusted anyone since.

And how weird was it that the thought made him want
to bunch his fists and dispense a little rough justice to the
guy who'd hurt her? Angel McKenzie seemed quite capa-
ble of looking after herself. She didn't need a tame thug.
Besides, Brandon didn't settle arguments with fists: there
were much better ways to sort out problems.

Angel made him feel slightly off balance, and he
couldn't work out why.

He scanned the room. Her office was super-neat and
tidy. There were photographs on the walls; some were of
cars he recognised as being iconic McKenzie designs, but
there was also a picture on her desk of a couple who were
clearly her parents, and one more on the wall of someone
he didn't recognise but he guessed had something to do
with the business—maybe her grandfather?

He unpacked the picnic basket, put the bread on a plate
and cut a few slices, then handed her a plate and his other
sharp knife. 'Help yourself to cheese.'

'Thank you.'

'It's not much of a choice, but I wasn't sure if you were a vegetarian,' he said.

'No, though I do try to do meat-free Mondays.' She paused. 'It's nice of you to have brought lunch.'

There was definitely a hint of suspicion in those beautiful violet eyes. She was clearly wondering what he wanted, because there was no such thing as a free lunch.

He wasn't quite sure he could answer her unasked question. He wanted McKenzie's. That was the main reason he was here. But he also wanted her, and that threw him. 'Think of it as a sandwich at your desk,' he said.

She took a nibble of the cheese and then the bread. 'A very nice sandwich, too.'

'So who are the people in the photographs?' he asked.

'The one on the wall over there is my grandfather Jimmy, back in the early days of McKenzie's.' She gestured to her desk. 'My mum and dad, Sadie and Max.'

Just as he'd guessed; but there were no pictures of Esther, who'd been at the centre of the rift between Barnaby Stone and Jimmy McKenzie. He wondered if Angel looked anything like her. Not that he was going to ask. He kept the conversation light and anodyne, then cleared away when they'd both finished.

'So,' he said. 'We managed to have a civilised meal together.'

'I guess.'

'We've done breakfast and lunch.' But the next words out of his mouth weren't quite the ones he'd intended to say. 'Would you like to come to a gala dinner with me?'

CHAPTER THREE

ANGEL REALLY HADN'T expected that, and it flustered her. 'You're asking me on a date?' she queried, hoping she looked and sounded a lot calmer than she felt.

'I guess so,' he drawled.

'No.'

'Why?'

Because gala dinners tended to be noisy and she found it wearing, having to make small talk and being forced to concentrate really hard to hear what people said.

Plus Brandon Stone dated a lot and he wasn't the serious type. She didn't want to get involved with him, professionally or personally. 'You're a Stone and I'm a McKenzie,' she said finally.

'"A rose by any other name would smell as sweet."'

'Don't quote Shakespeare at me.'

He raised his eyebrows. 'I thought you were an engineer?'

'I did *Romeo and Juliet* for GCSE. Besides, doesn't everyone know that line?'

'Maybe. So are we Montagues and Capulets?'

She scoffed. 'I have no intention of swooning over you on a balcony. Or drinking poison. And,' she pointed out, 'at thirty, I'm also more than twice Juliet's age.'

'Ouch. Thus speaks the engineer.'

'And that's why I don't want to date you. You'd spend all evening either flirting with me or making smart, annoying remarks.'

'Firstly,' he said, 'you're meant to flirt with your date.'

'Flirting's superficial and overrated.'

'Clearly nobody's flirted properly with you.'

That was a little too near the mark. 'I don't need to be flirted with.'

He held her gaze. 'No?'

'No.' She looked away.

'When was the last time you dated?' he asked.

Too long ago. 'Wasn't that in your dossier?' she retorted.

'Now who's making the smart remarks?'

At her silence, he continued, 'The gala evening is a charity dinner. The proceeds go to help the families of drivers who've been hurt or killed on the track.'

Was he trying to guilt her into agreeing? It was for a cause she knew was close to his heart, given that his brother had been killed; and it was a cause she'd be happy to support. But going to a posh dinner with Brandon, where she'd have to dress up and she'd feel totally out of place among all the glamorous socialites...

He sighed. 'At least think about it.'

She made a noncommittal noise, which she hoped he'd take as meaning 'maybe' and would back off.

Brandon was furious with himself. There were plenty of women who'd love to go to the gala dinner with him, so why was he spending this much effort on someone who'd made it quite clear that she didn't want to go anywhere with him?

He should never have mentioned the gala dinner.

He should've stuck to business.

At least if they'd been talking about cars, they would've

had something in common. Maybe that was the way to get this conversation back on track. 'Would you show me round the factory?'

Those beautiful violet eyes widened in surprise. 'That's direct. Don't you prefer other people to look things up for you and report back?'

Maybe he deserved that one. 'I'm not spying on you, if that's your implication. Anyone who works in our industry would be itching to look round, and sit in one of your cars and pretend to be its owner.'

She scoffed. 'My cars are very affordable. If you wanted one, you could buy one. In fact, you could buy a whole fleet for the price of just one of yours.'

'If that's your best patter,' he said, 'you should sack yourself as head of sales.'

She narrowed her eyes at him. 'What do you want from me, Mr Stone?'

A lot of things. Some of which he hadn't quite worked out. 'First-name terms, for a start.' He paused. 'Angel.'

She looked as if she was warring with herself, but then finally nodded. 'Brandon. OK. I'll show you round the factory.'

Walking through the factory with Brandon felt weird. Tantamount to parading her flock of lambs in front of a wolf. Though at least she'd already warned her staff that he'd made an offer and she'd refused. She'd reinforce that later

Please let that contract come through today.

She knew that the Frost prototype was in a partitioned-off part of the factory, safely away from his gaze. But he could see the areas where the body parts were sprayed, the leather seats were hand-cut and hand-sewn, the engines were built and the final cars were assembled. If he saw the process for himself he'd understand what was so

special about McKenzie's, and why she was so adamant
about keeping things as they were.

'This is the Luna,' she said. 'This one's being built by
Ernie and Ravi. Ernie, Ravi, this is Brandon Stone.'

Ernie gave him a curt nod, but Ravi shook his hand enthusiastically and smiled. 'I've seen you race. I was there
when you won the that championship, six years ago.'

'A lifetime ago,' Brandon said softly. 'I'm on the other
side of the business now.'

Ravi looked awkward. 'Sorry. I didn't…'

'It's fine.' Brandon clearly knew what the other man
wasn't saying. He hadn't meant to trample over a sore
spot and bring up Sam's death. He patted Ravi's shoulder
briefly. 'I really like the lines of this car. Is it OK for me
to have a look at the engine?'

'Sure.' Ravi popped the catch on the bonnet.

Ernie gestured to Angel to step to the side while Ravi
was showing Brandon the engine. 'What are you doing,
Angel?' he asked in an angry whisper. 'I thought you said
you weren't selling?'

'I'm not. He turned up today. I'm showing him round
the factory so he can see our processes for himself,' Angel
said, 'and to prove we're not compatible with Stone's.'

'You're a good boss, lass, but you're no match for a company that ruthless.' He shook his head. 'You be careful.'

'I will.' Even though Ernie should've retired a couple of
years back, Angel appreciated the fact he'd decided to stay
on, training their younger staff and making sure the quality control lived up to their brand's promise. And she knew
he had the company's interests at heart; he'd accepted her
as his boss because he knew she paid the same attention
to detail that he did, and she wasn't afraid to get her hands
dirty and work on the factory floor if she was needed.

As they walked through the different stations, she could see Brandon looking intrigued. 'This is very different from the way we do things at Stone's,' he said.

'Exactly. I'm glad you see your business is completely incompatible with mine.'

He raised an eyebrow. 'I didn't say that.'

'I'm saying it for you.'

He just looked at her as if to say he knew something she didn't. She brushed off her worries by switching the conversation back to technical issues. 'I guess you need more tech in a race car than in a roadster. Doesn't its steering wheel alone cost as much as we charge for a basic Luna?'

'There are a lot more electronics in one of our steering wheels than in a Luna's,' he said, and she noticed that he avoided the question. 'Maybe you should come and take a look at our place in Oxford and see how we do things.'

See where he planned to change her beloved hand-built into mass-produced monsters? She fell back on a noncommittal, 'Mmm.'

'Thanks for showing me round,' he said as she walked him back to the reception area. 'But, before I go, I thought you might like to see my favourite car ever.' He took his phone from his pocket and showed her a photograph of a gorgeous iridescent turquoise car with outrageous tail fins.

She recognised it instantly as her own favourite car. Did he know that from his dossier? Was he playing her? 'That's a McKenzie Mermaid. My grandfather designed it in the early sixties.'

'I know.'

She narrowed her eyes at him. 'I would've expected you to prefer one of your own family's cars, or one of the classic 1960s sports cars.'

'I like the classics,' he said, 'but I fell in love with the Mermaid when I saw a picture of it as a kid.'

It had been the same for her. If only there had been more than a hundred of them ever produced. The only one she'd ever seen had been in a museum, years ago, and even the fact that she was a McKenzie hadn't been enough for the curators to allow her to touch it, let alone sit in it. And because Mermaids were so rare they almost never came up for sale.

His next comment floored her completely. 'Which is why I bought one, six years ago. After I won the championship race.'

She stared at him, not quite believing what she was hearing. 'That picture... Are you telling me that's actually *yours*?'

'Uh-huh. It was a bit of a mess when I first saw it. It'd been left in a barn for years. There was more rust than anything else, and mice had eaten their way through the leather.'

'So you picked it up for a song.' That figured.

'Actually, I paid a fair price,' he said.

Why did she suddenly feel so guilty? She pushed the thought away. All her life, she'd been told that Stones were ruthless asset-strippers, and what she'd read in the business press had only confirmed that. Hadn't Barnaby walked away from the original company with way more than his fair share?

'I thought about having it restored here,' Brandon continued, 'but then I decided it'd be too much like rubbing your dad's nose in it, a Stone asking a McKenzie to restore one of their most iconic cars.'

Which was a fair point: but, actually, her father wouldn't have minded. He would've loved the chance to get his hands on a Mermaid.

So would she.

And then she thought about what he was telling her. 'So you're saying the factory at Stone's restored it?'

'No. I did it myself at home. Little by little, over a few months.'

If he'd restored it himself, by hand, that mean he had to understand craftsmanship. Everything from the precision of the angles in the spokes of the chrome wheels through to the cut of the leather in the seats and the walnut of the dash.

'Do you want to see it?'

Absolutely. Though she knew better than to appear too eager. 'And the price of seeing it is going to this gala thing with you?' She still couldn't work out why he even wanted her to go with him to a gala dinner. He had a string of super-glamorous women queuing up to date him. Why would he want to date a nerdy engineer?

Though she already knew the reason for that: one particular nerdy engineer who happened to head up his rival company, and whom he was trying to charm into selling to him.

He didn't answer her question. 'I drove over here in it today.' He shrugged. 'It's sunny. The perfect day to drive a Mermaid.'

Along a coast road, with the roof down and the radio playing upbeat early sixties' pop tunes, and he'd be wearing the coolest pair of sunglasses in the world, looking sexy as hell. Like a young Paul Newman, albeit with longer hair and grey eyes instead of blue. She could imagine it all too easily.

To stop herself thinking about that, she asked, 'You *really* own a Mermaid?'

'Don't you?' he parried.

'Unfortunately not,' she said dryly. 'Are you going to tell me that you have every single model that Stone's ever produced?'

'We have all bar one of them, actually,' he said, making her wonder which one he was missing. 'We have a museum at the factory. They're all on display.'

Something she would've loved to do here, too. But they couldn't afford the building for a museum, let alone the cars to go inside. Her dad had sold off most of his personal collection to prop up the business during the last recession, and she knew how much it had hurt him.

'Come and see the Mermaid,' Brandon said, giving her the most sensual smile she'd ever seen. Her knees almost buckled. That smile; and her grandfather's iconic design. How could she resist such a combination?

The paint sparkled underneath the sun, looking even more gorgeous than the car she'd seen all those years ago in the museum. 'It's so pretty.' Her hand went out instinctively to touch the paintwork; then she stopped herself.

'I don't mind touching,' he said.

For a second, she thought he meant touching *him*, and she went hot all over at the thought.

But of course he meant the car.

'It's the iridescent paint,' she said. 'It actually shimmers in the light.'

'That's what I loved about it, too. When I was little, I thought it ought to be an undersea car.'

So had she.

Unable to resist the lure, she ran her fingers over the bodywork. 'It's a lovely finish.' Given what he'd said about the rust, he would've had to respray it, but she could barely tell what was original and what was new. She bent down to inspect the wheels. 'And the chrome's perfect.' She ought to give credit where it was due. 'You did a good job.'

'Thank you.' He popped the catch on the bonnet. 'I guess you'd like to see the engine?'

'Yes. Please.' This time, she couldn't quite contain her eagerness.

And it was everything she'd hoped it would be. She skimmed the lines of it, memorising every detail. When she'd looked her fill, she put the bonnet back down again. 'Thank you,' she said. 'That was a really kind thing to do.'

'I'm not your enemy, Angel.'

His voice was low and husky, and his eyes had grown so dark they were almost black. For a moment, she thought he was going to kiss her. Worse still, she actually wanted it to happen. Her mouth tingled, and she felt her lips parting ever so slightly.

How ridiculous was she to feel disappointed when, instead, he took a step back?

Then he handed her the keys. 'Want to take it for a spin?'

She couldn't quite believe this. 'Seriously?'

'Your grandfather designed this car. In your shoes, I'd be pretty desperate to drive it.'

She was. And she didn't need a second invitation. She slid into the driver's seat. 'It's perfect. 'Though I could do with being a few inches taller,' she added ruefully.

'That's the thing about vintage cars. Fixed seats.' He gestured to the passenger seat. 'May I?'

'It's your car,' she said. 'Is it OK to take it round the test track?'

'The place where it was driven for the very first time? I like that idea.'

She drove the Mermaid very, very carefully over to the test track, a long thin right angle around two sides of the factory land. And then very, very carefully she drove it along one of the straights.

He smiled. 'It's a Mermaid, not a snail. You can put your foot down a bit if you want.'

Suppressing the urge to yell, 'Whoo-hoo,' she grinned and did so.

Driving this car was just like she'd always imagined it would be, with the wind whipping through her hair and the sun warming her skin. The wooden steering wheel felt almost alive under her fingers, and driving round the racetrack made her feel full of the joys of summer. The speed, the sound of the engine, the scent of the pine woods around the edge of the track… This was perfection in a single heartbeat.

Brandon had been pretty sure Angel would like the car and it would make her talk to him—but he was gratified that she liked it this much. Her hair was streaming behind her as she put her foot down along the straight, and she was laughing as she hurtled the car round a hairpin bend. She clearly loved this as much as he'd once loved racing cars. He'd forgotten that feeling. He'd barely been out in his garage, tinkering with his private collection of classic cars, since Sam died; he certainly hadn't added to the collection. But being in the passenger seat beside her reminded him of the sheer joy he'd once found in driving.

He was still catching his breath when she'd done a second lap and brought the car gently to a halt, not sure whether it was the thrill of the speed or the thrill of seeing quiet, serious Angel McKenzie all laughing and lit up and knowing that he was the cause of that smile.

And then he knew exactly what to do.

'This gala dinner,' he said.

The look on her face told him she thought he'd only let her drive the Mermaid to soften her up.

'Here's the deal. You and me—we race for it. If you win, I shut up about it. If I win, you go to the gala with me.'

CHAPTER FOUR

IF ANGEL WON the race, Brandon would leave her alone. If he won, she'd have to go to the gala dinner with him.

It was tempting. She knew the track like the back of her hand, and she knew her car even better. On paper, she should win the bet pretty easily. Yet, on the other hand, Brandon had won several championship races and he'd almost been the world champion. Twice. Even though he didn't know the track at McKenzie's, there was a risk that she was underestimating him very badly. He'd be able to drive pretty much any car, on any track, and he'd acquit himself well even if it was the first time he'd got behind the wheel of that particular model.

'Are you talking about driving side by side, or a time trial?' she asked.

'Your choice.'

'Time trial,' she said, 'and we use the same car. My Luna.'

'Nought to sixty in six seconds and a top speed of one hundred and seventy miles an hour,' he said.

She could just imagine him as a little boy, earnestly learning all the stats of his favourite cars. Funny how endearing she found it. Though she wasn't going to underestimate him—or play unfairly. This was going to be done strictly by the book.

'But I know the track and the car really well,' she said. 'Which gives me an unfair advantage. I should give you a ten-second lead.'

'And I spent years working as a racing driver,' he said, 'which gives me an unfair advantage. Especially as you've just driven me round the track, so I already know where the hairpins are and where the sharp turns are.'

She noticed that he didn't talk about how good he'd been during his career, how many races he'd won and his two world championship bids. He'd stuck to the facts rather than taking the opportunity to boast, and she rather liked that. 'I guess the advantages cancel each other out,' she said.

'We'll do three laps,' he said. 'Do you want to count just the time of the fastest lap, or average the times out over the three laps?'

Go for broke, she thought. 'The fastest. And we'll toss a coin for who goes first.'

He pulled a coin out of his pocket. 'Heads or tails?'

'Heads.'

He spun the coin, then caught it mid-air and slapped it down on the back of his hand. 'Heads,' he said, showing her.

His hands were beautiful.

Which was ridiculous. She was supposed to be thinking about the race, not about Brandon Stone's hands and what they might feel like against her skin. And since when did she fantasise about men anyway? There wasn't time to think about anything else except her work. Especially now, when she was trying her hardest to save her family business. She needed to concentrate. 'OK. The track's one and three-quarter miles long. We'll do three laps in the Luna, timing each one, and whoever does the fastest lap wins.'

'Agreed,' he said.

'Do you need to borrow a helmet, overalls or gloves?'

He smiled. 'This is a road car, so no. But if you're happier in a helmet, overalls and gloves, that's fine by me and I'm happy to wait while you get ready.'

'No.' She wrinkled her nose. 'Sorry. That was a stupid thing to ask. This isn't like professional driving. Of course you don't need racing driver stuff.'

'So do you have a transponder on the front of your car for timing the laps?' he asked.

She shook her head. 'Our test track isn't an officially accredited racing track. Yes, it's smooth enough for us to test that the car performs at high speed, and the bends are sharp enough for us to test the steering, but we tend to do lap timing here the same as we do everything else: the old-fashioned way. With a stopwatch.'

He took his phone from his pocket. 'OK. Are you happy to use my phone as the stopwatch, or would you rather use yours?'

'Yours is fine. Let's do this.'

It didn't really matter whether she won or lost. The important thing was that McKenzie's carried on. And, if the worst happened and she ended up having to sell the business to Brandon Stone, she wanted to convince him that he didn't need to change the way McKenzie's built their cars. If that meant meeting him on his own terms and acquitting herself well enough in the race to make him respect her opinion, so be it.

She ignored the other thing riding on their bet, because he couldn't possibly be serious about wanting to date her.

Butterflies did a stampede in her stomach as she led him over to her car. And again that was weird, because this was work—kind of—and she was always confident about her work. Maybe it was just adrenaline because of the race. She didn't want to think of any other reason why her heart was beating faster.

'I thought you'd pick grey,' he said, gesturing to the car's paintwork.

'Because it's mousy and boring?' The words were out before she could stop them.

'No. Because it's classic, understated—and usually underestimated.'

Was he saying that he thought she underestimated herself, or that she was trying to make him underestimate her? She didn't want to ask for clarification, because she wasn't sure she wanted to know the answer.

She unlocked the car and he climbed into the passenger seat. She could feel him assessing the car as she drove them back to the test track.

'If you want to know which options I chose,' she said, 'it was to have the wing mirrors and vents body-coloured, graphite spoke wheels, heated seats, air conditioning, and the touchscreen GPS.'

'So you're all about comfort and efficiency, then.' He touched the walnut dash, then grimaced. 'Sorry. I should've asked first, and I've probably put fingerprints on it now.'

What was it he'd said to her when she'd been itching to get up close to the Mermaid and touch the iridescent paint? 'It's OK. I don't mind touching.'

She gave him a sidelong glance and was gratified to see a slash of colour across his cheeks.

So did he, too, feel this weird pull between them? she wondered. Had he asked her to go to the gala dinner with him because he actually wanted to spend time with her, rather than it being some kind of tactic to charm her, soften her up and persuade her to sell McKenzie's to him?

The possibilities made her tingle.

But she rarely dated. The last thing she wanted to do

was start discussing the subject, only to find that he wasn't interested in her at all.

Better to stick to a safe subject. Cars and driving. The stuff she knew about. The stuff they had in common. There was more to this than met the eye, and she was going to be careful what she said to him.

'So you've never driven a Luna before?' she asked when she brought the car to a halt.

'No,' he admitted.

'I know you've probably driven many more different cars than I have, but I still don't think it's fair to race you without you taking the Luna round the track a couple of times first.'

'In business,' he said, 'you take your advantages where you find them.'

'In business,' she countered, 'McKenzie's has always believed in fairness.'

He gave her an assessing look. 'I'm going to assume that was a straightforward comment on your family's way of doing things and not an aspersion on mine.'

'It was,' she said. There had been enough bitterness between the two families. She wasn't planning to add to it. 'Just humour me and take the Luna round the track a few times.' She climbed out of the car.

He did the same, and moved the seat back before sliding in behind the steering wheel. He ran his fingers lightly round the polished wood of the steering wheel. 'I think,' he said softly, 'I'm going to enjoy this.'

Oh, help. Was he flirting with her again? What did he expect her to say?

She fell back on, 'Have fun,' and walked to the side of the track.

She watched him drive and noticed that he took the first lap very slowly; he was clearly thinking about the circuit and the angles he'd need to take the turns as fast as possible. The second time, he drove faster, handling the car perfectly.

Yup. It was pretty clear that she was going to lose this race.

But she was going to give it her best shot. This was her car, her track.

He did one more lap, then pulled up next to her and climbed out of the car. 'OK. Let's do this.'

Angel had always enjoyed driving, but she was surprised by the adrenaline surge as she took Brandon's place in the driver's seat. This wasn't just driving. And there was more than just their bet about the gala dinner resting on this.

She did the first lap and knew it wasn't fast enough. The second lap was worse, because she made a stupid error and had to overcompensate with the steering. The third lap, she knew she had to really give it her all—to get her angles right as she drove round the sharper turns, to ease off the throttle enough to let her make the turn smoothly, and to accelerate at the right time so she could make the most of the straights.

If she won, he'd leave her alone.

But did that mean he'd leave McKenzie's alone?

'Shut up and do it,' she told herself, and drove the very best she could on the last lap.

It definitely felt better than the previous two, but was it good enough?

She took a deep breath and went to face him.

'Your best lap was the last one,' he confirmed. 'One minute, fifteen point six seconds.' He showed her the stopwatch on his phone, so she knew he was telling the absolute truth. And it was a respectable time. Though she had a nasty feeling that it wouldn't be good enough.

'Your turn. May the best driver win,' she said.

His eyes crinkled at the corners. 'It's not just about driving.'

And why did that comment make her pulse speed up?

She concentrated hard as he drove off. His first lap was a careful one minute and eighteen seconds. Two seconds slower than her best. The next lap surprised her because it was even slower: one minute twenty.

Was he deliberately trying to lose?

If so, why? Had he changed his mind about going to the gala dinner with her? Or was he softening her up?

But then, on his final lap, his driving seemed different: much more focused, and very smooth.

The stopwatch confirmed what she already knew.

He'd won.

When he pulled to a halt beside her, she climbed into the passenger seat. 'I'm not sure I even need to show you this, but...' She handed his phone back.

'One minute, fourteen point nine seconds. So it was close. Closer than a breath,' he said.

Almost as close as a kiss....

She pushed the thought away and narrowed her eyes at him. 'Are you telling me you could've driven it faster than you did? That you were planning to let me win?'

'No. I'm saying the result was close. I don't know many people who could have driven it in your time.'

She scoffed. 'On my home track, in my own car?'

'Or on their home track of a similar length, in their own car.' He rolled his eyes. 'It was a good time and I'm trying to pay you a genuine compliment here, Angel. Why do you have to be so difficult about it?'

'Oh.' She felt a mixture of shame and embarrassment heating her face. She'd assumed he'd had all kinds of motives that he didn't actually have. 'Sorry.'

'You drove well. It's good to race against an opponent who's worth it.'

She felt herself flush even more because his grey eyes were serious. He really meant it. 'Thank you.'

Somehow they'd both twisted their upper bodies so they were facing each other, and he seemed to have moved closer.

The air suddenly felt too thick to breathe. What would it be like if Brandon Stone kissed her? Her heartbeat spiked at the thought.

He reached across and tucked a strand of hair behind her ear, and the touch of his skin against hers made every nerve-end tingle.

'Angel,' he said, his voice soft and husky and incredibly sexy.

And then he leaned forward and brushed his mouth against hers.

Soft. Sweet. Asking, rather than demanding.

Then he pulled back and looked at her.

She was unable to resist resting her palm against his face; she liked the fact that he was clean-shaven rather than sporting designer stubble to go with the rock-star effect of his hair. His skin was soft and smooth under her hand, and somehow the pad of her thumb seemed to be tracing his lower lip.

His lips parted and his pupils dilated.

Could she do this?

Should she do this?

But her body wasn't listening to her head. She closed the distance between them and kissed him back. This time, her arms ended up wound round his neck and his were wrapped round her waist.

She couldn't remember the last time she'd been kissed,

but she knew she'd never felt like this before. This hot, drugging need for more.

Time seemed to stop, and there was nothing in the world except Brandon Stone and the warmth of his body and the way his mouth teased hers: but then he broke the kiss. 'Sorry. That wasn't supposed to happen.'

So he regretted it already? It had been a stupid mistake. And she'd been the more stupid of them for letting it happen. Disappointment sagged through her, and she pulled away. 'It wasn't just you. I'm sorry, too.'

'Put it down to the adrenaline of the race.'

'Yeah.' Though she'd never actually wanted to kiss anyone senseless after driving a car round a track. Not until today.

'Thank you. It was good to drive round a track again.'

'Do you miss racing? Because you haven't raced since—' The words were out before she could stop them, and she grimaced. It wasn't fair to stomp all over past hurt. 'I'm sorry about your brother. That must've been rough.'

The worst feeling in the whole world. And nothing had been the same ever since. 'It was.' Brandon paused. She'd asked him a straight question. He'd give her a straight answer. 'And yes, I do miss racing. I occasionally take a rally car round the track in Oxford for a test drive, but it's not the same thing.'

'Why don't you go back to it?'

He shrugged. 'I'm getting on a bit, in terms of driver age.'

'You're only thirty-two.'

'Which is getting on a bit,' he said.

But the way she looked at him told him that she could see right through him. She knew as well as he did that it was a feeble excuse. Plenty of professional racing drivers carried on until at least their forties. True, you needed to be at the peak of your fitness to drive a car well, but age wasn't a real barrier.

Of course he missed racing.

But he'd seen the way his mother and his sister-in-law had fallen apart when Sam was killed. And there was always that risk, no matter how good a driver you were. Your car might malfunction and there would be nothing you could do about it. Someone else's car could malfunction and you might not have time to avoid the fallout from it.

He couldn't put his family through that again.

So, the day after Sam's funeral, Brandon had talked to his family and agreed to give it up.

It wasn't as if he was totally cut off from the world of racing. Stone's made excellent racing cars. Just Brandon happened to be making them for their own drivers and other teams rather than driving them himself.

He liked running the business, but it didn't give him the same adrenaline rush as driving. Which was one of the reasons why he wanted to develop a road car: to help himself push some boundaries and remind him that he was still alive, but without taking all the risks that came with professional racing.

He could change the subject.

Or he could give in to this weird impulse and tell her something he'd never told anyone else.

It was a risk. She could go to the press with what he told her. But he somehow didn't think she would.

'All right. If you want the truth…' For a moment, the words stuck in his throat. But then she squeezed his hand. Just once. Not in pity: he could see that in her expression. She was just letting him know without words that it was OK to talk—and that it was also OK not to talk. She wasn't going to push him.

And that made it easier to speak. 'When Sam died, I saw my sister-in-law Maria fall apart. I saw my mum fall apart,' he said. 'And I saw the fear in their eyes every time they looked at me. Sam was always the careful one out of the two of us, and he died.' And it had been his fault, though he didn't want to tell Angel that. He didn't want her to think less of him.

'I was the fearless one, so it was more likely that I'd be the one to take a stupid risk and have an accident.'

'Maybe,' she said, her voice gentle, 'but, by not driving any more, you're denying part of yourself.'

Was that the reason he always felt so restless? But he'd been restless before Sam's death, too, never finding the real contentment that Sam had found with Maria. He'd been ruthless about ending things with his dates. Three dates, and if he still felt restless he'd leave.

It had been so much worse since Sam's death, because he felt he didn't deserve the future he'd taken from his brother—love and a family. He just hadn't been able to let himself connect emotionally with anyone, so it had been easier to focus on the business and keep his relationships short.

'Surely there's some way you can compromise?'

He shook his head. 'If I drive again, my family's going to be sick with fear for the entire race. Watching it through their fingers, willing nothing bad to happen, flinching every time they hear a report of someone coming off the track. I can't do it to them.'

'So instead you're suppressing yourself?'

'Plenty of people would love my life.'

'But if *you* don't love it,' she said, 'there's a problem.'

Those violet eyes were deceptive, pretty enough to lull you into a false sense of security and letting you forget how sharp the brain was behind them, he thought ruefully.

Angel McKenzie could be seriously dangerous to his peace of mind. 'I find other ways to challenge myself.'

'Like trying to buy me out?'

'Or talk you into working for me.'

'And then buying McKenzie's.'

'Would it be such a bad thing?'

'My grandfather built up this business from scratch. If I sell, I'm letting him down, and I'm letting Dad down,' she said. 'If it was the other way round, wouldn't you feel the same?'

'I guess.' And wasn't that most of the reason why he was so insistent on buying McKenzie's? To make his family feel that he'd pulled out all the stops and restored their family honour? That in some way he'd made up for causing his brother's death? 'So what's your plan B?'

'Confidential,' she said.

He wasn't entirely sure that she had a plan B. 'You can't carry on as you are.'

'I know. I'm stubborn,' she said, 'but I'm not daft.'

He smiled. 'Your education is quite a few rungs above mine. I don't have a first degree, let alone an MA. You're the last person I'd dare to call daft.'

'You're not exactly an airhead yourself,' she said. 'You understand velocity, angles and wind speed. And you know your way round an engine.'

He'd had all kinds of compliments showered on him in the past. But this one was the most genuine—and it was odd how much it affected him. 'I guess,' he said gruffly, hoping she hadn't worked out how much she unsettled him.

And now was definitely time to change the subject. 'Have you always worn this?' He traced the edge of her ear with the tip of his finger. Mistake, because touching her made him want to kiss her again.

'No.'

'So what happened?'

She winced. 'It's a terrible story.'

'Tell me anyway,' he coaxed.

'OK. You know when you're five years old, you do some really stupid things because you're too young to think about the risks?'

He nodded. At thirty-two, he still did stupid things without considering the risks. Kissing her being his most recent one.

'Well, I was playing ghosts with my oldest cousins on Mum's side of the family—which basically meant walking around with a tablecloth over your head, waving your hands and saying, "Whoo, whoo, I'm a ghost," and pretending to be scary.'

He could just imagine young Angel throwing herself earnestly into the game and trying to be just as good at it as her older cousins, and grinned. 'It's the sort of thing Sammy and I would've done, too.'

'Because obviously I couldn't see where I was going with a cloth over my head, I walked into a table,' she said, 'and the corner hit me just behind my ear. Obviously I cried a lot, but everyone thought I'd simply bumped myself a bit hard, and we were banned from playing ghosts for the rest of the day.' She took a deep breath. 'But apparently that night a lump the size of an egg developed behind my ear and I became delirious, so my parents took me to hospital.'

Brandon frowned. 'That doesn't sound good.'

'They gave me some medicine and I was kept in overnight for observation, but I was fine. We didn't really think more of it. But after then, if I was drawing or had my nose in a book, I wouldn't hear my parents calling me. They thought I was just really focused on what I was doing and tuning them out, but a couple of years later I was getting really low marks on my spelling tests, even though I never spelled things wrong outside tests, and my teacher noticed that the words I was writing down weren't actually the ones she was reading out. They sounded like the words she was saying, so she thought I might have a problem with my hearing. She got my parents to take me for a hearing test.'

'And then they discovered you can't hear in that ear?'

She nodded. 'The audiologist said it was caused by impact damage, and my parents were horrified. They said there was no way they'd ever hit me, so they had no idea how it could've happened. Then they remembered the table incident, and the audiologist said that was the most likely cause.' She grimaced. 'My parents felt so guilty about it— even though it wasn't their fault, it was mine.'

'You were five, Angel. It wasn't anybody's fault, just an accident.' But he could guess the rest. Angel was only child and she'd still been quite young when her hearing problem had been diagnosed; no doubt her parents had overprotected her and sheltered her too much, just as his own mother had been overprotective with him ever since Sam's death.

And it also made him wonder something else. He looked at her. 'So it wasn't just because I'm a Stone that you didn't want to go to the gala with me?'

She looked puzzled. 'I'm not with you.'

'I remember what you said in the hotel restaurant about wooden floors making it hard for you to hear properly. It must be much worse at a party, where there's a constant background drone of noise from people talking.'

Her expression told him that he'd hit the nail on the head. That was precisely why Angel didn't enjoy parties.

She lifted her chin. 'You won the bet and I said I'd go with you if you won. I won't go back on my word.'

'If you're going to hate every minute of it, I'd rather not make you go,' he said.

She blinked. 'I didn't expect that.'

'What?'

'You. Being sensitive. Given how many girlfriends you go through.'

'Don't judge me by what the press says about me,' he said with a sigh. 'They like a good story, and half the time they make up quotes.'

'Uh-huh.' Though she didn't look quite convinced.

'And don't judge me by our family history, either,' he said.

'Didn't you judge me that way?' she asked.

'Fair point.' He reached over and took her hand. 'Let's agree to be nice to each other.'

'I'm not selling McKenzie's,' she warned. 'Or coming to work for you.'

He was pretty sure she'd do both. Because, from the look of her balance sheet, she didn't really have any other option. But he'd try to make it as easy as he could for her. 'That wasn't under discussion. This is about…' What the hell was it about? He'd never met a woman who flummoxed him like this enough to lose his train of thought totally. 'Getting to know each other, I guess,' he finished.

'Do we even want to do that?'

It probably wouldn't be tactful to point out that, just a few minutes ago, she'd been kissing him back, so it was pretty obvious that they were both interested.

'I want to get to know you,' he said. 'Imagine if you weren't a McKenzie and I wasn't a Stone. Look at what we have in common. We like cars. We like engines.' 'And my guess is that if we'd met without actually knowing who each other was, we might've liked each other.'

'You,' she said, 'have had more girlfriends than I've had hot dinners, so you'd get bored and dump me within a week. And I'm not interested in a relationship in any case. Right now, my focus is on my business.'

That stung. She made him sound like a tomcat. And he wasn't. He never led his girlfriends on or pretended he was going to offer them more than just fun for now. 'I don't sleep with everyone I date.'

'Even so, I'm not your type. You go for leggy models and actresses. And they're just the ones you're photographed with.' She shook her head. 'Maybe you're right. Maybe if our grandparents didn't have a history, we'd like each other. But we do have that history. Plus I'm not your type and you're not mine.'

'So what is your type?' he asked.

'That's for me to know and you to wonder.'

In other words, she didn't date. If he goaded her, she might eventually slip up and tell him what her type was. On the other hand, there had to be a reason why she didn't date. Maybe she'd had a really bad breakup, and her ex had crushed her ability to trust. He didn't want her to tar him with the same brush as whoever had hurt her.

'So currently we're at stalemate,' he said.

'You won the race. I agreed to your terms. So just let me know when and where I have to show up, and the dress code, and we'll leave it at that,' she said.

He had no intention of leaving it at that, but now was a good time to regroup. 'OK. Thank you for the hospitality.'

'You provided most of it,' she said. 'Thank you for lunch. And for letting me drive the Mermaid.'

'Pleasure.' He itched to kiss her again, but he knew it wouldn't be appropriate. He didn't want to give her an excuse to back away. Instead, he drove them back to the staff car park and parked the Luna next to his Mermaid. 'I'll be in touch, then.' His hand brushed against hers when he gave her car keys back to her, and every nerve-end tingled.

Her beautiful violet eyes had grown darker, he noticed; so did she feel it, too? Not that he was going to ask her. Right now he needed to tread carefully.

'OK. I, um… Drive safely.'

For a moment, he thought she was going to kiss him on the cheek. He even felt himself swaying slightly towards her. Ridiculous.

'Laters,' he drawled, and climbed into the Mermaid.

Though he was gratified to note that she stayed to see him drive off and she even gave him the tiniest wave as he reached the end of the driveway.

Angel McKenzie was a puzzle.

As she'd said very openly, she wasn't his type. She was very, very different from the women he usually dated. She wasn't fussed about appearances, and he'd just bet she was happiest wearing a boiler suit with her sleeves rolled up, getting to grips with an engine, or sketching out a design at a draughtsman's board.

His tour of the factory had left him in no doubt that she really loved McKenzie's, and her staff felt the same way about her. Ernie, the older guy who'd obviously worked out who Brandon was and didn't approve of her fraternising with the enemy, had looked concerned about her when he'd talked to her while Ravi showed Brandon the Luna. Almost like a grandfather keeping an eye out for a favourite grandchild: and there really had been a kind of family feel about the place. Nothing like the way his own factory was.

He didn't think Angel's team would respond to his uncle Eric in quite the same way as they did to her. Eric would throw his weight about and make it clear that he expected everyone to toe the line he drew, whereas Brandon had the strongest impression that Angel talked to her team and gave their ideas full consideration, and explained exactly why she did or didn't run with them.

She'd sell the company to him. Her balance sheet didn't offer any other option.

But he'd need to think hard about the best way forward and how to keep her team firmly on board—and then hopefully Angel would stay, too. Because that was the one thing he was very clear on, now: he didn't just want McKenzie's. He wanted Angel as well.

CHAPTER FIVE

'YOU HAVE TO speculate to accumulate, Miss McKenzie,' the lawyer drawled.

Which was a bit tricky when you didn't have anything to speculate with. 'Of course,' Angel agreed mildly. 'But would Triffid shoot a film on spec without a distribution deal? Because then you'd have to pay the actors and the crew up front, along with location fees and costumes and props, and you'd be spending all that money without even knowing if you'd see a return on your investment. You have to speculate to accumulate, yes—but you have to speculate *sensibly*.'

'I guess,' the lawyer said.

'So you understand that I can't just take one of my teams off their production rota for cars that have customers actually waiting for them, to make more Frosts for you that you might not use at all because you might want to make further changes to the spec. It'd be a waste of time and resources for both of us.' Resources she didn't have, and she was pretty sure Triffid wouldn't pay her for anything they didn't use, even if she pointed out that they were development costs specifically incurred for them.

'Noted,' the lawyer said. 'So are you saying you want to pull out of the deal?'

'No. I'm saying that I need to work out my factory production schedules for the Frost and my other models—just as Triffid has to work out how much time they need to film at each location, and how long they need for editing, and how long they need to get the films distributed to the various screens for the launch date,' Angel said. 'So I'd like to firm up numbers and dates, and I really think we should have everything signed off by the end of the week.'

'I'll talk to my people.'

Meaning more delay? Angel forced herself to smile and hoped that the lawyer couldn't see the anxiety in her eyes. Video conference calls could be tricky, but at least then she could be sure she was picking up every single word. Phone calls, where she had to concentrate super-hard because she had no visuals to work with, left her tired and cranky.

'I'd like to firm up the PR plans, too. To agree when we do the photoshoot of the car, when we draft the press release, and if you want to give anyone an exclusive interview. Perhaps we can have that signed off by the end of the week, too? I know the Internet makes things almost instant nowadays, but the car magazines still have lead times, and it'd be great to capitalise on this over the summer.'

'I'll talk to my people,' the lawyer said again.

'Great. I'll speak to you tomorrow, then. Same time?' Angel suggested brightly. 'Because then we can all get our ducks in a row and it'll be great for everyone.' And a signed contract would keep her bank manager happy and give her what she needed to refuse Brandon Stone's offer.

'Same time tomorrow,' the lawyer agreed. 'First thing.'

Ten a.m. in LA might be first thing, Angel thought, but it was six p.m. in England and she'd already been at her desk for ten hours. 'Lovely,' she said, and ended the call.

And please let the talking go quickly, this time. No more delays. She was running everything way too close to the wire.

Stephanie came in with a skinny cappuccino and a plate of chocolate biscuits. 'Given who you've just been talking to, I'm guessing you need this.'

'Thank you,' Angel said gratefully. 'Though you should've left an hour ago.'

'I knew you were calling Triffid—that's why I stayed behind,' Stephanie explained. 'I thought you could do with this when you were finished.'

'I could. Thank you.'

'Oh, and Brandon rang while you were on the phone to LA.'

Not 'Mr Stone', Angel noticed. So he'd clearly charmed her PA.

'Can you give him a call on his mobile?' Stephanie gave her a sticky note with the number written down.

'I will. Thanks, Stephie. Go home. And come in an hour later tomorrow morning to make up for this.'

'Yes, boss.' Stephanie smiled at her.

Angel was really too tired right now to concentrate on a phone call. Instead, she texted Brandon.

Stephie said you rang.

His reply came back immediately.

Busy or can you talk?

There was her ready-made excuse. All she had to do was say she was busy. But she surprised herself by actually wanting to talk to him.

Skype? she suggested, and typed in her profile ID.

A couple of minutes later, he called her on Skype.

'You OK?'

'Just a bit tired,' she admitted. 'It's been a long day.'

'And having to concentrate on listening to someone on the phone is hard work when you're tired.'

Again she was surprised by how perceptive he was. Since when did a Stone have a soft centre like this? 'A bit.'

'OK, then I'll keep this brief. Are you busy tomorrow night?'

'Why?' she asked carefully.

'Because I have a suggestion for you. I thought we could maybe meet halfway.'

'Halfway?' she repeated, feeling a bit stupid. What was he talking about? Selling the company to him? Because there was no halfway where McKenzie's and Stone's were concerned.

'St Albans is roughly halfway between Oxford and Cambridge.'

'St Albans?' So he'd been talking about geography after all.

'There's an outdoor performance of *Romeo and Juliet* tomorrow night in the Roman Theatre of Verulamium.' He gave her the sweetest, cheekiest smile. 'I thought it might be appropriate for us.'

The two warring houses he'd once compared them to: Montagues and Capulets. He had a point. They probably ought to keep well away from each other. But that smile was irresistible. 'Can you even get tickets for the performance, this late?' she asked.

'I can get tickets. And it'll be fun.'

'Fun.' There hadn't been a lot of that in her life, lately, with all her worries about the business. She'd almost forgotten how to have fun. It was tempting: but she simply didn't have the time.

As if he guessed at the excuse she was about to give, he said, 'You work hard. An evening off will do you good— refresh you, so you can work harder the next day.' The way he looked at her made her knees go weak. 'Are you up for it?'

She ought to say no.

She wasn't meant to be fraternising with the enemy. Or letting herself think about what it might be like to date Brandon Stone properly.

But completely the wrong word came out of her mouth. 'OK.'

'Great. Apparently they have food stalls, so we can grab dinner there. I'll bring a couple of foldaway chairs for us.'

'What time?'

'It starts at seven, so I'll meet you outside the gates at half-past six?'

Which would mean leaving work early to get there on time. As she was expecting a call from the lawyers in LA at six, it just wasn't doable. 'Sorry. I can't get there by then,' she said. But it felt mean to just knock him back. He'd been thoughtful. And she did actually want to go to the play with him. 'Can you make it another night?'

'How about Friday?' he suggested.

'Our factory finishes at half-past three on Fridays.'

'So does ours,' he said. 'Then Friday would work for both of us. Excellent. Friday it is. *Ciao.*' And then he hung up.

Ciao? *Ciao?*

She should've had him pegged as corny and ridiculous. Nobody English said *ciao* nowadays. It wasn't quite old enough to be retro, and it was cheesy and… And… That smile made it so charming.

That was the problem.

With Brandon, she still couldn't be sure what was charm and what was substance. She hated herself for being so suspicious but, given their family history and his offer to buy out her company, was he schmoozing her or did he really like her? If she'd dated more, maybe she would've had more of a clue. As it was, Brandon left her in a spin.

On Wednesday night, Angel's call to LA went much better. 'I'll email the contract over now,' the lawyer said. 'We have a digital signing system. I'll send you a link, and you can sign it once you've read it through.'

Once her own legal team had read it through, to make sure there weren't any last-minute changes, she thought. 'Thank you. I will.'

'Pleasure doing business with you, ma'am.'

'And you,' she said, lying through her teeth. The delays had driven her crazy. She definitely wouldn't have been able to cope with a career in law, where the wheels ground so very slowly. Give her the straightforwardness of engineering any day: either it worked, or it didn't—in which case you could work out how to fix it.

It was nearly two hours before the contract arrived in her inbox. But she was able to open the document without a problem, and she scanned it through quickly to make sure that everything she'd agreed was roughly there.

And then she sagged in relief.

She wasn't going to have to sell the company to Brandon after all. As long as her legal team was happy with the terms, she could sign the contract, and then she'd be able to start talking about the Frost. She could work with Triffid's PR team on a teaser campaign that would have people flocking to their dealers and asking to be put on the waiting list for a McKenzie Frost, or maybe a Luna if they couldn't wait for a Frost to be built. She'd be able to offer her staff overtime if they wanted it. Expand the business, maybe. And hopefully the Frost would become the iconic design of her generation, just as the Luna was her father's and the Mermaid was her grandfather's. She'd do McKenzie's proud.

Nobody would be at the bank at this time on a Wednesday night, she knew, but she dropped an email to James Saunders saying that the contract was now in her hands and her lawyers were looking through it.

By the time she got home, she was too tired to bother cooking dinner, opting for a bowl of cereal instead. Once she'd changed into her pyjamas, she thought about her date with Brandon on Friday night. And again the ugliest question raised its head: was this a real date, or was he simply softening her up to persuade him to sell to her?

Except she didn't have to sell the company any more.

She didn't want to make a fool of herself. Even allowing for press exaggeration, Brandon had dated a lot of women. On average, she was pretty sure he had more dates in a month than she'd had in her entire life so far. He was so far out of her league, it was untrue.

Maybe she should call it off.

Or maybe she was just tired and overthinking it. Maybe she should just go and have some fun.

The next day at work, Angel was mulling about what to wear on her date. She didn't often go to the theatre. Were you supposed to dress up? Or, given that it was an outdoor production and it might get cold as the evening went on, should you dress for comfort?

A call from the bank distracted her for a little while. This time James Saunders seemed prepared to discuss her business plan, and to her relief there was no more talk about calling in her overdraft. But then her lawyer called, wanting to make a change in one of the clauses.

'I know it means you'll have to stay after normal office hours here to talk to LA, because of the time difference,' she said, 'but you're the expert on contracts. Maybe it'd be best if you liaised with LA directly, rather than me acting as a kind of postman between you and getting it wrong?' She really couldn't face any more delays and excuses to drag things out.

Finally, on Friday lunchtime, she was able to call into her lawyer's office to sign the contract and it was sent electronically to LA.

And all the worry was over at last. She didn't have to let her family down and sell the company. Triffid's PR team would talk to her next week about the shoot and interviews, and then things would start to look up in the sales department.

She finished locking up the factory at four, and then headed for St Albans.

There were a thousand butterflies doing a stampede in her stomach as she drove to meet Brandon. Was she doing the right thing, or making a fool of herself? Though it was too late to change her mind, now.

She parked the car and texted Brandon to let him know she'd arrived.

He replied instantly.

Am in the queue by the gates. Will look out for you.

As she reached the group of people by the gates, she scanned the queue for him. He clearly spotted her first because he raised his hand to her and gave her that rock star smile.

'Hi.' She could see that he had a couple of fold-up chairs in bags slung over his shoulder; and he was dressed much more casually than she was. So she'd got the dress code well and truly wrong. 'Sorry. I came straight from work.'

He kissed her cheek. 'You look lovely.'

Was that gallantry, she wondered, or did he mean it? 'Thank you. How much do I owe you for my ticket?'

'Nothing. My treat. And no strings,' he added swiftly.

'Then I'll buy the pizza,' she said firmly, not wanting to be beholden to him. 'Especially as you've already bought me breakfast and lunch.'

'I'm not totting it all up, you know,' he said.

It made her feel even more awkward. And it must have shown in her expression, because he smiled and touched her cheek briefly with the back of his hand. 'Relax, Angel. We're just going to see a play together. Have you decided which of us is the Montague and which the Capulet, by the way?'

Strange how suddenly she felt so much more at ease. 'A rose by any other name, hmm?'

'Indeed. I brought a blanket as well as the chairs, because I thought the temperature might drop a bit once the sun sets.'

Was he suggesting that they'd share the blanket? It sounded cosy. *Intimate.* And it made her feel hot all over. She just about managed to cover her confusion.

Finally they were through the gates and Brandon set up their chairs with the minimum of fuss.

'What would you like to eat?' she asked.

'The pizza smells good,' he suggested.

'Pizza it is.'

His hand brushed against hers as they walked over to the stripy tent, sending a spike of adrenaline through her. His fingers caught hers and then curled round hers. This was definitely starting to feel like a date, she thought. A real one.

They chose from the menu chalked on a sandwich board, but when they reached the front of the queue Angel didn't quite catch what the pizza guy said to her through all

the chatter round her; his face was in the shadows, and his
beard meant that she couldn't lip-read what he was saying.

Without making a fuss, Brandon took over the conversation and ordered their pizzas. Angel was grateful and
frustrated at the same time; most of the time, she could
work round her hearing loss, but sometimes it made her
feel just as she had as a child: stupid and useless.

Back at their seats, he asked gently, 'Are you OK?'

'Sure.' Though he knew he'd rescued her from a struggle, so she could hardly pretend that everything had been
totally fine. She looked away. 'Thanks for helping me out.
Occasionally my hearing lets me down. I could probably
do with a reassessment and maybe a tweak to my hearing
aid program, but I haven't had the time.'

'Make the time,' he said, 'because you're important.'

Part of her felt nettled that he was bossing her about; but
she could see that his motivation was concern for her. She
was used to her parents wrapping her in cotton wool, and
some of the team at McKenzie's—particularly the older
ones—were a bit overprotective of her, but she'd put that
down to them having known her since she was a toddler.

But Brandon showing that same consideration... It actually felt good that he seemed protective of her. It made
her feel cherished. Which she knew was ridiculous, because she didn't need anyone looking after her: she was
doing perfectly well on her own.

Angel thoroughly enjoyed the play; and it was particularly lovely to see it in the old Roman amphitheatre with
minimum props, just as plays had been produced here
nearly two thousand years ago.

It started to get chilly after the sun set and, although
Angel tried really hard not to shiver, Brandon noticed that
she was cold. He tucked his blanket round them both and
slid his arm around her.

'Do you want me to get you some hot chocolate?' he asked.

'No, I'm fine, thanks. Don't miss any of the play for me.' A cup of hot chocolate would've been nice, but she had to admit to herself that she much preferred sitting there with his arm round her.

She knew he'd chosen *Romeo and Juliet* as a nod to the rivalry between their own families; but there was a serious side to the issue, too. She had no idea how her parents would react to the idea of her dating him, or how his family would react to him dating her. On balance, as long as he treated her well, she was pretty sure that her parents wouldn't mind that he was a Stone. The rift between their families had happened seventy years ago, so it was way past time that the breach was healed.

But would his family mind that she was a McKenzie? Would they welcome her, or would they mistrust her? Especially as Brandon was now their only child?

She pushed the thought away and concentrated on the performance.

Sitting here with his arm round Angel, snuggled together under a blanket, felt oddly domestic. Brandon knew he ought to be running a mile. Domestic wasn't in his vocabulary.

But this was actually *nice*. He liked being with her. And that really surprised him.

This whole thing had been supposed to be a way of getting under her skin and talking her into doing what he wanted. But Brandon had a nasty feeling that he'd miscalculated this badly; if he wasn't careful, he could actually lose his heart to Angel McKenzie. There was so much more to her than the focused businesswoman, the engineer who did everything by the book. She was shy and sweet, and he really liked the woman he was getting to know be-hind her shell.

Was it possible that he was looking at this completely the wrong way round—that maybe he should be dating her properly and just forget about the business? The whole idea of dating someone seriously scared him: he'd backed away from it for so long, and a large part of him thought he didn't deserve to be loved. But for the life of him he couldn't think of an excuse to pull away; if he was honest with himself, he didn't want an excuse. And at the end of the play, when he had to pack away the blanket and the chairs, it felt a real wrench to move away from her.

He covered his confusion by playing the clown, just as he'd always covered his nerves when racing by making everyone else laugh. '"A rose by any other name would smell as sweet."' He looked at her. 'A Stone by any other name would…' He wrinkled his nose. 'The only thing I can think of would sound wrong if I said it. I'm not mean-ing to be smutty.'

She grinned, picking up what he hadn't said. 'Sand-stone's soft.'

He gave her a pained look. 'Please.'

'Best leave it to Shakespeare,' she advised, laughing.

Like this, she was irresistible. Those eyes. If they were anything like her grandmother's eyes, he could quite un-derstand now why his grandfather had totally lost his head over his best friend's girl.

Worse still, he found himself holding her hand when he walked her back to her car. Just as if this was a real date.

'Thank you for this evening,' she said. 'I really en-joyed it.'

'Me, too.' And to his horror he realised that he meant it. It freaked him slightly when he realised that he couldn't take his eyes off her mouth. A perfect rosebud.

For pity's sake, what was wrong with him? He didn't do soppy, and he always kept that little bit of distance between himself and his girlfriends.

The last thing he should do right now was kiss her.

Yet it was inevitable. With her looking up at him like that, all cute and soft and sweet, he simply couldn't resist dipping his head to brush his mouth against hers. Or to hold her: she was so soft and warm in his arms. The perfect fit.

One kiss wasn't enough, and he knew this shouldn't be happening, especially when she kissed him back. He never, but never, let himself get deeply involved.

Angel was the one who broke the kiss, and Brandon was actually shaking. What on earth was wrong with him? Had he gone insane? He needed to keep control of the situation. Not seeing her wasn't an option, at least not until she'd agreed to sell the business. But maybe he'd be able to be more in control of himself on his home territory.

'Can I see you again?' he asked.

She actually blushed, and Brandon wanted to pick her up, carry her off somewhere very private and make her blush even more. This really, really wasn't good.

'When were you thinking?' she asked.

My house. Now. And breakfast tomorrow morning.

He stopped himself saying it. Just. 'Next week. You showed me round McKenzie's, so I thought maybe you'd like to come to Oxford to see how we do things.'

'So I get a private tour of this famous museum of yours? I'd like that.'

His mouth was really on a roll. 'And maybe you'd like to take one of our cars round a track.'

She blinked. 'I'd be driving an actual racing car? The one whose steering wheel costs more than a whole one of my cars?'

'It'd be a rally car, if you want to drive,' he said. 'Or we have a two-seater racing car we use for "experience" days. I could drive you.'

And why on earth had he said that? He didn't drive racing cars any more.

'I'd like that,' she said.

Too late. He couldn't back out of it now. Not without explaining—and all of a sudden it was important to him that she didn't think he was a lowlife. If he told her he was responsible for his brother's death, she'd think a lot less of him. Just as he thought a lot less of himself for it.

'When's your diary free?' he asked. If those violet eyes were focused on her phone screen rather than his face, he might have a chance of getting his common sense back for long enough to deal with this properly.

To his relief, she took her phone from her bag and checked her diary. 'I've got a couple of meetings I can move on Wednesday.'

'That works for me,' he said, knowing he could ask Gina to move things around in his diary. 'Wednesday it is.'

'OK.' She looked awkward, as if wondering what they did now.

He knew what he wanted to do. He also knew it wouldn't be sensible. 'I'd better let you go. The traffic could be bad,' he said.

'Yes.'

'Text me to let me know you got home safely?' And again, where had that come from? It was more than just polite concern. He really wanted to know she was home safely.

'I will. You, too.'

And that was weird, too. He wasn't used to his girl-friends being concerned about him. It should make him want to run a mile, especially as he'd given up driving racing cars to stop his family worrying about it. He'd told himself for years that he didn't want to feel trapped by other people's emotions. But it actually felt nice that someone else cared what happened to him.

He waited for her to get into her car and drive off before he went to find his own car, but it made him antsy. Why on earth did waving goodbye to her make him feel as if he ached physically? Was he actually *missing* her? And all this after a first official date that he'd organised so casually that it wasn't supposed to be a *date* date.

And yet he'd held her hand. Snuggled with her under a blanket. Kissed her goodnight.

Somehow he was going to have to get himself under control. This was all about getting her out of his system and talking her into selling to him. Nothing more than that.

Nothing at all.

CHAPTER SIX

THE FOLLOWING WEDNESDAY morning, Angel drove to Oxford. The rush-hour traffic on the M25 kept her too busy to think about the stupidity of what she was actually doing—practically going into the lion's den.

She was still trying to work out whether she and Brandon were actually dating or not. She didn't have a clue about the etiquette of dating; as a teen, she'd been so shy that nobody had ever asked her out. She'd developed an unfair reputation as an ice maiden at university, so she knew that the men who'd asked her out had seen her as a challenge rather than actually wanting to date her, and were probably boasting about it to their friends; she'd turned them down.

After her Master's degree, she'd concentrated on work; dating Brandon was out of her comfort zone. She was surprised to realise that actually she was a little bit nervous about today. How ridiculous. Brandon had invited her here to see round the factory. She needed to think about this as business.

When she arrived at Stone's, the first thing she noticed was that the site was much larger than her own. But then again Brandon's business was more diverse than hers; as well as making the cars here, there was an accredited race track which she knew was used by other local manufacturers, and he'd talked about the museum next to the factory.

Though it set her to thinking that this was how McKenzie's could be. And maybe diversifying the business a little might help with cash flow. She definitely needed to think about how they could make the most of the Frost—an exhibition, maybe an experience day where people could drive a Frost...

But first she needed the money from the contract to come through from Triffid. And if that took as long as the paperwork had, her bank manager would be nagging her again.

She parked her car where the man on the security gate had directed her, but before she had the chance to call Brandon to let him know that she'd arrived, he came walking over to her.

In a dark grey suit and with his hair brushed back from his face, he looked every inch the businessman.

So would today be all about business?

Or would he kiss her again? Because he didn't just look like a businessman. He looked sexy as hell, with that perfectly cut suit and crisp shirt and understated tie.

She pushed the thought away. She wasn't even sure what she was really doing here anyway. He was out of her league and she'd better remember that.

'Thanks for coming,' Brandon said as she climbed out of her car.

He smiled at her, and she was cross with her knees for going slightly weak on her. Yes, he was gorgeous, but she shouldn't let herself get distracted. 'Well, who's going to turn down a personal tour of the factory of someone who's planning to be their business rival?' she asked brightly.

He coughed. 'Not necessarily rival. Where would you like to start? The museum? Coffee in my office?' Then he smiled again. 'Scratch that. You've just driven two hours to get here. Let me show you to the restroom first and sort out some coffee for you.'

When he was thoughtful like this, he was utterly irresistible. But did he know that? Was he really pleased to see her—or was he schmoozing her?

Brandon was surprised to discover how relieved he was to see Angel. He'd half expected her to call off today at the last minute, pleading pressure of work. He resisted the urge to curl his fingers round hers—after all, this was supposed to be a kind of business meeting—and led her to his office. Gina was sitting at the desk in the anteroom.

'Angel, this is my PA, Gina,' he said. 'Gina, this is Angel McKenzie.'

Gina stood up and shook Angel's hand. 'It's lovely to meet you. And you've had to drive such a long way this morning. Can I get you tea, coffee, or a fruit infusion?'

Angel gave one of those shy smiles that set all Brandon's nerve-ends tingling. 'Coffee would be lovely, thanks—milk and no sugar, please.'

'Coffee. Would that be cappuccino, latte or Americano?'

Oh, help. Gina was definitely overdoing the hospitality thing.

But Angel didn't seem in the least bit fazed. 'Cappuccino, please.'

'I'll be right in.' Gina gave Brandon her sweetest smile. 'I know how you like your coffee, sir.'

Sir? *Sir?* Oh, no. The last thing he wanted was to give Angel the impression that he was one of those bosses who insisted on being called 'sir', especially after he'd seen the way she was with her own staff.

'She never calls me that usually,' he muttered as Gina left the room. 'Do you need the restroom?'

'I'm fine,' Angel said with a smile.

Was she amused by all this? Had she worked out that his PA was teasing?

And, more to the point, how come he felt so flustered when he was on his home territory and should be feeling totally at ease and confident?

'Come through,' he said, and ushered her into his office.

The room was very neat and tidy, Angel noticed, and Brandon's desk was immaculate. Was he a figurehead, or did he just have a tidy mind?

And then she noticed the blueprint on the wall. Unable to resist, she went over to it for a closer look. 'That's a beautiful car.'

'I can show you the car itself in the museum,' he said. 'It's my favourite of all the ones we've produced. But I'm probably biased because I drove it for a couple of years.'

She looked at the date on the blueprint and realised what it was. 'The one you drove for your first world championship.'

'I didn't actually win,' he reminded her. 'I came second.'

'Which still makes you in the top two drivers of the world, that year.'

'There's an element of luck as well,' he said, 'and it depends on how the others drive on the day.'

She liked the fact that he wasn't arrogant about his success. Funny, she hadn't expected him to be humble.

Like her, he had photographs on his desk. One was clearly of his parents. The second showed a young man with a shy smile—a kind of toned-down version of Brandon, so she had a pretty good idea who he was. 'That's your brother?' she asked.

'Sammy. Yes.'

'He looks like you.' She wanted to give him a hug, but

it felt like the wrong place and the wrong time. Instead, she said, 'I'm an only child, so I can't even imagine what it must be like. But you must miss him horribly.'

'Every day.' His words were heartfelt. Then he looked shocked, as if he hadn't meant to say that out loud.

Before he could backtrack, Gina brought in coffee and a plate of posh chocolate biscuits.

'Since when have we had these in the office?' Brandon asked, gesturing to the biscuits.

'They're strictly for visitors. Mind your manners and don't have more than your fair share,' Gina said crisply.

Brandon groaned. 'Gina, can't we have *one* meeting where you're just my PA?'

'No.' Gina added to Angel in a stage whisper, 'I've known him since he was a baby. And I've changed his nappy on more than one occasion.'

Brandon put his head in his hands and groaned even more. 'I can't even sack you for being over-familiar, because my mum's your best friend and she'd kill me.'

'Exactly,' Gina said with a grin.

Angel thoroughly enjoyed the teasing; here she was seeing another side to Brandon, one with a soft centre and one she liked very much. If he'd been simply an arrogant, cocky playboy, he wouldn't have such a good relationship with his PA. Gina clearly adored him and was perfectly comfortable teasing him. And she liked the fact that at least one corner of Stone's had the family feel of McKenzie's rather than being a ruthless money-making machine.

She grinned. 'I'm glad to see I'm not the only one bossed around by my PA. Stephie's having a baby in five months and she's practising her parenting skills on me.'

Gina grinned back. 'Good for her.'

'I really like your PA,' she said when Gina had closed the door.

'Don't get any ideas of poaching her for Stephie's maternity cover,' Brandon warned.

'Because she adores you so much that she'd never leave you?'

'More like she really enjoys being my mum's spy,' he said ruefully. 'You can expect to be reported on later.'

'Is that a good thing, or a bad?' The words were out before she could stop them.

'You got the approving look—and she brought in the special biscuits I didn't even know she kept. So on balance I'd say that's a good thing.' He sighed. 'Though my mother's going to be asking a lot of questions about my intentions.'

'Parents,' she said lightly. Her own were careful not to pressure her, but she knew her mother in particular was hoping for future grandchildren.

The trouble was, Angel hadn't even met anyone she wanted to date over the last few years, since she'd taken over from her dad, let alone settle down with. Apart from going out with Brandon Stone: who was just about the worst person she could date in the first place.

To distract herself, she said, 'So tell me about your roadsters.'

'You're asking me to talk to you about confidential business stuff?'

'If someone asks me to head up their R&D department and suggests developing a new car for them, I'd kind of want to know what sort of thing they have in mind.'

'You turned the job down,' he reminded her. His eyes glittered. 'Or have you changed your mind and you're thinking seriously about it?'

She took a sip of coffee. 'That would be confidential business stuff,' she retorted.

He laughed. 'I deserved that. OK. I want a new range.

Everything from the affordable sports car—' *her* market '—through to the top end.'

'Super-expensive?'

'Luxury and super-technical,' he said.

Which is the same thing,' she said dryly.

He gave her another of those knee-melting smiles. 'I guess. Basically I'm looking at working with the newest materials, and at a range of fuel options. But what I most want is to give my clients the experience of driving a racing car. Except *safely.*'

The ends of Angel's fingers tingled at the possibilities and she itched to start sketching.

It must have shown in her face, because he took a pad and pencil from his desk and handed it to her. 'Feel free.'

'You,' she said, 'are not playing fair.'

'I'm not talking to Angel McKenzie, the CEO of a very old manufacturing company who's sort of our rival. I'm talking to Angel McKenzie, the designer. The one who loves the Mermaid.' He paused. 'Imagine bringing the Mermaid up to date. New aerodynamics, new materials. Carbon fibre and titanium.'

'That's going to be seriously expensive.'

He nodded. 'And I'm looking at a good ride quality. Maybe a different kind of suspension system.'

'So not really the Mermaid at all.'

'The feel of it,' he said. 'But brought right up to date.'

'With materials like you're suggesting, that's the opposite of what I do: making beautiful cars that ordinary people can afford. And I can tell you now, I am *not* going to design an affordable car for a rival company.'

'Think about the super-techy one instead, then,' he said. 'And, when you've finished your coffee, I'll show you round the museum.'

'Deal.' She didn't touch the pencil and paper, but pictures were forming in her head as he took her over to the museum. A joint design. The first McKenzie-Stone car in years.

It was oh, so tempting.

But it would be the start of a slippery slope. One where she couldn't predict the final destination. Way, way out of her comfort zone.

The museum was a gorgeous building, light and airy. The cars were displayed well, too; even though it was clear that you couldn't touch the exhibits, you could still see everything.

'So which is the model you're missing?' she asked.

'A very early one,' he said. 'I might have sourced one. But I need to be a little more persuasive.'

'You mean, you need to offer more money,' she said dryly.

'The seller isn't bothered about money.'

'So the seller's just bothered about selling it to you? Tsk. And who was it who told me my sales patter was rubbish?' she teased.

'Yeah.' He gave her a considering look. 'Maybe we'll talk about that later. Come and see the factory.'

When he showed her round Stone's, she could see just how far apart their production techniques were. 'So your bodies are all pre-cut.'

'Precision cut,' he said.

'And put together by robots.'

'So we can pinpoint any problem immediately on the computer instead of having to wait until we do a test drive and then narrow it down—which you know can take days.'

'Uh-huh.' It wasn't the way she would want to produce a car. She liked the way they did things at McKenzie's. But she did enjoy poking around the engines in the factory and seeing just how they did things here.

'That's what I'd plan to use for the new car. Precision cutting,' he said.

'My team does precision cutting,' she pointed out. 'By hand.'

'But they haven't worked with the materials I want to work with. Not the new top-end stuff.'

The pictures flickered in her head again, and she could clearly see the new car being produced at her factory, side by side with the Frost. 'Supposing,' she said, 'you mix the old and the new. Old-fashioned craftsmanship and new materials.'

He regarded her with interest. 'Are you suggesting a joint venture?'

Was this what he'd been after all along? she wondered. And was it something that could work? Then again, now the Triffid contract was signed, McKenzie's were going to be at full capacity. She didn't have the space to produce a new car for Brandon—even though she was seriously tempted. She loved the idea he'd come up with: a cross between the Mermaid and a racing car, with aerodynamic lines.

Before she could reply, a voice boomed behind them. 'So Golden Boy's showing you round, is he?'

Angel straightened up and faced the man who'd just addressed her. 'I—er—yes.'

'Angel, this is my Uncle Eric,' Brandon said. 'Eric, this is Angel McKenzie.'

'I know who she is.' Eric's voice was full of contempt. For her, Angel wondered, or for Brandon? Or both?

She flinched on Brandon's behalf. None of her aunts and uncles on her mum's side would ever be rude to her like this, in public or in private.

'She looks like her grandmother,' Eric continued.

Ah. Was that the problem? If so, no wonder he was talking about her rather than to her.

But then he looked straight at her. 'So you've finally decided to see sense and sell to us, have you?'

Clearly he'd been discussing it with Brandon. And maybe that was why Brandon had invited her over today: for a charm offensive to persuade her round to his way of thinking. His uncle was completely the opposite of charming; hostility radiated out of him.

'McKenzie's isn't for sale,' she said quietly. She knew she really ought to be diplomatic, but that remark about seeing sense rankled so much that she couldn't just be polite and keep her mouth shut. 'But thank you for your concern about my mental state,' she added. 'I can assure that you I'm just fine.'

His eyes narrowed as he registered that she wasn't cowed by him. 'So why are you here?'

'I'm discussing possible business with Brandon,' she said. Which was true to a point. Poor Brandon, having to deal with so much resentfulness and rudeness every day.

'It looks more like he's giving you a factory tour,' Eric said. 'Golden Boy here's not bad as a factory tour guide.' He gave a nasty little laugh. 'We should probably put him in charge of the factory tours.'

And let Eric be the CEO of Stone's instead? Hardly. And if Angel had been forced to sell McKenzie's to Brandon, her staff would all have resigned rather than work for someone like Eric Stone, who blundered about totally uncaring of how the people around him felt. She smiled sweetly at him. 'A good manager understands how every job in a place fits in—so he understands the problems his staff face and the potential solutions. Plus there's a little thing called empathy. I've found it quite useful.'

'Humph,' Eric said, giving her an assessing look. 'Carry

on with the tour, Brandon.' And then, to Angel's relief, he stomped off.

'I'm sorry about that,' Brandon said, looking as if he wanted to punch the nearest wall.

And she couldn't blame him. In his shoes, she'd feel the same. His uncle had just been totally unprofessional, and it hadn't shown Stone's in a good light at all. 'It's not your fault.' She grimaced. 'I can't believe he was so rude to you.'

Brandon shrugged. 'I guess he thought he'd take over, after Dad's heart attack. He hasn't quite forgiven me for getting the top job.'

'But you've been here for three years or so. That's more than long enough for you to prove yourself. Especially as your balance sheets have improved every year since you took over.'

He raised an eyebrow. 'Been checking me out, Ms McKenzie?'

And now she was on surer ground. She'd keep this light and teasing, just as it had been before Eric's interruption. 'Pots and kettles, Mr Stone,' she parried. 'Your balance sheets are in the public domain, too.'

He smiled. 'I guess. OK. So what would you like to see now?'

'What would you like to show me?'

She regretted the question the instant she asked it, because then he looked at her mouth and she remembered how he'd kissed her in St Albans. It made her want him to do it again, and she really, really hoped he couldn't guess what she was thinking right now. 'You said something about showing me the track?' she mumbled.

'I probably should've told you to wear jeans today,' he said. 'But we can do something about that. Come with me.'

He took her over to an area with cupboards that contained bright blue overalls with the words 'Stone Racing' in white on the back, and a rack of helmets. He glanced at her shoes. 'Obviously you can drive in those?'

'Not all women wear high heels all the time, you know.'

'I'm not judging you,' he said, holding both hands up.

She grimaced. 'Sorry. I was being over-defensive.'

'That's OK—and I didn't mean to make you feel awkward,' he said. 'Find something that fits and is comfortable, so you don't get oil on your business clothes. Meet me outside through that door there—' he indicated the door at the other end of the room—'and then I'll take you round the track in the racing car.'

As soon as Brandon climbed into the driving seat, he wished he hadn't suggested this. Maybe he should've just stuck to driving her in the rally car. But she'd stood up to Eric and it had been nice to have someone bat his corner, for once. He'd wanted to show her the joy of racing round a track.

Even though it wasn't really a joy for him any more. Driving and racing was spiked with guilt.

Grimly, he brought the two-seater racing car round by the door to the changing rooms, then switched off the engine, climbed out and leaned against the car until she was ready.

She emerged a couple of minutes later in overalls and helmet. The outfit should've made her look totally unsexy, but for a moment she distracted him from his misery because the whole thing made her look so hot.

Then he remembered where they were—pretty much the last place where he could kiss her until they were both dizzy. Not unless he wanted his uncle slinging his weight around, and his mother calling him to ask him why he was kissing that nice young lady Gina had just told him about, right in the middle of the test track.

'Hey. Ready?' he asked.

'I think so.' She smiled at him. 'Would you believe I've never done anything like this?'

'Not even when someone else brought their car to your track?'

'Not even then,' she said.

'OK. You're going to be sitting very low down and the adrenaline level's going to be high, but I'm not going to show off or drive stupidly,' he reassured her. 'You'll be perfectly safe with me.'

She regarded the tyres, looking suddenly nervous. 'Slicks.'

'It's what we use in dry weather. It's the best tyre for the car. And the track's bone dry.'

'All right.' She took a deep breath. 'Let's do this.'

He helped her in and made sure her seat belt was fastened properly, then climbed into his seat. He took the first lap slowly, knowing that the seating position was very different from a road car's and could feel intimidating if you weren't used to it, and then he sped up.

Funny. He'd driven round this track so many times over the years. But it had lost its magic for him, and it felt plain *wrong* to be whizzing her round in the racing car. He'd just have to ignore it, because he'd promised to drive her in the car and it wasn't fair that she should have it spoiled by the misery that ate at him. 'Suck it up, buttercup,' he mouthed.

And he forced himself to get out of the car and smile at her when he helped her out of the back. 'So what did you think?'

'Um—adrenaline, as you said.'

'Too much?'

'Being hemmed in like this is a bit claustrophobic,' she said, 'and being this low down takes a bit of getting used to. But you're right—it was fun. Thank you.'

Fun? No. Not any more. He dredged up his best smile. 'Want to take the rally car round? You'll probably enjoy that a bit more. And this time you can drive.'

'Great. That sounds good.'

'OK. I'll take this car out of your way, first.'

Was it her imagination, Angel wondered, or had Brandon's mood changed since he'd taken her round the factory? She was pretty sure she hadn't put her foot in it, but something definitely felt wrong.

When he parked the rally car next to her, she climbed into the passenger seat before he had a chance to get out and asked, 'Are you OK?'

'Sure.' He gave her the full megawatt smile, but it didn't reach his eyes.

'Engineers are pretty good at noticing big fat lies, you know,' she said softly. 'What's wrong?'

He was silent for so long that she thought he was going to stonewall her. But then he sighed. 'I guess I owe you the truth. I've hardly sat in a racing car since Sam died. I've done the odd test drive round this track, but my heart just hasn't been in it any more.'

And yet he'd admitted to her back at McKenzie's track that he missed racing. If she asked him whether he wanted to talk about it, he might clam up—but at the same time she couldn't just sit there and watch him suffer and say nothing at all. She wanted to help him.

She reached over and squeezed his hand. 'Damned if you do, damned if you don't?'

'Something like that.' He looked anguished.

'Talk to me, Brandon,' she said softly. 'Whatever you say isn't going anywhere but me.

He paused for so long, she thought he was going to refuse. But then he swallowed hard. 'It's the guilt. It chokes me every time I get in a racing car.'

'Guilt?' she prompted, not understanding what he was talking about.

He dragged in a breath. 'Because it's my fault that my brother died.'

CHAPTER SEVEN

It was Brandon's fault that Sam had died? Angel stared at him, not understanding.

'And that my little niece is growing up knowing her dad as just a photograph,' he continued miserably, 'instead of as the man who taught her to swim and ride a bike and made sandcastles with her and took her to the park.'

'How was it your fault?' she asked. 'You weren't driving.'

'But I should've been driving,' he said. 'The week before the race, I'd gone skiing. I'd gone on a black diamond run, showing off—and I came a bit of a cropper. I broke a rib, and that meant the officials said I wasn't fit to drive in the race, so Sam had to be my substitute.' He shook his head in apparent self-disgust. 'If I hadn't been so bratty and selfish and stupid, Sam wouldn't have been anywhere near that car—he wouldn't have been on the track at all, and he wouldn't have been killed.'

'OK, maybe I can see at a stretch that it's your fault that Sam was behind the wheel—but it's *not* your fault that the accident happened,' she said. 'What about the driver who caused the crash in the first place?'

'Micky?' Brandon wrinkled his nose. 'It wasn't really his fault. The car steering malfunctioned and there was nothing he could do about it. And he didn't exactly get off lightly. He was in plaster for months and the poor guy hasn't been able to drive professionally since.' He sighed. 'No matter how good a driver you are, you can't always get out of trouble if a car goes wrong.'

'Exactly. So the accident was just that, Brandon—a freak event that nobody could've foreseen. It *wasn't* your fault. If you'd been driving in the race, you might not even have been involved in the crash anyway, because you might not have been in exactly the same position on the track that Sam was, plus Micky's car might not have gone wrong at all. There are so many variables, Brandon. You can't blame yourself.'

He said nothing, merely grimacing.

She took his hand. 'It really wasn't your fault.'

'In my head, I can see that. But my heart's saying something different,' he said. 'I can't forgive myself. I miss him every day. I see him in the way my niece smiles, and I hate myself for what I took from her.'

And the despair in his grey eyes went deep.

Angel had no idea what to say or how to make him feel better. Wanting to convey at least some kind of sympathy—fellow-feeling rather than pity—she placed her palm gently against his cheek.

He twisted slightly so he could press his lips into her palm, and her skin tingled where his mouth touched her.

Helplessly, she slid her other arm round his neck and reached up to kiss him.

And he kissed her back as if he were drowning and she was the only thing keeping him afloat. Her heart broke for him. He'd spent the last three years convinced that he was at fault for his brother's death; how did you live with a feeling like that?

'I'm sorry,' he said when he broke the kiss. 'I'm supposed to be driving you round the circuit in the rally car.'

'It's OK. You don't have to if you don't want to.' She bit her lip. 'If I'd had any idea how painful it would be for you to get behind the wheel of that racing car this morning, I would've suggested we skip it.'

He leaned forward and kissed the corner of her mouth. 'Because you're a much nicer woman than I deserve.'

Was that why Brandon seemed to date his way through such a long line of women? Because he didn't think he deserved love, so he never stayed with anyone long enough to let them love him? Her heart broke for him just a little bit more.

'No. Because I think you're hurting enough without me adding to it,' she said softly. And she wasn't that nice. She was a coward who'd buried herself in work rather than dealing with her shyness in her personal life.

'You're nice,' he said softly.

'And you're nicer than you give yourself credit for,' she said. OK, so maybe bringing the Mermaid to show her had originally been part of a plan to talk her into selling her the company, but he'd still let her sit in it and actually drive it. He hadn't had to go that far.

'I'm not as nice as you deserve.'

She went still. Was this his way of ending their fledgling relationship? Was she about to get the 'it's not you, it's me' speech?

Then she shook herself. This wasn't about her. This was about him feeling horrible and not being able to deal with it. And she really wanted to make him feel better. 'You know what?'

'What?'

'You're a Stone and I'm a McKenzie. We're not supposed to think each other is nice.'

That earned her a wry smile. 'Maybe.'

'Sam was your older brother, right?'

He nodded.

'So I'm guessing he bossed you around?'

Brandon smiled then. 'When I was little. Before I was old enough to be stroppy and do things my way.'

'But he loved you as much as you loved him?'

'He worried about me. Nagged me about burning the candle both ends and taking risks,' Brandon admitted.

Just as she'd thought. 'I didn't know him, but from what you'd told me I'd guess that he would've been livid with you for blaming yourself for his death.'

'Maybe.'

'Definitely,' she corrected. 'And I also think he might've been sad that you'd lost the joy you once had in driving.'

'Probably.' Brandon's face was tight.

'Hating yourself isn't going to bring him back. And in the end that hatred is going to tarnish your memory of him,' she said softly. 'My dad's sister died when he was little. He always says she would want us all to remember her with smiles and focus on the good stuff.'

'But how do you do that?' Brandon asked.

'Be kind to yourself, for a start. Block out how bad you feel and think of something that makes your heart feel light.'

'That sounds,' he said, 'like personal experience.'

'It is,' she said. 'When I was a teen, I was crippled by shyness. I hated people treating me as if I was stupid and useless just because I was deaf. I didn't know how to talk to people and I clammed up. I saw a counsellor about it, and she suggested that when I felt bad, I should focus instead on something I loved talking about—engines, cars, that sort of thing.'

'And it worked?'

She nodded. 'It's as if this lump in my throat just dissolves and I can talk easily again.'

'So you had to make a real effort.'

'I didn't say it was easy,' she said. 'Just it's a method that works for me. So maybe look at what you're good at. What you love. Focus on that and distract yourself.'

He stole a kiss. 'Angel McKenzie, you're amazing.'

'I'm very ordinary,' she said. And, because the look in his eyes made her heart feel as if it was doing anatomically impossible things, she went for distraction, too. 'And I can tell you something else. Right now, you need cake.'

He blinked. 'Cake?'

'Let's go into Oxford and I'll buy you afternoon tea. Anywhere you like—I'm assuming you know where they do the best scones in the city?'

'I guess.' He paused. 'You know what would be even better, in May?'

'What?'

'How are you in boats?' he asked.

Where was he going with this? 'Boats?'

'Punting, to be precise.' He gestured outside. 'It's sunny. The river will be gorgeous today.'

'I've never been punting,' she admitted.

'What, when you live in Cambridge?'

She saw in his expression the moment he realised why. 'Your parents were worried about you falling into the river, getting an ear infection and losing the rest of your hearing?'

'Something like that,' she agreed. 'Though they didn't wrap me up in cotton wool to constrain me; they just wanted to keep me safe. Besides, if I fall in and get my hearing aid wet, it'll stop working.' Leaving her with hearing on one side only, which wasn't quite enough to let her follow every nuance of a conversation. She could manage for a couple of days, but it would be a struggle and she'd be bone-deep tired and frustrated at the end of it.

'I promise faithfully,' he said, 'not to let you fall in.'

There was enough of a smile on his face to let her know that they'd pulled back from the danger zone. She took the risk of going a little further and teasing him. 'So as well as being a super-hot racing driver, you're an expert at punting, then?'

'Honey,' he drawled, 'I'm good at everything.'

Their gazes met, and suddenly she couldn't breathe.

He was certainly good at kissing; and she went hot all over at the thought of what it would be like if they took this thing between them any further. What it would be like if they actually made love.

Except... Would she have to tell him about her woeful, embarrassing inexperience? But, if she did, maybe he'd think there was something wrong with her.

Maybe there *was* something wrong with her.

She pushed the thought away. She'd just given him a lesson on avoidance tactics. Going over the top and flirting outrageously was clearly his way of doing that.

'OK. Let me get changed and we'll do the river. And then we're doing cake,' she said.

By the time Angel had changed back into her business suit and he'd changed out of his own racing overalls, Brandon had got himself back under control. He was still shocked that he'd actually confided in her; he never talked about his feelings to anyone, especially when it came to Sam's death. Yet there was something about Angel that made him feel grounded, safe enough to talk about the dark things in his head.

That in itself was worrying. He didn't want to get close to her. This was all meant to be about getting her to sell McKenzie's to him. He was on his home ground; it should be easier to resist his attraction to her here.

Yet it wasn't.

He needed to keep this light and easy. Play on their differences. Bring up the Oxford-Cambridge rivalry, maybe, rather than the Stone-McKenzie one.

'Ready to go?' he asked, giving her his best full-wattage smile.

'Ready,' she confirmed.

'Great.' He drove them into the city and managed to find a parking space. As they passed the Ashmolean Museum, he gave her a sidelong look. 'I should probably point out the Ashmolean. We have rather better museums in Oxford.'

'Than Cambridge, you mean? Nope. Raise you the Fitzwilliam,' she said.

He was relieved that she was playing along with him, so he could push all the emotions back where they belonged—in the locked box around his heart. 'Raise you the Pitt-Rivers,' he said. 'And we have the Bodleian Library—which is one of the oldest libraries in Europe, and the second-biggest in Britain.'

'I'll give you that,' she said. 'But in Cambridge we have one of the four remaining round Templar churches in the country.'

'We have a Saxon tower in St Michael's church,' he said.

'And we have St Bene't, which also has a Saxon tower.' She smiled. 'I think we're going to have to declare a tie on that one.'

'Perhaps.' That smile was irresistible. And he really wanted to hold her hand. What on earth was wrong with him? He wasn't a teenage schoolboy. He didn't do soppy.

But something about Angel made him feel different.

Brandon managed to keep himself under control until they got to Magdalen Bridge, where the punts were all set out waiting for business. He paid for their punt, and then he glanced at Angel's business suit. Her skirt was definitely too narrow to let her clamber into the punt. 'Can you forgive me for doing something a bit troglodytish?'

She looked surprised. 'What?'

'I'm still not with you.'

He gestured to her skirt. 'Short of asking you to hike that up...' And then, before she could protest, he picked her up and climbed into the punt with her.

She felt really, really good in his arms.

But they were in public, so that was enough to stop him giving in to the urge to kiss her until they were both dizzy—which would be a stupid thing to do on a boat in any case, especially as he'd promised to make sure he wouldn't let her fall in.

'Sorry about that,' he fibbed. 'It was just the safest way of getting you into the punt.

Her violet eyes were wide with shock and the expression on her face told him she didn't think he was sorry in the slightest. It was a real effort to hold himself back from stealing a kiss.

'Take a seat, my lady, and I'll punt you down the river.'

'As long as you don't try to sell me down the river,' she said dryly.

'As if I'd even try.' He smiled at her. 'Right. Note that I'm punting from the Oxford end.'

'There's an Oxford end and a Cambridge end of a punt?' she asked.

'There is indeed. Here, we punt from the sloping end. It's also less slippery as well as being traditional.'

'Right.'

She sat on the padded red velvet seat, and he gently steered them out into the middle of the river. 'I feel as if

I ought to be wearing a stripy jersey and singing "*O Sole Mio*".'

'Oxford is hardly Venice,' she teased back.

He liked this light-hearted side of her. 'Ah, but we have a bit of Venice in Oxford, and I don't mean the punting. I'll show you later. All righty, my lady. Your tour of Oxford starts here at Magdalen Bridge.' He pointed up at the golden stone bridge with its gorgeous parapet.

The sunlight sparkled on the river Cherwell; the river looked almost as green as the trees in the summer afternoon light, and the ducks and swans were out in full force, paddling lazily between the punts.

Funny how being on the river made him feel grounded again. He'd spent so much of his earlier life trying to drive as fast as he could and stay ahead of the pack, yet the slow pace of punting and the sound of the water lapping against the banks and the sight of the swans gliding always made him feel better. Right now he really wanted to share that with her. But sharing his favourite places didn't mean he was letting her close—did it?

'And this is Christ Church College Meadows,' he said. He gestured to the golden stone building in the background. 'This is where Lewis Carroll taught when he wrote *Alice in Wonderland*.'

'It's beautiful,' she said. 'I think it'd inspire anyone.'

Even though the conversation between them lapsed, it didn't feel awkward. He liked the fact that Angel didn't need to chatter on and on—something that had grated on him with quite a few past girlfriends.

Not that Angel was his girlfriend, exactly.

He didn't want to let himself think about what she could be to him, and instead concentrated on punting, on the slow steady strokes of the pole that propelled the boat forward past the college buildings, all red roofs and mellow golden stone, and under the little white bridges.

Finally, he glided the punt into a berth at the station.

'You are *not* lifting me out of the boat,' she said.

Because she didn't want to be close to him?

Maybe the question showed on his face, because she said, 'I'm not a helpless little princess.'

No. She was independent, stubborn and bright. And he liked that about her, too.

'Can I at least offer you a hand? Simply because it's tricky for anyone to get out of a punt, and not because I'm trying to make you feel pathetic. I did promise not to let you fall in, and I don't want to break that promise.'

'Hmm,' she said.

And then she hiked her skirt up.

Not too much, but enough to let her climb out of the boat. Though she did at least hold his hand for balance. And somehow he forgot to let her hand go again.

'Cake?' she asked.

'Soon. I want to show you what I meant about Venice, first.' He took her to New College Lane. 'Behold the Bridge of Sighs.'

'Except it's over the street and not over a canal.' She looked at it thoughtfully. 'And it looks more like the Rialto than the Bridge of Sighs.'

He smiled. 'Trust the engineer to notice that. And I suppose you're going to tell me that the one in Cambridge looks more like the one in Venice?'

She grinned. 'No. It's kind of like this one: it's simply the fact that it's a covered bridge. Though at least ours is over the Cam and not over a road.'

'Noted,' he said dryly. 'Score another to Cambridge.'

She smiled back. 'So was the bridge always part of the college?'

'No, it was built in 1913 to join the two parts of Hertford College.' He smiled. 'According to legend, someone did a health survey of the colleges and the students here were the heaviest, so they closed the bridge to make the students take the stairs and get more exercise.'

She laughed. 'You're kidding!'

'Sadly, it's just an urban legend. Apparently you end up taking more stairs if you use the bridge than if you don't, and the bridge has never been closed to students.' He smiled. 'I think it'd be better if they pinched the legend from the proper Bridge of Sighs—that love lasts for ever if you kiss under the bridge at sunset.'

Love lasts for ever if you kiss under the bridge at sunset.

Angel looked at Brandon. She didn't think that he even believed in love, let alone that he thought it could last for ever.

And then she thought about kissing. Remembered what it had felt like when his lips had teased hers, the way he'd sent her pulse thrumming.

She really didn't know what to say. All the words had gone out of her head.

He was still looking at her. And she could see the second his gaze dropped to her mouth. So he was thinking about it, too...

Then he seemed to shake himself. 'Cake. We're supposed to be looking for afternoon tea.'

She seized on the suggestion gratefully. 'Yes. Tea. I take it you know somewhere?'

'Oxford,' he said, 'had the oldest coffee shop in England. Pepys mentioned it in his diary.'

She couldn't quite come up with a Cambridge quote to match that. 'So does it still exist?'

'No,' he admitted. 'But there is another café on the site. And actually I do know somewhere that does good tea.'

The café he took her to turned out to be a stunning building with pillars, lots of gold leaf, chandeliers and potted palms. The waiters were all wearing black suits and white shirts. And the high tea was delightful, a tiered plate with a selection of finger sandwiches, still-warm scones served with clotted cream and strawberry jam, tiny lemon tartlets with a raspberry on top, pistachio macaroons and tiny sticky ginger cakes studded with stem ginger.

'This is perfect,' she said.

He gave her an impish smile. 'Better than Cambridge?'

She rolled her eyes. 'As if I'm ever going to say that.'

'We're on opposite sides in so many ways,' he said.

And yet they were on the same side, too. 'Maybe,' she said, and refilled her cup with Earl Grey tea.

She'd still been thinking about his idea for an updated version of the Mermaid. And she was itching to sketch. 'Can I be rude?' she asked.

'An important phone call you need to make?' he asked wryly.

'No.' She pulled a pad and pencil from her bag. 'Give me five minutes. Drink your tea.'

Brandon rather liked Angel's occasional little flashes of bossiness. And he liked the fact that she'd asked if she could take her attention away from him for a few moments. Too many of his past girlfriends had spent a meal out checking their phones for texts or social media notifications, or taking endless selfies. He'd guess that Angel had never taken a selfie in her life.

It looked as if she was sketching, and her face was really animated as she worked. Clearly she loved what she did. And Brandon wondered when the last time was that he'd felt that kind of passion for something.

Though he knew the answer. It had been before Sam's crash. Brandon had loved driving more than anything else. Racing. Using all his skills to anticipate his competitors' moves and when to make a bid for the front spot. Seeing the chequered flag come down as he went over the line.

He'd lost that along with his brother.

And he didn't know if he'd ever get it back. If anything would ever fill the holes in his life that he didn't usually let himself think about. Angel had suggested focusing on what he loved, but the guilt still got in the way.

Angel finished sketching, then pushed the pad over to him. 'Were you thinking about something like this?'

He stared at the picture. It was only a rough sketch, but it was incredibly close to the picture he'd had in his head when he'd talked to her about the high-end car he wanted to produce.

'I was thinking teal iridescent paint,' she said, 'with chrome accents on the curves here and here.' She pointed out the areas on her sketch. 'Or we could mess about and make it two-tone—say, black and red.'

'And you kept the fins. That's going to affect performance.'

She nodded. 'I guess it depends on the angles. We can tweak the aerodynamics.'

We.

So was she going to work with him? Were they going to turn this whole thing on its head and do something new, instead of concentrating on the old Stone's and McKenzie's firms? Did this mean they'd be partners—and not just in business?

The thought made him feel dizzy.

He hadn't expected this—for them to be this compatible, to see things the same way. It scared him and thrilled him at the same time.

'A rear spoiler would work better,' he said.

'Yes, you're right. Give me a minute.' She took the pad back and did a second sketch.

Brandon couldn't take his eyes off her. Her hands were deft and sure, and he couldn't help wondering what they'd feel like against his skin. And when she was all serious and concentrating like that, she looked stunning. It made him want to lean over the table and kiss her, regardless of who was around them.

This was bad.

Really bad.

He needed to get himself back under control. He didn't *do* relationships. Falling for the CEO of his family's bitter rival would be very stupid indeed.

She pushed the pad back across the table to him. The second sketch was very similar to the first, but this time she'd drawn a spoiler instead of the fins.

'That's brilliant. Can I keep these?' he asked. And then he frowned. 'I mean for *me*. Not because I'm going to run off to another designer and ask them to work on this or anything like that.' But because working closely together, she'd made him remember how much he'd loved cars. How much he still loved them, deep down. And it was the first time he'd felt this kind of lightness of spirit in years.

She smiled. 'Sure you can.'

'Thank you.' He folded the pieces of paper and put them into his wallet.

When they'd finished their tea—which she insisted on buying, and he decided not to argue because he knew how independent she was, plus then he could claim it was his turn to pay for whatever they did next—they walked back to his car. Somehow his fingers ended up tangling with hers, but she didn't pull away and neither did he.

Weird.

He just wasn't the soppy sort.

Yet here he was, walking hand in hand with her through Oxford. He'd taken her punting. She'd bought him afternoon tea. They'd talked about their mythical joint car and come up with a first design tweak to it. And his heart felt lighter than he would've ever thought possible.

Funny how he didn't want today to end.

She just made polite conversation with him on the way back to the factory. He didn't invite her in, after he'd parked next to her car—the last thing he wanted was for Eric to appear and come out with some stupid comment and ruin the mood—but, before she could get out, he said, 'I've really enjoyed today.'

She turned to face him, her violet eyes all huge and beautiful. 'Me, too.'

'Maybe,' he said carefully, 'we could do something at the weekend. If you're not busy.' Which was a bit disingenuous of him, he knew, because she'd more or less admitted to him that she didn't have a social life.

'I'd like that,' she said, rewarding him with that gorgeous shy smile.

'Can I call you?' God, he sounded like a seventeen-year-old. The weird thing was, she made him feel like a seventeen-year-old, ready to conquer the world. When had he last felt like this—as if there was hope and light at the end of the tunnel, instead of a black hole dragging him in?

'Yes.'

He smiled, leaned forward and touched his mouth to hers. Just once, enough to remember the feel of her lips against his but not for long enough to let him lose control. 'Drive safely. Text me when you get home.'

'I will.'

He got out of his car and leaned against it, watching her drive away. Once she was out of sight, he headed for his desk.

Gina smiled at him as he walked back into his office. 'Angel not with you?'

'She's gone home.'

'I see.' Gina paused. 'I liked her.'

Which sounded to Brandon as if Gina had been talking to his mother. 'Uh-huh,' he said, trying to sound casual.

'I mean *really* like her—and I think you do, too.'

He groaned. Yes, she'd definitely been talking to his mother. 'We're not discussing this, Gina.'

'She's nice. Really nice. And I think she understands you a lot better than those clothes horses you normally date.'

She did. Which was one of the things that worried him. He didn't want to get close to her; yet, at the same time, he did. 'This wasn't a date.'

'No?' Gina scoffed.

He smiled. 'This morning was business.'

'But this afternoon was a date?'

'She hadn't been to Oxford before. We did some touristy things. As you'd do with someone you're trying to sort out a business deal with,' he said.

'Hmm,' Gina said.

Busted. But he still wasn't going to admit to it, because he really wasn't sure how he felt. Angel McKenzie was nothing like he'd expected her to be. She made him feel all kinds of things he couldn't quite pin down, and it made him feel ever so slightly out of control.

'It's purely business,' he said again, knowing that he was lying to himself as well as to his PA. 'I'll make the coffee.'

'You do that, sweetie.' Gina wrinkled her nose at him. 'It'd be good to see you happy.'

'No matchmaking.'

''Course not,' she deadpanned.

She'd *definitely* been talking to his mother. 'Coffee,' Brandon said, and fled before Gina could grill him any further.

CHAPTER EIGHT

ON FRIDAY MORNING, Brandon texted Angel.

When are you free for me to Skype you?

She really appreciated the fact that he'd remembered she preferred to speak face to face rather than struggle with the phone.

Lunchtime? she suggested. Around twelve?

OK. Talk to you then.

He was as good as his word. 'Hey. I've found something we can do this weekend.'

'What?'

'It's a surprise.'

She narrowed her eyes at him. 'I'm an engineer. I'm not keen on surprises.'

'It's something you'll definitely like,' he said. 'But it does mean staying away overnight. Is that OK?'

Overnight.

Did that mean he wanted to take things further with her—and this soon?

Her worries must've been obvious, because he said, 'I planned to book us separate rooms.'

'OK,' she said cautiously. 'As long as I pay for my own room.'

'We'll talk about that later,' he said. 'Can I pick you up at nine tomorrow morning?'

Meaning he'd have to leave Oxford at the crack of dawn? It still gave her no clue about where they were going; but she had to admit to herself that she was looking forward to spending time with him. They'd definitely become closer, this last week, and she was starting to feel comfortable with him. 'All right.'

'Good. I'll see you then.' His voice and his eyes were filled with warmth. 'Text me your address so I can put it in the satnav.'

'Will do. What's the dress code?'

'Casual. And do you have good walking shoes?'

'Yes.'

'Excellent. Bring them,' he said. 'I'll see you tomorrow.'

So they were going walking? But where? And wouldn't it make more sense for her to meet him wherever it was, rather than make him drive for two hours to her place first? Surely she was out of his way?

Though Angel was pretty sure that if she asked him straight out, he'd come up with some excuse that told her even less.

On Saturday morning her doorbell rang at nine o'clock precisely.

Brandon was wearing faded jeans, boots, and a white shirt with the sleeves rolled up halfway to his elbow and the neck unbuttoned. He looked utterly gorgeous; but he also seemed to be unaware of it rather than preening like a peacock. A couple of weeks ago, she'd had him pegged as arrogant and vain, but she was learning that he was nothing of the kind. And she really liked the man she was getting to know.

'Hi.' He leaned forward and kissed her on the cheek. 'Ready to go?'

She indicated her small overnight bag, and he grinned. 'That's another good thing about dating an engineer. She packs sensibly.'

She pulled a face at him. 'That's horribly sexist. That, or you've been dating the wrong women.'

'Probably true on both counts,' he said with a smile. 'My car's parked a couple of doors down from you.'

She set the alarm, locked the front door and followed him to what turned out to be a newish and very expensive sports car.

'How many cars do you actually own?' she asked. There was the Mermaid, the car he'd driven to St Albans, and the one he'd driven in Oxford; this made at least the fourth different one.

'I've always liked cars. And I've been lucky enough over time to afford to indulge my whims without making life hard for anyone else. It's an entirely un-guilty pleasure.' He looked totally unabashed. 'Come and see my collection some time.'

'Is that as in "come and see my etchings"?' she asked wryly.

'It wasn't a ruse to get you into bed.' He paused. 'Though now you've made me think about doing precisely that.'

That made her think about it, too, and she went hot all over. She was glad of the excuse to put her bag in the boot of his car to cover her confusion.

Brandon noticed that Angel had gone quiet on him by the time she climbed into the passenger seat, and he wondered if he'd just pushed her too far. He needed to get the easiness back with her.

'You can pick the music, if you like,' he said.

She raised an eyebrow. 'You're telling me you don't already have a driving playlist sorted out?'

'Like the compilations you can buy which have the same songs on, just in a different order? No.' He smiled. 'There is something I like to drive to, but you have to promise to sing it with me.'

She shook her head. 'I'm not a good singer.'

'Neither am I. But we're the only ones who can hear us,' he pointed out, 'so who cares?'

'I guess.'

He put on the track and gave her a sidelong glance; OK, so it was retro, but she had to know it? 'Mr Blue Sky' never failed to put him in a good mood when he was on a long business drive; hopefully it would have the same effect on her.

To his relief, she joined in, albeit a little hesitantly at first. But when he hammed up the falsetto bits of the song, she was smiling—laughing with him rather than at him. And then suddenly the easiness was back between them. They were just a girl and a guy, driving down the motorway for a weekend away, and life felt good. Enough for him to forget that he was supposed to be keeping her at a distance.

When they stopped at the service station for a comfort break, Angel asked, 'Do you want me to drive for a bit?'

'No, it's fine—unless you're tired of being a passenger?'

'I just thought you might want a break, especially as you had to drive for two hours to get to me first.'

He liked the fact that she'd considered that. His previous girlfriends had always taken for granted that he'd do all the driving. Or maybe he'd chosen them partly because he knew they'd take him for granted and wouldn't get close to him, and he'd be able to walk away from them with barely a second thought.

'I know, but I like driving.' Particularly with her, though he wasn't going to spook her—or himself—by saying it. He didn't want her to back away. Or for him to lose that feeling and slide back into the darkness again.

Finally, they turned off the main road onto a series of narrow, winding rural roads which led them through pretty Cumbrian villages.

'This is a really gorgeous part of the world,' she said, 'but where exactly are we going?'

'The satnav claims it's about half a mile further,' he said, and turned into a very long driveway.

At the end was a sprawling ancient farmhouse built of grey stone. 'Here we are,' he said when he'd parked, and climbed out of the car.

'Who lives here?' she asked, joining him.

'Bill Edwards.'

Which left her none the wiser. Why did Brandon want to visit this mysterious Mr Edwards, in the middle of nowhere? And why was he being so secretive about it?

He rang the doorbell, and an elderly man answered, a black Labrador with a grey muzzle at his heels. 'Mr Edwards? Brandon Stone,' he said. 'And this is Angel McKenzie.'

'Good to meet you.' Mr Edwards shook their hands warmly. 'Come in, come in. Martha, we need tea for our guests.' He ushered them into the kitchen and indicated for them to sit down at the scrubbed pine table; his wife greeted them and bustled round the kitchen, preparing tea.

'Is there anything I can do to help?' Angel asked.

'No, love, you sit down and relax,' Martha said with a smile.

The dog sat at Brandon's feet and rested his chin on

Brandon's knee; Brandon absently scratched behind the dog's ears, and Angel found an unexpected lump in her throat. The dog clearly liked him, and didn't they say that animals were good judges of character?

'So you're a relative of Jimmy McKenzie, Miss McKenzie?' Mr Edwards asked.

'His granddaughter,' she confirmed, 'and please call me Angel.'

'Then you can call me Bill,' he said. 'And you work in the family firm?'

She nodded. 'Dad retired a couple of years ago. I took over from him.'

'And you head up Stone's,' Bill said to Brandon.

'I do,' Brandon said.

Bill's weathered face creased with a smile. 'Well, it's a surprise you're even in the same room as each other, let alone driven all the way up here together.'

'We're…' Brandon looked at Angel. 'Friends.'

Their relationship was a good deal more complicated than that, but she wasn't about to contradict him.

'Well. It's fitting that you should come here together.'

Angel was still mystified, until after Bill and Martha had made them drink two cups of tea and eat a slice of the lightest, fluffiest Victoria sponge she'd ever tasted. And then Bill led them outside.

'Here she is,' he said with pride as he ushered them through a door.

Angel blinked as she saw the ancient car sitting in the garage. 'Is that what I think it is?'

'Did Brandon not tell you he was bringing you to see it?' Martha asked.

'No. I wanted it to be a surprise,' Brandon explained.

'I can't quite take this in. That's the first McKenzie-Stone car,' Angel said. 'I've only ever seen photographs of one. I wasn't even sure there were any left in existence.' And to see one in such perfect condition, obviously well loved, was incredible.

'Brandon here's been trying to persuade me to sell it to him for months,' Bill said.

And then she understood. This was Brandon's 'missing' car from his collection. The one he wanted for the museum at Stone's. He'd said that the owner couldn't be persuaded to sell by offering more money; clearly he'd hit on a strategy that he thought might be rather more effective.

Using her as a kind of leverage.

Bitterness filled her mouth, but she forced herself to smile. 'It's lovely to see it, and especially in such amazing condition. So have you had it for very long?'

'It's been in the family since day one,' Bill said. 'My grandfather bought one of the first ones they ever made, and he handed it down to my dad, who handed it down to me.' He looked regretful. 'Me and Martha, we lost our lad when he was tiny, or it would've gone to him.'

'I'm sorry,' Angel said.

'No, lass, don't cry for us. We've had a good life,' Bill said. 'But our nephew, he's not really one for classic cars. He'd rather have the money to use on some newfangled equipment for the farm. And it's time this old girl went somewhere she'll be appreciated.'

'Brandon will look after her properly,' Angel said. Even though she was furious with him for using her to get his own way, she couldn't deny that he'd do right by the car.

'It was a shame they didn't make more,' Bill said. 'But your grandfathers fell out.'

'Yes.' And she and Brandon would be having a big falling-out, once they'd left here, she thought crossly. 'It's a shame that they let love get in the way. I didn't really know my grandparents, but my mum once let it slip that Esther really regretted the rift between Jimmy and Barnaby. I think she wanted to do something to heal it.'

'But I think both our grandfathers were too stubborn to make the first move,' Brandon said.

'Something like that,' Angel agreed. Before today, she'd thought that maybe she and Brandon could change things and heal the rift between their families. But maybe not. She'd believed that he'd wanted to go away for the weekend with her, whereas clearly he'd seen this whole thing as a business opportunity. He'd opened up to her in Oxford, or so she'd thought; but maybe he'd just been playing her all along. What a naive, stupid fool she was. He was a Stone. Ruthless to the bone.

'You came here together to see the car,' Bill said thoughtfully. 'Does this mean there could be a new McKenzie-Stone car in the future?'

The car she'd sketched for Brandon. Their joint idea.

That definitely wasn't going to happen now.

Before she could open her mouth to say no, Brandon said, 'We're talking. Which is more than our families have done for decades.'

'And that's a good start.' Bill held out his hand. 'I'll sell the car to you, Brandon. It's a deal.'

Brandon shook his hand warmly. 'Thank you. I'll take good care of it.'

'I know,' Bill said. 'Because your young lady vouched for you.'

She was absolutely not his young lady. No way was Brandon Stone ever going to kiss her again, let alone anything else. But Angel would prefer to have this particular fight in private.

Once Brandon had wrapped up the terms of the deal—and Angel had insisted on washing up the tea things—they left the farmhouse.

As soon as they were out of sight of the farmhouse, Angel said, 'I don't appreciate being used.'

'Used?'

Was he going to deny what he'd done? Angel felt her temper snap. 'You told me about this car, but you said the owner wouldn't sell to you. Clearly you worked out that family and history mean a lot more to him than money, and that's why you brought me along. As leverage. And I don't appreciate it.'

'Actually, I didn't use you.'

She scoffed. 'Come off it.'

'Bill told me he wouldn't sell the car, and I'd pretty much given up trying to persuade him. But I wanted to see the car for myself anyway, and I thought you might like to see it, too—considering that your grandfather built it with mine.'

Which was true. Part of her had been thrilled to see a piece of their joint family history, something from happier times. But she also knew that Brandon was competitive and he liked to win. He'd use every business advantage he could get. 'So are you saying you *didn't* use me to get him to change his mind?'

'No. If I'd thought that strategy would work, I would've contacted you months ago, when I first started talking to Bill, and I would've discussed it with you first.' His mouth thinned. 'Actually, I'm pretty upset that you think I'd be so underhand. I thought we'd got past our family rift and all the nonsense the press writes about me, and we were actually getting to know each other for who we are, not who we thought each other might be.'

His words made Angel feel guilty, but she still couldn't get rid of the suspicion. Not knowing how to deal with the situation, she lapsed into silence. He was clearly just as angry, because he didn't try to make conversation all the way to Keswick.

But when he parked outside the hotel, he turned to her. 'I really wasn't using you today, Angel. We're in separate rooms, so technically we can ignore each other for the rest of today—but then we're going to have a really horrible drive home tomorrow.' He folded his arms. 'I don't want to fight with you. And I'm sorry for not being honest with you right from the start. You told me you didn't like surprises and I didn't listen to you. I thought I was being so clever. I should've just told you that Bill owned one of the first McKenzie-Stone cars and I wanted to see it, and I wanted to share it with you because I thought you'd like to see it as well.'

His eyes were utterly sincere, and guilt flooded through her. Maybe she'd got it wrong after all. And if he'd told her in advance what they were going to see, she would've been really pleased that he'd asked her to go with him. She took a deep breath. 'Then I'm sorry for jumping to conclusions—and for judging you without listening to what you had to say first.'

'Apology accepted,' he said.

'I accept your apology, too.'

'So we're good?'

'We're good,' she confirmed. 'Though I still kind of want to smack you for making me feel used.'

'It sounds to me as if I'd be taking the smack for someone else,' he said. 'Who hurt you, Angel?'

'Nobody.'

He looked as if he didn't believe her; but how could she explain without telling him the shameful truth about her past? The college students who'd seen her as the ice maiden, a challenge to boast about. She couldn't remember their names or their faces now, but she still remembered the hurt when she'd realised they weren't interested in her: they were only interested in boosting their egos and their reputations by being the one who conquered the girl who said no.

To her relief, he dropped the subject and they booked into the hotel. He'd been true to his word and booked them separate rooms. She'd just finished unpacking when there was a knock at her door. Brandon stood in the corridor. 'I, um, was wondering if you might like to go for a walk. Considering we're about ten minutes away from the Derwent and the weather's good.'

And he had pretty much told her about this bit of the weekend in advance, asking her to bring walking shoes.

Guessing that this was a kind of peace offering, she nodded. 'I'll just change my shoes.'

'Come and get me when you're ready,' he said.

She felt awkward, knocking on his door.

'Have you forgiven me yet?' he asked when he opened the door. 'Because I really didn't do anything wrong.'

'I guess.'

She walked alongside him towards the lake, and eventually his hand brushed against hers. Once, twice. She let her hand brush against his. And then finally he linked her fingers with his. Neither of them said anything, and walking in silence among such beautiful scenery eventually lifted her mood.

'It's lovely out here. I haven't been to the Lakes since I was small.'

'Me, neither,' he said. 'We took a boat out. Not here—I can't quite remember where. I was desperate to help row the boat, but I wasn't strong enough. Then Dad sat me on his knee and suddenly I could move the oar.' He smiled. 'Dad was doing all the work, but he let me think I could do it.'

'You're close to your parents?' she asked.

'Yes. That's why I don't race any more. Dad hid it better than Mum, but I know how much he worried. When he had that heart attack and I thought I was going to lose him as well as Sammy, only a couple of weeks apart...' He shuddered. 'Thankfully he recovered. They're both doing OK now.'

'I'm glad.' She tightened her fingers round his. 'And I meant what I said to Bill Edwards. You'll do right by his car.'

'It'll be in pride of place at the museum,' he said. 'What about you?'

'Me?'

'You're close to your parents?'

She nodded. 'I see them or speak to them most days, though they're on an extended tour of Europe at the moment, seeing all the places they've always wanted to see but didn't have time because Dad was so busy at the factory. Mum sent me a selfie of them at the Colosseum yesterday.'

He smiled. 'My mum hasn't quite got the hang of selfies. And the family dog's not very co-operative when she tries to take his picture.'

She smiled back. 'Bill's dog liked you.'

'I like dogs,' he said. 'I've been thinking about getting one. But I'm away on business a lot, so it wouldn't be fair.'

'I can imagine you punting with a spaniel sitting patiently on the deck.'

'Yeah. I'd enjoy that.'

And all of a sudden she had the weirdest picture in her head. Brandon standing on the platform of a punt, the dog sitting on the deck, and herself on the red velvet seat—accompanied by a little boy who was the spitting image of Brandon and desperate to help his father propel the punt along the river, and a baby cradled on her lap.

Where on earth had that come from?

She'd been so focused on the business that she hadn't really thought about her future relationships. She'd never really been one for fantasising about weddings, even when she was small and playing with her cousins. So why was she thinking about it now? And why Brandon?

It spooked her slightly, but she couldn't make the picture in her head go away.

'Everything OK?' he asked.

'Sure.' She gave him her brightest smile, not wanting to admit to what she'd been thinking about.

They stayed by the lake long enough for dusk to fall, then headed back to the hotel for dinner.

'You know what Bill was saying, about the first new McKenzie-Stone car in decades... We could do that,' he said. 'The one you sketched for me.'

'That was just a sketch,' she said. 'It's very different from a full design spec.'

'I know.' He paused. 'You've already said no to my job offer, so I'm not going to ask you again. But maybe we could do this one thing together. You design it, I make it, and it goes out under our joint name.'

It was so very, very tempting.

But they were going to have to heal the rift between their families first. 'We'll see,' she prevaricated.

'Isn't that what people say when they don't want to come straight out with a no?' he asked wryly.

'It'd be a big project. A couple of years, maybe, from the initial thoughts to final production. I'm not sure either of us could fit it in.'

'We could make the time.'

'Maybe.'

'So what's your big ambition?' he asked.

'For McKenzie's or for me?'

'Both.'

'I guess it's the same thing,' she said. 'I want to design the iconic car for my generation. Granddad made the Mermaid, Dad made the Luna, and I...' She stopped, realising how close she'd come to telling him about the Frost.

'You,' he said, 'will make something amazing, because your ideas are great.'

Should she tell him?

But they were still business rivals. And the Frost was still under wraps. Better to say nothing for now. Though it warmed her that he actually seemed to believe in her.

After dinner, they sat in the hotel's garden and watched the stars come out. As the night air began to cool, she shivered.

'Cold?'

'A bit,' she admitted.

He slid his arm round her shoulders. 'Better?'

'A little.'

'That was a polite fib,' he said. 'Let's go inside.'

But he didn't take his arm away as they walked back into the hotel.

Outside the door to her room, he said, 'Come and sit with me for a while.'

Her mouth went dry.

'Just sit with me,' he said. 'I'm not going to push you into anything you don't want.'

She believed him. The problem was, she was starting to want more. 'OK.'

'Your choice,' he said as he unlocked the door. 'Chair or bed?' He paused. 'Or we could both sit in the chair.'

'Both?'

'Like this.' He scooped her up, sat down and settled her in his lap.

To keep her balance, she slid her arms round his neck.

'You know what you said to me about hating myself being pointless because it won't bring Sam back?'

She winced. 'Sorry. That was a bit harsh.'

'Don't apologise. It was something I needed to hear.' He leaned his forehead against hers. 'It's true about the car, too.'

'The car?' She didn't quite understand.

'It was Sammy's dream to complete the museum collection,' he said. 'So when this opportunity came up… It's why I wanted to buy the car. For Sammy.'

'And it doesn't make any difference?' she asked softly.

'It doesn't make any difference,' he confirmed. 'The hole in the centre of my world's still there.'

She stroked his face. 'I'm sorry. But I bet he's proud of you.'

'What, for haranguing an old man for months?' He lifted one shoulder in a half-shrug.

'If you'd told Bill Edwards why you wanted the car so much, he probably would've sold it to you months ago.'

He frowned. 'Why?'

'Because you weren't doing it for you, you were doing it for Sam. Meaning you're not one of the ruthless Stones.'

'Ruthless?' He stared at her for a moment, then sighed. 'OK. I guess you have a point. After your grandmother broke my grandfather's heart, apparently he was pretty focused on the business.'

'But he must've fallen in love with someone else, or you wouldn't be here,' she pointed out.

'I guess.' He paused. 'I didn't really know Barnaby. He died when I was too young to remember him. But Dad was always pretty focused on the business, too.' He grimaced. 'I know he tried to buy McKenzie's in the last recession.'

'That kind of explains why my dad always muttered about your family being ruthless,' she said thoughtfully.

'He sold his entire private collection of cars to make sure he didn't have to sell McKenzie's.'

'A whole collection at short notice?' Brandon grimaced. 'The sharks would've circled and he would've got less than it was worth.'

'It was enough to keep the bank happy,' she said dryly. 'So is that why you want to buy McKenzie's now? For your dad, or for Sam?'

'Maybe,' Brandon said. 'I don't know if Sam would've wanted to buy you out or not. We never discussed it.' He sighed. 'You're right. Sam was the best of us, but nearly all the Stone men are ruthless. Dad was—until Sammy died. It changed him.'

She could believe that. But Brandon... Brandon was different. 'I'm not so sure that you're ruthless,' she said.

He shook his head. 'I always went out on the track with the aim of being first past the finishing line. There have been times when I could've let someone win a race. When maybe I should've let them win, because I knew they'd been having a hard time; winning a race might've helped them turn things around.'

'And what if they'd found out the truth later—that their own skill and efforts weren't really enough to let them win? It would've punched a hole right through their victory and probably made them feel worse than if they'd come second,' she pointed out. 'Anyway, if you were really ruthless, you would've replaced Gina ages ago with someone younger and with longer legs.'

He scoffed. 'Gina's an excellent secretary. I don't need to replace her.'

'She's a bit more than that,' Angel said. 'She mothers you.'

He raised an eyebrow. 'I can hardly sack my mum's best friend. Particularly as she does a good job.'

'I think you like having her around.'

'Gina's been good to me,' he said softly. 'She's the only one at the factory who believed I could do it when I took over from Dad.'

That truly shocked her. 'Didn't your parents believe in you?'

'Sammy's death broke them.' He looked away. 'I don't think they could believe in anything, right then. So I had to step up to the plate. I couldn't let my family down.'

'Even though Sammy's death broke you, too?' she asked softly.

'I thought working until I was practically comatose from tiredness would get me through it. It kind of did. That and burning the candle the other end and still doing all the racing driver social stuff. But I still don't know how to make the empty spaces go away,' he said, his grey eyes filled with sadness. 'Nothing works.'

She didn't know how to make him feel better, but she had to try. There was only one thing she could think of that might fill the empty spaces.

It was a risk.

A huge risk.

But one she was prepared to take. She leaned forward and kissed him.

His eyes went very dark. 'Angel, my self-control's pretty good, but it's not perfect.'

She felt the colour flood through her cheeks. 'Sorry.'

He stole a kiss. 'Don't apologise.' Then he sighed and traced her lower lip with the pad of his thumb. 'Maybe this is a bad idea. Maybe I should just see you back to your room.'

'Or maybe,' she said, 'this is a good idea.'

His eyes widened. 'Are you suggesting…?'

For a moment, she couldn't breathe. This might be the

most monumentally stupid thing she'd ever done. Or it might be the best idea she'd ever had.

There was only one way to find out.

'Yes. Make love with me, Brandon,' she whispered.

She could feel the tension in his body. 'Are you sure about this?'

Not entirely. But she was tired of being a coward. 'Yes.'

CHAPTER NINE

AFTERWARDS, BRANDON LAY with Angel curled in his arms.

And he was absolutely terrified.

He'd always kept emotional distance between himself and his girlfriends. Always. But he'd let Angel closer than he'd ever let anyone in his life. Told her things he never even discussed with his closest family. He hadn't even sat at Sammy's grave and spilled this kind of stuff, and his brother's grave was the place where he went to spill things. When nobody could hear.

What made him even antsier was that, at the same time, he felt at peace with the world. And it wasn't just the sweet relaxation he usually felt after sex. This was something different. As if something had shifted inside him. As if the empty spaces weren't empty any more.

Was he falling in love with Angel McKenzie?

And what was he going to do about it? Particularly as there was something he and Angel really had to discuss.

OK. Time for a reality check. 'Angel,' he said, stroking her hair. 'We need to talk.'

'Uh-huh.' There was a pause, and then her voice sounded all super-bright. 'Is this where you tell me this was a mistake, it's your fault and not mine, and I need to go back to my own room?'

She hadn't pulled her punches. He dragged in a breath. 'No. Do you really think I'm that cold?'

Her silence confirmed his worst fears.

He sighed. 'The press has a lot to answer for. That's not who I... Well, I admit, I have done that in the past, and it wasn't very gallant of me. But I don't want you to go.'

'So what do you want to talk about?'

'The elephant in the room.'

'What elephant?'

He stole another kiss. 'OK. If you want me to be the one to say it. You just gave me your virginity.'

She blushed. He'd never seen anyone go so red before. 'It's so ridiculous, being a virgin at the age of thirty in this day and age.'

'No, it means...' That it was important to her. And he felt incredibly guilty. How could he explain that without making her feel awkward?

She bit her lip and looked away. 'I'm just not good at relationships. I was too shy to date anyone at school, then somehow everyone at university thought of me as an ice maiden, and I didn't want to be just a challenge that people boasted about conquering.'

'That,' he said, 'shows incredible strength of character. You didn't let anyone push you into doing anything you didn't want to do.'

'So you don't think I'm—well—pathetic? Or there's something wrong with me?'

'What?' He stared at her in utter shock. 'You're kidding. You're not pathetic in the slightest and there's nothing wrong with you.' He dragged in a breath. 'I feel honoured, actually. That you trusted me. And I feel guilty, because if you were saving—'

'—myself for my wedding night?' She cut in. 'I wasn't. And I wasn't using you to get rid of my virginity, either.

I… I could see you were hurting, and I wanted to make you feel better, and…'

'One thing led to another,' he finished.

She lifted her chin. 'I don't regret it, so don't feel guilty.'

'I don't regret it, either.' He stroked her face. 'I talk too much.'

'Agreed. Sometimes it's easier to sweep things under the carpet, but you don't do things the easy way, do you?'

'I probably do. That's why Eric calls me Golden Boy.'

'Eric's bitter,' she said. 'And wasn't King Midas—the original golden boy—lonely, when all he had was gold?'

'You scare me,' he said, 'because you see things that other people miss.'

'Comes of lip-reading,' she said lightly.

'Stay with me tonight,' he said, surprising himself.

'Is this a good idea?'

'Probably not,' he admitted. 'But I don't want you to go.'

'I don't want to go, either,' she said.

'Then let's stop talking and just go to sleep.'

She chuckled.

'What's so funny?' he asked.

'You're the one who said we needed to talk.'

'Sometimes,' he said, 'I'm wrong.'

She laughed. 'I'm glad you can admit that.'

'Me, too.' He kissed her.

He reached over to turn off the bedside light, then moved so that his body was curled round hers and his arm was wrapped round her waist, holding her close against him. Her breathing slowed and she relaxed back against him as she fell asleep, but Brandon stayed awake for longer. This was the first time in years that he'd actually shared a bed with someone and it didn't involve just sex. Why had he asked her to stay? Guilt, because he'd taken her virginity? Or was it that her obvious trust in him had made him relax enough to trust her with himself?

He couldn't quite work out how he felt about Angel McKenzie. What he did know was that she'd changed him. She made him feel as if maybe he had a soft centre after all, instead of a heart of granite wrapped around an empty space. He wasn't sure if that was a good thing or a bad, but for now he'd go with it.

The next morning, Brandon woke first and kissed Angel awake. He was rewarded with confusion in those beautiful violet eyes clearing, and then she gave him a smile of pure unadulterated warmth, as if she was glad to be waking in his arms. Weird that it suddenly made him feel as if he were ten feet tall.

'Good morning,' he said softly.

She stroked his face. 'Good morning.'

'Did you sleep OK?'

'Yes.'

'Good.' He couldn't resist stealing another kiss. 'Do you have to be back home as soon as possible?'

'Do you?'

'No. And as we're in one of the most romantic places in England, I thought it might be nice to go for a walk— oh, and holding my hand is obligatory.'

'Are you always this bossy?' she asked, but her eyes were lit with amusement.

'Pretty much.' He grinned. 'So are you, so this is going to be interesting.'

She bit her lip. 'About last night...'

'I stand by what I said,' he said softly. 'I don't regret a second of it. And I still feel really honoured that you trusted me that much.'

He saw her eyes fill with tears, even though she blinked them away immediately.

'Don't cry,' he said. 'Or was it that bad?'

'No, it was…' She paused, as if not knowing what to say.

'If you tell me I'm like your favourite engine…' he teased.

She laughed. 'Ah, but aren't you meant to do nought to top speed more slowly in this sort of thing?'

He liked the fact that she could laugh at herself, even though he knew she'd felt awkward about her inexperience. He held her close, laughing, and kissed the top of her head. 'Let's have a shower and breakfast, and go for that walk.'

Over breakfast, they pored over his phone and discovered that one of the prettiest sights in the Lakes was only a short drive away. The road, being a narrow single track, was busy and they had to wait at several passing places, but finally they were able to park by Wastwater.

'Oh, now that's definitely worth the wait,' Angel said, gesturing to the way the mountains reflected in the water. 'I can see why it's listed as one of the best views.'

'The deepest lake in England,' he said, referring to a page on his phone. 'And that bit over there is Scafell Pike, England's highest mountain.'

'Don't tell me—you've climbed it?' she asked.

He smiled. 'No. And I don't think we have time to do it today. But maybe we could come back, if you want to climb it?'

'I'm happy just to look at it and admire it,' she said, smiling back.

'OK.' He paused. 'Can we…?' He waved his phone at her.

'Selfie? Sure.'

He took a quick snap of them together. Again, it was

weird: he never did this sort of things with his girlfriends. But with Angel, it felt right.

'Send it to me, please?' she asked.

'Sure.' This was definitely starting to feel official. Even six months ago, that feeling would've sent him running as fast as possible in the opposite direction. But he was actually enjoying this.

He enjoyed the drive back to Cambridge even more, because Angel seemed so much more relaxed with him. This time, he shared the driving with her, and it was so good to talk to her about the car and discuss its pros and cons. Particularly as Angel was talking from an engineer's viewpoint, giving him a completely different perspective.

And he enjoyed the fact that she was comfortable with him looking through the music on her phone and choosing what to play. 'This is really retro stuff,' he said. 'Half of this would go better with the Mermaid.'

'If that's an offer…' she teased.

He grinned. 'Oh, it is. If we pick a time when the weather's good, we can have the roof down and drive along the nearest coast.'

'Oxford's pretty much smack in the middle of the country,' she said. 'And Cambridge is a good ninety minutes from the coast. You'd be looking at Norfolk or Suffolk.'

'Fish and chips, ice cream and candy floss,' he said promptly. 'It's a deal.'

She laughed. 'And a kiss-me-quick hat?'

'I'd prefer you to kiss me slowly,' he said. 'But the coast would be fun.'

'I'd like that,' she said.

'Then it's a date. An open-ended one because it's weather-dependent, but a definite date,' he said. And how weird it felt to be planning things in the future with her. Normally he didn't let people that close. But Angel…

Angel was different. She made him want to do this kind of thing.

When they arrived in Cambridge, she turned to him. 'I would offer to cook you dinner before you go back to Oxford, but, um…'

'You have work to do?'

'It's much more shameful than that,' she said. 'I have an empty fridge. And I'm not much of a cook anyway. I normally get in a stack of ready meals from the supermarket to keep me going during the week, but I forgot to go shopping on Friday night.'

'Well, I'm not leaving you here with an empty fridge,' he said. 'The supermarkets are all closed by now, so either we find a nice little pub somewhere or we get a takeaway.'

'Either's fine.' She paused. 'I've got milk.'

'Milk?' He wasn't quite following her line of thought.

'I normally have a protein shake for breakfast before the gym,' she said. 'But the baker round the corner opens really early in the morning. They do the best croissants in Cambridge.'

He caught his breath. 'Are you asking me to stay for breakfast?'

'Inviting you, yes.' She gave him the shyest, cutest smile. 'If you want to.'

Oh, he wanted to. He smiled. 'Provided you let me do the washing up.'

'I thought you said you had troglodyte tendencies?'

'I'm domesticated. To a point.' Though it spooked him slightly how domesticated he wanted to be with her. He could imagine waking up with her on Sunday mornings, lazing in bed with coffee and the papers and a bacon sandwich.

Her little Victorian terraced house turned out to be totally what he'd expected: neat, with everything in its place. There were family photographs everywhere, and arty black and white prints of close-up details from classic cars. And it felt way more like home than his own, much larger house. Personal. Full of warmth.

Then again, it was his own fault for using an interior designer instead of spending the time to make his house feel like a personal space.

Just as she'd promised, the croissants at breakfast were superb. And leaving her after he'd insisted on doing the washing up after breakfast turned out to be a real wrench. He actually missed her all the way to Oxford, and the only time the ache went was when he threw himself into work.

A few unexpected glitches meant that he didn't have time to meet up with Angel during the week, even if they'd driven to a halfway point. And he was shocked by how much he missed her and wanted to be with her.

Dating her had been supposed to be a way of getting her out of his system and persuading her to sell McKenzie's to him, but it hadn't worked out that way. If anything, he wanted to spend more time with her. The sensible side of him knew that he ought to back off right now, before he got in too deeply.

But then he found himself video-calling her.

'Hey,' she said, and smiled at him.

Oh, man. He'd never understood before when people said that someone made their heart flip. Now he did. Angel's smile did exactly that. 'How are you doing?' he asked.

She laughed. 'Say that for me again, but this time in a Joey Tribbiani voice.'

'*Friends* fan, hmm?'

'Joey's the best. Indulge me.'

He grinned and did what she asked.

'Be still, my beating heart.' She fanned herself.

Brandon almost told her how cute she looked, but stopped himself just in time.

'So how are things?' she asked.

'Wall-to-wall meetings.' Some of them with staff who'd had a spat with Eric and needed their feathers unruffled, which drove him crazy. 'How about you?'

'Similar.'

He wasn't going to tell her he missed her.

He *wasn't*.

'Can I see you at the weekend?' He cringed inwardly as the words came out of his mouth. How needy was that?

But she went pink. 'OK.'

'Come to me?' he suggested. 'If you stay overnight Saturday, I'll cook dinner for you.'

'You cook?' She looked surprised. And then she gave him the cheekiest grin. 'Wait. I forgot. You're good at *everything.*'

The breathy little way she said that sent desire lancing straight through him. 'Nearly,' he said. Right now he didn't seem to be very good at keeping his feelings under control. And his voice had gone all husky. He really hoped she hadn't noticed—or, if she had, that she hadn't guessed why.

'I'll be with you at nine,' she promised. 'Send me your postcode for my satnav.'

'I will.' He stopped himself telling her that he missed her. 'See you on Saturday.'

'How does it go?' She wrinkled her nose at him. 'Ah, yes. *Ciao.*'

No. Just no. He was *not* supposed to find it super-cute that she was teasing him about the ridiculously corny way he'd once said goodbye to her. Or want to drop everything and drive for two hours plus whatever hold-ups he encountered on the motorway just to kiss her goodnight.

'*Ciao,*' he drawled, and cut the connection.

* * *

On Saturday morning, Angel drove to Oxford, tingling with anticipation. Would Brandon have changed his mind about their relationship by the time she got there? Because she was pretty sure the women he reportedly saw only lasted three dates, and they'd already gone beyond that. Was he even now rehearsing a speech? *It's not you, it's me...*

But all her doubts melted when she parked on the gravel outside his unexpectedly large house and he walked out of the front door to greet her. The warmth of his kiss told her that he hadn't been rehearsing any speeches at all—and that he'd missed her as much as she'd missed him.

Not that she was going to bring that up. Brandon Stone wasn't the kind of man who liked talking about emotions, and she didn't want to make things awkward between them. And she definitely wasn't going to tell him that she was falling for him. She knew it'd make him run a mile.

'Hey.' She stole another kiss. 'Flashy house, Mr Stone. Are you sure you're not a secret rock star?'

He laughed. 'No. You'll probably find the garage more interesting than the house.'

'Garage? That looks more like an aircraft hangar,' she teased.

'Yeah, yeah.' But he grinned and held her close.

'So do I get to see your collection?'

'Later,' he said. 'And I'm not fobbing you off—I'm looking forward to showing you.' He stole another kiss. 'It's your fault you have to wait.'

'How?' she asked.

'Because,' he said, 'you've given me back the joy I used to find in racing cars. I lost it for a while.'

Since his brother's death, she guessed.

'One of the local stately homes is having an open

day—usually they're not open to the public, but today it's a charity thing to show off their garden. And there just so happens to be a vintage car rally in their deer park. I thought you might like to go.'

'Great idea. I take it we're going in the Mermaid?'

'We are. Want to drive?'

'Stupid question,' she said, and kissed him.

Once he'd taken her bag inside and locked up the house, he handed her the car keys. 'I'll direct you,' he said.

Angel thoroughly enjoyed driving the car—and she enjoyed being with Brandon even more. The stately home's garden turned out to be amazing, full of cottage garden plants with butterflies and bees everywhere and a secret garden full of roses. She loved wandering round, hand in hand with Brandon—particularly when he managed to find several hidden alcoves where he could steal a kiss in private.

The vintage car rally was fabulous, too, and they had a wonderful time arguing over the merits of their favourites and trying to convince each other to change their mind.

'You know, the red car on the end there,' Brandon said, 'has been used in a film.'

Cars and films. Angel went cold for a moment. Was this his way of telling her that he knew about Triffid and the Frost? Triffid's PR team had put her in touch with several magazines for features, but they'd all been thoroughly screened and there was an embargo in place. Then again, no matter how careful you were, there were always leaks. News like that would filter through pretty quickly to fellow car manufacturers. Maybe that was how he knew.

But then he turned the conversation to something else, and it didn't feel like quite the right time to tell him about why she didn't need to sell McKenzie's to him.

Back at his house, Brandon proved that his flashy

kitchen wasn't all for show. He produced grilled bream, crushed new potatoes with mint and butter, and steamed asparagus and samphire, all beautifully presented.

'That was utterly gorgeous,' she said when she'd finished. 'If I hadn't been sitting at your kitchen table and seen you cooking this from scratch, I would've guessed that you'd hired a caterer.'

'I did cheat by buying the cheesecake,' he admitted. 'I'm rubbish at puddings.'

'Tsk—and I thought you were good at everything,' she teased.

'Just for that,' he said, 'you can wait for your pudding until you agree that I am.' And he hauled her over his shoulder and carried her off to his bed.

Back in Cambridge, Angel called her parents. 'Hey. So how's Florence?' she asked.

'Wonderful. Is everything OK with you?' Max asked.

'Yes. And you don't need to worry about the business. Everything's fine.'

'Of course it is, with my girl in charge.' She could practically hear the smile in her father's voice. 'But you sound a bit worried.'

'I, um… This might be a bit of a Romeo and Juliet moment.'

'We're in Florence, not Verona,' her father teased.

'I'm, um, seeing someone.' She swallowed hard. 'Brandon Stone.'

'Larry Stone's son?' Max asked, sounding shocked.

'Is it a problem for you, Dad?'

He blew out a breath. 'Actually, love, it is. The Stones are a ruthless bunch. I remember Mum saying once that she chose Dad over Barnaby, because Dad was kind and

Barnaby was driven. Barnaby's sons and his grandsons are chips off the old block—and I don't want you to get hurt.'

'I'm thirty, Dad.'

'I know. But you're my daughter, and I worry about you. If you really have to date the guy, date him. But be careful.' He paused. 'And if he hurts you, he'll have me to deal with.'

'Dad, it's not going to be like that. But thank you for—well, doing what dads do.'

'I meant it,' Max said softly. 'If he hurts you…'

'He won't. He's actually a decent guy.'

'Who's photographed with a different woman on his arm every week.'

'That's the press blowing stuff out of proportion, Dad,' she said softly.

Max sighed. 'All right. You're old enough to know what you're doing. But please be careful,' he said again.

She didn't exactly have her father's blessing, but she didn't quite have his opposition, either, Angel thought. He might have a point about her needing to be careful. She liked spending time with Brandon, but their families were at loggerheads. And Brandon himself had told her that he was about to start developing cars that would be in direct competition with hers. He could afford to drop his prices enough to undercut hers and torpedo her sales.

But she didn't think he'd do that. Brandon had integrity. She'd trusted him with herself, and he hadn't let her down. So could she trust him enough to talk to him about her business—to share the new design with him? It was a risk: it would mean breaking confidentiality, giving him what could be a business advantage. But he wasn't the ruthless, selfish playboy she'd originally thought he was. He had a heart—one that had been broken—and he kept people at a distance to protect himself. Yet he'd trusted her enough to let her close. Maybe she should do the same. She thought about it all week.

And thought about it some more over the next weekend, when Brandon swept her off to the coast in the Mermaid so they could walk hand in hand by the edge of the sea.

The way she felt when she was with him—it was like nothing else she'd ever experienced.

Love?

Maybe. But she'd spent so long struggling on her own, trying to keep everything together and yet unable to talk to her parents about the problems because she was trying to protect them and let them enjoy their retirement. Just for once it would be good to lean on someone, share her worries—and share the joy, too.

He'd said she'd given him back the joy he'd once found in cars. And she'd really value his opinion of the Frost. Maybe it was time to trust him back.

'Can we call in to the factory?' she asked on the way back to her house.

'Sure. Is there something you need to do for work?'

'No. There's something I want to show you.'

He gave her a sidelong look. 'Such as?'

'You'll see when we get there.'

'Should I be worried?'

She smiled. 'No.' But her own fears were back. Was she taking too much of a risk?

As if he guessed that she was warring with herself mentally, he didn't push her to talk further until they got to the factory and she took him into the partitioned-off area.

'This is confidential,' she warned. 'Strictly confidential.'

'Got it. So what did you want to show me?'

'This,' she said, and whisked the tarpaulin off her prototype.

'Oh.' He prowled round it, clearly analysing it and inspecting every little detail. And then he straightened up. 'I'm assuming the design is all yours?'

'And I helped put it together. The engine's all mine,' she said.

'It's *stunning*,' he said. 'May I?' His hand hovered above the bonnet.

She nodded, and he ran his fingers lightly over the paintwork. 'I love the lines of it. And I've never seen a colour like this. Did you use one of your granddad's paint techniques—something from the Mermaid years?'

'No. I wanted the car to be shimmery, like the Mermaid, but I wanted the effect to be otherworldly rather than undersea,' she said. 'It's plain ivory paint.'

'No way is that just ivory,' he said.

'With a little bit of silver pearlescence—I wanted it to be like the moonlight glittering on grass on a winter night.' She paused. 'It's called the McKenzie Frost.'

'And that colour's perfect for the name.' He indicated the door. 'Can I sit in it?'

'Sure.'

He climbed inside, and again there was silence while he looked at the interior.

And then he leaned over and opened the passenger door.

'I want one,' he said simply.

Then she realised how tense her muscles had been while she'd waited for his verdict. 'You like it?'

'More than like it,' he corrected. 'And I want one in my private collection.'

'Technically, it doesn't exist. This is the prototype. It's had a couple of photo shoots, but the world hasn't seen it yet,' she warned.

'Then put me at the head of your pre-order list because I mean it—I really, really want one. And I don't care how much it costs.'

She smiled. 'Are you telling me to overcharge you?'

'No. I'm telling you I want the first production model and I'm prepared to pay a premium for it.'

He was serious. She could see it in his eyes. And it made her heart sing. 'I can't do that, I'm afraid. The first five are already taken.'

'I thought you said you didn't have a pre-order list?'

'I designed this for a specific customer,' she said. 'Triffid Studios.'

'The movie company?'

She nodded. 'It's going to be in the next *Spyline* movie. The deal is they have exclusive use until next summer. But I'll be taking pre-orders when it's announced formally, in about six weeks.'

'I see why you said it's confidential.' He paused. 'And you trust me?'

'Considering our family history, I ought to say no,' she admitted. 'But, yes. I trust you.' The man she'd got to know over the last few weeks was honourable and decent.

'Thank you. I'll respect your confidentiality.' He ran his hands over the steering wheel. 'You know you said you wanted to produce the iconic design of our generation?'

'Uh-huh.'

'I thought it might be the car you started sketching in the tea shop.' *Their* car. 'But you've already done it with this.'

She felt her eyes film with tears. He really thought that highly of her design? 'You're not just flattering me?'

'I'm never more serious than when I'm talking about cars,' he said, and rubbed the steering wheel again. 'I probably shouldn't ask this, and I promise I'm not pressuring you… But I'm dying to know how it handles. Can I drive it?'

'It's a prototype, so it's not perfect,' she warned. 'There are a few things I want to iron out for when it goes into production.'

'Noted, and I'll keep the speed low,' he promised. 'Come with me?'

'Sure. I'll open the doors and you can take it round the track.'

As he'd promised, Brandon drove the Frost carefully, then returned it equally carefully through the hangar doors into its spot in the factory.

'I love the design,' he said. 'But you're right—there are a couple of things that need ironing out, and I think it could be improved from a driving point of view.'

'Tell me.'

He began to list them, and Angel said, 'Hang on a tick.' She grabbed her phone and tapped into the notes section. 'OK. Start again, please.'

He nodded, and went through his thoughts.

'Thank you,' she said when he'd finished. 'I did this as speech to text and it sometimes gets things wrong, so can I send you the text file to review?'

'Of course you can. And if I think of anything else I'll add it to the list.' He raised an eyebrow. 'Our grandfathers would never believe it. A McKenzie listening to a Stone.'

'An engineer listening to a professional driver,' she corrected.

'The same as when you started sketching the car I was talking about and pointed out the aerodynamic issues— that was a driver listening to an engineer.'

'No, it was a Stone listening to a McKenzie,' she teased.

He laughed. 'This is just you and me—and thank you so much for sharing this with me. It's amazing.'

'It's the reason why I don't have to sell the company,' she said. 'I couldn't tell you before. But I'm sorry. McKenzie's really isn't for sale.'

'I understand.' He looked sad. 'And with you putting this in production, you're really not going to have time to do some freelance stuff and work with me on our joint car. That's a pity, because I really would've liked working with you.'

'And I with you,' she said, 'Though I don't think I could work with your uncle.'

'Not many people can,' he said with a grimace, 'but I'm going to have to put up with him until he decides he wants to retire. He's too old to change the way he acts in business, and I'm not going to humiliate him by making him jump before he's pushed. But, just so you know, I wouldn't have let him anywhere near your team if I'd bought you out.'

'I'm glad to hear it,' she said dryly. 'And I'm also glad you don't have to buy me out.'

'The Frost,' he said, 'is beautiful. You're amazing. I'm so proud of you.' His grey eyes were completely sincere, and Angel's heart felt as if it had performed a somersault. 'And I mean it about wanting one when it goes into production properly. I want to be top of your list.'

'You've got it,' she said softly. And she was starting to think that he was top of her list in a lot of other ways, too. If she wasn't careful, she could lose her heart to Brandon Stone.

But would that be such a bad thing?

When Brandon drove back to Oxford on Sunday evening, he made a slight detour via the churchyard in the village. He didn't bother taking flowers, because he knew that between them his mother and Maria always had that covered, but he sat down in front of his brother's grave.

'Hey, Sammy,' he said softly. 'My original Plan A isn't going to work, because McKenzie's isn't for sale. But I think I might just have something even better.' He smiled. 'It's all about a girl. But this one's special. I really like her, Sammy, and I think she might like me back.' In a way he'd never expected, and never experienced before. 'Remember when I used to tease you about being all soppy over Maria? I think I could be like that about Angel McKenzie. No, actually, I think I already might be. Dating her was supposed to get her out of my system, but it's done nothing of the kind. I wanted to charm her into selling to me—but now I just want her to be with me.'

And he could really do with a bit of advice from his brother right now. Not that he'd get it. But he could at least talk to Sam, even if Sam couldn't talk back.

'You're the one person I could talk to about this,' he said. 'I think I might actually be in love. For the first time ever. And it makes me feel as if I don't have a clue what I'm doing. I've always been in control and I've always been able to walk away. But Angel… She's different. I want to be with her. I want to end this stupid feud between our family and hers, and I want a future with her smack in the centre of it.' He gave a wry smile.

'I can't imagine getting married without you as my best man. But until I met Angel I couldn't imagine getting married at all. I haven't asked her. She might even say no. But I think finally I know who I want to be, thanks to her. It's as if I've found my way back out of a black hole. And I'm a better man when I'm with her.' There was just one sticking point. 'Let's just hope we can talk the Montagues and Capulets round.'

CHAPTER TEN

ON FRIDAY AFTERNOON, Brandon arrived to drive Angel to London for the ball. He kept the conversation light, but Angel felt her nervousness growing as they neared the city.

The hotel was seriously posh: it actually had a doorman who wore a top hat and tails. Inside, there was an amazing marble staircase, and all the decor was rich greens and golds.

Parties were the things she hated most. Where people made small talk and she couldn't always pick it up because there was so much background noise and the lighting wasn't good enough to let her lip-read. Conferences, presentations, lectures and interviews were fine. Parties were the seventh circle of hell; if she couldn't fall back on her usual strategy of talking cars, she knew she'd struggle.

Brandon had clearly guessed what was worrying her, because he paused outside the door to her room. 'We don't have to do this, you know,' he said. 'We can skip it and do something else. Go to the theatre. The cinema. Just for a walk along the river. Anything you like.'

'No. You won the bet, and I agreed to go with you. I'm not reneging on that,' she said. 'And people will expect to see you there.'

'I know parties are difficult for you,' he said. 'Look, when you've had enough, let me know and we'll escape.

And I'm staying right by your side tonight—just squeeze my hand or arm twice if you think you've missed something and you need me to rescue you.'

Angel felt close to tears. She really hadn't expected Brandon to be this thoughtful. 'Thanks.'

'Let's get ready,' he said. 'And there's no pressure. Any time you want to leave, we leave.'

'OK.' She took a deep breath. She could be brave about this. She *would* be brave about this.

The room was stunning, with views over the River Thames; she could see the London Eye and the South Bank. Even though the building was very old, the room itself felt completely modern.

She'd just finished changing when he knocked on her door.

His jaw dropped when he saw her. 'Wow. You look stunning.'

Her dress was dark red and A-line, with a skirt that flared out to just below her knees, a sweetheart off-the-shoulder neckline and lacy sleeves that went down to her elbows; she'd teamed it with dark red patent high heels. Angel had spent hours online, trying to find the perfect dress; thankfully, it looked as if it had been worth the effort. 'Thanks. You look pretty amazing, too. The outfit really suited him: a dinner jacket, slim-fitting dark trousers, a crisp white shirt and a black bow tie.

'Sorry—I didn't mean to sound shallow. It's just I've never seen you dressed up like this before.' He smiled. 'I think a lot of people are going to want to dance with you tonight.'

'I hope they're wearing steel-capped shoes, then, or they're going to get bruises.'

He grinned. 'Good.' Then he frowned. 'Hang on, are you telling me you can't dance?'

'I've never really had any cause to,' she admitted.

'All right.' He stood in front of her. 'Let me show you the ballroom hold.' He put her left hand on his right shoulder, and supported her arm with his right arm; then he took her right hand and lifted it up. 'Just follow my lead and it'll be fine.' And, to her surprise, he danced down the corridor with her.

'I feel a bit like Cinderella,' she said.

'My very shy Cinderella.' He stole a kiss. 'Except there aren't going to be any pumpkins at midnight. And you're not going to lose a shoe.'

'I hope not.' She forced herself to smile.

Together they went into the ballroom where the gala dinner was being held. The tables were all laid with snowy white linen and decorated with beautiful arrangements of white flowers; the room itself was incredibly glamorous, with pillars around the edges, floor-to-ceiling windows with heavy velvet drapes, and metalwork chandeliers with delicate glass shades.

And the background noise, particularly when it was amplified by the wooden floor, was horrendous.

'Twice for help,' he said, making sure that she could see his mouth.

Dreading it, she nodded.

Brandon seemed to know just about everyone in the room—well, of course he would, because a lot of them came from the motor racing world. Angel noticed that a lot of the women were staring at them, and a tight knot of nerves formed in her stomach. She wasn't the best at small talk. Hopefully she could get people talking about themselves and it would take the spotlight off her.

She was relieved when Brandon introduced her to a couple of the other drivers, and they started talking about engines and aerodynamics. At least this was a subject she felt comfortable with. And although the other drivers looked surprised at first, they were soon chatting to her as if she was one of them.

Dinner was slightly more difficult, because Angel was placed opposite Brandon rather than next to him. The man sitting on her left had a beard and she really couldn't work out what he was saying, half the time, but she hoped that she was nodding and smiling in all the right places.

Finally it was time for the dancing. Just as Brandon had promised, he stayed with her the whole time, not letting anyone else dance with her. She followed his lead, as he'd directed, and was shocked to find that not only did she feel as if she could dance, she was actually enjoying it. The way he whirled her round the floor made her feel like a princess.

'Midnight,' Brandon said against her ear. 'And not a pumpkin or a glass slipper in sight. Want to stay a bit longer, or do you want to escape?'

'Both,' she admitted. 'I want to dance with you.' And she wanted to be alone with him, too, though it felt a bit pushy to say so.

He laughed. 'One more dance,' he said, and stole a kiss.

And then finally they slipped away together.

'Stay with me tonight?' he asked as they stood outside the doors to their rooms.

How could she resist her very own Prince Charming? She smiled. 'Yes.'

The next morning, Angel woke early. Brandon was sprawled out, still asleep, and she smiled. It was tempting to wake him; but she could really do with a swim and he looked as if he could do with catching up on his sleep.

She managed to climb out of bed without waking him, then scribbled him a quick note and left it on her pillow.

Gone for a swim. See you in the pool or next door.

Then she put on enough clothes to make her decent, tip-toed out of his room, and went next door to her own room to change into her swimming things.

When she dropped her bag on her bed, her phone fell out; she could see that she had several voicemails. She'd kept her phone on silent during the ball and had forgotten to switch the ringer on again afterwards, so she'd clearly missed a call.

Worried that it might be her parents, and something was wrong, she listened to the messages.

But they weren't from her parents.

They were from the legal team at Triffid. Half a dozen of them asking her to call them urgently, and then a longer one which she had to listen to twice before she could make sense of it.

'Miss McKenzie, you should have told us about the takeover. We made the contract with you, not with Stone's. You've also broken the contract terms by breaking the embargo. You've made it clear that the deal's off and we'll have to go with another manufacturer. We may have to look at compensation if it holds up the film.'

Compensation? What? Were they talking about suing her? She stared at her phone in horror. What takeover? And what did they mean about breaking the embargo? Was there something about the Frost in the news?

She flicked into her favourite news site to see if she could find out what had happened and saw the headline straight away: *Racing Champ's Successful Takeover.*

According to the lead paragraph, Brandon Stone was buying McKenzie's. There was a picture of them together from last night, at the ball; she was looking all gooey-eyed at him, and he looked like a predator.

She stared at it, totally shocked. Where had the story come from? The small print talked about 'sources close to the company'; did that mean Brandon himself? Had last night simply been a set-up?

Angel didn't want to believe it. She knew she'd got his motivations completely wrong before, when he'd taken her to Cumbria, and she'd learned from that not to jump to conclusions. Her father had warned her that he was as ruthless as the rest of his family, but the Brandon she'd got to know was one of the good guys. He wouldn't betray her like that.

But the final paragraph was the killer. It talked about the new car. The Frost. It even mentioned the iridescent shimmery ivory paint: a detail that hardly anyone knew. Nobody at McKenzie's would've said a single thing about the Triffid deal: her staff had always been incredibly loyal and they'd worked as hard as she had on the Frost.

She dragged in a breath. The evidence was all in the article. No matter how much she didn't want to believe it, everything pointed to Brandon being the source. And, thanks to his deliberate leak, she'd lost the contract with Triffid. All the work she'd done, the hours she'd put in and the worrying, had been for nothing.

McKenzie's was going to the wall.

He'd ruined her company.

Sick to her stomach, she didn't bother going for a swim. She simply showered, dressed and packed. And then, filled with anger, she went to bang on Brandon's door and confront him.

Brandon woke with a jolt, hearing a banging noise. For a moment, he was disorientated. Where was Angel? She'd fallen asleep in his arms last night. But the bed was empty and the bathroom door was wide open.

Then he realised that someone was still banging on his door. 'Coming, coming,' he mumbled, and grabbed a towel to cover himself.

When he opened the door, Angel stood there, looking ragingly angry. He frowned. 'Angel? What's the matter?'

'What's the matter? You know perfectly well what the matter is.' She thrust her phone at him. 'Look at this. Are you proud of yourself?'

His frown deepened as he saw the headline: *Racing Champ's Successful Takeover.*

'What? I don't understand.'

'Don't play cute with me—it says "sources at the company" told them that Stone's is taking over McKenzie's. They're not going to be stupid enough to print something like this without your agreement, because they know if it's not true they'll end up with a court ordering them to pay damages.' She dragged in a breath. 'And it talks about the Frost. In detail. You're the only one outside McKenzie's and Triffid who knew about it.' Her lip curled. 'You're a player, and I've been incredibly stupid.'

What? But he hadn't talked to the press. At all. He had no idea where this was coming from. 'Angel, I—'

'Save it. I don't want to hear any excuses. I'm making my own way home—and I don't want to see you again. Ever. But I suggest you contact your precious sources at the paper and get this story corrected, or you'll be hearing from my lawyers.' She lifted her chin. 'And if I can't talk Triffid out of dumping the Frost and McKenzie's, you'll be hearing from my lawyers anyway. Because doing something this underhand *has* to be against the law.'

'Angel—' he tried again.

'Goodbye, Brandon,' she said, and walked off.

He grabbed some clothes, but by the time he'd pulled

them on she was nowhere to be seen. It was pointless trying to follow her.

He dragged a hand through his hair and tried to focus. What did he do now?

First things first, he needed to look at the news report properly so he knew exactly what he was working with. And as he worked his way through it, he groaned. She was right. It did claim that the source was someone at Stone's— and she was also right that the paper wouldn't have printed that if it wasn't true. The media had to be careful about defamation law.

But how the hell had the press got the information about the Frost? He hadn't said a thing to anyone except Angel herself.

He pushed away the fact how hurt he was that she thought he could do something like this to her. The emotional stuff could come later. First, he needed to fix this.

Who at Stone's would break a story like this? Who had leaked the news about the Frost?

He had one nasty thought about the person at Stone's— but no, surely…

There was only one way to find out. He rang the newspaper. After being put through to four different people, eventually he got the answer he'd been dreading. Which left him no choice but to act.

And this wasn't something he could do by phone.

He desperately wanted to see Angel and sort things out between them, but he needed to fix things before he talked to her. He showered swiftly, changed, checked out of the hotel without bothering with breakfast and drove back to Oxford.

Finally, he pulled up outside his uncle's house and rang the doorbell.

'Oh. You,' Eric said when he opened the door, not even looking surprised to see Brandon.

'Yes, me. We need to sit down and talk.'

Eric scoffed. 'You're not even going to thank me for doing your job for you?'

'Doing my…?' Brandon looked at him in disbelief. 'You didn't do my job, Eric. What you did was to cause a huge amount of trouble. It was unprofessional, underhand and unacceptable. That's not how we do things at Stone's.'

'Rubbish. You were dragging your feet about the take-over. We all knew what the outcome was going to be, but you weren't man enough to seal the deal. So someone had to give her a push.'

'You didn't give her a push. She wasn't selling.' Much as Brandon wanted to shake his uncle until his teeth rattled, violence wouldn't make anything better. 'How did you get the information about the Frost?'

Eric shrugged. 'If you will leave your PC on with your mail program up, you can expect people to read it.'

Brandon stared at him, hardly able to believe what he was hearing. 'What? You went into my office and snooped?'

'It's something that affected Stone's, and I'm on the management team. I had a right to know.'

So that was what this was about. Brandon gritted his teeth. 'Eric, I know you're angry that I'm in charge, but this has to stop. Now. I don't want you in the factory any more.'

'Are you trying to sack me? You can't,' Eric sneered.

'Actually, as the CEO of Stone's, I could sack you for gross misconduct,' Brandon said. 'I've put up with you sniping at me for years, because you're my uncle and I've been trying to cut you some slack, but this isn't healthy for anyone, And, by telling the press we're going to take over McKenzie's when we're not doing anything of the kind, you've damaged both our companies. She could sue us for misrepresentation—and more, if her business goes under.'

Eric flapped a dismissive hand. 'She's a McKenzie, so who cares if her business goes under?'

'*I* care,' Brandon said.

'Because you've got the hots for her.'

'I'm not discussing my private life. I'm discussing the business.' He raked a hand through his hair. 'Eric, you need to retire.'

'Jump before I'm pushed, you mean?'

'You're not happy in the company.'

'Are you surprised, with you walking in and taking the place I should've had?' he snarled.

'But,' Brandon said, 'I'm making a success of it. If I was making a total mess of things, then you'd have every right to be fed up with me. But I'm not making a mess of things. I've got a vision for our company. And you're working against me rather than with me. It's not helping either of us.'

'But I've worked there all my life.'

'Maybe,' Brandon said, 'it's time for you to find out what actually makes you happy. Even before I took over from Dad, you weren't happy.'

Eric said nothing.

'I don't want to sack you. But surely you can see this isn't working.'

'So you want me to jump before I'm pushed,' Eric said again.

Brandon sighed. 'Eric, I need my team to work with me. You're clearly not prepared to do that. What other option do I have?'

'Let me take over—as I should've done when your father retired,' Eric said, his face suffused with anger and resentment.

'I'm a second son, too,' Brandon said softly. 'If Sam hadn't been killed—'

'If Sam hadn't been forced to race because you'd just had to show off on the ski slopes and broke a rib,' Eric cut in.

'I have to live with that every single day,' Brandon said. 'But, as I was trying to say, if Sam hadn't been killed, I would've been happy to work with him here in whatever capacity he wanted me. Or I might've chosen to go and set up my own business, find my own way. Maybe it would've made you happier if you'd done that.'

Eric said nothing,

'Why do you hate the McKenzies so much?' That was the thing Brandon really couldn't understand.

'Because of Esther,' Eric said, 'and Angel McKenzie is the spit of her grandmother.'

Brandon sighed. 'Two men fell in love with the same woman. She chose one of them. It was seventy years ago. Don't you think it's way past time we moved on from that?'

'Barnaby was my father,' Eric said, 'and I spent my childhood seeing how miserable my mother was because she never matched up to Esther in his eyes. It was why she used to drink. Why she died when I was five.'

Brandon knew his grandmother had died young, but he hadn't realised she'd had a drinking problem that had led to her death. 'That's really sad for both of them,' he said, 'and I'm sorry I never actually knew my grandmother. But don't you think it's Granddad's fault rather than Esther's that Alice drank? Plus my father's five years older than you and he saw it all, too, but he's not bitter towards the McKenzies.' Or was he? Was that why he'd tried to buy McKenzie's in the last recession?

'You'll never understand,' Eric said.

'No, because thankfully my parents were happy to-

gether.' Though Brandon could understand now why Eric
had never married, with his parents as such an unhappy
example. Brandon's father, being slightly older, had maybe
seen happier times that had prompted him to get married,
but he'd also obviously decided that he didn't want his
son's childhood to be as miserable as his own had been.
Even though Larry had followed in his father's footsteps
as a ruthless workaholic.

'I'm sorry you suffered, Eric, and I'm sorry my grandmother suffered, but it doesn't excuse what you've done
to Angel McKenzie. She worked really hard on designing
a car that was going to be used in a movie—the car that
would make everything all right again at McKenzie's. The
car's amazing.'

'So you've actually seen it?'

'Yes. She trusted me enough to let me see the prototype. I let her down because I was stupid enough to think
that nobody at Stone's would go and snoop on my computer and then use private emails against someone who's
totally blameless. And I hate to think that this family feud
is going to fester and ruin things for this generation, too.'

'But they're McK—'

'They're *people*. Like you and me,' Brandon cut in. 'I
understand now why you did what you did, but it's *wrong*,
Eric. And hurting other people isn't going to change what
happened in the past.'

'Nothing's going to change the past.'

'I know. But we can learn from the past and change the
future,' Brandon said. 'Which is what I'm going to try to
do. And I'd like you to do the right thing and retire right
this very second—and get some counselling, which I will
pay for personally.'

Eric lifted his chin. 'And if I don't?'

'Then,' Brandon said, 'I'll sack you for gross misconduct. And I'll face up to all the consequences of that, though I'm pretty sure Dad will agree with me. But whether you retire or I have to sack you, I want you to get counselling. You can't keep living with this kind of misery, Eric, and you can't keep making other people's life hell just because you're miserable. It doesn't help you and it doesn't help anyone else.'

'I…' The fight suddenly went out of Eric and his shoulders slumped. 'So you're taking a McKenzie's side against me. So much for blood being thicker than water.'

Brandon's patience was close to snapping, but he thought of Angel. How would she deal with this? Kindly, he'd guess. 'I'm trying to do the right thing,' Brandon said. 'And I really have to ring LA now and grovel my head off to see if I can fix this for Angel and persuade the film company not to cancel the contract. Because she really, really doesn't deserve what you did to her.'

'But I've got stuff at the factory.'

'Then I'll pack it up for you and bring it to you.'

'Scared I'm going to do something like burn the factory down?' Eric sneered.

'I sincerely hope you wouldn't,' Brandon said. 'But, actually, I'm trying to spare you any embarrassment or pain.'

'Bossing me around, like the jumped-up little—'

'Eric, this isn't good for you,' Brandon cut in. 'You need to let it go. And you need help.'

'I don't need anything from you.'

'If that's what you think, fine, but I need something from you before I go. Your keys to the factory.' He held his hand out.

'But—'

'You don't work there any more—you've retired,' Brandon said.

Eric suddenly crumpled. 'What am I going to do with my life now?'

'Make it happier,' Brandon said softly.

Finally, Eric handed over the keys. He looked as if he'd aged two decades in as many minutes. It made Brandon feel guilty, but he knew he was doing the right thing. Something he probably should've done years ago.

'Thank you,' Brandon said. Once he was back in his car, he called his father and filled him in on what had just happened. 'I don't think Eric should be alone right now,' he finished.

'I'll come over and see him. You did the right thing,' Larry Stone said. 'I'm sorry you had to deal with this, Bran. I should've done more when we were kids or realised how unhappy he was.'

'Dad, you were a kid yourself.' He paused. 'Would you have a problem with me seeing Angel McKenzie? After the way your dad was with your mum, I mean?'

'Because of Esther?' Larry paused. 'If you'd asked me that a few years ago, I might've said yes. But losing Sammy taught me a hard lesson. Love's always more important than business. So if that's how you feel about her, follow your heart. Go after her. Don't let business get in the way.'

'Thanks, Dad. I'm glad we're not going to have to do a Romeo and Juliet.' Brandon took a deep breath. 'You'll like her. She's bright and she's sweet. And her designs are amazing.'

'Gina likes her. That's good enough for your mother. And what's good enough for your mother is good enough for me,' Larry said. 'So what are you going to do?'

'Hope that I can fix things—and then that she'll talk to me.'

'Good luck. And we're behind you all the way,' Larry

said. 'I know you've got this, but call me if you need any-thing.'

'Thanks, Dad.' Brandon appreciated the support.

His next call was to Triffid's legal team. 'My name's Brandon Stone, and we need to talk,' he said.

'We're not looking to do business with you, Mr Stone,' the lawyer said.

'No, but you've been dealing with McKenzie's and you're under the misapprehension that my company's tak-ing hers over. We're not. And Angel had nothing to do with any of those leaks about the Frost. I'm getting a correction printed in the news.'

'What does that have to do with us?' the lawyer asked.

'That car's amazing. It'll be perfect for your film. And you'd be shooting yourself in the foot if you tried to get someone else to design you a car even half as good. Angel McKenzie is the best designer I've ever met, and she's got guts and integrity.'

'That's as may be, Mr Stone.'

'Think of the time and cost implications,' Brandon said. The bottom line was usually the one that worked in busi-ness. 'Your PR team could spin this so everyone wins. And I have some ideas that might interest you.'

'Go on,' the lawyer said.

It took another half hour, but finally the lawyer agreed to talk to his people and reinstate the contract.

Which left Brandon one last thing: to face Angel and persuade her to listen to him.

He tried ringing her, but he wasn't surprised that she refused to pick up. He left her a message: 'Angel, we need to talk. I understand why you're angry with me but things really aren't what they seem. I'm coming to find you so we can talk—and I'm not taking no for an answer.'

Where was she likely to be?

His guess was that she'd be at the factory, looking through her books and trying to work out where she could go next—which was just what he'd be doing in her shoes.

Grimly, he headed for the motorway. If he'd got it wrong and she wasn't at the factory, then he'd drive to her house and sit on her doorstep until she came home; and if that meant staying there all night then he'd do it.

Because he wanted a future with Angel.

The only thing that might work was if he opened his heart and told her everything.

And he'd just have to hope that she'd listen.

CHAPTER ELEVEN

WHEN BRANDON PULLED up at the factory, he could see Angel's Luna in the car park. So she was here: now all he had to do was persuade her to talk to him.

He pressed the intercom switch at the barrier to the car park.

'Hello?' a voice crackled.

'Hello—is that Security?' he asked.

'Yes.'

'Great. I've got a meeting with Ms McKenzie. Can you lift the barrier and let me in, please?'

'I'm afraid Ms McKenzie isn't here, Mr Stone.'

Uh-oh. He'd been careful not to mention his name, but Angel's security team knew who he was. So obviously she'd given them a description of him or his car, and told them not to let him in. He sighed. 'I appreciate your loyalty to her. But this is important.'

'I can't let you in, Mr Stone.'

'Have you ever really, really messed up?' he asked. 'Because I have. And I really want to make it right for her.'

The security guy said nothing.

'Please. I'm not going to cause a scene, I promise. I just want to apologise and ask her to let me explain. If she tells me to go, then I'll go without making a fuss,' Brandon said.

'I can't do that, Mr Stone.'

Brandon knew he was going to have to go for broke. 'If you realised that someone was the love of your life, and you only had one chance to tell them or you'd lose them for ever…'

There was silence, and he knew he'd blown it.

'OK. Thanks anyway,' he said. 'I'll have to resort to sitting on her doorstep until she talks to me. Even if it takes me a week.'

'If she tells you to go,' the security guard said, surprising him, 'then you go immediately.'

'Immediately,' Brandon agreed, relief flooding through him. 'Thank you.'

Angel was in her office, looking through some files on her desk, when he rapped on the door.

She looked up. 'I expressly told my security team not to let you in.'

'Don't blame them. It's my fault.'

'What do you want?'

'To talk to you.'

Her lip curled. 'I don't want to talk to you.'

'Angel. Please. Just give me five minutes, and if you still want me to leave after that, I'll go without a fuss.'

'Why should I even give you that?' she asked.

'Because you were right, and I owe it to you to grovel properly. Plus, if I go, you won't ever know the truth.'

She paused for so long he thought she was going to refuse. But then she nodded. 'All right. You've got five minutes.'

'The most important thing you need to know is that I've spoken to Triffid. They know the truth, and your contract's back on.'

'Supposing I don't want to work with them now?'

'That's your decision,' he said. 'But at least they know now the story wasn't true.'

'Why did you lie about it in the first place?'

'I didn't,' he said. 'I know the evidence all looks as if it points to me being the leak, so in your shoes I'd be livid with me too, but it wasn't me. The paper was quite specific: they spoke to a source close to the company. Not the CEO.'

She still didn't look convinced, and he sighed inwardly. How could he make her understand the truth, but without dragging Eric into it?

'The person who talked to the press no longer works for me,' he said carefully. 'And because I'd got to know you and thought about the way you deal with things, I dealt with the situation slightly differently than I would have done if I hadn't met you. I wanted to be fair, not ruthless.' He paused. This was the really sticky bit. But they didn't have a hope in hell of a future if he wasn't completely honest with her now. 'But I did lie to you about something else.'

She frowned. 'What?'

'When I first met you,' he said. 'I tried to play you.'

She went white. 'So you never wanted to date me in the first place. It was all to get me to sell to you.'

'When I met you,' he said, 'I'd lost my way. I felt responsible for Sam's death, and I didn't feel I deserved love. So, yes, I was cynical about it. I was cynical about everything. I dated you as a way to get close to you and charm you into selling the company to me.'

'I think you've said enough,' she said. 'Get out.'

'I haven't had my five minutes.'

'You don't need it.'

'Oh, but I do,' he said. 'Because that was just the starting point, and I've moved further than I ever thought possible. You've changed me, Angel. All the while I thought I was charming you, actually you were the one who charmed me.'

'Me? Her face was filled with disbelief. 'But I don't play with people like that.'

'I know. It's just how you made me feel. I'm a different person when I'm with you. I like who I am when I'm with you. And all the time I kept telling myself I wasn't falling in love with you and I'd get everything under control, I was in total denial. Because I fell in love with you, Angel. You helped me find my way back. You helped me see that Sam's death was an accident—yes, it was my fault that he was racing, but it wasn't my fault that the accident happened.' He paused. 'And Cumbria. When you and I—'

She went bright red. 'Do you have to bring that up?'

'Yes. Because you gave me something really, really precious.'

'My virginity?' She flapped a dismissive hand. 'It's just an embarrassment in today's world.'

'No. It meant something to you. And it means something to me, too. It means you trusted me.'

'While you were lying to me all along.'

'I,' he said, 'am a first-class idiot. I don't know how to make things right between us. I need your help—I need you to show me the way.'

'There isn't a way.'

'You once told me that there's always a way.'

'Not this time.'

He sighed. 'OK. I can't fix it between us, but I can fix the damage done to your company.' He paused. 'If you change your mind about working with Triffid, you've still got financial problems. I've seen your books. So here's my proposal: if you don't go with Triffid, I'll give you the backing you need.'

She shook her head, looking disgusted. 'So you're still trying to buy McKenzie's?'

'No. I'm offering you an interest-free loan,' he said. 'Not from Stone's but from me personally.'

'Why would you do that?'

'Because the Frost is an incredible car that deserves to be out there in the market, and I believe in you.'

Brandon believed in her.

Or so he said.

He'd already lied to her. Multiple times. How did she know he wasn't lying now?

Her suspicion must have shown on her face, because he said, 'There aren't any strings. I'd also like to marry you, but that's a separate issue. Whatever happens between you and me, I'm still backing your business, because I love you and I believe in what you're doing. I don't want McKenzie's to go under. You rescued me from my private hell. Now it's my turn to rescue you.'

She couldn't get her head round this. Someone at his company had done their best to destroy hers—and he was trying to tell her he *loved* her and wanted to marry her?

More like he'd seen her in the same way as her fellow students had seen her at college: a challenge to be conquered. She'd been so flattered that she'd let him charm her into bed. Worse still, she'd instigated it. How he must have laughed at her. Hadn't he just told her that it had been his original plan to charm her into selling McKenzie's to him? Her virginity had been a cushy little bonus.

And now he was trying to make her believe that he loved her.

Of course he didn't.

She'd just been a means to an end. Only she wasn't selling.

'You've had your five minutes,' she said. 'Please go.'

'I'm sorry you've ended up hurt because of something

that Stone's did,' he said. 'Hurting you is the last thing I wanted to do. And I don't know how to make it better. All I know is that I love you, and I don't want our family history getting in the way.'

'It isn't our family history. You *lied* to me, Brandon. You used me.'

He raked a hand through his hair. 'And I apologise for that. I've been lying to myself, too. But I swear I would never intentionally do anything to hurt you. I love you, Angel. I respect you. You know your business inside out, you're a first-class manager and you've kept McKenzie's going for much longer than anyone else I know could've done in your position. You're an amazing designer whose ideas really inspire me. And more importantly you're an amazing woman. The woman I want to spend the rest of my life with.' He dragged in a breath. 'Except I don't know how to convince you that I mean it. How to get your trust back.'

She didn't know how he could convince her, either.

As if her agreement with him showed in her face, he sighed. 'OK. I've had my five minutes. I don't have any flashy gestures or flashy words or flashy *anything* left. I could go and buy the biggest diamond in the world and offer it to you on one bended knee, but it wouldn't even begin to tell you how I feel about you. All I can do is tell you that I love you and I want to fix it. But I can't do it on my own. I need you to meet me halfway, to show me how to bridge this gap between us.'

Angel wasn't sure she knew how to bridge the gap, either. How could she learn to rebuild her trust in him, when he'd admitted that he'd lied right from the start?

'I've done the best I can to fix things. But please think about what I said. And if you want to talk—well, you know where you can find me.' His grey eyes filled with sadness, and he turned on his heel and left.

Angel wasn't sure how long she sat there just staring at the empty doorway and wondering how her life had turned so upside down, but then her video call buzzed.

Triffid's legal team.

She thought about ignoring it; but then again maybe she could salvage something for McKenzie's from the call. Her personal life might be in shreds, but that was no excuse for letting her staff down. With a sigh, she accepted the call.

'Miss McKenzie, I'm glad I caught you. I've been talking to our people since Mr Stone called me this morning, and…'

So Brandon hadn't lied about that. He really had called LA to tell them the story about the merger wasn't true.

'Sorry. Can you run that by me again?' she asked, when it became obvious that the lawyer was waiting for an answer and she'd missed most of what he'd said to her.

When she'd finished the call, she leaned back against her seat. Brandon hadn't just corrected the story, he'd come up with a host of ideas to spin it in McKenzie's favour. He wouldn't have done that if he'd been the person trying to bring McKenzie's down with rumours.

So maybe he'd been telling her the truth.

He'd said some things that had really hurt her. Things that had shown him in a horrible light. But he'd also said that she'd changed him and changed the way he saw things.

Now she'd thought about it, he'd changed her, too. From a quiet, nerdy engineer who was happiest in her overalls and with no social skills into a woman who wore a red dress and danced at a glittering ball. He'd given her confidence in herself.

And maybe he did love her. He'd let her drive the Mermaid; he'd stepped in when her hearing let her down, but without making her feel useless or stupid; he'd thought about her and what she'd like to do on their dates.

Brandon Stone was a decent, thoughtful, caring man who also just happened to be one of the most gorgeous men she'd ever seen. He made her heart beat faster, but it wasn't just because of the way he looked. It was because she liked being with him. She liked who she was when she was with him.

If you want to talk—well, you know where you can find me.

She did indeed.

She locked up the factory, stopped by her security team to thank them, and headed for Oxford.

Brandon was right where she expected to find him: in his aircraft hangar of a garage, dressed in scruffy overalls, polishing chrome on the Mermaid.

'You missed a bit,' she said, pointing to a tiny area on the rear bumper.

'Engineers. So picky,' he said.

'Yeah. We expect the best.'

'Which is no less than you deserve.'

She knew she was going to have to be the one to broach the issue—because she was the one who'd refused to discuss it before. 'I've been thinking.'

'Uh-huh,' he said, as if he was trying really hard to sound careful and neutral and not scare her away.

'Triffid called me. What you did—you didn't have to.'

'I rather think I did,' he said. 'It was Stone's fault that McKenzie's was damaged.'

'Temporarily.'

'My company. My responsibility to fix the damage.'

'But not,' she said, 'your *fault*. That's the second thing you've taken the blame for. Don't let there be a third.'

'Too late. I hurt you. And you can't deny that's my fault, Angel.'

'True,' she said, 'but you were also being honest. If I'd found out in six months' time that you'd only starting dating me to get your hands on McKenzie's, it would've hurt me a lot more. I'm glad you told me now, because it means we're starting with a clean slate. With the truth.'

His eyes brightened with hope. 'So does this mean I get a second chance?'

'There's been bad blood between our families for too long,' she said. 'I know my dad wrote your dad a letter when Sam was killed, but maybe your dad was too upset to reply.'

'I don't think he got the letter. Eric was helping to deal with all the corr—' Brandon stopped and grimaced. 'Eric again.'

'Eric *again*?' she queried.

'I'm guessing he threw the letter away.'

'I gathered that,' she said gently. 'But what I didn't get was the "again" bit—do you mean Eric was the one who talked to the press about the buyout and the Frost?'

'He thought I wasn't doing a good enough job at making you sell McKenzie's to me, so he put the pressure on. He knows now he did the wrong thing.' Brandon sighed. 'And it didn't help that he was so bitter about the past.' He filled her in on what Eric had told him about the family history.

'That's really sad,' Angel said. 'I'm sorry he had to go through that. Though it's not been a total bed of roses for my family either; my dad's older sister died from scarlet fever when he was five, and I'm an IVF baby.'

'I'm sorry, too. I didn't know all of that,' Brandon said.

'Why would you? I'm guessing maybe one or the other wanted to try to mend things at different points along the way, but they were all too stubborn. Maybe your grandmother wanted to come to my aunt's funeral, but thought it would be rubbing it in because she still had two children and Esther and Jimmy didn't. Or maybe she was afraid that if Barnaby tried to comfort Esther, it might end up…' She grimaced. 'Just as I'm guessing that Esther felt bad when Alice died, but maybe she and Jimmy didn't want to hurt Barnaby by rubbing their own happy marriage in his face.'

'They all wasted so much time,' Brandon said.

She sighed. 'The way I see it, life's so short. You just have to muddle through things together.'

'I agree.'

'So what did you do? You said that the person who talked to the press doesn't work for you any more. Don't tell me you sacked your uncle?'

'No. I asked him to retire—though I didn't actually give him a choice,' Brandon admitted.

'Maybe he could—'

'Be redeemed?' He nodded. 'That's why I'm making him have counselling, and I'm taking him to the counsellor myself. He needs to find what he really loves in life. And only then will he be able to be happy.'

'I hope so,' she said.

Brandon looked at her. 'I've found what I really love in life. You. And I admit I had underhand motives when I first met you, but I fell in love with you along the way. Cumbria was real.'

'I know.' She took a deep breath. 'But our families hate each other. My grandfather married the woman your grandfather loved, your dad tried to buy mine out, and…'

'I spoke to my dad,' Brandon said. 'He said that losing Sammy taught him that love's more important than business. He told me if I loved you, to go after you.'

'I spoke to my dad,' Angel said. 'He says if you hurt me, you have him to deal with.'

Brandon grinned. 'Which is exactly what I'd say to our daughter's boyfriend. That's what dads are supposed to do, be all gruff and protective.'

'Maybe we made a tactical error and should've talked to our mums, and got them to talk our dads round,' Angel said.

'Or we face them together and tell them the family feud ends now. They can judge us on our terms. Which is at face value,' Brandon said.

'You know, seventy-odd years ago, we started as the same company. Maybe that's how we should end the feud.'

He blinked, looking surprised. 'Are you offering to sell to me?'

'No. I was thinking more along the lines of a merger,' she said.

'Professional or personal?' he asked.

She spread her hands. 'Do you have a preference?'

'I'm greedy. I'll go for both,' he said. 'I love you, Angel. And I'm sorry things went bad.'

'Me, too. I didn't want to believe you'd betray me like that.'

'Pretty much any jury in the land would've convicted me on that evidence,' he said wryly. 'Including me. I don't blame you.'

'You said I made you see things differently. You make me see things differently, too,' she said. 'I like who I am when I'm with you.'

He coughed. 'You're missing three words, you know. I've said it to you at least three times.'

'True.'

He groaned. 'Do you want me to beg?'

'Depends.' Her heart did a tiny little flip. 'Would that be on one knee?'

'You engineers drive a hard bargain.' He fished a key

ring from his pocket and removed the key. 'Are you quite sure you don't want this to happen in some flashy restaurant overlooking the sea at sunset, with us both dressed up to the nines and vintage champagne on ice?'

'How can that possibly compare with this—the things we both love?' she said, gesturing to the classic cars around them. 'And I don't need vintage champagne. That mug of tea on your workbench looks good enough to me.'

He grinned, and dropped to one knee. 'Angel McKenzie, I love you. I want to design cars with you and have babies with you and be a better man just because you're by my side. Will you marry me?'

'I love you, too, Brandon. And I want to design flashy high-end cars with you, and have babies with you, and be braver than I think I am because you're by my side. Yes,' she said, and he slid the Mermaid's key ring onto her finger.

'This is only temporary, you know,' he warned. 'You get to choose whatever you want as an engagement ring.'

She smiled. 'This would do me.'

'You can't have a key ring as an engagement ring, Angel.' He paused. 'Though you can have it as your engagement present.'

She laughed. 'The perfect present for an engineer—something useful. Thank you.'

'It comes with a key, though,' he said, and pressed the key to the Mermaid into her hand.

Her eyes widened as she realised what he meant. 'You're giving me the Mermaid?'

He shrugged. 'Looks like it.'

'Brandon, you can't—'

He silenced her by standing up and kissing her. 'It's your grandfather's design. I spent months restoring it. And

I think my favourite person in the world should have my favourite car in the world—right along with my heart.'

'I… Thank you. I'm a bit overwhelmed. And I can't afford to give you anything nearly so expensive,' she said ruefully.

'I don't want a present,' he said softly. 'I just want you. Right by my side.'

'You've got it.'

He held her close. 'So we're agreed: it's a merger?'

'McKenzie-Stone,' she agreed.

'Maybe,' he said, 'we should double-barrel our names. *Both* of us.'

She stared at him in surprise. 'You'd change your name for me?'

'If it means I get to marry you, yes. And it'll show that our families are truly one.'

'I like that idea.' She kissed him. 'It's a deal.'

He kissed her back. 'The deal of a lifetime.'

EPILOGUE

'ALL SET?' ASKED Sadie McKenzie. 'Something old?'

'Esther's pearls,' Angel said.

'Something new's your wedding dress. Something borrowed?'

Angel lifted her left arm. 'Lesley lent me Alice's bracelet.'

'That leaves something blue.'

Angel grinned. 'Brandon sent me a package this morning.'

'Right.' Sadie paused. 'I'm going to ask you about this while Lesley's sorting out Jasmine's fairy wings and can't hear me. You're totally sure about this?'

'I am,' Angel said. 'More sure than I've ever been in my life.'

Sadie hugged her. 'He's lovely and he's crazy about you, and that's all that matters.'

'Mum, don't. You'll make me cry and Maria spent ages doing my make-up this morning.'

'I know, love. She's a sweetheart,' Sadie said. 'And I'm glad the rift between the Stones and McKenzies has finally been healed. I know your dad was a bit worried that it was all going to go wrong, but I think he and Larry have surprised themselves by actually liking each other.'

Brandon and Angel's doubts had vanished as soon as

their mothers had started talking. There was only one Stone who hadn't been welcoming. The one who also hadn't responded to the wedding invitation. Angel had talked Gina into giving her Eric's private mobile number and had called him, but when he hadn't picked up she'd left a message that she hoped would make him put aside his anger for one day and come to the wedding.

Between them, the mothers had taken over to organise the wedding. They'd agreed that it wouldn't be tactful for Brandon and Angel to marry in the Cambridge church where her parents and grandparents had been married; instead, they'd chosen a local stately home which had a small and very pretty fourteenth-century church on the estate. And the McKenzies and the Stones were all getting ready at the McKenzie family home.

There was a knock on the door. 'Can I come in?' Lesley Stone asked.

'Of course,' Angel called.

Lesley walked in. 'The bridesmaids and flower girls are all rea— Oh, my. You look beautiful,' she said to Angel.

Angel smiled. 'Thank you. And so do you. So Maria, Gina, Stephie and Jas are all done? We're done, too— aren't we, Mum?'

'Then I think it's time for the girls to have champagne,' Lesley declared, linking arms with both Sadie and Angel.

Downstairs, the bridesmaids, flower girl and matron of honour were waiting; all were wearing simple deep violet dresses with a sweetheart neckline and wide straps, slim-fitting and falling to their ankles. Jasmine was wearing fairy wings and a sparkly tiara, which made Angel smile even more. The perfect outfit for a perfect day.

'Look at you! Turn round, Angel,' Gina directed. 'Brandon isn't going to know what's hit him.'

'You look like a princess,' Jasmine said, her grey eyes wide.

Her dress was ivory, strapless and with a sweetheart neckline. There was lace on the bodice, and then layers of organza falling to her ankles. Her shoes, for once, weren't flat but were strappy high heels to match the bridesmaids' dresses.

'That's because your mummy's very good with make-up,' Angel said.

'No, it's because you're beautiful,' Stephie said. 'Don't argue. You're not allowed to argue with pregnant women.'

'Aren't our girls all gorgeous?' Sadie said to Lesley.

'Aren't they just?' Lesley said. 'And I'm so glad our family's going to be one.'

There was just enough time for one glass of champagne, and the cars were ready to take them to the church.

'You look beautiful,' Max said outside the church. 'And best of all I know Brandon's going to be exactly the kind of husband I want for you—a man who really loves you.'

There was a lump in her throat a mile wide. 'Thanks, Dad. It means a lot, knowing we have your approval.'

'He's a good man. And his family's all right. I think we understand each other, now,' Max said. 'Ready?'

'Ready.'

Angel walked through the doors holding her father's arm. The church was all soaring arches, full of light, and the ancient box pews were crammed full of their family and friends. There were white and lilac and deep purple flowers everywhere and the organist was playing 'Here Comes the Sun'.

Brandon was standing at the top of the aisle next to his father, who was his best man. Larry looked round and saw her, then nudged Brandon and whispered something.

Brandon looked round and his eyes were so full of love; Angel could see him mouth, 'I love you.'

And then she was at the aisle by his side, plighting her troth, repeating the words after the vicar.

Finally, the vicar smiled. 'You may now kiss the bride.'

'About time,' Brandon said with a grin, and gently peeled back her veil before bending her back over his arm and kissing her soundly, to the applause of the congregation.

The signing of the register was a blur, but then they were walking back down the aisle, and the church bells were pealing as they came outside. Everyone was pelting them with white dried delphinium petals and cheering as they walked down the little path to the gate through the wall to the ancient hall next door.

The house itself was a beautiful eighteenth-century mansion with pale gold bricks and white sash windows, a porticoed entrance, a red-tiled roof with dormer windows jutting out, and wisteria on the walls. The photographer took photographs of family groupings by the car, next to the wisteria and on the steps, then finally went up to the parapet on the roof of the house and took photos of the whole group from above.

'The perfect day,' Brandon said.

'Absolutely,' Angel agreed, though she was aware that one person from his family was missing. The one person they hadn't seen at the church.

They lined up with both sets of parents to do the meet-and-greet. Angel was humbled to realise how many people there were to wish them well: family, old friends, staff from both their factories, and some of Brandon's old racing colleagues. Everyone hugged them soundly, all wishing them every happiness for the future.

'I don't think he's coming,' Brandon said softly.

'Trust me, he will,' Angel said. 'I left a message on his voicemail. He'll be here.'

And then, at the end of the line, there he was.

Angel greeted Eric with a hug.

'I'm sorry I didn't make the church,' Eric said. 'And I'm sorry about…'

'It's fine,' Angel said.

'I just wanted to wish you both well for the future.'

'I'm really glad you came,' she said. 'I meant what I said in that message.'

'That it wouldn't be the same without me? Even though I wrecked everything?' He looked shocked.

'It was fixable,' she said, 'and we all wanted you here. All of us. Because you're part of our family.' She paused. 'And you had a point. We're merging the businesses. And I meant what I said about coming back to the factory as a consultant. I've been looking through some of your paperwork and I really like your ideas about new fuels. We want you on our team to build the first McKenzie-Stone car in seventy years.'

Eric blinked away the tears in his eyes. 'If Esther was half the woman you are, I can quite see why my grandfather lost his head over her.' He turned to Brandon. 'Look after her.'

'I'd never make the mistake of wrapping my wife up in cotton wool,' Brandon said with a smile. 'But I'd lay down my life for her. So, yes, I'll look after her.'

'And the same goes for me,' she added.

'You'll be good for each other,' Eric said, and gave them both a hug.

And then he shocked everyone by hugging Angel's parents, who reacted by hugging him back.

'I have a feeling,' Brandon said, 'that everything's going

to be just fine. Come and sit down for our wedding breakfast, Mrs McKenzie-Stone.'

She smiled. 'I'd be delighted, Mr McKenzie-Stone.'

'To us,' he said softly at the table, lifting a glass. 'And our families. Joined at last.'

* * * * *

A MILLIONAIRE FOR CINDERELLA

BARBARA WALLACE

To Peter, who has the patience of a saint come deadline time, and to the revitalizing powers of coffee and snack-sized candy bars. I never would have written this book if not for you all.

CHAPTER ONE

How LONG DID it take to examine one little old lady? Patience paced the length of the hospital emergency room for what felt like the hundredth time. What was taking so long?

"Excuse me." She knocked on the glass window separating the admissions desk from the rest of the emergency waiting area. "My…grandmother…has been back there for a long time." She figured the lie would get her more sympathy than saying "my employer." Luckily there'd been a shift change; the previous nurse on duty would have called her on it. "Is there any way I can find out what's happening?"

The nurse gave her a sympathetic smile. "I'm sorry, we're really busy today, and things are backed up. I'm sure a doctor will be out to talk with you soon."

Easy for her to say. She hadn't found her employer crumpled at the foot of a stairwell.

Ana's cry replayed in her head. Frail, weak. If only she hadn't been in the other room…if only she hadn't told Nigel he needed to wait for his dinner, then Ana wouldn't be here. She'd be having her tea in the main salon like she did every afternoon.

Patience couldn't help her sad, soft chuckle. A year

ago she didn't know what a salon was. Goes to show how much working for Ana had changed her life. If only Ana knew how she'd rescued Patience, taking her from the dark and dirty and bringing her into a place that was bright and clean.

Of course, Ana couldn't know. As far as Patience was concerned, her life started the day she began cleaning house for Anastasia Duchenko. Everything she did beforehand had been washed away.

The hospital doors opened with a soft whoosh, announcing the arrival of another visitor. Immediately, the atmosphere in the room changed, and not because of the June heat disrupting the air-conditioning. The conversations stilled as all attention went to the new arrival. Even the admissions nurse straightened. For a second, Patience wondered if a local celebrity had walked in. The air had that kind of expectancy.

His tailored shirt and silk tie screamed superiority as did his perfect posture. A crown of brown curls kept his features from being too harsh, but only just. No doubt about it, this was a man who expected to be in charge. Bet he wouldn't be kept waiting an hour.

The man strode straight to the admissions window. Patience was about to resume her pacing when she heard him say the name Duchenko.

Couldn't be a coincidence. This could be the break she needed to find out about Ana. She combed her dark hair away from her face, smoothed the front of her tee shirt and stepped forward. "Excuse me, did I hear you ask about Ana Duchenko?"

He turned in her direction. "Who's asking?"

For a moment, Patience lost the ability to speak. He was looking down at her with eyes the same shade as the blue in a flame, the hue so vivid it couldn't possibly be real. Lit with intensity, they were the kind of eyes that you swore were looking deep inside your soul. "Patience," she replied, recovering. "I'm Patience Rush."

She didn't think it possible for his stare to intensify but it did. "Aunt Anastasia's housekeeper?"

His aunt. Suddenly Patience realized who she was talking to. This was Stuart Duchenko, Ana's great-nephew, the one who called twice a week. Actually, as far as she knew, the only Duchenko relative Ana talked to. Patience didn't know why, other than there'd been some kind of rift and Ana refused to deal with what she called "the rest of the sorry lot." Only Stuart, who managed her financial affairs, remained in her good graces.

"I thought you were in Los Angeles," she said after he introduced himself. Ana said he'd been stuck there for almost a year while some billionaire's family argued over a will.

"My case finished yesterday. What happened?"

"Nigel happened." Nigel being Ana's overly indulged cat.

She could tell from Stuart's expression, he didn't find the answer amusing. Not that she could blame him under the circumstances. She wondered, though, if he would find the story amusing under *any* circumstances. His mouth didn't look like it smiled much.

"He was in the foyer meowing," she continued. "Letting everyone know that his dinner was late. Near as I can guess, when Ana came down the stairs, he started weaving around her ankles, and she lost her balance."

He raised a brow. "Near as you can guess?"

Okay, the man was definitely an attorney; Patience felt she was on trial with all the questions. Of course, that could also be her guilty conscience bothering her. "I was in the dining room polishing the silver. I heard Ana cry out, but by the time I got there, she was already on the floor." She shuddered, remembering. The image of Ana crumpled at the foot of the stairs, moaning, wouldn't leave her soon.

Ana's nephew didn't respond other than to stare long and hard in her direction before turning back to the admissions nurse. "I'd like to see my aunt, please," he said. It might have been said softly, like a request, but there was no mistaking the command in his voice.

The nurse nodded. "I'll see what I can do."

Finally, they were getting somewhere. "I've been trying to get an update on Ana's condition since we arrived, but no one would tell me anything."

"Nor would they," he replied. "Privacy laws. You're not family."

Well, wasn't somebody feeling territorial. Never mind that she was the one who'd brought Ana in and filled out the admissions paperwork. Anyone with two heads could see she cared about the woman. What difference did it make whether she was family or not?

She had to admit, Ana's nephew wasn't at all what she expected. Ana was always talking about how sweet "her Stuart" was. Such a pussycat, she'd coo after hanging up the phone. The man standing next to her wasn't a pussy anything. He was far too predatory. She could practically smell the killer instinct.

Apparently, his singlar request was all they needed, because less than a minute passed before the door to the treatment area opened, and a resident in pale green scrubs stepped out.

"Mr. Duchenko?" He headed toward Stuart, but not,

however, before giving Patience a quick once-over. Patience recognized the look. She folded her arms across her chest and pretended she didn't notice. The trick, of course, was to avoid eye contact. Easy to do when the man wasn't looking at your eyes to begin with.

"I'm sorry to keep you waiting," the doctor continued. "We were waiting for the results of your great-aunt's CAT scan."

"How is she?"

"She's got a bimalleolar fracture of her left ankle."

"Bi what?" Patience asked, her stomach tightening a bit. Hopefully the medical jargon sounded more serious than it actually was.

The doctor smiled. "Bimalleolar. Both the bone and her ligaments were injured."

"Meaning what?" Stuart asked the same question she was thinking.

"Meaning she's going to need surgery to stabilize the ankle."

Surgery? Patience felt horrible. She should have been paying closer attention. "Is it risky?"

"At her age, anything involving anesthesia has a risk."

"She's in terrific health," Patience told him, more to reassure herself than anything. "Most people think she's a decade younger."

"That's good. The more active she is, the easier her recovery will be. You know, overall, she's a lucky woman to have only broken her ankle. Falls at her age are extremely dangerous."

"I know," Stuart replied. For some reason he felt the need to punctuate the answer with a look in her direction. "May we see her?"

"She's in exam room six," the doctor replied. "We'll be taking her upstairs shortly, but you're welcome to sit with her in the meantime."

Exam room six was really a curtained area on the far left-hand side of two rows of curtains. Stuart pulled back the curtain to find Ana tucked under a sheet while a nurse checking the flow of her IV. The soft beep-beep-beep of the machines filled the air. Seeing Ana lying so still with the wires protruding from the sleeve of her gown made Patience sick to her stomach. Normally, the woman was so lively it was easy to forget that she was eighty years old.

"We just administered a painkiller, so she might be a little out of things," the nurse told them. "Don't be alarmed if she sounds confused."

Stuart stepped in first. Patience followed and found him standing by the head of Ana's bed, his long tapered fingers brushing the hair from the elderly woman's face. "Tetya? It's me, Stuart."

The gentle prodding in his voice reminded her of how she would wake her baby sister, Piper, before school. It surprised her. He honestly didn't seem like the gentle type.

Ana's eyelids fluttered open. She blinked, then broke into a drunken smile. "What are you doing here?"

"That fall-alert necklace you refuse to wear notifies me when 911 gets called. I was on my way back from the airport when I got a message."

The smile grew a little wider. "Back? Does that mean you're home for good?"

"It does."

"I missed you, *lapushka*."

"I missed you, too. How are you feeling?"

"Good, now you're here." Her gnarled hand patted his. "Is Nigel okay?"

"Nigel is fine."

"He was a naughty boy. Make sure you tell him I'm disappointed in him."

"I'll let him know." There was indulgence in his voice.

"Don't make him feel too guilty. He didn't mean it." The older woman's eyelids began to droop, sleep taking over once again. "He's stubborn, like you."

"You go ahead and get some sleep, Tetya. I'm back home now. I'll take care of everything."

"Such a good boy. Not at all like your grandfather, thank goodness." She closed her eyes only to open them wide again. "Patience?"

Until then, Patience had lingered at the foot of the bed, not wanting to crowd Ana any more than necessary. Upon hearing her name, she drew closer. "Yes, Ana?"

"There you are," Ana replied. "Thank you."

"You don't have to thank me," she said.

"Yes, I do," the older woman insisted. "You take such good care of me."

Out of the corner of her eyes, she saw Stuart shift his weight and felt the moment his gaze slid in her direction. She kept her attention on Ana and pretended she couldn't see him. "I was only doing what any person would do. Now, why don't you get some rest?"

"Take care of Nigel while I'm here?"

"I will."

"Stuart, too."

She assumed Ana meant for her nephew to help take care of Nigel. Either that or this was the confusion the nurse mentioned, because the man next to her definitely didn't need taking care of. Certainly not from someone like her.

From the tick in his cheek, Stuart thought the same thing.

They stayed until a different nurse came to check Ana's vitals. The small space was barely big enough for two visitors, let alone three, so Patience stepped outside. To her surprise, Stuart followed.

"You know what's crazy?" she remarked. "That foolish cat causes her to break her ankle and he's still going to get gourmet cat food for dinner." A dinner that, she realized as she did the math in her head, was now several hours late. Hopefully he didn't kick cat litter all over the kitchen floor in retaliation. Or worse, break her ankle.

Stuart was watching her again, his face as dour as before. Apparently drawing the exam room curtain closed off more than Ana's bed. "Are you positive Nigel tripped Ana?" he asked.

That was dumb question. "Of course, I'm sure," she replied. "I mean I don't know *for certain*. But, it was dinnertime, and the cat does have this annoying habit of bothering the nearest warm body when he wants to eat. Why are you even asking?" Ana had already told him that the cat had caused the accident.

"Just want to make sure I have all the facts."

Facts? For crying out loud, he sounded as if they were in one of those hour-long detective dramas. "Trust me, you've got all the facts. Nigel is one horrendous pest." Not to mention spoiled rotten. "Besides, who else would trip her? I was the only other person in the house and I…"

He didn't...

She glared up at him through her bangs. "You think I had something to do with Ana's accident?"

"Why would I think that? Ana blames Nigel."

"Because Nigel *tripped* her." His mistrust was serious. Unbelievable.

No, actually, it was very believable. A guy like him, used to the cream of everything. Of course, he'd suspect the help. "Are you suggesting your aunt is lying?"

"Hardly."

"Then why would I be? Lying, that is."

"Did I say you were lying? I told you, I was simply gathering facts. You're the one who read deeper meaning into my questions." Immediately, she opened her mouth to protest, only to have him hold up a finger. "Although," he continued, "you can't blame me if I am suspicious."

Oh, couldn't she? The guy was practically insinuating—not practically, he *was* insinuating that she had pushed a helpless little old lady down a flight of stairs. "And why is that?" She folded her arms across her chest. This she had to hear.

"For starters, Aunt Ana hired you directly while I was in Los Angeles."

So that was it. The man was territorial. "In other words, you're upset because Ana didn't talk to you first."

"Yes, I am." Having been expecting a denial, Patience was surprised to hear him agree. "Normally, I vet my family's employees and you, somehow, managed to bypass the process. As a result, I don't know a damn thing about you. For all I know, you could be hiding some deep, dark secret."

Patience's insides chilled. *If only he knew...*

Still, no matter what questionable decisions she'd made in her life, there were lines she'd never dream of crossing. Hurting a defenseless old lady being on top of the list. "You're right," she told him, "you don't know me."

Yanking back the curtain, she returned to Ana's side.

My, my, quite the bundle of moral outrage aren't we? Stuart ignored the twinge from his conscience as he watched Patience sashay behind the curtain. He refused to feel guilty for taking care of his family. After all, until eight months ago, he'd never heard of Patience Rush. Suddenly, the housekeeper was all his aunt could talk about. Patience this, Patience that. *No need to worry about me, Stuart. Patience will take good care of me. Patience is moving into the brownstone.* And the final straw... *Patience takes care of writing out the checks now.*

With Aunt Ana incapacitated, Patience would have an awful lot of power. Or rather, she would have, if he hadn't come home. He kicked himself for not being around the past eleven months. Now his aunt was attached to a stranger he knew nothing about. Ana might be sharp for her age, but when all was said and done, she was still an old woman living alone who had a soft spot for sob stories. Her big heart made her vulnerable to all sorts of exploitation.

It certainly wouldn't be the first time a pretty young thing had tried to grab a piece of the Duchenko fortune.

Unfortunately for Miss Rush, he was no longer a lonely twenty-year-old looking for affection. Nor was he still naive enough to believe people were as guileless as they appeared. Ana was the only family he had left. He'd be damned if he'd let her be burned the way he had been.

There was the rustle of a curtain, and Ana's gurney appeared on its way toward the elevator. As she passed by, the older woman gave him a sleepy wave. Stuart grabbed her hand and pressed the wizened knuckles to his lips. "See you soon, Tetya," he whispered.

"The surgical waiting area is on the third floor," the nurse told him. "If you want to stay there, we can let you know as soon as they're finished."

"Thank you."

Patience's soft voice answered before he had the chance. Immediately, his mouth drew into a tight line. "You're planning to wait, too?"

"Of course. I'm not going to be able to sleep until I know you're okay," she told Ana.

Ana smiled. "But Nigel…"

"Nigel will be fine," he said. While he wasn't crazy about Miss Rush hanging around, he wasn't about to start an argument over his aunt's hospital gurney. "Don't you worry."

"Besides, it'll do him good to wait," Patience added, "seeing as how this whole accident is his fault." She raised her eyes, daring him to say otherwise. "I promise, I'll go home and feed him as soon as you're out of surgery."

The sedatives were starting to kick in. Ana's smile was weak and sloppy. "Such a good girl," she murmured before closing her eyes.

Oh, yeah, a real sweetheart, he thought to himself. The way she so casually referred to the brownstone as home rankled him to no end. It was like ten years ago all over again, only this time, instead of a beguiling blonde worming her way into their lives, it was a brunette with hooded eyes and curves that wouldn't quit.

Interesting that she chose to downplay her sexuality. A tactical decision, perhaps? If so, it didn't work. A burlap sack couldn't mute those assets. Even he had to admit to a stir of appreciation the first time he saw her.

She was hiding more than her figure, too. Don't think he didn't notice how she looked away when he mentioned having secrets. There was a lot more to Patience Rush than met the eye. And he intended to find out what.

They spent the time Anna was in surgery on opposite sides of the waiting area, Stuart moving chairs together to create a makeshift work area while Patience made do with out-of-date women's magazines. Having read up on last fall's fashions and learned how to spot if her spouse was having an online affair, she was left with nothing to do but lean back in her chair and shoot daggers at Ana's nephew.

Who did he think he was, suggesting she had something to do with Ana's fall? Like she could ever. Anastasia Duchenko saved her life with this job. Every morning, she woke up grateful for the opportunity. To be able to walk down the street with her head held high. To not have to scrub herself raw to feel clean. Finally, she had a job she could be proud of. Be a *person* she could be proud of.

Even if the whole situation was built on a lie, she thought, guilt washing over her the way it always did.

She wasn't proud of her behavior—add it to a long list of regrets—but she made amends every single day by working hard and taking care of Ana. You wouldn't find a better housekeeper and companion on Beacon Hill. She would never—ever—jeopardize the gift Ana had given her.

Tell Stuart Duchenko that, though. If he learned she'd lied her way into the job, he'd kick her to the curb before she could say *but*... And who knows what he'd do if he learned what she used to do for a living before finding Ana? She shuddered to think.

The sound of rustling papers caught her attention. Looking over, she saw Stuart pinching the bridge of his nose. The man looked worn-out. Patience had to admit, for all his jerkiness, he appeared genuinely concerned for his great-aunt. The adoration Ana talked about seemed to run both ways.

"Mr. Duchenko?" A small African-American nurse in a bright pink smock rounded the corner, bringing them both to their feet. "Dr. Richardson just called. He'll be down shortly to talk with you, but he wanted you to know that your aunt came through the surgery without problem and is on her way to recovery."

"Oh, thank goodness." The words rushed from Patience's mouth, drawing Stuart's attention. Their eyes met, and she saw agreement in their blue depths. In this, they were on the same page.

"Can we see her?" he asked.

"She'll be in recovery for several hours, I'm afraid," the nurse replied with a shake of her head. "In fact, considering the hour, they might not move her until morning. You're better off getting some sleep and coming back tomorrow."

Patience watched as a protest worked its way across the man's features. She had a feeling if he insisted, he'd

get his way. Better judgment must have stepped in—
either that or fatigue—because he nodded. "How long
before Dr. Richardson gets here?"

"He said he was on his way down, so I don't think
it'll be more than five or ten minutes."

It turned out to be closer to twenty. When he did
arrive, Dr. Richardson gave a succinct report, without a whole lot of new information. They'd inserted a
plate and some screws to stabilize the break. Ana came
through the surgery without issue. They'd monitor her
throughout the night for complications. No, he wasn't
sure how long she'd need to stay in the hospital.

Still, Patience left the waiting room feeling that Ana
was in good hands. Another plus: Stuart was on the
phone so she was spared any more accusations. From
here on in, she'd do her best to avoid the man.

A pair of angry green eyes greeted her when she unlocked the door to Ana's brownstone. Patience wasn't
intimidated. "Don't give me attitude, mister. This whole
night is your fault."

With what Patience swore was a huff, Nigel jumped
down from the entryway table and ran toward the
kitchen. An urgent wail traveled back to her ears a second later. "Puleeze," she called, "like you were ever in
danger of starving."

Arms hugging her body, Patience made her way
along the corridor, thinking the slap of her sandals
against her feet sounded abnormally loud. It felt weird
being in the brownstone alone. While Ana went out
a lot, the woman was seldom gone past eight o'clock
and so her absence hung thick in the emptiness. A
gleam caught Patience's eye as she passed the dining
room. The silver set she'd been polishing when Ana

fell still sat on the table, the cloth on the floor where she'd dropped it upon hearing Ana's cry. The moment replayed as she curled her fingers around the soft material, the image of her savior crumpled at the base of the stairs making her nauseous. Thank goodness, Ana was going to be all right. Tomorrow she would work on making the house perfect for her return. Starting with making sure the tea set gleamed.

Nigel had resumed his meowing. Patience tossed the cloth on the table. "Oh, for goodness' sake, I'm coming. Five minutes will not kill you."

She turned around only to walk into a tall, muscular wall. "What the—" Why hadn't she brought the teapot along with her as a weapon?

Stuart Duchenko arched a dark eyebrow. Even in the partially lit hallway, his eyes shone bright. "Did I startle you?"

He knew perfectly well he had. "How did you get in?"

"Same way you did. With my key." He held up a key ring. "Or did you think you were the only one Ana gave access to?"

"Don't be silly. I didn't hear the doorbell is all." They were way too close. Close enough she could smell the breath mint he'd obviously just finished. She wasn't used to sweet-smelling breath, not from men anyway. It caught her off guard, which had to be the reason she didn't step back at first contact. She stepped back now, and spied a pair of suitcases at the base of the stairs.

Seeing where her gaze had gone, he gave a shrug. "I sold my condominium before leaving for LA. Until I find a new place, this is more convenient than a hotel."

Convenient for what? Keeping an eye on her?

It was as if he read her thoughts. "Ana made the suggestion back when I first left. Of course, I'm sure she wasn't expecting to be in the hospital at the time. My being here won't be a problem for you, will it?" he asked. The gleam in his eye dared her to say that it was.

Patience would be damned if she'd give him the satisfaction. "Of course not. Why would your staying here be a problem for me?"

"Extra work for you. I know you're used to it being only you and Aunt Ana."

Another veiled comment. The man was full of them, wasn't he? "Extra work won't be a problem. Cleaning is cleaning. Besides, like you said, it's temporary, right?"

"We can only hope. I figure I'll stay until Ana gets back on her feet. Make sure there aren't any problems."

What kind of problems? Was he afraid Patience would take off with the silver? Why didn't he just come out and say what was really on his mind?

"You don't trust me, do you?"

"No, I don't."

Finally, the truth was out in the open. She appreciated the bluntness. Beat phony friendliness any day. Didn't mean she wasn't going to set him straight though.

"Your aunt trusts me. Are you saying Ana isn't a good judge of character?"

She stepped back into his personal space, making sure to maintain eye contact and letting him know his answer didn't intimidate her one bit. The posture brought her close enough that she could smell his skin. Like his breath, his body smelled clean and fresh, despite having been traveling all day. An antsy, fluttering sensation started in the pit of her stomach. Butterflies, but with a nervous edge. The notion that she was out of her league passed briefly through her mind.

Stuart's eyes stayed locked with hers. A Mexican standoff, with each of them waiting for the other to blink. "My aunt has a generous heart. I, on the other hand…"

"Let me guess. You don't."

Patience sensed rather than saw his smile. "I prefer to lead with my head. Less chance for mistakes."

"Except, in this case, you're already mistaken."

"We'll find out, won't we?" he said. "Since I'll be living here, we'll have plenty of time to get acquainted. Who knows what secrets we'll learn about each other?"

Patience managed to wait until he disappeared upstairs before hissing. What was it with him and secrets?

You didn't exactly help your cause, did you? Challenging him like that. A smart person would have let his comments pass, refused to give him the satisfaction of a reaction. But, *nooo*, she had to call him out. Might as well hold a sign over her head reading I've Got a Secret!

So much for leaving her past behind. She should have known that a future built on a lie—even an innocent one—wouldn't last. Ana was going to be so disappointed in her.

She bit her knuckle, forcing down her panic. No need to start packing just yet. This bluster was probably nothing more than a scare tactic to put her in her place. To make up for not having a say in hiring her, no doubt. A few days from now, after seeing how well Patience did her job, he'd back off and leave her alone.

It could happen, right?

CHAPTER TWO

THERE WAS A weight vibrating on his chest. He must have left the door open when he came upstairs. "It better be light out, Nigel," he muttered. Freeing a hand from under the covers, he felt around until his fingers found fur. Immediately, the purring increased as Nigel leaned into the touch. A sad voice in his head noted this was the most action he'd had in his bed in way too long. "Hey, be careful with the claws, buddy," he said when the cat began kneading the blanket. "I might need those parts someday." You never knew. A social life might spontaneously develop. Stranger things had happened.

At work, people considered him a workaholic, but the truth was, he'd never been what people would call popular. He discovered early that being a Duchenko heir meant being judged and misunderstood. As a kid, his awkwardness was labeled snobbery. As he got older, his social desirability was measured in terms of his bank account. He had to be constantly on guard, assessing the motives of every person that crossed his path. The one time he hadn't…well, that had taught him two more lessons: Don't let sex cloud your judgment and even family members will screw you over. Except for Ana, that is. Ana was the one family member who loved him for him.

Nigel's head butted his hand, a not so subtle way of saying *more petting, less thinking*. Giving a half sigh, Stuart opened his eyes, then blinked when he saw Nigel in perfect focus. He'd forgotten to take out his contact lenses again. No wonder his eyes felt as if they had sand in them. What time was it anyway? Yesterday had wiped him out so badly he barely remembered falling into bed.

Not too wiped out to go toe-to-toe with the house-keeper, though. It was a bit arrogant of him showing up without warning, but he'd wanted to catch her off guard. To see how she'd react to learning she wouldn't have the run of the brownstone.

Turned out she reacted to the blind side better than most of his legal opponents.

Most of his legal opponents didn't have eyes that lit up like chocolate diamonds, either. Dark and sinfully rich, their spark got his adrenaline going in a way practicing law sure didn't. A guy could make a career out of looking for ways to make those eyes light up.

What was that about not letting sex cloud his judgment? Ignoring Nigel's protest, he rolled onto his side and reached for the phone on the nightstand. It was early, he thought, noting the time, but not so early to reach an associate. The ambitious ones practically slept at the firm. A few minutes of scrolling through his contacts found him the name he wanted.

Just as he expected, Bob Cunningham answered on the first ring. "Welcome back. I hear congratulations are in order." He was referring to the LA case.

"Too bad the former Mrs. Wentworth didn't come

to her senses last year." Instead, she'd put her late husband's family through hell and sentenced Stuart to months of aggravation, not to mention opening the door for Patience Rush. "There are a couple details to iron out that I'll talk to you about later. In the meantime, I need some background research done. A woman named Patience Rush."

"Is that her real name?"

Good question. Strangely enough, he hoped the quirky moniker was real. "That's for you to tell me." He gave him what details he knew.

"You're not giving the investigator much to work with," Bob replied.

"He's worked with less."

"True. What client number should I bill?"

"SD100." On the other end of the line, there was a soft intake of breath. Stuart seldom used his discretionary fund, but the firm's investigator was the best around. He'd reimburse the firm later.

"Um…"

"What?" Stuart asked.

The associate paused. "This might take a while. We've tapped him for a couple other projects."

And clients always came before personal. Stuart understood. "Just tell him to get to it as soon as he can."

In the meantime, he'd just have to keep a close eye on Patience Rush. Thinking about her eyes, he couldn't help but smile. There were worse jobs in the world.

A short while later, having showered and changed, he headed downstairs only to hear muffled voices coming from the kitchen. One muffled voice actually. He found Patience crouched over Nigel's food dish, brandishing a dustpan and broom. "You'd think a cat who acts like he's starving wouldn't drop pieces of food all over the place," she muttered. "One of these days, I'm going to toss the whole bowl out. Let's see what you do then."

A chuckle rose in his throat. Nigel had a way of making all of them talk as if he understood. He leaned a shoulder against the door frame. "Not a cat person, I take it."

She gasped before looking up at him with a glare. "Do you always sneak up on people?"

There they were again, those chocolate-diamond eyes. He crossed his legs to keep his jeans from growing tight. "I didn't know walking around the house was considered sneaking."

"Then you should walk louder," she replied. "Or wear shoes."

He looked down at his bare feet. "I'll keep that in mind. May I ask what the cat did to earn your wrath?"

"Nigel isn't a cat. He's a four-legged spoiled brat."

As had been all of Ana's cats. His aunt tended to overindulge the strays she adopted. Pushing herself to her feet, Patience swayed her way across the room to the trash can. Stuart found himself wondering if the seductive gait was natural or on purpose. "Sounds like the two of you have a great relationship," he remarked.

"Mine and Nigel's relationship is just fine. Why?" She took her foot off the receptacle latch, causing the lid to close with a loud slap. "Afraid I'll try to push him down the stairs, too?"

"Nah. A woman as smart as you would know hurting Nigel is the quickest way to getting on Ana's bad side."

She gave him a long look. "Was that supposed to be a compliment?"

In a way, yes. He did think she was smart. "If you want to take it as such."

"Gosh, thanks. I'll try not to let it go to my head."

Smart and quick-witted. She was dressed similarly to yesterday in jeans, a T-shirt and a cardigan sweater, her hair pulled back with one of those plastic hair bands. For the first time he looked closely at her features. Yesterday, he'd been too distracted by her eyes, but today he noticed more intricate details like the long slope of her nose and the way her teeth met her lower lip in a slight overbite. A two-inch scar cut across her right cheekbone. Time had caused it to fade. In fact, with makeup, it'd be barely noticeable, but since she was again bare faced, he could see the jagged edges of a cut that should have had stitches. The scar bothered him, like seeing a crack on the surface of a crystal vase. It didn't belong.

Patience cleared her throat. Realizing he'd been staring, he covered his action by adjusting his glasses. This might be one of those rare moments when he was grateful for them. He detested wearing the heavy black frames. The look might be considered stylish now, but it simply reminded him of his younger, awkward days. Then again, maybe a reminder was a good thing, given the awareness swirling around his insides this morning.

He reached for a change of topic. "Do I smell coffee?" There was a distinct aroma of French roast in the air, a unique scent in his tea-drinking aunt's home.

Patience nodded her head toward a stainless steel coffeemaker tucked in the faraway corner. "Cream and sugar are in the dining room. Do you prefer a full breakfast or continental."

"Neither." Was she offering to make him breakfast? Considering the circumstances, he wasn't sure if he should be flattered or suspicious. "Are you waiting on me?" he asked when she took a coffee mug from the cupboard. "Why?"

"Because it's my job," she replied. "I serve breakfast every morning. So long as someone's here, I'll keep on serving it." Filling the cup, she handed it to him.

Stuart stared into the black liquid. What gives? Last night, Patience had made it quite clear that she didn't appreciate his staying at the brownstone, yet here she was pouring him coffee and offering breakfast. Citing her job. Was she truly that dedicated or was this some kind of tactic to throw him off his game? If the latter, it was working.

"Something wrong?" she asked. "Would you feel better if I drank the cup first?"

"All right, you've made your point," he said, setting the coffee cup down. "You didn't appreciate my questioning Ana's accident."

"Not the accident—me. You all but accused me of pushing your aunt down the stairs."

Yes, he had. Now that he thought about it, the accusation wasn't his finest moment. Treating the woman like a hostile witness wouldn't accomplish anything. A situation like this called for a more delicate touch. "I'm sorry," he said. "I tend to be wary when it comes to strangers around my family."

"Well, I tend to have a problem with being accused of crimes I didn't commit," she replied, snapping his olive branch in two. "Now if you'll excuse me, I've got a job to do."

"Can you believe the guy? I think he actually considered that comment an apology."

"Some people aren't very good with apologies." Her sister Piper's face filled the screen of her smartphone. Thank goodness for Wi-Fi and internet chat apps. She so needed a friendly ear right now and Piper was the one person in this world she could trust. Patience called her as soon as she sat down at Ana's desk.

"Maybe he's one of those people," her sister continued.

"Probably because in his mind he's never wrong." She sighed. "I can't believe I'm going to be stuck working for the man while Ana's in the hospital. Talk about a nightmare."

"Oh, come on, it won't be that bad."

"Are you kidding? We're living under the same roof. How am I supposed to avoid him?"

"I doubt he's going to be hanging around the house."

Wanna bet? Patience caught the smirk in his eyes last night. He probably considered the arrangement the perfect opportunity to vet her. Who used words like *vet* anyway? Couldn't he say *check her out* like a normal person.

"I don't like him," she said. "He's…"

"He's what?"

Too imposing. With his unwavering blue eyes and long lean torso. "There's something about the way he looks at me," she said, keeping her thoughts to herself.

"Guys are always looking at you."

"Not like this." Those guys were skeevy. All hands and leers. "It's like he's trying to read my mind." She wasn't used to a man looking at her as anything more than a chick with a nice rack. It was unnerving to have a man look deeper. "Plus, he keeps talking about secrets. I'm worried one of these times I'll slip up and say something incriminating."

"So, don't talk to him. There's no rule that says a housekeeper has to be chatty."

"True." Except she seemed unable to help herself.

"If it helps," Piper added, "I watched a movie the other night where the woman drugged her husband's dinner so he'd leave her alone. You could always try that."

"Oh, sure." It was exactly the laugh she needed. "Because my life isn't enough like a made-for-television movie. Seriously, though, what am I going to do?"

"You could try telling the truth."

Patience shook her head. "I can't."

"Why not? I bet Ana won't care, especially once she hears the whole story. I mean, it's not like you had other choices. Surely, Ana would understand that you did what you had to do."

Maybe, but what about the reason Patience stayed for as long as she did? There were some secrets Piper didn't know and was better off never knowing. That particular shame was Patience's and Patience's alone.

Again, she shook her head. "I'll just have to stay on my toes is all. Hopefully, when Ana starts to feel better, he'll lose interest. A rich, handsome lawyer? I'm sure he's got better things to focus on than the hired help."

"You didn't mention he was handsome," Piper said, giving her a smirk.

"He's…good-looking," Patience replied rolling her eyes. *Handsome* wasn't the right word. "Not that it makes a difference. I'm more concerned about keeping my job."

"You're going to be fine, You're one of the most resilient people I know."

Patience wished she shared her sister's confidence. "Let's talk about something else," she said. She was tired of whining. "How's school?"

"Um…good. French pastries are turning out to be a challenge."

"Bet yours taste fantastic. Any way you can mail me your homework?" She was so proud of Piper. Winning a scholarship to study cooking in Paris. Piper's success made everything worthwhile. "And how's work?" Her sister was earning room and board as a live-in maid. "Your boss must be psyched to have a gourmet cook on staff."

"Frederic doesn't eat home much."

The grainy camera image failed to mask the shadow that crossed Piper's face, immediately sending Patience's maternal instincts into high alert. "What's wrong?" she asked.

"Nothing," Piper replied quickly. "I'm just bummed not to have someone to cook for is all. I miss you."

Homesickness. Of course. Patience should have realized. This was the longest the two of them had ever been apart. Hard as it was on her, it had to be doubly hard on Piper, alone in a foreign country. "I miss you too Pipe. But, hey, we've got Wi-Fi. You can call me anytime you want."

Piper smiled. "Back at you." Offscreen, a noise occurred, causing her sister to look over her shoulder. "Hey, I've got to go," she said. "The boss just walked in. Don't let Ana's nephew intimidate you, okay? You're just as good as he is."

"Thanks. I love you."

BARBARA WALLACE33

"Love you, too."

Patience's smile faded as soon as she clicked off. Piper had such faith in her. It wasn't that she was completely ashamed of everything she'd done in life, she thought, setting the phone aside. Raising Piper, for instance. She couldn't be prouder of the woman her baby sister had become. Giving Piper a chance for a real future had always been what mattered the most. Her baby sister would never have to degrade herself to pay the bills.

A knock sounded behind her, making her start. "You can't accuse me of sneaking up on you this time," Stuart said. "I knocked."

Yes, he had, and he now stood in the doorway with his arms folded like a long, lean statue. It wasn't surprising that he managed to look as regally imposing in jeans and bare feet as he did in a suit. Patience had a feeling he could wear a bunch of rags and still look wealthy. Even the glasses that, on someone else would look geeky, looked more geek-chic on him. Actually, much as she hated to admit it, the frames looked adorable on him.

Some of her bangs had slipped free of her hair band. She brushed them aside to disguise her reaction. "Do you need something?" she asked.

"It dawned on me that I sounded—are you writing out checks?"

His gaze had dropped to the ledger that lay open on the desk. What now?

"I'm reconciling the checkbook. Ana likes a paper record in addition to the online version." She considered adding that his aunt had asked her to take over the task because her math was getting a bit fuzzy, but that would only make her sound more defensive than she did, and she refused to feel guilty for doing her job.

"I never did understand her insistence on two records," He replied. She'd expected a far more snide comment. Walking over to the desk, he studied the laptop screen from over her shoulder. "Seems like way too much opportunity for mistakes."

"I've tried to tell Ana the same thing." As much as she tried not to be, Patience found herself acutely aware of his chest hovering behind her ear. The scent of his body wash lingered in the air. Clean. Crisp. She couldn't help herself; she inhaled deeply.

"You forgot to record check number 3521," he said, pointing at the screen.

Sure enough, there was an unrecorded check. "This is the biggest problem," she said. "Ana always forgets to mark the checks in both places."

"I thought you wrote the checks?"

"I write out the monthly checks for the bills. That doesn't mean your aunt doesn't write out her own occasionally. Especially when she want to give money to the humane society. See?" She pointed to the written ledger. "Check 3521 in her handwriting."

She shifted in her hair, so she could better confront him. "Are you going to question everything I do while you're living here? Because if so, it's going to make for a very long stay."

"I wasn't questioning anything. All I did was point out you missed a check."

Right. And his pointing out had nothing to do with his distrust. "Look," she said, "I know you don't like me—"

"I never said I didn't like you."

Patience blinked. "You didn't?"

"No. I said I didn't trust you. There's a difference."

Not much. "Gee, thanks. I feel so much better."

A hint of color found its way to his cheeks. It, along with his quick, sheepish smile, dulled her annoyance. "I'm not saying this right at all," he said. "I came in because I realized what I said back in the kitchen didn't come out as apologetically as it should have. What I should have said was that I'm sorry for treating you like a trial witness last night. I should have let the matter drop after Ana corroborated your story."

"Actually," Patience replied, "what you should have said was that you're sorry for even suggesting I'd hurt your aunt."

Stuart grabbed the edge of the desk, trapping her between his two arms. Body wash and heat buffeted the space between them, the combination making Patience's pulse quicken. She looked up to meet a gaze that was bright and resolute. "Ana is the only family I have," he said. "I won't apologize for trying to protect her."

This was where Patience should retaliate with angry defiance. Unfortunately, she understood where Stuart was coming from. When it came to keeping your family safe, you did whatever you had to do. No matter what.

Still, she wasn't ready to let him off the hook. "Let's get something straight," she said, straightening her spine. "I like Ana. She's been good to me. Real good. I would never hurt her. I don't care how good your reason is—you are a jerk for thinking otherwise."

They were back to Mexican standoff territory, with their eyes challenging one another. Patience focused on keeping her breath even. She didn't know if it was his scent, his close proximity, or the thrill of having held her ground, but she could feel the adrenaline surging through her. When Stuart broke the moment with a slow, lazy smile, her heart jumped. The thrill of victory, she decided.

"Yes, I was," he said. "A jerk, that is."

"Finally, we agree with something." She sat back, only to realize the new posture placed her in the crook of his arm. Instinct screamed for her to straighten up again, but that would imply she was nervous, and since she wasn't nervous she forced herself to look relaxed. "Apology accepted."

Stuart responded with a low chuckle before—thankfully—shifting positions and releasing her. Patience was surprised how much she missed his scent when it disappeared.

"How about we start over with a clean slate?" he said. "Hi. I'm Stuart Duchenko."

She stared at his extended hand. For some reason, the gesture kicked off warning bells. "Why?" she asked.

"Why what?"

"Why the one-eighty?" A dozen hours ago, he was smirking with suspicion. Now he wanted to be friends?

He'd obviously expected the question, because he chuckled again. "Because you're right, I was being a jerk. And, because Ana would have my head if she saw the way I was acting. Our bickering like a couple of twelve-year-olds won't help her. Therefore, I'm hoping we can be civil for her sake."

He had a point. Ana would expect better of her, as well. "Does this mean you've decided to trust me?"

"Let's not go crazy. I am, however, willing to give you the chance to prove me wrong."

"Well, isn't that mighty big of you." Although, in truth, they had something in common. She didn't trust him, either.

His hand was still extended, waiting for her acceptance. Fine. She could be the bigger person, too. For Ana's sake.

"I'm Patience Rush," she said, wrapping her fingers around his palm.

His grip was firm and confident, more so than she expected. Patience was shocked at the power traveling up her arm.

You're playing with fire, a tiny voice whispered in her ear. Stuart wasn't some sour-smelling creep she could hold off with an expressionless stare. He was a man whose clout and influence could ruin her life. But, like a shining red sign blinking "Do Not Touch," she couldn't resist the challenge.

"Nice to meet you, Patience. I look forward to getting to know you."

"Same here."

She wasn't sure what to say next and, based on the awkward silence, neither did he. The strangest energy had begun humming around them. Wrapping them together, as if the two of them were suddenly on the same page. Weird. Other than Piper, Patience had always made it a rule to keep an invisible wall between herself and the rest of the world. To feel a connection of any kind left her off balance.

Stuart's smile mirrored her insides. Tentative and crooked. "Look at us being all civil."

"Let's not go crazy," she replied, quoting him. "It's only been a minute. Let's see how we do at the end of the day."

"I'm up for the challenge if you are."

Oh, she was more than up for it. If being civil led to him dropping all his talk of "secrets," then she'd civil him to death.

CHAPTER THREE

To HER COMPLETE and utter amazement, he didn't insist on supervising her work. Instead, he left her with a friendly "Don't forget to mark down check 3521." Probably planning to double-check her work later, Patience decided. She took more care than usual to make sure the ledgers were perfect.

After lunch, Stuart went to the hospital to spend time with Ana while she stayed behind to wage war with the brownstone windows. She thought about visiting as well, but decided to wait until evening so Stuart would see how seriously she took her job.

And, okay, maybe part of her wanted to avoid him. Being civil would be a lot easier if they didn't see each other. The energy shift when they shook hands still had her thrown. Ever since, there'd been this inexplicable fluttering in her stomach that no amount of window cleaning could shake. A reminder that she wasn't dealing with an ordinary man, but rather someone a class above the creeps and losers who'd crossed her path over the years. Talk about two different worlds, she thought with an unbidden shiver. All the more reason to avoid him as much as possible.

And so, armed with cleaner and crumpled newspaper, she polished glass until the smell of vinegar clung to her nostrils and there wasn't a streak to be found. As she stretched out the small of her back, she checked the clock on the parlor mantel. Five o'clock. Time to feed the beast. She was surprised Nigel wasn't upstairs with her, meowing up a storm. He wasn't in the hallway, either.

"You better not be hiding somewhere thinking about pouncing on me," she called out as she trotted down the stairs. "I can tell you right now scaring me won't get you on my good side."

"I'll keep that in mind," Stuart replied. He looked impossibly at home, standing at the counter with a cat food can in his hand and Nigel weaving in and around his legs.

"What are you doing here?" she asked, only to realize how abrupt she sounded. They were supposed to be acting civil after all. "I mean, I thought you were visiting Ana." That sounded much nicer.

"I got home a few minutes ago and Nigel met me at the door. Nearly broke my ankle demanding supper."

"No way!" She purposely exaggerated her disbelief. "Good thing you weren't on the stairs." Her smirk couldn't have faded even if she wanted it to. *Go Nigel.* Kitty earned himself extra tuna.

To his credit, Stuart had the decency to look apologetic. "Point made. I was wrong."

"Told you so." Since they were being civil, she kept the rest of her gloating to herself. Instead, she bent down to retrieve Nigel's bowl, making sure she gave the cat an extra scratch under the chin when he ran over to see her. "How is Ana?" she asked.

His expression changed in a flash, growing somber. "They've got her on pain medicine so she mostly sleeps, and the couple times she did wake up, she was confused. The nurses told me that's pretty common, especially at her age." He breathed hard through his nostrils. A nonverbal *but*...

Patience felt herself softening toward the man even more. Seeing Ana so weak had upset her, too, and she had been around to see how active Ana had been. Goodness only knows how shocked Stuart must have felt having missed the last eight months. "I'm sure she'll be back to her feisty self in no time," she said, trying to reassure him. And herself, too, maybe.

"That's what the nurses said."

"But...?" There was a hesitancy in his response that once again left the word hanging in the air.

"Did you know one-fourth of senior citizens who break a hip die within six months?"

"Not Ana." No way was he going down that road. "She'd kill you if she heard you. Besides, she broke an ankle, not a hip, so your statistic doesn't apply."

"You're right. It doesn't." A smile graced his features. Forced maybe, but it erased the sadness from his face. Patience was glad. He looked much better with his dimples showing. Not that he didn't look good when serious, but his appeal definitely increased when his eyes sparkled.

"And Ana would kill me," he added, and they shared another smile before Stuart looked away to finish feeding Nigel. Patience waited until he'd scraped the sides of the cat food can before placing the bowl back in its place. "I was planning to visit Ana tonight," she told him.

"Me too. Right after dinner."

Shoot! She'd completely forgotten about dinner. Normally, by this point in the day, she'd have started cooking, but she'd been so engrossed in cleaning the windows—and trying not to think about Stuart—that everything else slipped her mind. "I…um…" Combing the bangs from her eyes, she caught a whiff of vinegar and winced at the odor. "I hope you don't mind simple. I forgot to get the meat out to thaw."

"Don't worry about it. I'll grab something on the way. I've been dying for an Al's Roast Beef."

"No way."

"What, you don't like Al's?"

"No, I love it." She was surprised he did. Al's was a little hole-in-the-wall near the subway overpass. The kind of place you weren't one-hundred-percent sure passed the health inspection, although it did have the most amazing burgers and roast beef sandwiches. She would have pegged Stuart as preferring something more upscale and elegant, like the wine bar up the street. "Can't beat their barbecue special."

"Would you like to join me?"

Join him? The hair on the back of her neck started to rise, much the way it did when he'd suggested they start over. She didn't trust this warmer, gentler Stuart. Especially since he said he still didn't trust her.

What was he up to?

"We both need to eat," he replied, picking up on her hesitation. "We're both going to the hospital. Why not go together?"

Why not? She could give a bunch of reasons, starting with the fact she should be avoiding him, not giving him an opportunity to dig for information.

"Plus, I owe you an apology for being wrong about Nigel."

"You do owe me that," Patience replied.

"So, is that a yes?" His expectant smile was so charming it caused her stomach to do a tiny somersault. As sure a sign as any that she should say no. Playing with fire, the voice in her head reminded her.

Except that smile was too darn hard to refuse. "Sure," she replied. "Why not?"

She regretted her response as soon as they arrived at Al's. Actually, she regretted it as soon as the words left her mouth and Stuart flashed a knee-buckling smile, but arriving at the restaurant sealed the deal—*restaurant* being a loose description. Beacon Hill types considered the banged-up booths and ketchup stains "atmosphere." Patience considered it dirty. The place reminded her too much of the old days.

"We could do takeout if you'd rather," Stuart said, correctly interpreting her expression. "Go eat by the river."

Patience shook her head. "No. Here will be fine." A picnic by the river sounded too nice, and, frankly, the situation was strange enough without the atmosphere feeling like a date.

This kinder, gentler Stuart made her nervous. They weren't friends—not by a long shot—and she wasn't really sure she bought his apology excuse. So why were they out to dinner together?

After placing their orders, they took seats in a booth toward the rear of the restaurant. One of the cleaner tables, if that was saying anything. Immediately, Patience took out a package of hand wipes and began cleaning the crumbs from the surface, earning a chuckle from Stuart.

"You do realize you're off the clock, right?" he asked.

"You want to eat on a dirty table?" she shot back. She was beginning to dislike his laugh. Rich and thick, the sound slipped down her spine like warm chocolate syrup, making her insides quiver every time she heard it. Doubling down on her cleaning efforts, she did her best to wash both the crumbs and the sensation away. "I don't even want to think about what the kitchen looks like," she continued.

There was a splash of dried cola near the napkin dispenser. She went at it with vigor. "Piper would have a nutty if she saw this place."

"Who's Piper?"

Drat. She didn't realize she'd spoken aloud. This really was a mistake. Not five minutes in and she'd opened the door to personal questions. Fortunately, Piper was the one personal subject she could talk about forever. "She's my sister."

"Let me guess, she's into cleaning, too?"

"No, cooking." Her chest grew full. "She's studying to be a chef. In Paris." She made a point of emphasizing the location.

"Is that so?"

Based on the spark in Stuart's eye, Patience decided it was admiration and not disbelief coloring his voice, and her pride expanded some more. "She was accepted last fall. It's always been her dream to become a famous chef."

"You must be proud."

"Proud doesn't begin to cover it. I think she's going to be the next Top Chef, she's that talented. Ever since she was a kid, she had a knack for taking ingredients you'd never thought would go together and turning them into something delicious. Once, I came home and found her making jalapeño pancakes."

"Were they any good?"

"Believe it or not, they were. Although she got flour everywhere. Took me all night to clean the film from the countertop." A waste of time since the roaches came scrounging anyway. The thought only made her smile fade a little. As always, her pride in Piper's talent overruled the bad.

Their conversation was interrupted by a group of college students settling into the booth behind them. Their laughter barely disguised the popping of beer cans.

"I forgot this place was BYOB," Stuart remarked. "We could have brought a bottle of Merlot to go with our meal."

"I'm not sure this is a Merlot kind of place," Patience replied.

"Good point. Beer then."

She tried and failed to stop her grimace.

"You don't like beer?"

"I don't like the smell." He wouldn't either if he'd spent years breathing sour, stale air.

Stuart was clearly curious, but thankfully he didn't push. At least not right then. Instead, he stretched his arms along the back of the booth, the position pulling his shirt taut across his torso and emphasizing the contours beneath the cotton. Patience wondered if he realized he was the most superior-looking man in the place.

"So, your sister's dream is to become a famous chef," he said. "What's yours?"

To make sure Piper's dream came true. Patience busied herself with pulling napkins from the dispenser. "I don't know what you mean."

"Oh, come on. Surely you didn't always want to be a housekeeper?"

He was fishing. Looking for clues about this so-called agenda he thought she had regarding his aunt. What would he think if she told him her childhood hadn't allowed for dreams or aspirations? Or that there was a time when even being a housekeeper seemed out of her reach? Would he trust her more or less? Patience could guess the answer.

"I thought we called a truce," she said, dodging the question.

"Hey, I was just making conversation. I didn't realize I'd asked you to reveal a state secret."

He had a point. Maybe she was overreacting just a little. It certainly wasn't his fault he'd stumbled too close to a bad topic. "Teacher," she said softly. "When I was little, I wanted to be a teacher."

"There now, that wasn't so hard, was it?" Damn him for having a charming smile as he spoke. "What changed your mind?"

"I grew up," she replied. The words came out sharper than she intended, causing a stunned expression. "And my mother died, leaving me to raise Piper." She was probably telling him way too much, but she figured revealing some facts was smarter than acting prickly. "Hard to go to school and raise your kid sister." Not that there was money for school to begin with, but he didn't need to know that.

"I'm sorry. How old were you?"

"Eighteen."

"That must have been tough."

"We managed. How about you?" She rushed to change the subject before he could ask anything further. "Did you always want to be a lawyer?"

He laughed again. "Of course not. No little boy wants to be lawyer. I wanted to be a professional baseball player."

"What happened?"

"I grew up," he said, repeating her answer. In his case, instead of sounding prickly, the words came out sad, despite his clearly trying to sound otherwise. "Turns out you have to have athletic ability to be a professional athlete—or a child athlete, for that matter."

Looking at him, she found his protest a bit hard to believe. "You look pretty athletic to me," she said. His arched brow made her blush. "I mean, I'm sure you weren't as bad as you make it sound."

"I had bad eyes, allergies and childhood asthma. Trust me, no one was ever going to confuse me with Babe Ruth. Or John Ruth for that matter."

"Who's John Ruth?"

"Exactly." He grinned, and she got the joke. He was worse than a guy who didn't exist.

"So," he continued, "with the Hall of Fame out of the picture, I found myself steered toward the family business."

"I thought your family business was mining?" Ana was always talking about Duchenko silver.

"Not since the turn of the century. Grandpa Theodore turned it into law. Thankfully. Can you see me coughing and squinting my way through a silver mine?"

No, she thought with a laugh. He definitely belonged to suits and luxury surroundings. His choice of words did make her curious, however. "You said steered. You didn't choose?"

"Sometimes you find yourself on a path without realizing it," he replied with a shrug.

Patience could sure relate to that, although at its worst, his path couldn't hold a candle to the one she'd landed on. "Do you at least like it?"

"For the most part. There are days when I'd rather be in the mine."

"No offense," she told him, "but I'll take the bad day of a rich lawyer over the bad day of a poor maid anytime."

"Don't be so sure," he said. "You've never had to draft a prenuptial agreement for your step-grandmother."

At that moment, the girl at the counter called out their order, and he slid from the booth, leaving Patience to wonder about his answer. Writing some document hardly seemed a big ordeal.

Stuart returned a few minutes later with a tray laden with food. The smell of fresh beef made her stomach rumble. Grimy location or not, Al's did have good burgers.

She waited until they'd divided the burgers and French fries before picking up the conversation. "How is writing a prenuptial so awful?" she asked him. "It's not like unclogging a toilet or something."

"You wouldn't say that if you met Grandma Gloria."

"Harsh."

"Not harsh enough," he said, biting into his burger.

So Patience wasn't the only person Stuart had issues with. Maybe he didn't like outsiders in general. Or was it only women? "She had to have some redeeming quality. I mean if your grandfather loved her…"

"Grandpa Theodore *wanted* her. Big difference."

"She must have wanted him too," Patience replied. She wasn't sure why she felt the need to defend this Gloria person, unless it was because exonerating Gloria might improve her own standing in his mind.

"She wanted Duchenko money." There was no mistaking the venom in his voice. "And she went after it like a heat-seeking missile. Didn't matter who she got the money from, or who she had to hurt in the process."

Like who? The way his face twisted with bitterness made her think he was leaving something out of the story. It certainly explained why he had issues with her befriending Ana.

"This Gloria woman sounds lovely."

"Oh, she was a real peach. Did I mention she turned thirty-four on her last birthday?" he added abruptly.

"Thirty-four?"

"Uh-huh."

"Hasn't your grandfather been dead for…"

"Ten years," he supplied. My grandfather died ten years ago."

Making Gloria…ew. Patience wrinkled her nose at the image.

"Exactly. And now I'm stuck dealing with her for the rest of eternity."

Patience took a long sip of her cola. His comments had opened the door to a lot of questions, about many of which she had no business being curious, and yet seeing his frown, she couldn't help herself. "Ana doesn't talk much about her family," she said. "Other than you, that is.

"Unfortunately, there wasn't much love lost between Ana and Grandpa Theodore. From what I understand, they stopped speaking to each other around forty or fifty years ago. People were shocked when she traveled to his funeral. She told them it was only out of respect for me."

"Wow." To not speak to your sibling for decades? She couldn't imagine going more than two or three days without talking to Piper. "That must have been some fight."

"True. I asked Ana once, but all she said was Grandpa Theodore stole her happiness."

"How?" Ana seemed like one of the happiest people she knew.

"Beats me. I remember my father grumbling once that he wished my grandfather would make things right this one time, so whatever happened was his fault. Unfortunately, unless Ana decides to open up, we might never know."

"Your poor dad. Sounds like he was stuck in the middle."

"For a little while anyway. He uh…" His eyes dropped to his half-eaten meal. "He and my mom died in a car accident when I was fourteen."

"Oh." Patience kicked herself for bringing up the subject. "I'm sorry."

"It was a long time ago."

Time didn't mean anything. There was nothing worse than having the ground yanked out from under you, leaving you with no idea where you belonged, what would happen next, or who would catch you if you fell. The teenage Stuart would have held in the pain, put on a strong face. She could tell by the way he held himself now, closed and protected.

Just like her. *No one should be forced to grow up before they're ready.*

Again, it was as if she'd spoken her thoughts out loud, because Stuart looked up, his blue eyes filled with a mixture of curiosity and gratitude. "I'm going to go out on a limb and say you grew up earlier than I did."

His words twisted around her heart. If only he knew... For a crazy second, she longed to tell him everything, thinking that he, having been in her shoes, might understand. Reality quickly squashed her fantasy. He'd never understand. The two of them came from two different worlds. Rich versus poor. Clean versus dirty. Sitting here, sharing childhood losses, it was easy for that fact to slip her mind.

"It's not really a contest I wanted to win," she heard herself answer.

"I don't suppose anyone ever does." Picking up his soda, he saluted her with the paper cup. "To happier subjects."

That was it? No questions? No probing? Patience studied his face, looking for evidence that the other shoe was about to drop. She saw nothing but sincerity in his smoky eyes.

"To happier subjects," she repeated. She'd gotten off easy this time.

Or had she? Stuart smiled over the rim of his glass, causing her insides to flip end over end. All of a sudden, Patience didn't feel she'd gotten off at all. More like she was falling into something very dangerous.

"Ana seemed a little more with it tonight," Patience remarked a few hours later. They were walking along Charles Street on their way home from the hospital.

"Yes, she did," Stuart replied. The change from this afternoon made him hopeful. Interesting, how his aunt's improvement seemed tied to Patience's arrival. Much as he hated to admit it, the housekeeper and his aunt had a real rapport. Patience was so, well, patient, with the older woman. Gentle, too. Getting Ana water. Making her comfortable. Everything about Patience's behavior tonight screamed authenticity. If her kindness was an act, Patience deserved an award.

Then again, he'd seen award-worthy performances before, hadn't he? He'd purposely brought up Gloria over dinner to gauge Patience's reaction, thinking the topic of fortune hunters might at least cause her to reveal some kind of body language. Instead, he got sympathy, felt a connection...

"You're frowning." Patience remarked.

"Sorry, I was thinking how little Ana ate this evening."

"She never eats much. You know that."

Yes, thought Stuart, but he needed something to dodge her question.

They walked a few feet in silence. The night was balmy and clear. Combined with the warm breeze, it created an almost romantic feel to the air around them. Stuart stole a glance in Patience's direction. She had her arms folded across her chest, and her eyes were focused on the pavement. Even so, he could still sense the undulating of her hips. It was, he realized, unconscious and natural. Otherwise, he suspected she'd attempt to downplay the sensuality the way she did her figure and her looks. Hell, maybe she was trying and failing. She certainly wasn't having much luck minimizing the other two.

That plastic hair band was failing, too. Strands of hair had broken free, and covered her eyes. One of them needed to brush the bangs away so he could see their sparkle again.

He rubbed the back of his neck instead.

Patience must have mistaken the action for him being warm. "You can definitely tell it's going to be the first day of summer," she remarked.

"Longest day of the year. Did you know that after tomorrow, every day gets a few seconds shorter? Before you know it, we'll be losing two and a half minutes a day. Sorry," he quickly added. "I did a graph for a high school science fair. The fact kind of stuck with me."

"In other words, you were blind, asthmatic, unathletic and a science nerd. No wonder you gave up on baseball."

He felt his cheeks grow warm. "For the record, I'd outgrown the asthma by then."

"Glad to hear it."

"Hey, we can't all be homecoming queens."

If he didn't know better, he'd swear she hugged her body a little tighter. "I didn't go to many school dances," she said.

Another piece to what was becoming a very confusing puzzle. One moment she was sexy and sharp-witted; the next, her eyes reminded him of a kitten— soft and innocent. What the heck was her story? He was no closer to knowing if Patience had an agenda than he was this morning. They might say you get more flies with honey, but all he got was more questions.

Along with a dangerously mounting attraction.

Cool air greeted them upon entering the brownstone. Stuart shut the front door and turned on the hallway light. Nigel, who had been sitting on a table by the front window greeted them with a loud meow before running toward the kitchen.

"For crying out loud," Patience called after him. "It's only been a few hours."

At the other end of the hall, the meows grew louder and more indignant—if such a thing was possible. She rolled her eyes, earning a chuckle from Stuart. He said, "You think he's bad, you should have met the other Nigels."

There were more? "You mean he's not the first."

"Actually, he's the third. Nigel the Second lived here while I was in law school."

"Wow, Ana must really like the name Nigel." Either that or the woman wasn't very good at pet names.

"I asked her once why she gave them all the same name,' Stuart added. "She told me it was because they all have Nigel personalities."

"If that's true, remind me to avoid guys named Nigel."

Their chuckles faded to silence. Patience toed the pattern on the entryway carpet. What now? There was an awkward expectancy in the air, as if both of them knew they should do or say something. The problem was, neither knew what.

At least Nigel had stopped his meowing.

"Thank you for dinner,' she said finally.

"You're welcome." He smiled. "Maybe we've got this being civil thing down."

"Maybe. I have to admit, you're not bad company when you aren't accusing me of things."

"Never fear, tomorrow's another day," he replied. Patience would have laughed, but there was too much truth to his comment. This temporary truce of theirs could break at any time.

"By the way," he added, you're not such bad company yourself. When you aren't dodging questions."

"Like you said, tomorrow's another day." She turned to leave only to have her left foot tangle with something warm and furry. Nigel. She maneuvered herself awkwardly, trying to avoid stepping on the darn cat. Her ankle twisted, and she pitched sideways, toward the stairway. That caused her right knee to buckle, and before she knew it, she was falling in a heap.

Stuart caught her before her bottom touched the floor. "Stupid cat," she muttered.

"Are you okay?"

"I'm fine. Nigel on the other hand might have used up another one of his nine lives." She looked around, but the creature was nowhere to be found.

"He ran upstairs," Stuart replied, helping her to her feet.

"With his tail between his legs, I hope. If you didn't believe me before about Nigel causing Ana's fall, you have to believe me now."

"The evidence is definitely in your favor. Are you sure you're okay?"

"Positive. My butt didn't even hit the ground."

"Good. Hate to see you bruise something you might need," he said with a smile.

That's when she realized he still held her. His arm remained wrapped around her waist, pulling her close, so that their hips were flush. The odd angle gave Patience little choice but to rest her hand on his upper arm,

They might as well have been embracing.

He smelled of soap and laundry detergent. No aftershave—a testimony to his innate maleness that he didn't need anything more. Awareness—no, something stronger than awareness—washed over her, settling deep in the pit of her stomach.

Fingers brushed her bangs away from her temple. Barely a whisper of a touch, it shot straight to her toes. Slowly, she lifted her gaze. "I've been wanting to do that all night," he said in a voice softer than his touch.

"I—I'm growing out my bangs. That's why they keep falling in my face." Why did she think he wasn't talking about her bangs?

Maybe because his attention had shifted to her mouth. Staring, studying. Patience caught her lip between her teeth to stop it from trembling. All either of them needed to do was to move their head the tiniest bit and they would be close enough to kiss.

"I should check on Nigel…" She twisted from his grasp, combing her fingers through her hair in a lousy attempt to mask her abruptness. She needed to…she didn't know what she needed to do. The blood pounding in her ears made it hard to think.

She needed space. That's what. Turning on her heel, she headed upstairs, forcing herself to take one step at a time. She lasted until the second flight, when Stuart was out of sight, before doubling the pace.

Smooth going, Patience, she thought when she finally closed her bedroom door. Why don't you break out in a cold sweat while you're at it?

What on earth was wrong with her anyway? She'd dealt with literally dozens of unwanted advances over the years. Losers, pushy drunks, punks who couldn't keep their hands to themselves And she freaks out because Stuart touched her hair? The guy didn't even try anything.

Oh, but you wanted him to, didn't you? That's why

she'd bolted. In spite of everything that had gone on between them in the past twenty-four hours, she actually wanted Stuart Duchenko to kiss her.

Heaven help her, but she still did.

CHAPTER FOUR

THE NEXT MORNING, Patience woke up with a far clearer head. Tossing and turning for half the night did that for a person.

When she thought things through, Patience wasn't really surprised that she was attracted to Stuart. Along with being handsome, he was the polar opposite of every man who had ever crossed her path. Sadly, that difference was exactly why she had no business kissing or doing anything else with him.

Throwing back the covers, she stretched and headed for the shower. Back in her and Piper's old apartment, a long hot shower was her way of scrubbing away life's dirt. The close, fiberglass stall had been her oasis. This morning, she was using Ana's Italian marble shower to rinse away last night's fantastical thoughts. There was probably some kind of irony in that. All she knew was she had to go back to keeping her distance before she made a fool of herself or, worse, said something she shouldn't.

The brownstone was empty when she finally came downstairs. A quick look toward his bedroom door—because she needed to prepare breakfast, not because she was thinking about him—showed Stuart was already awake. Up and out, apparently. A good thing, Patience told herself. She still wasn't sure how to explain her behavior last night, and Stuart's absence gave her the space she needed to come up with one.

Nigel was sitting by the kitchen door. The food littering his mat said he'd already had breakfast. There was coffee in the coffeepot, too.

"He sure is making it hard to stay unaffected, isn't he, Nigel?" She gave the cat a scratch behind the ear. "But we're going to do our best."

Just then the front door opened, signaling the end of her solitude. With a soft meow, Nigel trotted toward the entryway. "Hey, Nigel," she heard him greet. "Told you I'd be back."

Patience rubbed her arms, which had suddenly developed goose bumps. Amazing the way the air seemed to shift every time he entered a building. Like the atmosphere needed to announce his arrival.

And thank goodness, too. She turned to the door at the same time he entered, and if she hadn't been forewarned, her knees would have buckled underneath her completely.

He'd lied last night. No way the man walking into the kitchen was an unathletic nerd. His thin cotton tank might as well be nonexistent, the way it clung to his sweaty body. She could see every muscle, every inch of nonexistent fat. His arms alone…were lawyers allowed to have biceps that illegal? All those thoughts she had about his being commanding and superior? They doubled. And she'd thought he might kiss her last night? Talk about being a fool.

"Good morning." He barely looked in her direction as he made his way to the refrigerator. "Going to be a scorcher. You can feel the heat in the air already." Grabbing a bottle of water, he downed the contents in one long drink. "Did you sleep all right?"

Clearly last night's encounter hadn't affected him. "Fine," she lied, ignoring the hollow feeling threatening to take hold of her insides. "You?"

"As well as anyone with a furry bed warmer can sleep. Nigel has apparently appointed me the substitute Duchenko."

"I noticed you fed him. And made coffee. Thank you."

"Since I was awake first, it seemed only logical. Plus, Nigel would never have let me leave the house, and I wanted to get a run in before it got too humid."

"I didn't know you were a runner."

"Grandpa Theodore's idea. He thought it would help keep my lungs strong. The habit just sort of stuck." As he talked, he crossed the kitchen to the side where she stood. Patience gripped the counter a little tighter. Even sweaty, his skin smelled appealing. Instead of stale and dirty, it was the fresh, clean scent of exertion.

"I called the hospital before I left. Ana had a good night," he said, reaching into the cupboard for a mug.

He offered her a mug, as well, but Patience shook her head. Sharing coffee together felt too domestic and familiar.

"Oh, good. I was thinking of taking her some of her favorite tea and cookies when I visited her today. Since you were concerned about her eating and all… what?"

He was giving her one of those looks, where he seemed to be trying to read her mind. "That's very thoughtful of you."

"You sound surprised."

"Actually..." His expression turned inward. "I'm beginning not to be."

"Thank you. I guess." Maybe he was finally realizing she wasn't some kind of criminal mastermind out to take his aunt's money or whatever it was he suspected her of being. Maybe this meant he would back off and her insides could unwind.

Or maybe not, she corrected, taking in his muscular arms.

"Don't get too comfortable. I'm still keeping an eye on you." Damn, if the smile accompanying the remark didn't make her insides grow squirrelly. He finished pouring his coffee and headed toward the door. "I'm planning to stop by the hospital before work this morning. If you'd like, I can give you a ride."

"Thanks," she replied as Stuart left to get a shower. Sitting in close quarters with him while they wove through traffic was not her idea of fun. She'd bet he had a tiny Italian sports car so their knees could bump on every turn, too.

"Like I said," she remarked to Nigel, who had returned and was weaving in and out of her legs, "he's making it awfully difficult."

Stuart took the stairs two at a time. So much for the restorative powers of a good run. Five miles and his thoughts were still racing.

Not just his thoughts. All he could say was thank goodness Patience wasn't trying to look sexy or he'd have a heart attack.

It was time he accepted the fact that he'd gone from finding the woman attractive to being attracted to her. His fate was sealed the second his arm slipped around her waist. She fit so perfectly, her hips aligning with his as though they were meant to be connected...

Giving a groan, he kicked his bedroom door shut. It was all that damn tendril's fault. If the strand had stayed tucked in her band where it belonged, he wouldn't have been compelled to brush the hair from her face, and if he hadn't brushed her hair, he never would have considered kissing her.

And oh, did he consider. He owed her a thank-you for bolting upstairs. Kept him from crossing an improper line with his aunt's employee.

Raised a few more questions, too. Mainly, what made her flee in the first place? Stuart swore that for a few seconds before Patience took flight, he saw real desire in her eyes. Did she back off because she realized the mistake they were about to make or because of something more? The lady sure had her secrets.

Maybe he could find out what they were. That is, if he could keep his attraction—and his hands—to himself.

Surprisingly—or perhaps not so surprisingly—Patience left for the hospital without him. The hastily scrawled note pinned to the coffeemaker said she needed to stop at the tea shop to buy Ana her Russian caravan tea. "A reasonable excuse," he said to Nigel. But the tea shop was only a block away, and in the direction of the hospital. He would have gladly waited while she ran her errand.

No, more likely, she wanted to avoid being in the car with him. For him to care about her decision was silly, but care he did. Why didn't she want to ride with him?

Unfortunately, any answer had to wait because when

he arrived at the hospital, his aunt was awake. Someone had raised her bed so she was sitting upright. Patience stood by her head, brushing out her hair. Stuart watched as her arm moved with long, slow strokes, each pass banishing the tangles of hospitalization. "Do you want to leave the braid down or wear it coiled?" he heard her ask.

"Coiled," Ana replied. "Of course."

He smiled. His aunt always insisted on looking as regal as possible. She was wearing the serenest of expressions. Her eyes were closed and the hint of a smile played across her lips. For the first time since he'd come home, she resembled the Ana he remembered.

His chest squeezed tight, his heart and lungs suddenly too big for his body. He was afraid to cough lest he spoil his aunt's moment.

"Good morning." The moment ended anyway, as Dr. Tischel, Ana's primary care physician boomed his greeting from behind his shoulder. *"Lapushka!"* Ana greeted with a smile. "How long have you been standing there?"

"Not long. I didn't want to disturb your beauty session." He locked eyes with Patience only to have her break the gaze and resume brushing. "How are you this morning, Tetya?" He kissed Ana's cheek.

"I don't know," she replied. "How am I, Karl?"

"Remarkably lucky, for one thing. You're too old to be rolling down staircases. We all are."

All the more reason not to stare at women two-thirds your age, thought Stuart. The good doctor's gaze had locked itself to a spot below Patience's neck. The housekeeper had angled her body toward the wall, but that didn't stop the man's blatant assessment.

"Will she be able to go home soon?" Stuart asked in a loud voice, drawing the man's attention. A question to which he already knew the answer, but then he wasn't asking because he wanted information.

"I'm afraid not," the doctor replied. The man didn't even have the decency to look embarrassed. "You took a nasty fall, Ana."

He lifted the sheet from where it covered the upper part of her legs. On the leg without a cast, a large bruise turned Ana's kneecap purple. Dr. Tischel touched around it, causing Ana to wince.

"Knee's pretty tender," he said, stating the obvious. "You're definitely going to have to stay off your feet for a little while."

"Are we talking about a wheelchair?" Stuart asked. He was having trouble imaging his great-aunt managing crutches as the moment.

"At the very least," the doctor replied. "For a little while anyway."

"Don't worry," Patience said. "I'll push you around the house."

"Oh no, the brownstone has way too many stairs," Dr. Tishcel said. "That's what got you in trouble in the first place. The rehab hospital has a terrific orthopedics wing. They'll take good care of you."

"What?" In spite of her pain, Ana stiffened. "You're sending me to another hospital? For how long?"

"Depends," Dr. Tischel replied. "At least a couple of weeks."

"A couple weeks!" Patience and Ana spoke at the same time, although he was pretty sure their furor was for two different reasons. Stuart tensed at the announcement himself, and he'd been expecting the news since the day Ana fell. Two weeks sharing a house with Patience. Alone.

"I'm afraid so," Dr. Tischel replied. "We want to make sure that ankle heals properly. I'll give them a call this afternoon and check on availability. With luck there's a bed open and we can transfer you tomorrow.

"In the meantime," he said, pulling the sheet back over her legs, "I want you to try and sit up in a chair for a few hours."

Ana gave an indignant cough. "Don't know why if I'm just going to be laid up in another hospital bed."

"Because the movement will do you good. You don't want to develop blood clots, do you?"

"No, she does not," Stuart answered. Seeing the doctor was getting ready to leave, he rose from his chair, hoping to keep the man from giving Patience another once-over. Granted, he shared Dr. Tischel's appreciation of her beauty, but the woman wasn't standing there for his viewing pleasure. He held out a hand. "Thank you for your help."

The gambit failed as the older man shook his hand only briefly before reaching across Ana to grasp Patience's. "It's my pleasure. Ana has always been one of my favorite patients."

Ana coughed again. "Favorite, my foot," she grumbled once the doctor left. "Stupid old fool wants to stick me in a nursing home."

"Rehab facility, Tetya." Stuart replied. Out of the corner of his eye, he caught Patience wiping her hand on her jeans. Apparently, she wasn't impressed with Dr. Tischel's behavior this morning, either. "It's only for a little while. You'll be back at the brownstone before you know it."

Ana shrugged. She looked so sad it made Stuart almost want to tell her Dr. Tischel had made a mistake. In a way, he understood. The news probably did sound like a sentence. She was losing her freedom.

He grabbed her fingers. "I'll visit every day, I promise."

"And me," Patience said. "I'll even find out if I can bring Nigel so you can see him, too."

"Will you?" Ana's face brightened. "I've been so worried about him. He acts tough, but on the inside, he's really very sensitive."

"I'll do everything I can. I promise."

Stuart watched while the two women talked about the cat, his chest squeezing tight again. The soft, caring tone in Patience's voice mesmerized him. She sounded so genuine; it made him want so badly to trust her intentions.

Could he?

Just then, Patience reached over to brush a strand of hair from Ana's face, sending his mind hurtling to the night before. Parts of his body stirred remembering how soft Patience's hair had felt sliding through his fingers. How on earth was he going to spend two weeks with Patience, get to know her and keep his attraction under control?

"Oh, no!"

Ana's cry shook him from his reverie. She sat straight, her face crumpled in distress. "What's wrong, Tetya?" he asked.

"The humane society dinner dance. I totally forgot, but it's tonight."

Was that all? Stuart let out his breath. "Looks like you'll have to miss this year's festivities."

"But I can't," Ana said. "I'm being honored as the volunteer of the year. I'm supposed to be there to accept my award."

"I'm sure people will understand why you're not there, Tetya. You can have your friend, Mrs. Calloway, accept on your behalf."

"Ethyl Calloway is not my friend," his aunt snapped.

Stuart should have remembered. Ana and Ethyl weren't friends so much as friendly society rivals. The two of them had worked side by side at the Beacon Hill Humane Society for years, competing to see who could do more to further the organization's good work. As a result, hundreds of homeless cats and dogs had found new homes. Personally, he thought it incredibly fitting that Ethyl accept the award on his aunt's behalf, but what did he know?

"Missing the ceremony isn't going to diminish what you've done for the shelter," Patience said. "People will still know about your hard work."

To Patience's credit, her comment worked. Ana settled back against her pillow, her agitation fading. "Will you accept the award for me?" she asked.

Stuart cringed. The humane society dinner dance was a nightmare of society women and their spouses who made it their mission to offer up single granddaughters to every eligible bachelor who had the misfortune of attending. Those without granddaughters used their time to strong-arm donations. The last time Ana had convinced him to attend, he'd left four figures poorer and with a pocket full of unwanted phone numbers. But the organization was Ana's pride and joy. Accepting her award was the least he could do.

"Of course I will," he told her.

His aunt and Patience exchanged an odd look. "What?" he asked.

"I think she meant me," Patience said.

The blush coloring her cheeks couldn't be as dark as the one heating his. "Oh. I didn't…"

"I had no idea you'd be home this week," his aunt said, her eyes looking deeply apologetic, "and you know how I hate to attend alone."

"You're more than welcome to go in my place," Patience added. "I don't mind."

No kidding. Her eyes were practically begging him to say yes, they were so hopeful-looking.

Unable to see the silent exchange, Ana waved the offer away. "Nonsense. You never go out. This is your chance to dress up and have a good time. Stuart will go with you."

"I will?" The painkillers had to be making Ana loopy again. Take Patience to an event where holding her in his arms would be encouraged? Bad idea.

"Someone has to keep the men from pestering her," Ana said. "You know how persistent some of those people can be."

Yes he did. In that sea of gray hair and pearls, Patience was going to stand out like a star. A welcome distraction for every senior man there.

Stuart wasn't sure if what he felt was jealousy or wariness on their behalf. "Ana's got a point," he said. "There is no reason why we shouldn't go together."

"See, dear? Stuart's on board."

He could see the moment Patience accepted her fate. Her shoulders slumped ever so slightly and she nodded. "All right."

"Good, it's settled. Stuart will go with you to the

dance, then tomorrow you can both fill me in on all the gossip." Ana relaxed a little more, the smile from earlier returning to her face.

"If you don't want to attend together, I'll understand," Stuart said when they stepped into the corridor a short while later. "I know Ana backed you into a corner. I'll be glad to deal with these people on my own."

Why? Was he trying to do her a favor or did he think she wouldn't fit in at the society function? Patience had to admit the second question had crossed her mind more than once.

She also had to admit that Ana hadn't backed her into anything. As soon as she suggested Stuart go along, her entire body broke out in excited tingles. Which, now that she thought about it, was a far bigger problem than not fitting in. Unfortunately...

"It's too late to back out now. Ana's expecting a report from both of us."

Patience wished she could read what was behind Stuart's long sigh. He ran a hand over his features, and when he finished, the face he revealed was an expressionless mask. "Very well," he said. "We'll go, collect her award, and make it an early night. That way, neither of us has to spend more time at this party than necessary."

Good idea, thought Patience. Less time for her to get into trouble.

So why did she feel disappointed?

CHAPTER FIVE

PATIENCE SMOOTHED THE front of her dress, then smoothed it again. Why hadn't she gone shopping this afternoon when she had the chance? The little black dress she pulled out of the closet was too short, too tight and too tacky. Everything about her screamed *cheap*.

It hadn't mattered when she'd thought she was attending with Ana. Or maybe it hadn't mattered *as much*. While naturally she wanted to please Ana, the older woman didn't make her stomach tumble.

Stuart shouldn't either, remember?

A knock sounded on her door. "Patience?" So much for not affecting her stomach. The sound of his voice made the butterflies' wings beat faster.

She draped a scarf around her shoulders, hoping that the draped material might camouflage her cleavage, smoothed her dress one more time and slipped into her pumps.

The heels were way too high. Would anyone notice how banged up her black flats were?

"Patience?"

Face it, she'd look out of place no matter what she wore. Best she could do was wear a smile and hope Stuart wasn't too horrified by her appearance.

Taking a deep breath, she opened the door.

Afraid of what she might see in Stuart's face, she avoided raising her eyes past his torso. That view was intimidating enough as it was. He was in full lawyer mode in a black suit similar to the one she remembered from the emergency room. This time, he finished off the outfit with a blue tie, the color of his eyes. To her embarrassment, Patience noticed her scarf matched. Made them look coordinated. *Like a couple.*

Maybe he wouldn't notice.

"Sorry to keep you waiting," she said.

"No worries. It was…worth the wait." There was an odd hitch to his voice. Mortification, maybe? Still afraid to look up and see, she pretended to pay attention to the steps as they headed downstairs.

"The Landmark isn't too far from here," he said. "Would you like to walk or drive?"

Once again, she faced the specter of being in a dark closed space with him. "Would you mind walking? I could use the fresh air." Anything to get the butterflies to settle down.

"Are you sure?" She didn't need to ask to know he was referring to her high heels. If only he knew how many hours she'd logged in shoes like these. A few blocks' walk would be a piece of cake.

The night air was surprisingly comfortable. A gentle breeze greeted them as they stepped onto the stoop. While Stuart locked the door behind them, Patience looked up at the darkening sky. A handful of early stars twinkled hello, and she made a quick wish that the night would turn out all right. Remembering their conversation from the night before, she asked, "How much daylight did we lose today?"

Stuart chuckled. "None, actually. The drop in daylight doesn't start for a few more days."

"So yesterday's explanation was wrong?"

"Generalized. I didn't realize I was going to be quizzed."

His hand hovered by the small of her back, guiding her down the steps. Patience made sure to walk quickly so as to avoid contact. "I'm sorry Ana strong-armed you into coming with me."

"I thought we covered this at the hospital. She strong-armed both of us."

"Yeah, but still I thought I should apologize. To be honest, I'm surprised you haven't said anything about the fact she and I were going together. I thought for sure you'd comment on it being part of my agenda."

"I thought about it, but since I know how badly Ana likes to have someone attend these things with her, 'll give you a pass." He flashed a smile. "Don't get used to it, though."

Patience added it to her list. Right after "going to parties with Stuart."

They stopped to wait for the traffic light. "I've never been to one of these kinds of events before," she said, while they waited for the light to change. "Any chance they'll present Ana's award early?"

"Nope. They need incentive for people to stick around. How else would they get them liquored up enough to bid on the silent auction items?"

"You ever bid?"

"Are you kidding? Those society women are worse than mob enforcers. You'd be amazed at the stuff they've convinced me to bid on. And for how much."

Patience fought a smile picturing Stuart fending off a parcel of senior citizens. "Did you win?"

"Twice. Once I won a gym membership. That was useful. The other time it was a romantic getaway to Newport, Rhode Island."

"Romantic weekend, huh?" She fought back the intense curiosity that rose up with his answer. Who was the lucky woman? In her mind, she pictured someone smart and sophisticated and who always wore the perfect outfit. Since his dating life wasn't her business, she settled for the blandest response she could think of. "At least you won something fun."

"So my secretary said."

"You took her on the trip?"

"No, I gave it to her as a bonus. She took her husband."

There was no need to feel relieved, but she was anyway.

They reached the Landmark just as a limousine pulled to the front door and a couple stepped on to the curb. Seeing the way the woman's diamond cocktail ring sparkled from a block away, Patience's palms began to sweat. She was supposed to mingle with these people? What was she going to talk about with them? By the way, what furniture polish does your cleaning lady use?

"Hey, you okay?"

She nodded, and adjusted her scarf. "I'm glad you're here is all. I'm a little…" Why not admit the truth? "I'm a little out of my league."

"Why?" he said. "It's just a lot of people dressed up and showing off."

A lot of people who hired people like her. No, correction. Who hired cleaning ladies. They wouldn't let her in the door, let alone hire her, if they knew her story.

"What you should really worry about is whether the chicken will be any good." His hand molded to the small of her back. The warmth of his touch spread up her spine, giving her courage. It was only for a few hours. She could do this.

The couple they saw were waiting for the elevator when they entered the lobby. It took less than ten seconds for Patience's confidence to flag. The same amount of time it took for the husband to smile and check out her legs. She wished Stuart's hand was still on her back. Then she could pretend he was with her by choice, and, by extension, the entire room would think so too. Instead, his fingers barely brushed her as they boarded the elevator.

Ethyl Calloway greeted them at the ballroom door. She was a tall, handsome woman who, like their companion on the elevator, was decorated with expensive jewelry. "Stuart! It's so good to see you." She kissed the air by his cheek. "How is Anastasia doing?"

"Much better," Stuart replied. "Already chomping at the bit to get back to her volunteer schedule. We had to practically tie her to the bed to keep her in the hospital."

"Well, at her age, it's best she not push herself too soon."

Her age? Ethyl wasn't much younger. The way the corner of Stuart's mouth was fighting not to smile, he was thinking the same thing. "Knowing Ana, she'll recover so fast she'll make the rest of us look lazy," Patience said.

Ethyl looked over as though she was noticing her for the first time. "Hello—Patty, isn't it?"

"Patience."

"Right. Ana mentioned she gave you a ticket. I'm glad you could make it. You'll be accepting Ana's award for her, right?" The older woman turned her attention back to Stuart. Actually, she physically turned toward Stuart and, in doing so, turned her back to Patience. Not on purpose, she told herself. Even so, she found herself blocked from the conversation. While Stuart nodded and went over details, she stood awkwardly to the side, smiling at the people who glanced in her direction.

"Lucky us," Stuart said, once Ethyl freed him from her attentions. "We're sitting at the front table."

"What does that mean?" From his sarcasm, she guessed not anything good.

"We get our rubber chicken first."

"Oh."

"And we get to sit with Ethyl. Take good notes. Ana's going to want a blow-by-blow recap." He pointed across the crowd to a congregation in the corner. "Looks like the bar is over there. I'll buy you drink."

They wound their way through the crowd, a difficult task as every ten feet some acquaintance of Ana's stopped them to ask for a medical update. After one very familiar-looking man inquired, she touched Stuart's arm. "Was that…?"

"The mayor?" He nodded.

Yep, she was out of her league. *Please don't let me do something stupid*

"Wine?" Stuart asked when they finally reached the front of the bar line.

Patience shook her head. "Sparkling water, please." Alcohol would go straight to her head, and she needed to keep her senses as sharp as possible. Another man walked by and checked out her legs. She gave the hemline a tug, on the off chance she could cover another quarter inch or so.

"You look fine." Stuart's breath was gentler than the breeze as he bent close and whispered in her ear. "Just a bunch of people…"

"Dressed up and showing off." She repeated his lesson for his benefit. Certainly her insides weren't listening. Her skin crawled, positive she was being evaluated by every person in the room and coming up short. What was that phrase about putting lipstick on a pig?

How she envied Stuart and the effortlessness with which he fit into his world. "I bet you go to a lot of these kinds of parties," she said to him.

"Only when I absolutely have to. Crowds and parties aren't really my thing."

"Really? But you look so at home." Everyone did, except for her.

"I'll tell you a secret." He leaned in close again. Damn, if he didn't smell better than the flower arrangements. "It helps if you think of all this as one big game," he said.

Distracted by the way his lips moved when he whispered, Patience nearly missed what Stuart said. "A game?"

"One big contest. Society's version of who's the biggest. Everyone's trying to prove they're better than the other."

"You make it sound like the whole room is a big pile of insecurity."

"Isn't it?"

"Including you?" she asked, although she couldn't imagine Stuart ever having a reason to be insecure.

"I've had my moments. Hard not to when you're raised by Theodore Duchenko." His eyes looked down at the glass in his hand, studying the contents. "My grandfather would make anyone feel insecure. He was what you'd call 'larger than life.'"

She was beginning to think life under Theodore Duchenko wasn't much of a picnic. "And step-grandma?"

A shadow crossed his features. It might have been a shadow from one of the people in the crowd, but Patience couldn't be sure. Whatever it was, the passing left his expression darker than before. "Gloria is a case unto herself."

What did that mean? Before she could ask, he was steering her toward a group of tables lining the side wall on which were displayed a collection of wrapped baskets, photographs and other items. "The infamous silent auction," Stuart announced. "Everything a person couldn't want, dutifully accompanied by a heaping serving of guilt." He pointed to an easel next to the table where a large poster sat. Above the photograph of a big black Labrador, a caption read, "He's got so much love to give; if only someone would love him back." The dog's big brown eyes grabbed Patience's heart and squeezed.

"Admit it," Stuart said. "You want to adopt a puppy now, don't you. Or at least bid on a membership to the wine-of-the-month club." Patience took a long drink from her glass. The puppy and the wine weren't the only things she wanted and couldn't have.

The two of them spent time reviewing the various items up for auction, with Stuart predicting how much he thought the final bid would be for each one. Despite his sarcastic commentary, he too bid on a few items, including a customized kitty tree for Nigel and, to Patience's surprise, a braided gold bracelet. "This is for Ana right?" she teased. "Because I'm not sure your assistant's husband would like you giving his wife jewelry."

"Who says I wasn't planning to give the bracelet to you?"

She laughed. Wistful quivers aside, that was hardly likely. "Exactly what you give the girl you don't trust."

"You don't think I would?"

"I think…" His eyes dared her to believe his offer. "I hope you're joking," she said.

"You're not into expensive jewelry?"

Not if it came with strings attached, and that was the only kind of expensive jewelry she knew of. "I think Ana would enjoy the gift more."

There was something very off-putting about the way he reacted to her response. Rather than laugh or look disappointed, he gave her one of those soul-searching stares.

She was about to ask him if she'd said something wrong when Ethyl Calloway reappeared with a silver-haired gentleman behind her. "This is Bernard Jenkins from WZYV," she said, stepping in front of Patience—again. "He's emceeing tonight's award presentation. Since you're accepting Anastasia's award, I thought you two should meet."

On the emcee's arm was the most statuesque blonde Patience had ever seen without a stripper pole.

The woman introduced herself as a Natalie Something. "We met last year at the bar's program on the revised probate laws," she said, pumping Stuart's hand with enthusiasm.

"That's right," Stuart replied. "You're with Ropes Prescott. Good to see you again."

The conversation moved into a mishmash of names and companies Patience didn't know. She could see why Bernard became a deejay. The man knew how to talk. And talk. Patience put on a pretend smile and used the time to examine the lovely Natalie. Her little black dress was current. In fact, Patience was pretty sure she'd seen a picture of the dress in a fashion magazine last month. The woman knew all the "in" jokes too. Every time she laughed, she would toss her mane of blond curls and let her fingers linger on Stuart's jacket sleeve. Patience squeezed her glass. She'd wanted to know what kind of woman Stuart would date. She had a pretty good idea now. Her stomach soured.

Meanwhile, Bernard Jenkins gave her a wink.

"Excuse me," she murmured. Without bothering to see if anyone heard her, she slipped away in search of a few quiet moments in the ladies' room. The draped tables used for guest check-in were empty save for a solo volunteer who was packing unused papers into a box. She smiled as Patience walked by, the first smile she'd received outside of Stuart's all night.

"People dressed up and showing off," she repeated to herself. Was it really all a game, like Stuart said? If so, he had to be one of the winners. It was so obvious when you compared him to everyone else in the room.

"Isn't this a pleasant surprise."

Dr. Tischel came strolling out of the ballroom, with a smile as broad as the rest of him. "Twice in one day. Fortune must be smiling on me."

"Hello, Dr. Tischel."

"Karl, please." Spreading his arms, he drew her into

an unexpected hug. Pulling her close, he held on so tightly Patience had to angle her spine to prevent his hips from pressing against hers. Antiseptic and cologne assaulted her nostrils, making her grimace.

After a beat longer than necessary, she managed to extricate herself. "Is Mrs. Tischel here, too?"

"Last I heard she was in Salem with all the other witches." He laughed at his joke.

Patience took a step backward. His eyes had that glassy sheen she knew too well. She looked to the check-in table, hoping the volunteer might help, but the woman had conveniently disappeared. And she could forget Stuart. He was probably so busy talking to the lovely Natalie he didn't realize she was missing. Looked like she would have to deal with the situation the same way she'd solved problems her whole life. On her own.

She took another step backward. Distance was always the first solution. "Ana was looking better when I left her this afternoon." A safe topic always helped, too.

"Ana? Oh, Ana." He waved a sloppy hand through the air. "She's a tough old bird. Are you here alone?"

Thank goodness, a way out of this conversation without causing a scene. "No, I'm here with Ana's nephew, Stuart. In fact, he's probably—"

"The one whose girlfriend dumped him?"

"I wouldn't know anything about that," she replied. Other than thinking that if true, the woman was a fool. "I should be getting back—"

The doctor grabbed her upper arm, preventing her from passing. "Let me buy you a drink."

His hot, stale breath made her want to gag. "No."

Shoving the man with enough force that he tottered sideways, she broke free and hurried back into the ballroom.

A half dozen pairs of eyes turned in her direction. Of course. Pay attention now, after she no longer needed anyone's assistance. Wasn't that always the way? For crying out loud, but she was tired of being stared at. She looked down at her dress. Her scarf had been pushed aside during her scuffle with Dr. Tischel, revealing her ample cleavage for all the world to see. No wonder the good doctor had hit on her. She looked like a two-bit hooker.

"There you are."

The crowd parted and there was Stuart threading his way through the guests, his eyes glittering with a different kind of brightness. One that suggested he was actually glad to see her. "I was wondering where you went. Is everything all right?"

He was looking her up and down, taking in the disheveled scarf and goodness knows what else. "What happened?"

"Nothing." Patience didn't want to talk about it. Her arm hurt from where Dr. Tischel had grabbed her, and she was starting to get a headache. "I'm not feeling well is all."

He arched a brow. Why, she didn't know. She was telling the truth. She didn't feel well. "I'm—"

As if on cue, Dr. Tischel lurched by them, his shoulder striking her shoulder blade and pitching her forward. Stuart caught her by the arms before she crashed into him.

"We meet again," the doctor said. A lewd smile unfurled across his face as his eyes locked onto her exposed neckline.

In a flash, Stuart was between them, blocking the doctor's line of sight. "Maybe you should get some coffee," he said, his tone making it clear he didn't expect an argument. When the doctor had left, Stuart turned back to face Patience. "Are you all right?"

Everyone was looking at them. Patience could feel the stares on her skin, worse than before. A tiny sob escaped before she could stop it. "No," she said.

"Come on." A warm arm wrapped itself around her shoulder and guided her toward the door. "Let's get some air."

Stuart led her to an unused conference room down the hall. There weren't any chairs, but it was private. "Was he the reason you wanted to leave?"

"I ran into him outside and he got a little grabby."

"Jeez. What is it with old guys and young girls? Did he hurt you?"

"No. I'm fine." Wrapping her arms around her body, she stared out the window at the traffic on Newbury Street. She hated that she let Dr. Tischel's leering get to her. The old guy was no worse than any of the others. "I thought these people would be different."

"Different how?"

"Better, I suppose. Stupid, I know." She should have known better.

Stuart joined her at the window. His nearness made her feel warm and safe, and, while she knew she shouldn't, Patience let the sensation surround her. "Sometimes I wonder if I'll ever be more than a hot body to people."

"Hey—you are more." Gripping her shoulders, he forced her to turn around and look at him. "Way more."

If he knew how dangerously good his words made

her feel… "Not to guys like Dr. Tischel," she said. As far as she knew, there were way more of his kind than anyone else.

"Dr. Tischel is a drunken moron," Stuart replied "In fact, first thing tomorrow, I'm going to talk to Ana about switching physicians. A guy who drinks like that? I don't want him anywhere near her."

"Can we not tell her about the grabbing part? I don't want to upset her."

"I suppose that means punching him out on the dance floor is out of the question too?"

He was being purposely outrageous, and it worked. Patience smiled. "Yes, it is."

"Too bad. It'd be fun to watch the old guy fall. Nice to see you smiling again though. There's nothing worse than seeing a pretty woman looking sad. I can say you're pretty, right?"

Color flooded her cheeks. He could say anything he wanted. The man had her completely under his spell at the moment. "Thank you," she said.

"For what?"

"Being so nice. You didn't have to be." It was true. He could have let her go home in a taxi cab and wiped his hands of her. Instead, here he was making her feel… special.

"What can I say? Didn't you watch me at the silent auction table? I'm a sucker for sad brown eyes."

Patience tried to blush again, but fingers caught her chin, forcing her to hold his gaze. "I can't help myself."

"Sorry." She couldn't think of another response, her brain having short-circuited as soon as he touched her. The connection reached far deeper than her skin. Stuart didn't know it, but he was the first person besides

Piper to ever talk to her this way, as if she was a person, whole and worthwhile. Cracks formed in the wall she'd so carefully built to keep the world from closing in.

"Don't be." His touch shifted, fingers tracing their way along her jaw and across her cheek. Patience knew exactly what he was tracing. Like so much about her, the jagged line could be covered but never completely erased. She'd cut herself falling off a table. A painful reminder of what happened when a person got too close.

Stuart was breaking that rule right now. Scary as the thought was, she longed to sink into his touch.

"You still want to go back to the brownstone?" he asked.

"No,"

"Good." One word, but it—and the smile that came along—made her feel more wanted than all the words in the dictionary could.

The cracks grew wider.

He held out his hand. "Let's go get Ana her award."

Stuart still wanted to punch Karl Tischel in the nose. What was it with rich old men and young women—did they think that every woman belonged to them?

Or just the women Stuart was with?

Thinking of how many times he'd caught Tischel leering at Patience, his fingers curled into a fist. Three strikes and you're out, Doc.

When had the fight become so personal? Was it when she'd answered her bedroom door looking like an eleven-point-five on a ten-point scale? Or when he saw her walk into the ballroom pale and shaken? When had he gone from being attracted to the woman to caring about her feelings? Damn if her likability wasn't getting to him, too.

They managed to get through dinner and the awards presentation without incident. Unless you counted Bernard Jenkins's pompous droning. Honestly, did the man ever come up for air? The guy spent the entire meal giving Patience and Ethyl a grape-by-grape account of his recent trip to the Tuscan vineyards.

Bernard's date, Natalie, wasn't much better. When she wasn't agreeing with Bernard, she was laughing and tossing her hair as though every word Stuart said was the most fascinating thing she'd ever heard. The woman reminded him of Gloria. Continually on the lookout for a brighter horizon. Aging local celebrity or rich lawyer. Nerdy law student or elderly silver magnate. They made their decisions based on whatever put them on top.

Ethyl was at the podium announcing the winners of the silent auction when a flash of movement caught his eye. Turning, he saw Patience texting away on her cell phone. Suspicion tried to take hold but failed. Tonight, he was suspicioned out.

"I'm sending Ana a picture of you accepting her award," she said when she noticed he was watching.

"I don't think she's awake at this hour."

"No, but this way she'll see it first thing in the morning, and I get extra brownie points." Her smile knocked the wind from his lungs.

"And finally, the gold bracelet donated by Basmati Jewelers was won by Paul Veritek." A smattering of applause floated across the room.

"You didn't win," Patience said. "Sorry."

"I'll live." He wasn't sure what had possessed him to bid on the bracelet in the first place. Seeing Patience's bare wrists had him offering up a bid without thinking. In a room filled with expensive jewelry, the simplicity stood out. But then, she didn't need jewelry, or makeup for that matter, to stand out, did she?

"And that concludes our program," Ethyl announced. "We look forward to seeing you next year."

"Guess that means the evening is over," Patience said.

"All but the dancing." Right on schedule, a Big Band standard began to play. As he watched couples making their way to the dance floor, Stuart was suddenly gripped with the desire to join them.

"Feel like dancing?"

"I thought you said you wanted to leave right after the ceremony."

He did. He also told himself putting his arms around Patience again was the worst idea ever, but now he couldn't think of anything he'd rather do. "I changed my mind. A few dances might be fun."

"I—" He'd caught her off guard, and she was struggling with what to say. The hesitancy made his palm actually start to sweat like a high schooler.

"Okay," she said finally. "Why not?"

His thrill over her acceptance was like a high schooler's, too.

He led her to the far edge of the dance floor, where the crowd wouldn't swallow them up, and pulled her close. Last night's embrace had been tentative and accidental, but here on the dance floor, he was free to hold her as close and for as long as he liked.

They moved in sync, their bodies slipping together in a perfect fit. Not surprisingly, Patience moved with a natural rhythm, her lower half moving back and forth like the waves in an ocean. Or like a lover meeting his thrusts. Stuart rested his hand on her hip and savored every shift beneath his fingers.

The song ended, and another ballad began. And another. They danced and swayed until the deejay announced it was time to say good-night.

Patience lifted her head from his shoulder. Her eyes were as bright as he'd ever seen then, with a sheen that looked suspiciously like moisture. "Thank you for chasing Dr. Tischel out of my head," she whispered.

That was all it took. Something inside him started to fall.

They walked up Beacon Street in silence, both of them pretending to act matter-of-fact even though they both knew their relationship had changed. How and why could wait until later. Right now, Stuart was content listening to the click-clack of Patience's heels on the sidewalk and reliving the feel of her curves beneath his hands. As for Patience, she was letting her fingers glide along the fence lining Boston Public Garden. "A fancy cake for Mrs. F," she said in singsongy tone under her breath.

"Whose Mrs. F?" he asked.

She flashed him a nostalgic-looking smile. "It's from a bedtime story I used to read to Piper about a man delivering cakes around Boston. A fancy cake for Mrs. F who lived on Beacon Hill. I think of the line whenever I see this row of houses."

Another memory involving raising her sister. Interesting how easily she shared those memories yet said so little about her own childhood. Beyond what he'd pulled out of her over dinner, that is. It was as if she didn't have a childhood of her own, Considering the shadows he'd seen in her eyes last night, maybe she hadn't.

So many pieces of her he didn't understand, so many parts unrevealed.

The story she described was one you read to a young child. "How old is your sister anyway?"

"Piper? Twenty-two."

Eight years younger. "So you read your sister a bed-time story when you were a kid?"

There was a stutter in her step. "Yeah, I did."

"I'm guessing your mom worked nights."

"Um…not really. She was just…busy." The evasiveness had returned, only this time what she didn't say came through loud and clear. If he had to guess, he'd say she'd started raising Piper long before their mother passed away. A child raising a child. He'd been right; she hadn't had a childhood of her own. She *was* like those damn dogs on the humane society poster, only instead of sympathy or guilt twisting in his gut, he wanted to wrap Patience in his arms and hold her tight and tell her she never had to be on her own again.

"I'm—"

"Don't." Stepping in front of him, she cut him off. "You're about to say you're sorry, and I don't want the sympathy."

"Okay, no sympathy." He understood. Sympathy was too much like pity. "How about admiration?"

"How about nothing? I did what I had to do. Trust me, I didn't do anything special," she said, turning away.

Except that Stuart didn't trust her, or had she forgotten? Had he forgotten for that matter?

They kept walking until they reached the State

House, the moon reflecting off its golden dome. Around the corner, Stuart spotted a trio of staggering silhouettes making their way from Park Street station. Patience was walking a few feet ahead. Her curves made her the perfect target for drunken comments. Stepping up his pace, he positioned himself on her right, creating a buffer. The group came closer, and he saw that two of the three were women teetering on high heels. The pair clung to the shoulders of the man in the middle, a pasty-looking blond who looked like he spent most of his time in dimly lit places. Their raucous laughter could be heard from ten feet away.

Stuart stole a look in Patience's direction before slipping his arm around her waist. She looked back, but didn't say anything.

As luck would have it, the trio reached the signal light the same time as they did. The man made no attempt to hide his ogling. "Come join the pah-ty, baby," he slurred, alcohol making his Boston accent thicker. "We're gonna go all night."

Patience's body turned rigid. He tightened his grip on her waist, letting her know he'd keep her safe.

The drunk slurred on, oblivious. "This dude knows what I'm talking about, doncha? Life's too short. Gotta grab the fun while you can. I did." He slapped one of the women on the rear, and she let out a giggly yelp. "Me and these ladies are just getting started."

Just then, a public works truck drove up, its bright headlights lighting their slice of the street.

"Oh, my God," one of the women cried out. "I know you!" Pushing herself free, she stumbled closer, her oversize breasts threatening to burst free from her tiny camisole top. "You work at Feathers. I danced right after you. Chablis, remember?"

Patience didn't reply. She stared straight ahead. When the light changed, she stepped off the curb and started walking. Stuart had to step quickly to keep up.

"What's the matter, you too good to talk to me now? That it?" Chablis asked as she followed. "Hey, I'm talkin' to you."

A crimson-nailed hand reached out to grab Patience's shoulder, but she quickly turned and dodged the woman's touch. "You have the wrong person," she hissed.

When they reached the opposite side of the street, Chablis looked to make one more attempt at conversation only to have her friend tug her in the opposite direction. "Come on, baby," he slurred. "We don't need them. We got better things to do."

"Yeah, Chablis," the other woman whined. "Give it up. That witch ain't owning up to nuthin'."

"But I know her," Chablis insisted, as if her knowledge was the most important discovery in the world. As she let her friends drag her away, she continued to swear and complain about being ignored. "She always did think she was better than us," Stuart heard her mutter.

"Sorry about that," he said to Patience.

"It's no big deal. They're just a bunch of drunks."

Perhaps, but the pallor of her skin said they'd upset her more than she let on. Poor thing had probably had her fill of drunks by this point.

A beer can came hurtling in their direction, rattling the sidewalk a few feet shy of where they stood. "Hey!" Chablis yelled, her voice sharp in the night. "Does your boyfriend know he's dating a stripper?"

Stuart might have laughed if Patience hadn't stopped

in her tracks. When he looked, he saw the color had drained from her face.

A sick feeling hit him in his stomach. "She's got you confused with someone else, right?" he asked.

Even in the dark of night, Patience's eyes told him everything he needed to know. There was no mistake.

Chablis was telling the truth.

CHAPTER SIX

"IT'S TRUE, ISN'T IT?" he asked. "You were a—a…"

Stripper? He couldn't even say the word, could he?

Stupid Chablis. Patience never did like the woman. For a second, she considered blaming everything on the rambling of a drunken trio, but one look at Stuart's face snuffed that idea. The thought had been planted in his head, and no amount of denial would chase it away. Eventually, he would dig up the truth. No reason to drag the ordeal out longer than necessary.

How stupid for her to think the night would end on a good note. Like she would ever earn a fairy-tale ending.

Folding her arms across her chest, Patience held on to what little dignity she could. "We prefer the term 'exotic dancer,'" she said, pushing her way past him.

"Where do you think you're going?"

"Where do you think? To the brownstone to pack my things." With luck she would get there before the tears pressing the back of her eyes broke free. Now that Stuart knew about her background, he was bound to ask her to leave her job with Ana. Hadn't he said that he didn't want Dr. Tischel anywhere near his aunt. Surely he would feel the same about Patience.

Well, she might have just lost her job, and her home,

but she would not lose her composure—not on the streets of Boston and not in front of him.

There were footsteps, and Stuart was at her shoulder, grabbing her arm much like Dr. Tischel had. With a hiss, she pulled away. The look of regret passing over his features was small compensation.

"You're not even going to try and explain yourself?"

Patience had never felt more dirty and exposed as she did under his stare, but she managed to hold herself together. "Why should I? You don't want to listen." No, he would judge her like everyone else had. The same way she judged herself. Why stick around to listen to condemnations she'd said to herself?

Stuart blocked her path. "Try me." Between the shadows and his stony expression, it was impossible to read his thoughts

They weren't the words she had expected to hear, and Patience hated how they made her heart speed up with hope. "You're really willing to listen?"

"I said I would. Don't you think you owe us an explanation?"

Us, as in him and Ana. With the shock of discovery wearing off, guilt began to take hold. She owed Ana way more than an explanation, but the truth was a good place to start. "Fine, but not here. Please." Out of the corner of her eye, she caught the silhouette of a person standing in a window. "I'll tell you everything when we're at the brownstone." Then she'd move out and never bother him or Ana again.

Neither said a word the final few blocks. Such a different silence compared to when they had left the hotel.

Then, the air had hummed with romantic possibility. This long walk was nothing but cold.

Naturally Nigel was waiting for their return, meowing and running back and forth for attention. Without a word, they walked into the kitchen so she could give Nigel his midnight snack. Attending to a cat's needs had never taken so long.

"You ready to talk?" he asked when she'd finished rinsing the can.

"Not much to say." She'd already decided to give him the shortest version possible. Less misery that way. "I needed money and dancing was the only job I could find that would pay me enough."

Minus the part where she turned down the offer twice before finally giving in, and only then because her creepy boss at the burger place wouldn't give her more hours unless she slept with him.

"Interesting." He pulled out a chair and motioned for her to take a seat. "Now how about you give me the full version?"

The full version? Her heart hitched. She'd never told anyone the *whole* story. "Why do you care about the details? It is what it is."

"Because I care." The words warmed her insides, until she reminded herself he meant "about the details." He was, after all, a lawyer. Naturally, he'd want to collect all the facts.

Question was—how many facts did he need? She'd buried so much of her story that even she wasn't sure of everything anymore.

Taking a seat, she wiped the dampness from her palms on her dress. "Where do you want me to start?"

"Try the beginning."

"I was born."

"I'm serious."

"So am I." Where *did* she begin? "I suppose everything really started when Piper was born. My mom—don't get me wrong, she wasn't a horrible mother. I mean, she didn't beat us or let us starve or anything like that. She just wasn't into being a mom, you know?"

A quick look across the table said he didn't, but she plowed ahead. "I think she thought a baby would keep Piper's dad around, but…"

She shrugged. That was her mother's pipe dream, not hers. "Anyway, as soon as I got old enough, she left taking care of Piper to me. But I told you that already."

"'A fancy cake for Mrs. F,'" he recited. "How old were you?"

"Twelve or thirteen? Thirteen, I think. It wasn't that hard," she added quickly. As was the case whenever a person looked askance at the arrangement, her defensiveness rose up. "Piper was a good kid. She never caused trouble, always did her homework. Plus, she could cook."

"A thirteen-year-old taking care of a five-year-old. You didn't resent it?"

Her automatic answer was always no. For some reason—the way Stuart looked to be reading her mind maybe—the answer died in favor of the truth. "Sometimes, but I didn't have a choice. She was family. I had a responsibility."

From behind his coffee cup, she saw Stuart give a small nod and realized if anyone understood the importance of family responsibility, he would. After all, wasn't his devotion to Ana the spark that had led to this conversation?

She continued. "When my mom died, Piper and I were left alone. I promised her we would stay together no matter what."

"And that's why you needed the money? For Piper?"

"Yeah." She stared into her cup, unsure how to continue. Talking about Piper was the easy part. It wasn't until after their mom died that the story turned bad. "My mom left us broke. Worse than broke. Actually. I didn't know what else to do."

"What about assistance? There are programs…"

"You don't understand. It wasn't that easy." How could he? Man like him, who never wanted for anything.

"But surely—"

"We were living in our car!" She hurled the answer across the table, the first time she'd ever acknowledged what happened aloud. "We were afraid if we told anyone, Piper would end up in child services, and I swore that wouldn't happen." In her mind, she saw her sister's frightened face, heard the desperation in her voice. She squeezed her eyes shut, but the memories stayed all the same. "I couldn't break my promise to her. We were all each other had. Losing her would have been like…like…"

"Losing your own child."

"Yes." His answer gave her hope that he understood. Opening her eyes, she stared across the table, silently pleading her case. "I would have done anything to keep her safe. Anything."

This was the place in the story where she should stop. Having justified her actions, there was no reason to share any more. The problem was that talking about the past was like cracking a glass. Once begun, the crack didn't stop spreading until it reached its natural end. And so the words continue to flow. "There was this guy who lived near us. Named Ben. He was always hitting on me, telling me how hot I was. Used to tell me a girl built like me could rake it in at the club where he worked. I always ignored him. Until I didn't have a choice anymore."

Unable to sit still any longer, Patience pushed herself away from the table and crossed to the back window. Her distorted reflection stared back at her in the glass. "It was January. We hadn't eaten all day. I'd lost my job—we didn't have money. Piper had a cold. Sounds like one of those over-the-top TV movies, doesn't it?" she said with a hollow laugh.

"Go on."

"I didn't know what else to do," she whispered. The desperation and shame she'd felt that fateful day returned as fresh as ever, rising up to choke the air from her lungs. "I told myself it was only for a little while. Until Piper and I were on our feet." The delusion of youth and hopelessness.

"How long did that take?"

Why was he asking? He could guess the answer. Until she went to work for Ana.

"That's the trick life plays on you," she said, resting her head against the glass. "You tell yourself it's only for a few weeks, a few months tops. Next thing you know, a few months turns into a year. Two. After a while, you start to think maybe you can't do any better. I mean, you've got no experience, so any job you can get doesn't pay nearly as much and that's assuming you could even get another job. Who's going to hire someone who danced on a table?"

"Table? Is that—?"

"Yeah. A drunk grabbed my ankle." Her breath left a smudge on the pane. Using her scarf, she wiped the mark away. If only life could clean up so easily. "Sometimes I think, if only I'd held out one more day…

"I can still feel their eyes on me," she whispered. "At night. Watching me with their dull, glassy eyes. Fantasizing about what they want to do with me." She slapped a hand against her mouth to keep from gagging as the memories began to choke her. A sob broke through anyway. "They made me feel so dirty."

"Shh." Once again Stuart was there, his face joining hers in the glass. Didn't matter that he wasn't touching her, his proximity was good enough.

"But I kept my promise," she said. "I kept us off the streets and I gave Piper a normal life." Of all the regrets she had in her life, keeping Piper safe wasn't one. "Whenever things got really bad, that's what I would tell myself. *I kept my promise.*"

Behind her, Stuart let out a long, loud breath. An echo of her own exhaustion. She hadn't expected to share so much. Telling Stuart details she'd never told anyone…the ordeal left her raw and exposed. "You said you wanted the long version."

"Yes, I did."

There was another sigh. Patience imagined him washing a hand over his features as he tried to digest everything. What would he think if he knew the one detail she'd kept back? But how could she tell him when she could barely admit the secret to herself?

"I know you think I had some big agenda, but I didn't. I ran into Ana and she confused me with a job applicant. I let her believe that's who I was and interviewed for the job." She turned so he could see she was being as honest as possible. "Ana was the first person besides Piper who ever treated me like I mattered. I swear I would never hurt her. I just needed to get out."

"You do matter," Stuart whispered.

She hated the way his words warmed her from the inside out. More so, how she couldn't help following them up with a pitiful "I do?"

"Yeah, you do." His thumb brushed her cheek, chasing away tears she didn't know had fallen. "And you deserved better."

She was too tired to argue otherwise. He'd asked for her story and she'd told him. "If you want me to leave, I will," she told him. She'd lied, and deception came with a price. Thankfully she'd squirreled away enough money so she wouldn't have to worry about living on the streets this time around. If she kept her expenses low, she'd be all right. She was a survivor.

"You don't have to leave," Stuart told her. "We all have things in our past we regret."

Tears turned her vision watery, but they were happy tears this time. "Thank you...I know I should have told the truth from the start, but I was afraid if Ana knew what I was, she would want nothing to do with me. And then, of course, you arrived, talking about how you didn't trust me and..."

"I was pretty inexorable, wasn't I?"

"If that's your way of saying you were acting like a jerk?" She was finally beginning to relax. "Then yeah."

"I'm sorry about that. You can blame Gloria."

Right. The step-grandmother. "I think I'm beginning to dislike her as much as you do."

"Trust me, that's not possible."

It was, once again, a comfortable silence wrapping around them. Patience felt lighter than she had in months—since the day she accepted the job, really. It was as if a thousand pounds had been lifted from her shoulders. Maybe, if she was lucky, the rest of her story would die a silent death, and she could enjoy that relief, as well.

"It's late," Stuart said. "You look exhausted."

She was drained. And sad, in spite of her relief. This wasn't how she'd expected the night to end. There had been magic in the air on that dance floor. For a little while she'd felt like Cinderella at the ball. But it was time to come back to reality. Having told her story, there was no way Stuart would ever look at her the same way again.

How could he? She was no longer a housekeeper; she was a housekeeper who used to take her clothes off for money.

"If it's all right with you, I think I'm going to go to bed."

"Yes, of course. I'll see you tomorrow. Good night."

"Good night." She had moved to leave when the need to say one last thing stopped her. "Thank you again for understanding." He'd probably never know how much it meant to her. On so many levels.

She expected a simple *you're welcome* in return, mainly because there didn't seem to be anything more to say. But Stuart didn't utter a word. Instead, his hand reached out to cradle her cheek. Patience's breath caught. How could a man's touch be so gentle and yet so strong? Her body yearned to lean into his hand. To close her eyes and let his strength hold her up. He swept his thumb across her cheekbone, stopping at the top of her scar. After what felt like forever, his hand dropped away. "Good night."

Patience's heart was racing so fast she was convinced it would reach her bedroom first. Twice in two nights, she'd come dangerously close to breaking the rules when it came to keeping her distance. The third time, she might not be able to walk away.

He'd wanted to know her secret. He finally did and, man, was it a doozy. Never in a million years would he have imagined Patience was…had been…he couldn't even think the word. That she'd been forced to make those kinds of choices… It made him sick to his stomach to think that in this day and age she'd felt there was no other way.

Took guts, what she'd done. And strength. Real strength. She was barely an adult and yet she'd kept her family together.

If her story was true, that is, and not some ploy for sympathy.

Immediately, he shook the distrust from his head. Damn, but he'd become such a skeptical jerk. Patience was telling the truth. He saw it in her eyes. At least he wanted to believe that's what he was seeing. He wanted to believe her as badly as he wanted to hold her. Which, he thought, washing a hand over his face, was pretty damn bad.

They were two very scary realizations.

"Nigel, why do you insist on being in the one place that makes doing my job difficult?" Patience narrowed her eyes at the cat, who, as usual, was ignoring her question. He was too busy poking at imaginary enemies in Ana's dresser drawer.

It'd been twelve long days since the dinner dance,

and she was finally starting to believe that she was keeping her job. Stuart hadn't brought up the confession again. Of course, he also made himself as scarce as possible. He was on his way out the door when she woke up, and away until she went to bed. Except for that first morning when they'd recapped the dance for Ana, he'd even taken to keeping a different visiting schedule. None of his avoidance surprised her. Understanding was one thing, wanting to associate with her was another.

Back at the club, they had a saying: Prince Charming ain't walking through that door. No matter how good-looking or how amazing some guy might seem, the two of you weren't going to ride off into the sunset on his white horse. She was smart enough to know the same rule applied to housekeepers and their bosses. Say she and Stuart had slept together that night. It wouldn't have been anything more than a short-term fling, right? Being help with benefits wasn't her style. What self-respect she had, she'd like to keep, thank you very much.

So Stuart avoiding her was a good thing. Honestly.

"Will you quit it?" She found a way out of her thoughts in time to catch Nigel snagging the lace on a pair of Ana's undergarments. "I'm pretty sure Ana wants her clothes unmolested," she said. The cat pawed at the air as she took the panties away and refolded them. Feeling bad that she'd disturbed his fun, Patience scratched behind his ear. She had a feeling part of Nigel's more-than-usual peskiness was because he missed Ana. Their promise to bring him for visits, it turned out, had been a bad idea. Nigel treated the rehab facility as he did the brownstone and wandered at will. It had taken her almost an hour to find out what room he had moved into for naptime.

"Ana will be home in another few days. In the meantime, how about you give me ten more minutes, and then we'll have a good long petting session."

As usual, Nigel wasn't interested in bargaining. He wanted his attention and he wanted it now. Somehow he managed to wedge his head and paws into the drawer opening, and began chewing on something.

Patience rolled her eyes. "What are you doing now? Please tell me you're not trying to eat Ana's underwear." She opened the drawer and saw that the cat had found a box and was attempting to bite the corner of the cover. Her sorting and taking things the past few days must have unearthed it from the bottom of the drawer.

"You really do want to eat everything in sight, don't you?" Lifting them both free, she plopped Nigel on the bed before placing the box on the bureau. As soon as she was finished, she'd put the box back safely at the bottom of the drawer.

A knock sounded behind her. "Somehow I didn't picture you as a granny panties kind of girl," Stuart said. The sound of his voice made her stomach tumble. Swallowing back the reaction, she glanced over her shoulder. "I'm putting away Ana's laundry and packing some new items. You know, for a woman with expensive tastes, she has the most disorganized drawers I've ever seen."

It didn't skip Patience's notice that only a week before, he would have questioned what she was doing rather than make a joke. While she was touched by the show of trust, she sort of missed the protection her defensiveness gave her. When he was nice, it made keeping her distance that much harder.

"Surprised to see you here so early," she said. Here at all, really.

"We closed shop early for the holiday, and since Ana takes her post Physical Therapy nap around this time, I figured I'd work at home."

"That's right, tomorrow's Fourth of July." With all the coming and going, she'd forgotten the date. "Ana told me once how she usually has a barbecue on the roof deck."

"Barbecue in the sense that she has a caterer bring in barbecued chicken," Stuart replied. "She and her humane society buddies have been doing it for years."

"She must be devastated to have to cancel."

"Not as much as you'd think. Last I heard, Ethyl was moving the event to the rehab hospital."

Patience envisioned Ana, Ethyl and the others invading the rehab terrace with their catered dinner and cocktails. "Maybe I should be devastated on behalf of the hospital."

"Don't be. I'm sure there's a donation involved." He sat down on the edge of the bed. It was the longest and closest they'd been together since the dance. Patience studied the hands clasped between his legs. All too clear was the memory of those hands holding her close. Fingers burning a hole in the fabric of her dress. She turned back to the underwear drawer.

"Sorry I haven't been around much lately. Work has been slamming," he said.

Even the weekends? "You don't have to explain your schedule to me." Or make excuses, for that matter.

"I know, but…" The mattress made a settling noise, and she imagined him shrugging. "But I didn't want you to think that after the other night, I was…well, you know."

"Yeah." She knew. She wasn't sure she believed him, but she knew.

"Anyway, I was wondering what you were doing tomorrow."

Patience's stomach dropped. He was going to tell her he was hosting some kind of event himself, wasn't he? If she wanted a distance reminder, being asked to wait on his friends would certainly fit the bill. "It's a normal paid day off," she told him, "but if you are planning something…"

"Actually, I was wondering if you would mind checking out a condominium with me."

"What?"

"You know the new luxury tower they built near the Leather District? One of our clients is the developer. Sounds like a pretty awesome property."

"I'm sure it is." Weren't most million-dollar properties? Patience tried to ignore the pang in her chest. From the very start, Stuart had said this living arrangement was temporary. Now that Ana was close to being discharged, there was no reason for him not to look for a place of his own. What did the decision have to do with her, though?

"I was hoping you'd check out the property with me. Give me your opinion."

"The housekeeper's point of view?"

He grinned. "I was thinking more of a female point of view, but if you want to weigh in on how difficult the place will be to keep clean, feel free. Don't feel like you have to though. I know it's your day off, but if you do say yes, I'd make it worth your while."

"Worth my while, eh?" Talk about loaded language. She shivered at the potential prospects. "How?"

"I will personally show you the best seat in all of Boston for watching the fireworks."

Patience chewed the inside of her mouth. Goodness, but it was impossible to say no. Especially when the idea of sitting with him beneath the stars was so seductive.

"Sure." There'd be plenty of time to kick herself for the decision later. "What time?"

"After lunch. I figured we'd go see Ana, then meet up with Nikko. He's the developer."

"It's a—plan." She almost slipped and called it a date. Luckily she caught herself at the last moment.

What she should have been trying to catch was Nigel. Tired of being ignored, he leaped from the bed to the bureau. Problem was, he miscalculated the distance. His front paws connected with the box she'd set on the bureau, flipping it end over end. Off flew the cover, sending the contents flying.

"Bad kitty," she said. The admonishment was useless since Nigel had already bolted from the room in embarrassment.

"Here, let me help you." Stuart crouched by her on the floor, his unique Stuart scent filling the space between them. Patience had to struggle not to close her eyes and inhale. "The box was in Ana's drawer," she explained. "Nigel started chewing the cover so I moved it to the bureau." To keep it out of his reach. So much for that idea.

"Looks like a bunch of photographs."

Mementos was more like it. Patience spied newspaper clippings, tickets, playbills, what looked like drawings scribbled on napkins. Piper had kept a similar box when she was a kid.

She picked up one of the newspaper clippings. The article was written in a foreign language.

"French," Stuart said when she showed him.

"Don't suppose you can read it?"

"Sorry. Russian."

And she'd barely made it through Spanish. "This is where we need Piper."

The date said it was from the early fifties. Ana would have been just out of high school. Patience couldn't help wondering what had made her hold on to the article. The photo accompanying the article featured a trio of men standing together in front of a painting. Nothing very exciting. She was about to put the clipping in the box when one of the names jumped from the page.

"Stuart, look." She pointed to the caption. "One of the men is named Nigel Rougeau. Think it's a coincidence?"

"I don't know. The name Nigel had to come from somewhere." He slipped the clipping from her fingers and studied it closer. Like a lawyer examining evidence, Patience thought. "Looks like this was taken at some kind of art show. The wall is lined with paintings."

"But which one is Nigel?"

"Well, I can't say for sure, but based on the names listed in the caption, I'd say the one in the middle." He pointed to the bearded man with intense, dark eyes. "In fact…" He picked up one of the scattered photographs. "Here he is."

Sure enough, it was the same bearded man, only this time he was leaning against a motorbike. There were other photos, too. Nigel on the beach. In a café. One showed him standing in what looked to be an artist's studio, looking very serious and artistic as he dabbed paint on a canvas. Whoever he was, he'd obviously played a very important role in Ana's life. Important and personal.

"We should put these away," she said. It didn't feel right, poking through Ana's past. "This is obviously something very private or she wouldn't have stashed the box in her underwear drawer."

"You're right. This is none of our business." One of the pictures had fluttered a few feet away. Leaning forward, Stuart picked it up and was about to add it to the box when he froze. "Well, I'll be," he muttered.

"What?" Patience looked over his shoulder. It was another studio photo, not very different from the other one, except for maybe a few additional paintings on the wall.

"Check out the painting to the left of the easel."

It was nude portrait. A large one featuring a woman sprawled on a sofa. She was smiling at the artist, as if they shared a secret. Even in the background of a snapshot she could feel the intimacy. But why did Stuart want her to look?

"Don't you recognize the face. The smile?"

Patience studied it closer. "No way…" The smile was the same one that had greeted her the day she took the job. "Ana modeled for him?"

"More than modeled, I'd say. Which," he said, dropping the photograph into the box, "has me feeling extra slimy for poking around."

"Yeah, definitely." Looked like Ana had her own secrets. Patience could respect that.

With the items collected, she reached for the box cover only to have Stuart reach at the same time. Their hands collided, his fingers skimming the tops of hers. Patience stilled. It was but a whisper of a touch, but it brought her skin to life with a tingling sensation that enveloped her entire body.

For most of her adult life, Patience had avoided physical contact. Look, don't touch. That was the rule. But with Stuart, even the lightest of touches had her craving more. She longed for him to take her hand. Pull her into his arms and hold her like he had the night of the dance.

She needed to back away before she lost her head. One look at Stuart's eyes said he was fighting the same battle.

"I'd better put this away before the contents spill again," she said, her voice a whisper.

"Good idea."

They stayed put, each waiting for the other to move.

"I—"

"Yeah," Stuart completed for her. He pushed himself to his feet, then offered a hand to help her up. Patience declined. Better she stand on her own two feet.

"I'll let you know what time we're going to meet Nikko tomorrow."

Who? The condominium. How could she forget. "I'll be here," she told him.

Stuart looked about to say something, only to think better of it. With one last look, he turned and left the room.

She didn't realize how badly she wanted him to stay until his footsteps had faded away.

CHAPTER SEVEN

"WE APPRECIATE YOU opening the office for us on a holiday, Nikko. I hope we didn't screw up your plans."

"Are you kidding? My wife's got her sisters at the beach house for the weekend. I'd rather do this than deal with holiday traffic any day."

Stuart and Patience shared a smile as the realtor herded them onto the elevator. While Nikko chose the floor, Stuart made a point of positioning himself in the middle. It was no secret that his client had a roving eye. The man had already stolen a glance at Patience's behind. Stuart wasn't going to let him steal another.

From the start, it had bothered him to see men checking her out. Knowing her secret, however, added a layer of protectiveness. He felt compelled to keep her from being objectified. Especially by men like Nikko Popolous.

Okay, perhaps he was doubly compelled to protect her from Nikko, whose silver hair and good looks had half the women at the firm sighing with longing.

For her part, Patience dressed in her usual nondescript style. Flowing sleeveless top and cropped jeans. He wished he knew a way to tell her that disguising her figure wasn't working. It wasn't her figure that turned men's heads—it was the whole package.

He ran his thumb across his fingertips remembering how close he'd come to kissing her yesterday. Clearly a dozen days of keeping his distance had done nothing to kill his attraction. Like that was a surprise.

But wouldn't acting on his desire make him no better than Karl Tischel and the other creeps? Worse actually, since a week ago he'd been telling her he didn't trust her. She deserved more respect than that.

"This is one of our prime corner units," Nikko was saying as he unlocked the door. "The natural lighting is out of this world."

Patience let out a small gasp as they stepped inside. "This place is amazing!" A poker-faced negotiator, she was not.

She was right, though. The condo was nice. Hardwood floors, tons of windows.

"The open floor plan makes this a great place for entertaining," Nikko told them.

Stuart was more entertained by the sparkle in Patience's eyes as she ran a hand across the top of the kitchen island. "Everything is so clean and new."

"Top-of-the-line, too," Nikko told her. "The cabinets are solid cherry."

"There's a double oven! And a wine cooler." She smiled at Stuart. "Piper would go crazy if she saw this place."

"You need to check out the terrace. Wraps around the whole unit. Gives you another two hundred square feet. And the best part is, you don't have to share with the other tenants." The realtor slid open one of the window panels and stepped outside. "Check out this view," he said to Patience.

Stuart guided Patience out into the hot, humid air, resisting the urge to place his hand against the small of her back. The way her shirt fluttered when she walked suggested the material was light and thin. If he touched her back, he'd feel straight through to her skin and that would open up far too many problems.

"Great view, huh?"

It was nice; you could see Boston Common in the distance.

"Bet it's great at night," Patience remarked.

"Oh, at night it's spectacular," Nikko said. "There's another door that leads out here from the master bedroom. You think the kitchen was a nice setup, wait till you see the bathroom. My own bathroom isn't this fancy."

The sales patter continued while Nikko led him back into the condo and down the hall. Stuart didn't listen. A sales pitch was a sales pitch. All he wanted was a place to sleep that accrued a good return on investment.

Damn, but he'd grown jaded.

Once upon a time, he might have hunted for a home instead of an investment. When he was younger. Someplace like what he remembered sharing with his parents.

Of course, maybe things would be different if he were condo shopping with someone. Someone whose eyes sparkled with excitement.

The bathroom was impressive. Designer vanities, giant sunken tub in thecorner. "Beat's Ana's claw-foot tub, doesn't it?" he said to Patience.

There was no answer.

"I think she stayed on the terrace," Nikko remarked.

Indeed, when Stuart stepped through the bedroom slider, he found her in the same place as before, her attention fixed on some faraway point.

He had to stop and grab the railing as desire rolled through him. Why was keeping his distance a bad idea again?

It wasn't until he walked closer that he saw the sadness behind the faraway gaze. "Everything all right?"

"Great," she replied. "Why wouldn't it be?"

He settled in next to her. "You tell me. You looked a million miles away."

"I was thinking how you could fit my old apartment into this place's living room."

"It's the lack of furniture. Makes the space seem bigger."

"No, our apartment was that small."

There was regret in her voice that didn't belong. "Bet it was easy to clean," he teased.

He got the smile he was hoping for. "Didn't take long, for sure."

Nor, Stuart bet, did the apartment ever feel empty and cold. "And, you had your sister."

"True. I'd pick small over losing her in a second, even if she did take over the bathroom when she hit high school. There was only one electrical plug that could handle a blow-dryer," she said when he chuckled. "For four years, I was lucky to get my hair dried in time for work."

Patience would never believe him, but he envied her. Her closeness with her sister, that is. Despite everything the two of them had endured, they'd always had each other to cling to. He wished he had that kind of support. Sure, he had Ana, but their closeness hadn't really de-

veloped until he came east for law school. Before that…
well, no wonder Gloria was able to charm him blind.

Looking to the ground, he concentrated on plowing
little piles of grit and dirt with his shoe. "My grandfather's house was big," after a moment. "It actually
had wings."

"You mean like in west wing, east wing—that sort
of thing?"

"Uh-huh." Though his attention remained on the
ground, he imagined her eyes widening. "There were
literally days when I wouldn't see Grandpa Theodore
even though we were in the same house."

"Not at all?"

"Not unless I went looking for him." Attempts that
were met with varying degrees of success.

"I'm sorry."

No, he didn't want her sympathy any more than she
did. "He was…busy," he said too, to steal her word.

Patience slid her hand to the left until their fingers
aligned, her little finger flush with his. "I understand."

Yeah, she did, thought Stuart, but then he'd known
as much for a while. Same way he knew that as lonely
as his teenage years had been, they were a cakewalk
compared to hers.

He itched to cover her hand with his and entwine
their fingers. Would she pull away if he did?

"The view is irresistible, isn't it?" Nikko stepped
onto the terrace, making the decision for him. The realtor waved his phone. "Sorry. My wife couldn't find
the air pump. Don't know why—the thing's right in the
center of the garage."

"Are you telling this guy he needs to buy?" Nikko
asked Patience.

She laughed. "I think that's up to him."

"Maybe, but I did bring you here for input. What do you think?"

"I think this is the most amazing apartment I've ever seen outside of Ana's brownstone."

"Those brownstones are great, but they come with their headaches. Like parking. Brownstones don't come with parking," Nikko said. "And did you see the cedar closet in the laundry area? Solid cedar, not veneer. A moth would need a drill to get at your winter wardrobe. To put something like that in custom would cost you a fortune."

As opposed to spending a fortune on a condominium that already had one. Stuart was about to reply when he realized Nikko had been directing his remarks to Patience. He was assuming it would be her wardrobe hanging in the cedar closet.

Patience, staying here. The idea didn't strike him nearly as improbable as it should. On the contrary, the longing from earlier reared again, tendrils spreading up and across his chest. He hadn't realized until just now that when he left Ana's brownstone, he would be leaving Patience behind. Strange as it seemed, he'd grown used to sharing a space with her. He would miss her presence. That's what the ache in his chest was all about. He was going to miss having company.

"All I'm saying is that most people would have at least slept on the decision," Patience said when they got back to the brownstone.

"I don't know why you're so surprised. You said yourself the place was amazing."

"It is. But I didn't mean for you to whip out your

checkbook and write a down payment." Last thing she wanted was the responsibility of having influenced his decision. Picking up Nigel's dish, she headed to the cupboard. "How do you know there isn't someplace better out there?" she asked, pulling out a can of Salmon Delight.

"There might be, and if I were looking for the perfect apartment, that would be important, but I'm not. This place is close to my office, and a good investment. I had pretty much made up my mind to buy if the space was halfway decent."

If that was so, why invite her?

"I really did want a second opinion," he replied when she asked. "If both of us liked the space, then I knew the condo was a winner."

"Oh, sure, because I've so much experience buying luxury property. You do realize when I said it was the most amazing place outside of the brownstone that it was also the only other high-end place I've ever looked at."

"You sell yourself short. You zoned right in on the areas I wanted an opinion on. The laundry room, the kitchen, the living space."

All the cleaning woman areas of expertise. She winced and tried to take the compliment the way he meant. "The kitchen was nice."

"So I could tell by the way your eyes lit up." Okay, now she was blushing. He was studying her eyes?

"Here I thought I was being so calm and sophisticated."

"You were being yourself, which—before you make a comment—is exactly what I wanted. You'll argue otherwise, but you're not very good when it comes to hiding your thoughts."

"I'm not?" Impossible. She'd spent years cultivating her stone face. She knew how to block out the audience with the best of them.

However, she had been off her game since Stuart moved in. Did that mean he knew how badly she'd been struggling to keep her attraction at arm's length?

Luckily, Stuart couldn't see her face or he'd really be able to read her feelings. The overheated cheeks were a dead giveaway.

"How else do you think I figured out you were keeping secrets? Your eyes gave you away. They always do," he said. "I see it all the time in depositions. Body language is a killer. Although in this case…you weren't exactly hiding your enthusiasm."

"I did gush a little, didn't I?"

"A little?" Patience didn't have to be a body language expert to read the amusement on his face.

"Okay, a lot," she conceded. "That didn't mean you had to buy the place. I don't think I could be that impulsive." She had trouble buying anything on a whim. What if you needed the cash later on?

"I told you, I had already decided—"

"Before we got there. I know what you said, but this afternoon was still the first time you saw the place. That, to me, is impulsive. How do you know you got the best place?"

He shrugged. "It's just a condominium."

"Just?" His comment made it sound as if he was settling, and while Patience wasn't expecting him to gush about the place like her, she had expected him to at least care about where he lived.

"I work seventy to eighty hours a week," he explained. "I'm hardly ever home. As long as the place is close to my office and can fit a bed, that's all I care about."

So he was settling. Patience wasn't sure what saddened her more: that or how little he had in his life. Something Karl Tischel said at the dinner dance popped into her head. *The one whose girlfriend dumped him.* Was work the reason? Or did he work because he'd been dumped? Either way, his life sounded lonely. Correction. He sounded lonely, Patience realized.

Apparently, she wasn't the only one who couldn't hide her emotions.

Even so, she shouldn't want to reach out and comfort him the way she did. Certainly not after watching him spend a million dollars without blinking an eye. What more proof did she need that they were from different worlds?

And yet his loneliness spoke to a place deep inside her, making her feel closer to him than ever.

"What's with the take-out bag?" In Stuart's hand was a large white paper bag with handles. On the way home, he'd insisted they stop at the local market. He made her wait outside while he went in, only to return a few minutes later with a bag of food. Patience had been curious then, and she was doubly curious now. She leaped on the topic as the perfect change of conversation.

"Dinner," he replied. "I seem to recall promising you a picnic and fireworks."

"Yes, you did. The best seats in Boston, you said."

"Trust me, they are."

Nigel sauntered into the kitchen and crouched by his empty food dish, waiting for Patience to fill it. The minute Patience crossed his path, he began weaving around and between her legs. "You're lucky we aren't on the stairs," she told him.

"Don't you mean *you're* lucky?" Stuart replied. "As far as I can tell, Nigel isn't the one who gets hurt."

"True." Patience thought of the photographs they'd found yesterday. Ana had once said Nigel had a "Nigel personality." If the original was as pesky as his name-sake, that might explain why he wasn't around any-more.

Behind her, Stuart was unpacking the tote bag. She saw containers loaded with potato salad, fried chicken, fruit and chocolate cake—enough to feed a full army. "So where is this awesome picnic spot?" she asked. "Near the Boston Esplanade?"

"Nope. The roof."

"Ana's roof?"

"Sure. That's why the humane society insists she throw the summer barbeques here. You won't find a better view, not even on the Esplanade."

He pointed to the utility closet in the corner of the kitchen. "Is the portable radio still on the shelf?"

"I think so."

"Great. Grab it and a couple of glasses, will you? I'll go set up the table."

The rooftop deck had been something of a marvel to Patience. Before her accident, Ana had ocassionally taken afternoon tea up there. In Patience's old neigh-borhood, a deck meant a place to keep a couple plastic chairs or small table for eating outside, but Ana's deck was an outside living room. No plastic chairs or cheap furniture here. Instead, there was a love seat and match-ing chairs. Floor lamps, too. Four of them, one in each corner so as to light the entire space once the sun went down. Potted evergreens and other plants brought nature into the arrangement while a pair of heaters added warmth in the colder weather.

One of her first major housekeeping projects had been to bring the cushions indoors and cover the furniture. Then, as she did now, she found herself in awe that such a beautiful room could exist outdoors.

It was a perfect summer night, made for sitting under the stars. A three-quarter moon hung high and yellow in the cloudless sky. Before them a mosaic of rooftops and lights spread as far as the eye could see. The beacon atop old John Hancock Tower glowed blue, telegraphing the beautiful weather to anyone who needed reminding.

Stuart was opening a bottle of wine when she arrived. "You don't mind, do you?" he asked her. "If you'd rather, there's water..."

"No, wine would be great." Even if it did make the atmosphere feel more date-like. "After all, it's a holiday right?"

"Right. What's Independence Day without a toast to freedom?"

Walking over to the edge of the deck, Patience looked out across the city. "I can see your apartment building from here, I think. Over there." She pointed to a tower in the distance. "I can't remember if I could see Ana's roof from the terrace or not."

"We'll have to stand outside and wave to each other someday to find out." He appeared at her elbow, carrying a glass of wine in each hand. Handing her one, he raised the other. "To freedom."

Patience gave a slight smile as she raised hers in return. "One of us achieved freedom today. How long before you move?"

"The end of the month, I think. I want to make sure Ana's mobile enough before I go, so as to not put all the burden on you."

"That's sweet of you."

"I want to." Perhaps, but Patience didn't harbor any illusions. He was looking out for Ana because he loved his aunt, not her.

Not that love had anything to do with anything.

"Did I say something wrong?"

And here she thought staring at her glass would keep her eyes from giving her away. "Just thinking a month wasn't that far away. Ana will be sorry to see you go."

"Ana?" He moved in tighter, giving her little choice but to turn and meet his gaze. Questions hung in the back of their blue depths. He knew she meant both her and Ana, but she couldn't bring herself to admit it.

"Don't be silly. You know she adores you. It has to be killing her to be in the hospital while you're here in the brownstone."

"It's killing me," he replied. "Seeing her laid up reminds me of how old she's getting. And how frail."

"Part of me wants to think she'll be here forever," he added, contemplating the contents of his glass.

Patience could feel the regret pressing down on his shoulders and rushed to reassure him. "We always want to think that the people we love will stay forever. I'm as guilty as you are. I want to believe Piper will be part of my world forever, but someday she's going to have a life of her own. It's already started."

"You make it sound like she'll forget you exist."

"Forget no, but she'll have other priorities beyond her

big sister." The way it was supposed to be. She hadn't sacrificed in order for Piper to stay by her side.

"Maybe you'll be too busy having a life of your own to notice."

Doing what? Cleaning? "Oh, I'll have a life, but I want more for Piper. I want her to have everything. Love, family, a home."

"Who says you won't have those things, too?"

She'd love to have them, but they seemed too far out of reach. Easier to wish happiness for Piper. "Maybe someday," she said, speaking into her wine. "At the moment, I'm happy where I am. Working for Ana."

"You know you deserve more, right?" His fingers caught her chin and turned her face toward him. "Right?" he repeated.

Patience wanted to tell him to stop being so kind. Things were easier when he'd been suspicious. At least then she knew the dividing line. Attraction bad, distance good. When he was sweet and tender like this, the line blurred. She could feel the cracks in her invisible wall growing bigger. Pretty soon there would be no wall at all to protect her.

But she couldn't tell him any of that—not without admitting his growing hold over her. "Maybe someday," she repeated with a smile. Stepping away from his touch, she looked to the Esplanade, the long expanse of green lining the Charles River. "You're right, this is the best picnic spot. You can see the Hatch Shell," she said, jumping once again to a safe topic. The area around the open-air stage glowed white from all the spotlights and television trucks. "I swear I can hear the music."

"I'm not surprised. We're close enough." Behind her, Patience heard shuffling, and suddenly the music grew louder. He'd turned on the radio simulcast. "There," she heard him say, "that's better than straining to catch a stray chord. Sounds like the concert just started. Plenty of time before the fireworks."

"Do you know," Patience said, stepping away from the view, "that I've never seen the July Fourth fireworks live?"

"Really?"

"Nope. Just on TV. Piper was afraid of loud noises so I never took her. We stayed home and watched them on TV instead."

"How about when you were a kid? Sorry." He seemed to realize his mistake as soon as he spoke.

"That's all right. There are worse things to miss out on." She took a plate and started helping herself to the food. "How about you? What did your family do on Fourth of July?"

"Nothing. I was at camp, learning important wilderness survival techniques, like how not to lose your inhaler while hiking."

She laughed.

"I'm not kidding," he said. "I lost that sucker twice one summer. Kept falling out of my pocket."

"I'm sorry," Patience said, "but I'm having a hard time picturing you as this awkward asthmatic."

"Remind me to show you my high school graduation photo someday. You'll believe me then."

"Well, you're definitely not awkward now."

"Thank you." Stuart's smile had an odd cast to it, almost as if he didn't quite believe her. Which was ridiculous, because surely he knew what kind of man he was, didn't he?

They ate in silence, letting the music fill in for conversation. It never failed to surprise Patience how comfortable just being with Stuart could be. Simmering attraction aside, that is. Maybe it was more that she never felt uncomfortable with him. Never felt like he was trying to mentally undress her. Even those moments of intense scrutiny, when his eyes bore down on her, weren't about her figure, but rather what was inside. With him, Patience never felt like less than a person.

It was a gift she'd never forget.

Feeling a lump begin to rise in her throat, she reached for her wine. This wasn't the time for tears.

"How do you think Ana's party is going? She seemed pretty excited when we saw her this morning."

"Going great, I'm sure." Stuart smiled while wiping the grease from his fingers. "No doubt she and her cronies have commandeered the entire hospital sunroom and put the staff to work. Those ladies can be a force to be reckoned with. Don't be surprised if we show up tomorrow and hear they had the whole hospital involved."

Patience could picture the scene. "They'll miss her when she's discharged." She sipped her wine thoughtfully. "I'm surprised you're not at a party yourself."

"I promised you a picnic for viewing the condo with me."

"We could have done it a different night." He must have had better options than spending the night with her.

"No, I said I'd show you the best place to see the fireworks. Besides, I wanted to."

Patience tried not to get too excited by the remark. Unfortunately, she failed. The idea that Stuart had chosen her warmed her to the core. "I hope your friends aren't too disappointed."

"They'll survive, I'm sure." He stared at his drink, looking as if he was debating saying more. "I don't— I don't have a lot of friends. At least not close ones."

"I'm surprised."

He looked up. "Are you? In case you haven't noticed, I tend to be rather suspicious of people."

Because of Gloria? Wow, his step-grandmother had really done a number on him. Or was there someone else who'd hurt him, too? The woman who "dumped him" maybe?

"Dr. Tischel told me about your ex-girlfriend," she told him.

"What did he say?"

She was right—the way his spine straightened told her that his step-grandmother hadn't been the only woman to burn his trust. "Not much. Only that she broke up with you."

"He didn't say anything else?"

Like what? Seeing Stuart on alert had her curious. "No. He didn't even mention her name." The fact he'd brought up the subject at all had made Patience think she wasn't just any girlfriend but rather someone who had broken his heart.

Stuart's reaction all but confirmed her theory. Waving away the comment with exaggerated indifference, he sat back in his seat. "Dr. Tischel was drunk and looking to spread gossip is all."

Patience wasn't so sure. Dr. Tischel had spoken pretty offhandedly for a guy trying to gossip. In fact, he sounded more as if he was repeating news everyone already knew.

She was about to ask for Stuart's version when he held up his hand. "Listen," he said. The orchestra was playing a medley of Big Band songs. Memories of swaying in each other's arms came rushing back, the onslaught overwhelming all other thoughts. One look at Stuart's darkening eyes told her he remembered, too.

"Let's dance," he said, setting down his glass. It wasn't a request but a command. The assertiveness sent a thrill running down her spine. Her hand was in his before she could think twice.

"What are the odds?" she heard him murmur as he pulled her close.

"I don't know." And she didn't care. She would dance to anything if it meant being able to spend time in his arms. You are such a goner, she thought as she rested her temple against his shoulder.

"This is the first time I've ever danced without milehigh heels," she said. "I feel short."

His chest rumbled beneath her ear. "You could always stand on tiptoes."

"That's okay, this is perfect." More than perfect. Closing her eyes, she let the moment wash over her. Who knew when they'd share another one? "Much better than the dinner dance."

Stuart pulled back and his eyes searched hers. "You mean that, don't you?"

There was something about his voice. In a way he sounded surprised, but a bigger part of him sounded pleased, as if he'd made a great discovery.

"You still don't trust me to tell you the truth, do you?" After everything she'd shared about her past...

"That's just it, I do," he said, pulling her close again. "For the first time in a long time, I do."

They swayed in silence. Patience lost herself in the music and the sound of Stuart's breathing as they turned around and around, their feet and their bodies in perfect sync. The roof, the streets below, the entire city—all fell away except for the two of them.

The song ended, replaced by the slow mournful strands of the "1812 Overture," Boston's signal the fireworks were on their way. Patience clung tighter, wishing the moment would never end.

"Gloria," Stuart whispered suddenly. The name made Patience's insides chill.

"The girlfriend who broke up with me. It was Gloria."

CHAPTER EIGHT

DEAR GOD. WAS he saying…? "You had an affair with your step-grandmother?" It was a lousy question, but she had to ask. Gloria was, after all, married to a man sixty years her senior. It would be only natural that she might turn to someone young and virile.

Besides, the alternative would be that Gloria chose Theodore over…

"No affair."

Her stomach sank. Exactly what she'd feared. "She left you for your grandfather." The *ew* factor increased. What kind of woman would prefer an old man to…to Stuart?

She already knew the answer. "She was after the money."

"Yeah." He broke away. Patience tried to grab his hand to pull him back only to miss the mark. "I should have realized. I mean, she pursued me—that alone should have been my first clue."

"Why?" Patience didn't understand. She pictured women coming on to Stuart all the time.

He laughed at her question. A soft, sad laugh. "Asthmatic and awkward, remember? Well, awkward anyway. This was almost fifteen years ago," he rushed to add. He must have guessed she was about to argue the point. "I hadn't grown into myself yet. When it came to things like dating, I was pretty clueless. Gloria on the other hand…let's say she'd grown into herself years earlier. When she started showing interest in me, I thought I was the luckiest guy in the world. Couldn't wait to introduce her to Grandpa Theodore. Talk about a stupid mistake."

"She started chasing after him."

"Hey, why settle for the nerdy grandson when you can snag the mother lode, right?" The bitterness in his voice told the rest of the story. Along with his eyes. He could try to make a joke out of the betrayal, but she could still feel his hurt. As he'd said before, the eyes gave away everything.

Having told his story, or as much as he intended, he made his way back to the coffee table. "Although to be fair, Grandpa Theodore did his part, too." Snagging his wineglass, he drained the contents. "In a way I'm grateful to them," he said, reaching for the bottle. He started to pour, only to change his mind, and set it back down. "They taught me a valuable lesson."

"Be careful who you trust."

"Exactly. I promised myself I would never—ever— get taken in again. Wasn't long after that I came out here and connected with Ana."

Who became the one relative he could trust. Patience understood now why he'd been so suspicious of her when they'd met. Like her, Stuart had built himself an invisible wall. Granted, he'd built his for different reasons, but the purpose was the same: self-defense. So long as he kept the world at a distance, he would be safe.

He'd shared his history with her, though. To think he'd allowed her to see a part of him few people ever saw. Tears sprang to her eyes, she was so honored. What little there was left of the walls protecting Patience's heart crumbled to dust.

It was a mistake. Every bit of her common sense knew better. A woman like her, a man like him. Temporary, at best. But she couldn't help herself. The need for distance forgotten, she brushed her fingers along his jaw.

"Gloria was a fool," she whispered, hoping he could read in her eyes the words she wasn't saying.

"Are you sure?" Stuart whispered back. He wasn't asking about Gloria, but about her. Was she sure she wanted to cross the line they were toeing.

The answer was no, but surety had long since fallen by the wayside in favor of emotion. Patience melted into his arms as his lips found hers.

In the distance, fireworks exploded over the Charles River. Neither noticed.

The first thing Patience noticed in the morning was the pressure bearing down on her chest. She opened her eyes to discover Stuart lying next to her, his arm flung possessively across her body. Remembering the night before, she smiled. Funny, but she expected the morning after to be uncomfortable, with regrets darkening the light of day, but no. She was so happy she felt as if her chest might explode.

Her smile widened as Stuart gave a soft moan and moved in closer. "Morning," he murmured. With his voice laced with sleep, he sounded young and unjaded.

Blue eyes blinked at her. "I see you."

"I see you, too."

"No, I mean I can see you. I fell asleep wearing my contacts again."

"Again, huh? Happens often?"

"More than I want to admit." He rolled to his side. "In this case, though, I blame you."

"Me?" she asked, rolling to face him.

"Uh-huh. You distracted me."

"Oh." She was going to strain her cheek muscles if she kept smiling this way. "I didn't hear any complaints last night."

"Oh, trust me, there are no complaints this morning, either."

They lay side by side, his arm draped around her waist. The intimate position felt so natural it was scary. "But I better not hear any jokes about my glasses."

"I like your glasses. They give you a sexy hipster look."

Stuart laughed. It was a sound everyone should hear in the morning. "Maybe we should get you some glasses." His smile shifted, turning almost reverent. "You really mean what you're saying, though, don't you?"

"Doesn't make a different to me whether you wear glasses or not. You could wear a sack over your head for all I care. Well, maybe not a sack. I kind of like your face."

"I like yours," he said, brushing her cheek. Her face. Not her body. Patience loved the way he looked at her. He didn't see her as an object or even as an ex-stripper. As far as Stuart was concerned, she was a person. Someone worthy of respect.

But do you deserve it? The question came crashing

into her brain, reminding her that, in spite of all her confessions, there was still one secret she'd kept to herself. Stuart trusted her enough to tell his story. Maybe she should trust him with the rest of hers?

His fingers were moving south, tracing a path over her shoulder, tugging the sheet away from her skin.

"Stuart…?"

"Mmm?"

"I—" She arched into the sheets as he nuzzled the crook of her neck. "Nothing." He made it way too easy to give in.

Ana was talking a blue streak. "…need more events like last evening's. I asked Dr. O'Hara to get me the CEO's phone number. When I'm settled back home, I want to make a donation and tell him to earmark the money for entertainment. As I told Dr. O'Hara, patients need distractions, and he agreed. I have to say, I wasn't sure I was going to like him but he's much less condescending than Karl. Plus, he has a lovely wife, so he won't be bothering Patience. Are you listening to me?"

"Of course, I am. Dr. O'Hara's condescending."

He wasn't even close, was he? Stuart could tell from Ana's arched brow. "Sorry, I was thinking about… something else." This morning, to be exact. And last night.

"Obviously." His aunt settled back against her pillow. Time in the rehab facility had improved the sharpness of her stare, which she used to full advantage. "So what is it that has you smiling like the cat who ate the canary? It's unlike you."

"I'm in a good mood is all. I found a condo yesterday. On the other side of the Common."

"Does that mean you'll be moving out?"

"Not for a while yet."

The disappointment left Ana's face. "Good. I'm not ready for you to leave yet."

Neither was he. It had dawned on him this morning that leaving would mean leaving Patience behind. Unless they continued whatever it was they were doing at his place. Was that what he wanted?

Pictures of her standing on his terrace flashed through his head.

"You're smiling again. Must be a very nice apartment."

"It's not bad. Patience came with me to check the place out. She liked it."

"Really? I didn't realize you valued her opinion? I got the impression there was tension between the two of you."

"We…" Damn, if his cheeks weren't getting warm. "We worked that out."

"Did you, now?"

"We talked."

"I'm glad. She's a lovely girl, isn't she?"

"Um…" He pictured her face when she woke up this morning. Hair mussed. Sleep in her eyes. She was far more than lovely. She was genuine and honest. He could trust her.

The realization hit him while they were dancing. Scared the hell out of him. At the same time, he'd never felt freer.

"Stuart?"

"You were right, Tetya. She's terrific."

He could tell the second his aunt put two and two together. Her pale blue eyes pinned him to the chair. "Are you having an affair with my housekeeper?"

Stuart ran a hand across the back of his neck. His cheeks were definitely crimson now. Thankfully, his aunt took pity on him and waved her question off. "You don't have to say anything. I know a besotted look when I see one."

"I'm not sure I'd say besotted." A word from this century, perhaps.

"Use whatever word you want. I'm glad."

"You are?"

"Of course. You let what happened with Gloria keep you from falling in love for way too long. Killed me to think Theodore crushed *your* heart, too."

Who said anything about love? He was about to tell Ana she was reading too much into the affair when something his aunt said caught his attention.

"Too?" This was the first time his aunt had ever referred to the bad blood between her and his grandfather. He thought of the memory box buried at the bottom of her drawer, of cats all bearing the same man's name, and his heart ached for the woman he'd grown to love as a grandmother. What had his grandfather done? He had to ask. "Are you talking about Nigel?"

"Don't be silly? What would your grandfather have to do with my cat?"

She was a worse liar than he was. The way she suddenly became interested in smoothing her sheets gave her away. "I meant Nigel Rougeau," he said.

Her hand stilled. "Who?"

"I saw the photographs, Tetya. The ones in your drawer."

"Oh."

"I know it's none of my business…I've just always

wondered why. What could my grandfather have possibly done to make you cut us off?"

"Oh, *lapushka*, I was never trying to cut you off. What happened was a long time ago, before you were ever born."

"You mean what happened with Nigel?"

She nodded.

She didn't get to say anything further. Footsteps sounded outside the hospital door and, a second later, Patience appeared. Stuart couldn't believe the way his pulse picked up when he saw her.

"Hey," she greeted in a shy voice that screamed all the things they'd done overnight. "I was bringing Ana something to eat. I didn't realize you'd be here."

"I decided to visit during lunch so I could get home at a decent hour," he replied. His answer made her blush, probably because they both knew why he wanted to get home early. The pink ran across her cheeks and down her neck, disappearing into the collar of her T-shirt. She looked so incredibly delectable Stuart had to grip the sides of his chair to keep from kissing her senseless.

"I brought you a chicken salad sandwich," she said, setting a bag on Ana's bedside table. Then, noticing his aunt's distraction, she frowned. "Am I interrupting something?"

"Ana was about to tell me about Nigel Rougeau." That made Ana look up.

"She was the one who found the box," he explained.

"We weren't trying to pry, I swear," Patience said. "I put the box on the bureau while I was organizing your drawer and Nigel—the cat—knocked it on the floor. We saw the name when we were picking up the mess. I'm sorry."

"Don't be, dear. It was probably Nigel's way of demanding attention." Ana gave a long, sad sigh. "He never did like being kept a secret."

She meant Nigel Rougeau. Realizing this, Stuart and Patience exchanged a look. Apparently cats and their namesake shared personality traits after all.

"Maybe it's time I told our story," Ana said, smoothing the sheets again.

"Should I leave?" Patience asked. "Let you talk about family business…"

"No, dear. You can stay," Ana told her. "You're like family."

Stuart could tell Patience was still wavering, so he grabbed her hand and pulled her into the chair next to his. "Please stay."

She looked down at their joined fingers. "This is okay, too," he said. "She knows."

"Oh." The blush returned.

"Nigel loved when women blushed. He used to say every woman's cheek has its own special shade. He was a painter I knew in Paris."

"You were his model. The painting on the wall."

"He and I preferred the term *muse*. Our relationship was far deeper than artist and model." She sighed. "He had such talent."

The reverence in her voice took Stuart aback. "Why didn't you mention him before?" he asked. Why keep a man she so clearly worshipped a secret?

"Some things are too painful to mention." Next to him, Patience stiffened. They both understood all too well what Ana meant. "You don't have to tell us now, either," Patience said.

"Yes," he agreed. "We'll understand."

"No, I want to. I'm sure he's furious that I've stayed quiet this long." Ana spoke in the present tense, as if he were in the room with them.

"We met the summer I graduated high school. I was on a grand tour, being bored to tears with tours of cathedrals and palaces and had sneaked away to see some of the more forbidden parts of Paris. Instead, I met Nigel. It was love at first sight. When the tour moved on, I stayed behind."

Her voice grew gravelly. Stuart reached over and poured her a glass of water. As he handed the drink to her, he saw her eyes had grown wet. "We were going to do great things in the art world. He would paint, I would be the inspiration. The Diakonova to his Salvador Dali."

"What happened?" Patience asked. The two of them leaned forward, curious.

"Your grandfather happened, of course. You know our parents passed away when I was a child." Stuart nodded. Losing your parents young seemed to be Duchenko tradition.

"Because he was the eldest, Theodore became my legal guardian. When he found out Nigel and I were living together—Nigel considered marriage a bourgeois institution—he went crazy. He flew to Paris to 'bring me home.' Said he would not allow his seventeen-year-old sister to ruin the Duchenko name by living in sin with some two-bit, fortune-hunting painter. I always wondered whether if Nigel had been more successful, if Theodore might have had a different view."

She paused to take another drink before continuing. "And then, he saw Nigel's work."

"The painting hanging in the studio."

His aunt gave a wistful smile. "That was one of so

many studies. Nigel was a student of the human form and being his muse…"

"He studied your form the most." Patience's comment earned a blush. It was the first time Stuart ever saw his aunt color in embarrassment.

"Your grandfather was doubly furious. He told me in no uncertain terms that if I didn't come home and live like a proper lady, he would destroy Nigel's career before it had ever started."

Patience gave a soft gasp. "Surely, he didn't mean…"

"I'm sure he did," Stuart replied. "Grandpa Theodore could be ruthless when he wanted to be." Didn't matter who was involved. His sister, his grandson.

Reading his mind, Patience squeezed his hand, the gesture replacing the emptiness inside him with warmth. Grateful, he pressed her fingers to his lips.

"What did you do?" he asked Ana, knowing the answer.

"What could I do? I was only seventeen. If I refused, it would be the end of Nigel's career, and I couldn't do that to him. He was born for greatness."

So, instead, she sacrificed her happiness for his sake. Stuart wanted to strangle his grandfather.

"You must have loved him very much," Patience whispered.

"He was my soul mate." Ana smiled a watery smile, only to have it melt away seconds later. "I told Nigel, I'd come back. That as soon as I was eighteen I would find him. We could use my money to protect ourselves from Theodore's influence."

"But you didn't go back." She'd moved to Boston and never returned to Paris.

A tear slipped down Ana's face. "There was nothing

to go back to. A few weeks after I left, Nigel was killed in a motorcycle accident. He always rode too fast..."

Her voice grew wobbly, and the tears fell more frequently. "Later I heard Theodore had hired someone to purchase all his paintings of me and have them destroyed. All his work gone forever."

"Oh, Tetya." There were no words. Stuart jumped to his feet and wrapped his arms around her, anger toward his grandfather building as Ana shook silently against him. Here he'd thought marrying Gloria was the old man's low point. He couldn't be more wrong.

A comforting warmth buffeted him. Patience stood by his side, her hand gently rubbing circles on Ana's back. "I'm so sorry," she whispered.

Giving a sniff, his aunt lifted her head. While her eyes were red and puffy, Stuart saw the familiar backbone finding its way back. "My sweet child," she said, swiping at her cheeks, "why are you apologizing? You didn't do anything. Either of you."

Her absolution did little to alleviate the hurt he felt on her behalf. "But if I'd known..."

"What? You'd have called him on his behavior? Theodore knew what he was doing. He was a selfish man who didn't care who he hurt."

No, thought Stuart, he didn't.

She touched his cheek, tenderly, like the surrogate grandmother she'd become. "I'm just glad he didn't destroy your heart the way he did mine."

"Me, too." Although he'd come damn close.

Emotionally and physically worn-out, Ana dozed off a short while later. Patience waited by the doorway while Stuart tucked the older woman in and gave her a goodbye kiss.

* * *

"This explains why she named all the cats Nigel," Patience said, once they stepped into the corridor. "She was keeping her lover's memory alive." It broke her heart to think of Ana—sweet, gentle Ana—spending a lifetime mourning her only love. How could Theodore ruin his sister's happiness like that? All because she'd dared to fall in love with the wrong kind of man?

Life really did stink sometimes.

Out of the corner of her eye, she saw Stuart looking back over his shoulder. "I knew my grandfather could be cold, but I always thought what happened with Gloria was a case of him being seduced. Now I wonder…" Rather than finish the sentence, he looked down at the linoleum. Didn't matter. Patience could guess what he was thinking. In spite of what he said regarding his grandfather's involvement, he still placed the bulk of the betrayal on Gloria's shoulders. Ana's story shifted the blame more evenly. "Ironic, isn't it?" he said. "My grandfather being so intent on protecting the Duchenko name and fortune, only to make a spectacle of himself decades later by marrying a fortune hunter himself?"

"You heard Ana. He was selfish. Selfish people only care about what benefits them."

"True." He left out a deep breath. "Goes to show, you really can't trust anyone."

"That's not true." Patience rushed to keep the walls from reforming. "You can trust Ana. And you can trust me." Staring directly at him, she dared him to look into her soul and see her sincerity. "I swear."

"I know." He went back to studying the floor.

This morning, Patience had joked about his glasses looking sexy and hip. At the moment, however, he just looked lost. It felt like the most natural thing in the world to wrap her arms around her waist and hold him close. He started at first, but it wasn't long before he hugged her back, his chin resting on her shoulder. "I'm as bad as he was, you know that?"

"What are you talking about?" Pulling back, she frowned at him. "If you're talking about your grandfather, you couldn't be more wrong." The two men were day and night. "I've seen how much you care about Ana. For crying out loud, you've been in here visiting every day since the accident. You make sure she has the best doctors, the best therapy. Hell, you went to the humane society dinner dance for her."

She pressed herself tight in his arms. "You could never do what your grandfather did to Ana," she whispered in his ear. Or what his grandfather had done to him. "Not in a million years."

"You sound pretty confident."

"I am," she replied with a smile. "There's a reason Ana sings your praises so much. You're a good man, Stuart Duchenko." Her heart echoed every word.

Stuart squeezed her tight, and for a second Patience thought she felt his body shake. The moment didn't last. Slipping out of her embrace, he crossed the hall and moved to a new doorway. There he stood, staring into an unoccupied room. "My pity party must sound pretty pathetic to you."

Because, he was saying, she'd had it so much worse. Maybe so, but as she'd told him before, it wasn't a contest. "Everyone needs reassurance once in a while."

"That so?" A smile made its way to his face as he leaned against the door frame. "Well, in that case, I hope you know how awesome you are, Patience Rush. I'm damn lucky our paths crossed."

On the contrary, she was the lucky one. She was falling deeper and deeper by the second.

"Thank you for being here." Leaning forward, he kissed her. A long, lingering kiss, the tenderness of which left Patience's head spinning. "See you back home?"

Not trusting herself to speak, she nodded. If there was any chance that she could keep her heart from getting involved, that kiss chased it away for good.

CHAPTER NINE

THAT NIGHT, THE two of them lay on the deck's top sofa, legs and bodies entwined like spaghetti, making out like a pair of teenagers. Patience swore Stuart had turned kissing into an art form. One moment his kisses were possessive and demanding, the next they turned so reverent they brought tears to her eyes.

All the while Patience fought the voice in her head warning her that he'd eventually realize she wasn't good enough.

She was saved from her dark thoughts by Stuart tugging on her lower lip with his teeth. "I think I'm love with your mouth," he murmured.

Words muttered in the throes of passion, but Patience's heart jumped all the same. She forced herself to treat the remark as lightly as he intended it to be. Running her bare foot up Stuart's leg, she thrilled at the way her touch caused a soft groan. "What does *lapushka* mean?" she asked.

Stuart raised himself up on his elbows. "Seriously?"

"I'm curious." And she needed the distraction. He might have been only talking about her mouth, but the word *love* required her to take a step back. "I know *tetya* means aunt…"

"*Lapushka* means little paw. And before you ask, I have no idea why she calls me that."

"I like it. *Lapushka*." She drew out the second syllable. "It's sweet."

"Better than *mon petit chou*. French for my little cabbage," he added when she frowned.

"I thought you didn't know French."

"That was the extent of my knowledge."

"At least now I have something to call Piper next time she calls."

Stuart didn't answer. A faraway look found its way to his face. Patience touched his cheek to call him back to the present. "You're thinking about what Ana told us this afternoon, aren't you?"

"Grandpa Theodore took so much from her. She could have had a completely different life." He cast his eyes to the cushion, but not before she caught a flash of regret. "I keep wondering if there isn't some way I could fix the damage he caused."

"How? Unless you can turn back time, I don't think you can."

"Actually…" With a moan that could best be described as reluctant, Stuart rolled onto his side. The separation wasn't more than a few inches, but Patience felt the distance immediately and shivered. "I was thinking about that this afternoon."

"About turning back time?"

"Sort of."

Now he had her interest. She shifted onto her side as well, propping herself on one elbow so as to give him her full attention. "What do you mean?"

"I was thinking about the painting we saw in the photograph. Ana said Nigel painted all sorts of studies of her."

"Yes, but she also said your grandfather paid some-one to buy all of them."

"But what if he didn't? I mean, what if he wasn't able to buy them all. Ana made it sound like there were a lot of paintings and sketches. It's possible one or two of them survived. Grandpa Theodore was powerful, but he wasn't omnipotent. In spite of what he thought."

"Do you really think a painting exists?"

"It's possible, and if one does, then Ana could have back a piece of what she lost. Might not be much, but…"

It was a wonderful, beautiful gesture that deepened the feelings that were rapidly taking control of Pa-tience's heart. "But Nigel died years ago,' she reminded him. "How would we ever find out about his paintings?"

"We can at least try. I did a little searching on the internet this afternoon. Apparently Nigel had a sister."

"Really? Is she still alive?"

"Alive and living in Paris. If anyone knows what hap-pened to his artwork, it would be her. All we need is for someone to go talk to her. You wouldn't happen to have any ideas who we could call, do you?" he asked, brushing the bangs from her face.

"Funny you should ask—I do." She matched his grin. "I'm sure Piper would be glad to help. She knows how important Ana is to me. I'll call her tomorrow. With luck, she can arrange to talk to Nigel's sister this week."

"That would be great. Thank you."

He didn't have to thank her. "After everything Ana has done for me, this is nothing. I'd love to find this painting as much as you." And give back to the woman who saved her a piece of her soul mate that was big-ger than a box of memories and a string of cats bear-ing his name.

Thinking of the cats made her giggle. "What's so funny?" Stuart asked.

"Nothing. I was thinking, if the cats all had Nigel's personality, does that mean he never stopped eating?"

"Interesting question. We'll have to ask Ana someday.

"In the meantime," he said, rising above her. "It's still the middle of the night in Paris. We've got a few hours to kill before we can think about calling your sister."

"Is that so?"

"Uh-huh." He gripped her waist and quickly flipped her beneath him, causing Patience to let out a high-pitched squeal. "Looks like we'll have to find something to pass the time," he said, dipping his head.

Patience met him halfway.

Despite claiming her older sister "owed her," Piper was more than happy to visit Nigel's sister, just as Patience knew she would be. "Stuart and I really appreciate this," she said to the younger woman.

"Stuart, huh?" Piper's face loomed large as she leaned toward the screen. "How are things going with the two of you? Is he still cool with, you know, the club?"

Patience's mind flashed to a few hours before, in Stuart's bed. "Seems to be," she replied.

"See? I told you he'd understand. It's not like you went to work in that place because you liked dancing naked on tables."

"Of course, I didn't," Patience replied with a wince. She wondered if the memory would ever stop making her stomach churn. "And you're right. Stuart says he understands."

"Wait—what do you mean 'says he understands'? Don't you believe him?"

"No, I believe him. Stuart's been great."

"Then what's wrong?"

"Nothing." Patience shook her head. How could she explain that Stuart being great was the problem. He was too great while she was…well, she sure as heck didn't feel worthy. Sooner or later, this dream had to end. A soft sigh escaped her lips. Too late, she remembered Piper was on the other end of the line.

"Patience?"

Blinking, she came face-to-face with Piper's scowl.

"What aren't you telling me?" her sister asked.

"Um…" She bit her lip and prayed her sister's old cell phone camera wouldn't pick up her blush.

It was a fruitless wish. "Oh, my God! Is something going on between you and your boss?"

"He's not my boss," Patience said quickly. "He's my boss's great-nephew."

They were splitting hairs and they both knew it, which was why Piper asked, "What exactly is the difference?"

"The difference…" There was no difference, but she didn't want to admit it. Calling Stuart her boss only reminded her they weren't from the same world, a reality she was trying to ignore for as long as possible. Acknowledging that reality would only lead to others, like Patience not being good enough for him. "The difference would be the same as you dating either your boss or his next-door neighbor." she finally said.

Just as she knew she would, Piper rolled her eyes at the lame example. "Please. The only neighbor I've met is an eleven-year-old boy, and my boss doesn't even…"

"Doesn't even what?" For some reason, her sister had stopped midsentence, and her gaze was focused on a point off camera. "Piper?"

"Sorry, I lost track of what I was about to say. And you still haven't answered my question. Are you dating Stuart Duchenko?"

"For now, yes."

"No way! That's great!" Piper beamed from ear to ear. "I'm so happy for you."

"Don't go making a big deal. We're having fun together, that's all. It's nothing serious."

Of course she still hadn't mentioned the other thing. After Stuart distracted her yesterday—not that she'd fought too hard—there hadn't been another good moment. Then again, when was there a good time to share something so humiliating? It wasn't exactly something you could blurt out. *Hey, Stuart, by the way, dancing naked wasn't the only thing in my past I didn't tell you about. There's also this little police matter...*

She switched the subject back to Nigel Rougeau's sister and hoped Piper believed her.

At least one of them should.

"And this," Stuart said, "is the firm library. Home away from home for any decent first-year associate."

He snuck a kiss to Patience's temple while pointing out the shelves, causing her knees to wobble slightly. Not because of the kiss but from the intimacy it implied.

"Was it yours?" She pictured his dark head bent over the books late at night.

"Are you kidding? See that desk by the window? If you sit in the chair, you can still feel the imprint from my butt cheeks."

Patience choked back a snort, causing a pair of heads to look in their direction, only to return to their work as soon as they spied Stuart. "Don't look now, but I think they're afraid of you."

"Well, I can be pretty scary, you know."

"I know I was terrified when I first met you."

"I could tell by the way you sauced off."

"That's not even a real word." Giggling, she slapped his sleeve. One of the heads looked up again, and she couldn't help indulging in a moment of smug pride. *That's right*, she wanted to say, *your boss is entertaining me.*

It was an illusion, of course, this image of being a couple, but she was willing to let herself enjoy the fantasy for as long as it lasted. Later today, Ana would be coming home, and soon after Stuart would be moving out, bringing an end to their affair. When that happened, she would confront the emotions she was fighting to keep buried.

Until then, she'd let the illusion have control.

"The partner's dining room is next door," Stuart said. "Would you rather eat in there or in my office?"

That's why she was here. With Ana returning home, Stuart had invited her to lunch to discuss what she needed to do to get the brownstone ready. "You're the host. I'll let you decide."

"My office it is. That way I can ravish you after we eat," he whispered in her ear.

Patience's knees wobbled again. The way his voice grew husky, she could listen to his whisper all day long. "Sounds good to me."

"What part? The eating or the ravishing?" Either. Both. She welcomed the privacy, too. Previous moment aside, she felt uncomfortable walking around Stuart's law firm. Although she'd exchanged her jeans for an ankle-length skirt and tank top, she still felt out of place amid the power suits. "What are you talking about?" Stuart had remarked when she'd mentioned her fears. "No one expects my date to look like she's heading to court."

"They would if she was a lawyer," she countered.

"But she's not. She's you."

He had no idea how his response made her heart soar.

"Bob was looking for you," a woman called to them when they reached his office.

"I know," Stuart replied. "I got his emails. If it's about the Peavey case, tell him to send the brief directly to John Greenwood."

"He said this was about another project. A report you asked him to assemble."

There was a sudden stutter in his step. While they weren't touching, Patience could still feel Stuart's body tense. "Oh," he replied. "Tell him I'll talk with him later." Even his voice sounded tight.

"I'm keeping you from something important, aren't I?" she asked.

"Nothing that can't wait."

But she was. His whole demeanor had changed on a dime. Lighthearted Stuart had disappeared behind a shadow. All of a sudden, he was frowning, the playful gleam gone from his eyes.

"Seriously, if you have work to do, I can—"

"No." He practically shouted the word. For some reason, it made the hair on her neck stand on end. "Whatever Bob has to say can wait."

"But if he's trying so hard to talk with you..." Multiple emails and personal visits—it had to be important.

Stuart shook his head. "I already know what he wants to tell me, and it's not important at all."

"Okay. If you say so." No need pressing the issue, even though she wasn't sure she believed him. "Bob can wait."

"Exactly."

Stuart's office was a mirror image of him. Attractive and elegant. If this was the reward, no wonder those associates worked so hard.

She stood in the center of the room while he closed his office door and then turned to her with a mischievous grin.

"Are we planning to eat?" she asked him.

"Eventually." Taking her hand, he led her to the luxurious leather chair that dominated the back of his desk. "First things first. I believe I said something about ravishing."

"I distinctly remember you saying after we eat."

"Sue me. I lied."

She would have made a joke about being in the perfect place to do so had he not completely derailed her thoughts by slipping his arms around her waist. She tumbled onto his lap without argument.

His eagerness never ceased to amaze her. Every time he kissed her felt like the first time, passionate and needy.

She let out a whimper when he broke away. "Sadly, not being able to lock my door prevents a proper ravishing. That will have to wait until later."

"Your aunt will be home."

"She has to sleep eventually. And, if I recall, they're

installing her bed on the first floor, which means we can be as loud as we want." He slipped off the strap of her tank top and nipped at the exposed skin.

Goodness, but she would going to miss this when he left. Putting her hands on his shoulders, Patience pushed gently away. One of them had to add some space; otherwise, it wouldn't matter whether his door locked or not.

"I thought we needed to talk about Ana's new living arrangements," she said. Stuart groaned, but he didn't argue.

"The medical supply company delivered the bed this morning," she continued. "Is Ana okay with the arrangement?" After discussing it, she and Stuart had decided to move his aunt to the first floor for the next few weeks. Dr. O'Hara had been concerned about her going up and down stairs. Stuart and Patience were concerned she might trip over Nigel again.

"She's not crazy about the idea, but I think Dr. O'Hara convinced her she was doing the smart thing. I told her you'd bring down a lot of her personal items and set up the front sitting room as much like her bedroom as possible."

"Linens and nightstand are already down. And when I left, Nigel had taken up residence on the bed." She'd passed the cat curled up in the center of the mattress, the same location he claimed on Ana's regular bed.

"So long as she has Nigel, she'll be more than comfortable," Stuart replied. "Speaking of…have you spoken to your sister yet?"

"No. I got a message from her this morning saying she wanted to video chat, but we were unable to connect. I don't know if she's managed to look into Ana's painting, though."

"She has. I got an email from her just before you arrived."

"You did? Why didn't you tell me?"

The index finger trailing down her arm gave her the answer. He'd been distracted.

"Did she say if she learned anything?" she asked, ignoring the goose bumps ghosting across her skin.

A slow smile broke across Stuart's face. "Looks like we were right. A dealer did buy the contents of Nigel's studio right after his death—I'm guessing that's the man Grandpa Theodore hired—but it turns out that Nigel sold at least a couple pieces before his death. She gave Piper the name of the gallery owner who brokered the transaction. Piper and her boss were going to talk to him tomorrow."

"That's great! Wait." Patience paused. "Did you say her boss was helping her?" To hear Piper talk, the two of them barely had contact.

"Maybe he's helping her translate."

That would make sense. Piper's French was shaky. "Let's keep our fingers crossed the gallery owner kept decent records."

"Fingers, toes, and anything else you can think of," Stuart replied. "I really want to make this happen for Ana."

"Same here." Especially if success meant Stuart would have a smile, as well. Patience was pretty sure she'd do anything to see that.

Stuart didn't take two-hour lunches. Not unless there was a business meeting involved. But, with Patience, the time simply got away from him. Moreover, he didn't care. If he didn't have work to finish before Ana's discharge, he would have been perfectly happy to let the lunch go on for three or four hours. The woman was so damn easy to talk to.

Easy to do a lot of things with, he thought with a smile.

You, pal, are in deep, aren't you? For once, he let his subconscious speak freely. He *was* in deep, and, to his amazement, the thought didn't set off alarm bells. Why should it? Patience wasn't Gloria. Patience didn't pretend to be something she wasn't or tell him what she thought he wanted to hear. Instead, she was content to be with him—the real him. The one who wore thick glasses and talked about sunset differentials. Even at his most besotted, to steal his aunt's word, Gloria didn't make his insides feel light and joyful, the way Patience did. So, Stuart didn't freak out at the notion he might be falling. In fact, he could see himself falling a lot deeper.

Someone cleared his throat. Stuart looked to the door, saw who it was and cringed. "Hey, Bob. Come on in."

The overly tall, overly eager looking attorney stepped inside and closed the door behind him. No doubt meant as a gesture of confidentiality, it made Stuart wince nonetheless. "The investigator tracked down the information you needed," he said, brandishing a thin manila envelope. "I know it took a little longer than expected, but we had a couple big cases come through, and since this was personal and you hadn't followed up…"

"I thought I sent you an email telling you to cancel the investigation."

"You—you did?" The color drained from Bob's face. Associates hoping to be on the fast track hated to make mistakes, Bob more than most. "I didn't see one."

"A few weeks ago." The Saturday following the dinner dance. Stuart distinctly remembered typing out the message before going to bed. Right before Nigel jumped up and demanded attention.

Damn. Was it possible he hadn't hit Send? Now two people who didn't need to know were aware of Patience's secret.

Bob mistook his wiping his hand across his face for displeasure. "I am so sorry. The note must have gotten buried somehow...I..." He thrust the envelope at Stuart. "Are you sure you don't need this information? I mean, it's pretty interesting reading, I'll say that."

"You read it?"

Again Bob paled. "Um, only to make sure the report was complete. I wasn't trying to pry..."

Like hell he wasn't. The investigator's notes were probably too salacious to pass up. He gave Bob a dismissive look, letting the associate know he was unhappy with his performance. "Doesn't matter," he made a point of saying. "I already know everything the investigator might have found."

"You do?" Bob said. "Even the criminal record?"

Criminal record? Please no. Stuart squeezed the arms of his chair tight enough to snap them. It took every ounce of his control and then some to keep his face free of reaction. "Yes, even that."

"Oh. Okay. I'll go finish the brief for Greenwood then."

"You do that," Stuart replied. "And Bob?" Man, but it was hard to talk with nausea rising in his throat. "If you ever get a personal project from a partner again? Mind your own business."

The associate nodded before exiting as quickly as possible. Leaving Stuart alone.

With the manila envelope.

It had to be a mistake. Patience had told him everything, right? And he trusted her.

But what if…the possibility made him gag.

Only one way to be certain. He tore open the envelope.

"Dammit!" He slammed his fist on the desk, ignoring the pain shooting to his elbow. It was nothing compared to the hurt tearing through his insides. There, fastened to the top of the report, was everything he didn't want to know.

"All right, Nigel, let's get this straight. This is Ana's new bed, not yours. Meaning you will give her space to lie down when she and Stuart get home from the hospital, okay?"

Which, Patience checked the clock on the mantel, should be in an hour or so. She smoothed the wrinkles from Ana's comforter. The setup might not be ideal, but it would work for a month. Who knows? Ana might decide she liked living on the first floor.

We can be as loud as we want. A delicious shiver ran down her spine as she remembered Stuart's comment after Dr. O'Hara suggested the new arrangement. "Might as well make the most of what we have while we have it, right, Nigel?" she said, combing her fingers through Nigel's fur.

Suddenly, the front door slammed with a force so hard it made the frame rattle against the wall. Stuart appeared in the doorway, wild-eyed and out of breath.

"Stuart, what's wrong?" Instinctively, she took a step backward. He looked like a madman. The pupils in his eyes were blown wide, and while she'd seen them black with desire, she'd never seen them like this. "Did something happen to Ana?"

"Ana's fine."

"Then what?" This was not the man she had spent lunch sharing kisses with. This man looked like he wanted to…

Oh, no. She spied the crumpled papers in his fist. Pain began spreading across her chest, sharp like a heart attack. Why couldn't the past have stayed buried for a little while longer?

"I can explain," she said.

"Oh, I bet you can." His voice had gone dead. "I bet you have a whole slew of explanations at the ready."

"Stuart—"

"I trusted you," he spit. "When you said you told me everything, I believed you, but you were lying."

"No," she said, shaking her head. "I was telling the truth."

"Oh, yeah?" He stalked closer, waving the papers in his fist like they were a club. "Then tell me. Why do I have a police record telling me you were a prostitute?"

CHAPTER TEN

THE ACCUSATION HUNG between them, a fat, ugly cloud. Patience wished she could turn herself into Nigel. He'd run under the bed when Stuart slammed the door.

"This is what you were really hiding, wasn't it? You didn't want Ana to know who she'd hired. What she'd hired."

What she'd hired? How dared he? "I am not a prostitute."

"Your police record says otherwise."

"Police records don't tell the whole story." A few sentences typed on a form. How could it possibly cover all the details?

Tell that to Stuart, though. His outburst seemed to let out some of his steam, making the anger more of a slow boil. Patience preferred the outrage. Folding his arms, he settled in a nearby chair, his eyes burning holes in her skin.

"Then by all means, enlighten me," he said. "I can't wait to hear the long version."

"Why should I bother? You've obviously made up your mind." Worse, she wasn't entirely sure she could blame him after hiding the truth the way she had.

"Try me."

Patience almost laughed, the comment was so close to his words the night of the dance. The night she should have come clean. He'd been willing to listen then. Now she wasn't so sure.

In his chair, Stuart sat waiting. Her own personal judge and jury.

She took a deep breath. "You ever been to a place like Feathers? It's not some upscale bachelors' club. It's a dive, with divey people. Some of the girls—a lot of the girls—did stuff on the side to make extra cash."

"But not you."

"No!" she snarled. She got it. He was angry and hurt, but to even suggest… How many nights had she spent in his arms offering herself to him, body and soul? She didn't share herself like that with just anyone, and he should know that.

Stuart must have realized he'd crossed the line, as his voice lost its sharp edge. "How did you get lumped in with the others then?"

"One night, the cops raided the club, and hauled us all downtown. My lawyer said it would be too hard to fight the charge and I'd be better off pleading out to avoid jail time."

"Too hard for whom? You or him?"

It was the first civil thing he'd said since walking in, and it was a question she'd asked herself dozens of time. "I just wanted the whole thing to go away so I did what he said. I didn't want to risk breaking my promise to Piper.

"And that," she said, sinking onto the edge of the bed, "is the long version."

Neither of them said anything for several minutes. Patience stared at the floral duvet, counting the various blossoms. A tail brushed her ankle. Nigel making his escape to the kitchen. The lucky guy

Finally, Stuart broke the silence. "If all this is true, why did you lie? I might have understood if you'd told me first."

"Because I wanted to forget the night ever happened. I felt dirty enough. To admit I not only danced like a cheap whore, but I was arrested like one, too?" No matter how tightly she wrapped her arms around her midsection, her stomach still ached every time she thought about it. "Do you have any idea how it felt the other night, having to tell you about my pathetic past? I wanted to salvage a little bit of dignity." And also cling to him a little bit longer.

None of that mattered now. Patience had seen the loathing on Stuart's face when he walked in.

"All I ever wanted from this job was respect."

"You had my respect."

Had. Past tense. Her insides ripped in two. Hadn't she known from the beginning getting involved with Stuart was a bad idea. *Don't drop your defenses*, she'd told herself. *The crash would be worse if you let yourself care.*

Well, she hadn't listened, and the crash was killing her.

Stuart stood and crossed to the window. "I trusted you." The same words he'd said when he first came in. Violating his trust had been her biggest crime of all.

Except...

"Did you?" she asked suddenly. "Did you really trust me?"

"You know I did. I told you about Gloria, for crying out loud."

"Then how did you find out about my record?" Last time she looked, there wasn't a criminal record fairy handing out information. A person had to go searching for it. "I don't believe it. You had me investigated didn't you?"

"I—" He couldn't even look her in the eye.

"You did. Unbelievable." Sitting here, making her feel bad about her violating *his* trust, when all the time… "Face it, *lapushka*." She drew the word out as sourly as she could. "You never trusted me all, did you?"

"That's not true." Stuart shook his head.

Right. And she was the Queen of England. Suddenly, the brownstone was much too small for the two of them. She needed to leave right now.

"Where are you going?" Stuart asked when she stalked toward the foyer.

"Out." Unless she was fired, she still had the right to come and go as she pleased. "I need some air."

She noticed Stuart didn't try to stop her. Looked like the fantasy truly was over.

Well, like she always said, Prince Charming ain't walking through that door. Instead, *she* was walking out.

"Patience?" Soft though it was, Ana's voice still managed to echo through the brownstone. "Where is she? I thought you said she was waiting for us at home?"

"I thought she was," Stuart told her. A lie. He'd been *hoping* Patience was waiting for them. He had no idea if she'd ever come back after walking out.

This was his fault. If he hadn't been such a jerk when he'd found out about her arrest. But he'd been hurt, and he'd lashed out.

A soft meow sounded behind them. "Nigel, my sweetie pie. Did you miss Mommy?" His aunt hobbled over to the stairway. "He looks like he's lost weight. Don't you think?"

"Maybe. I don't know." At the moment, he was more concerned with Patience's whereabouts. "Maybe she went to the store."

Ana was trying to scratch an excited Nigel's head without falling over. "But she knew we were on our way. Why wouldn't she wait until we got here?"

"Perhaps she went to get something for your return. Tea, maybe." But he'd already discounted his theory soon as the words left his mouth. "Or maybe she's upstairs and can't hear us in her room." An equally lame suggestion, but he clung to the possibility.

"Tell you what," he said, scooping up Nigel. "Why don't I show you what we've set up in the front parlor? Then, while you and Nigel are having a good reunion, I'll go see if I can track down Patience."

But he was pretty sure he knew the answer. The air in the brownstone was different; the silence thicker than usual. By the time he went upstairs and spied Patience's open bedroom door, he was certain.

He stood in the doorway while his heart shattered. The bed where they'd made love this morning had been stripped to the mattress, the bedding folded in neat piles waiting to be washed. She'd left the closet door open. One lone hanger, the only sign the space had ever held clothes, lay on the floor.

A blue scarf hung on the doorknob. He recognized it as the one Patience wore to the dinner dance. Balling the cloth in his fist, he pressed it to his cheek, and inhaled deep. He remembered the way her scent had teased him while they'd danced. The memory mocked him now. The pain in his chest threatened to cut him at the knees.

Dear God, but the house already felt emptier. *And it was all his fault.*

On the bureau lay an envelope with Ana's name scrawled across the front. No goodbye for him, he thought sadly. He didn't deserve one.

"Is she upstairs?" Ana asked when he returned.

"No. She's gone."

"What do you mean gone? I don't understand." Her eyes narrowed when he handed her the envelope. He was doing a lousy job of hiding his feelings, and she knew it. "What's going on Stuart?"

"It's complicated," he replied. "You should read the letter."

"Do you know what's in it?"

"No." But he could guess.

"What does she mean she couldn't bear to face me after I found out?" Ana looked up with a frown. "Found out about what?"

It was the question he'd been dreading. "Patience…" Staring at his hands, he searched for the right words. "Turns out she was keeping secrets." Briefly, he told her about Patience's arrest and her job at Feathers, doing the best he could to leave out the gory details. When he finished, Ana looked back to the letter that was on her lap. "I'm sorry, Tetya."

"I figured her story had to be something pretty awful for her to lie about it."

"She was afraid—" He whipped his head around. "You knew she was lying?"

"Of course, I did. Surely you don't think I'm that

naive." Her glare chased off any possible response. "I could tell she was hiding something during her interview. It was obvious she didn't know a thing about being a proper housekeeper. And the way she stuttered on about forgetting her agency paperwork…the girl is not a very good liar, you know. After she left, I spoke to the agency, and they told me the real candidate had gotten stuck on the subway."

Stuart owed his aunt an apology. She was far sharper than he gave her credit.

"Wait," he said, backing off that thought. "If you knew she was lying, why did you hire her? Why didn't you call her out on the story?"

"Because the poor dear was clearly desperate. Leaping at the chance to clean house?"

"Still, for all you knew, she could have been trying to rob you." The questions were moot at this point. He was simply looking for grounds to justify his mistrust. Hoping for some sliver of a reason to prove he wasn't an arrogant, jaded fool.

"Nonsense," Ana replied. "Patience couldn't hurt a fly. Anyone who spends five minutes with her can tell that."

Yes, they could. Even he, with all his suspicion, had recognized her gentle sweetness. It's why he'd fallen so hard in spite of himself.

"Besides, Nigel liked her and he doesn't like just anyone. That alone told me I could trust her. As for not asking her story…I figured when the time came, she would tell me what I needed to know."

In other words, his aunt had decided based on the opinion of a cat who, sadly enough, was a better judge of character than he was.

"In a lot of ways, Patience reminds me of the animals at the shelter," she told him. "Lost and looking for a place to call home. I know it was a rash decision—a dangerous one, even—but I couldn't turn her away."

"When you put it that way…" It didn't sound so rash at all. Simply confident in the goodness of human nature. Something he'd always had trouble with. He thought he'd conquered his mistrust, but apparently not.

"She has a way of getting under your skin, doesn't she?" Now the guilt arrived, strong and harsh. He'd managed to do what his aunt couldn't: chase Patience away. He'd let her sweetness frighten him and turn him into a bully.

"I've really screwed things up, haven't I?" he said.

"Yes, you have."

Ana never did believe in mincing words. "What do I do?" He looked to her face, hoping in her wisdom she'd have a solution.

"For starters, you can get me my housekeeper back. I care too much for her to lose her."

"Me, too," Stuart whispered. He should never have overreacted the way he did when he'd read Bob's report. If he'd acted calmly, Patience might be here with him right now. Instead, he'd let his heart give in to suspicion. And she was gone.

"She's never going to forgive me."

"You'll never know until you try."

When he shook his head, she reached over and took his hands, her gnarled grip stronger than he expected. "Listen to me. I had the chance to fight for my Nigel. I didn't and I lost him forever. I don't want to see the same thing happen to you. You have already missed out on so many years of happiness because of Theodore and that gold digger he married. Patience is your second chance. Don't be like me, lapushka—fight for her."

His aunt was right. He couldn't give up on Patience. He had to find her if only to apologize for being an ass. How did he track her down, though? He doubted she'd left a forwarding address at the bottom of her goodbye note. But....

There was one person Patience would contact no matter where she ran off to. One person she would never desert. And he had that person's email address. A kernel of hope took root inside him.

Rising, he kissed Ana on the cheek. "I'll be right back."

"Where are you going?"

"I've got to send an important note to someone in France."

"You look lousy."

"Back at you." Patience knew exactly how she looked. Tired and depressed. Same way she felt. "The beds at this place are like boards on stilts. I was tossing and turning half the night." She missed the big comfy bed she had at Ana's.

She missed a lot of things she had back at Ana's.

But that was in the past. With a swipe of her hand, she brushed away her bangs and the painful thoughts. "I've got possible good news, though. The front desk clerk told me they're hiring at the new Super Shopper's Mart. I'm going to go apply today."

"Good luck."

"Thanks." She'd need it. She couldn't afford to hide away in a hotel room forever. Eventually, she was going to have to find a new job and a new place to live. Preferably soon, before she drained her savings and found herself living in her car. Again.

Funny how things came full circle.

"I just hope they don't ask for a lot of references. Or ask too much about my previous position."

"Maybe if you called Ana…"

"No." Patience cut that suggestion right off. That possibility died when she'd walked out.

She hadn't meant to leave so abruptly. Not at first, anyway. When she'd stormed out of the brownstone, she'd truly intended to just clear her head. Problem was, the more she walked around Beacon Hill, the more upset she got. At Stuart for being so damn suspicious of everybody. At the world for being so unfair in the first place.

But mostly at herself for being stupid enough to think she could bury the past. And for letting her guard down. She'd let herself care—more than care—and now her insides were being shredded for her foolishness. In the end, she'd decided she couldn't face seeing Stuart or Ana again, and so when Stuart had left for the hospital, she'd packed her things.

"Don't you think you're being drastic?" Piper asked.

"Trust me, I'm not. You should have seen Stuart's face," she added in a soft voice. For as long as she lived, she wouldn't forget how the betrayal and anger darkened his features.

"Probably because he was mad you didn't tell him. Stinks when people keep information from you."

Patience winced. "I know. I'm sorry." The other night she'd broken down and told Piper about the arrest. Her sister had been ticked off over being kept in the dark, too, although she'd softened when Patience had explained how it wasn't news you shared with your preteen sister.

The thing was, Piper was right. If she'd told Ana everything from the beginning, she wouldn't be in this position. Granted, she probably wouldn't have gotten the job, but she also wouldn't have had to deal with Ana's disappointment. Or with Stuart's. Which, when she thought about the past couple weeks, would have been the best thing of all.

Sure would hurt less, that's for sure.

"I'm not really upset anymore," Piper told her. "Stuart might not be, either. Maybe he decided that the past doesn't matter."

"Right, that's why he had me investigated. Because my past doesn't matter." She still couldn't believe he'd crossed that line. Well, actually, she could believe it. Stuart had said from the beginning he had trust issues. Still… "Who does he think he is, judging me? I may not have made fantastic decisions, but I always had the best intentions. I got you an education, and I kept us off the streets."

"Hey, no arguments from me," her sister replied. "I think you're awesome."

And to think she had been feeling guilty about not telling him. Turns out her subconscious knew best. The only thing telling him about the arrest would have accomplished would be to put the regret in his eyes that much faster. At least this way, she'd eked out a few more days with him.

"I never should have let myself…"

"Let yourself what?" Naturally Piper heard her. When would she learn to keep her thoughts quiet?

She considered brushing the comment off, but Piper wouldn't let her. When she was a kid, she'd made Patience repeat every under-the-breath phrase ever muttered. Maybe talking would lessen the ache in the chest. "Let myself start to care," she said.

"You really like him, don't you?"

Way more than liked. She missed him the way she would miss breathing. "Not that it matters. I told you before, we were having a fling, nothing more, I mean, face it—even if I'd told him everything from the start, he could never seriously love someone like me. We come from completely different places."

"So? Why can't people from different worlds fall in love?"

"Do they? When's the last time someone from our neighborhood got swept off their feet by a millionaire?" *Prince Charming ain't walking through that door.*

"That's not what you used to tell me."

"You're different," Patience immediately replied. "I raised you to be better than the neighborhood."

"I know. You always said I was just as good as the next person."

"You are."

"Then, aren't you?"

Closing her eyes, Patience let out a long, slow breath. "This is different."

"How?"

Because, she wanted to say, the world wasn't black-and-white. Equality in a human sense didn't mean equal in the eyes of society. And while Stuart had no right to judge her as a person, there was a huge difference between not judging someone and falling in love with them.

"Trust me, it just is. A guy like Stuart doesn't want to spend the rest of his life with an ex-stripper."

Before either sister could keep the argument going, a knock sounded on her hotel door. "Who on earth would be banging on my door this time of morning?" Patience asked, frowning. Housekeeping didn't start for another hour.

"Patience, are you in there?"

The sound of Stuart's voice came through the wood, causing her heart to panic. "It's Stuart," she whispered. "He's here." How had he managed to track her down? The only person who knew her location was...

"You didn't," she said with a glare.

"He asked me to contact him as soon as I knew where you were staying. He wants to talk with you."

"Patience, I know you're in there. Please open the door."

She looked over her shoulder before glaring at her laptop where her sister's face was the picture of apology. "What makes you think I want to talk with him?"

"How about the fact that you look like hell? Give him five minutes. What if he's sorry?"

"Sorry, not sorry—I told you, it doesn't make a difference."

"And I think you should hear him out."

"I'm going to keep knocking until you answer," Stuart called from outside.

He would, too. A knot lodged itself at the base of her skull. A ball of tension just waiting to become a headache. Patience squeezed the back of her neck, trying to push the tension away, but the feeling was as stubborn as the man banging on her hotel door.

"Patience?"

"Fine. One minute! I am so going to kill you when you get back to Boston," she hissed at her sister.

"I love you, too," Piper replied.

Whatever. Patience slapped the laptop closed. Might as well get this over with. A quick glance at the mirror told her she really did look terrible. She started to comb her fingers through her hair, thought better of it and went to the door.

"What?" she asked, through the chained opening.

Stuart's blue eyes peered down at her. "May I come in?"

"Anything you need to say, I'm sure you can say from out there." Where she was safer. The mere sound of his voice had her insides quaking. Goodness knows what standing close to him would do.

"You sure you want me airing our dirty laundry so everyone else in the place can hear us?" he asked.

Damn. He had a point. "Fine. Five minutes." Sighing, she unlatched the door and let him in. Immediately, she knew it was a mistake. He had on his weekend clothes. Faded jeans and a T-shirt. The look made him appear far more approachable than his suit. She didn't want him approachable. She wanted to keep her distance.

He jammed his hands into his back pockets. "How are you?" he asked.

"I was doing fine until you got my sister involved," she replied.

"You don't look like you're doing fine."

"How I look isn't your business anymore." Nevertheless, she pulled her sweater tightly around her, feeling exposed in her T-shirt and sleep shorts. "What's so important that you needed to track me down?"

"You left without saying goodbye."

"I left a note."

"For Ana."

"Maybe Ana's the only person I wanted to say good-bye to."

"Ouch."

If he expected an apology, he was mistaken. "Is that all you came about? To critique how I said goodbye?"

"No. I came to find out why you left."

He was kidding, right? "Isn't it obvious?" She started to make the bed, fussing with the sheets the alternative to losing her temper. Did you really think I would stick around so Ana could fire me for lying to her?"

"No one was going to fire you."

Patience stopped her fussing. "Okay, pity me then."

Stepping away from the door, Stuart walked to the opposite side of the bed. The queen-size space suddenly felt too small a buffer zone. The rumpled sheets did nothing but remind her what it felt like to be under the covers with his arms wrapped around her.

"No one was going to pity you, either," he said. "Ana knew from the very beginning. Well, not the specifics, but she knew you lied your way into the job."

"How?" She wasn't sure she should believe him.

"Apparently you're not that good an actress."

What did he say the other day? Body language always gives people away. Here she thought she was fooling everyone, when in reality the only fool was her.

She sank to the bed, her back to him. "If Ana knew... why did she hire me?"

"You know Ana and her thing for strays."

Yeah, she did. Ana believed all creatures deserved a good home. Obviously, she'd believed Patience did, too. A lump rose in her throat, bringing tears. Ana was a greater gift in her life than Patience ever realized.

Suddenly, she felt like the world's biggest jerk. "You're right. I owed her a better goodbye. I'll call her."

"Better yet, why not come back?"

"You know I can't do that."

"Why not? I told you, she doesn't care. *I* don't care."

Behind her, she heard his soft cough. "Look, Ana's not the reason I came. I came to apologize for the way I overreacted the other day. I was a jerk. I should have trusted that you had a good reason for not telling me about the arrest."

"You hired an investigator."

"Yes, I did," he said. "When I first got to town and was worried about Ana. But that was before I got to know you."

"Stop." Next, he'd start saying how much he'd come to like and admire her or some other meaningless sweet talk. Her heart was hurting enough as it was. "I get it. Really, I do. Shame on me for not expecting it."

"Excuse me?"

He came around the foot of the bed until he stood by her knees. Patience immediately fought the urge to scoot backward, to where their personal spaces couldn't merge.

With a swipe of her hair, she gave her best imitation of disinterest. "In a way, the timing couldn't have been better. I mean, we both know we were ending things soon. This way we got the messy part over with."

"What are you talking about?"

"Do you really need me to spell it out for you?" She had to give him credit—he actually sounded incredulous. "A millionaire and an ex-stripper who cleans toilets? Hardly a fairy tale. I knew from the beginning it was temporary."

He met her attitude with one of his own. Arms folded, he scowled down at her with eyes that pinned her to the spot. "Wow, you've got everything all worked out, don't you?"

"I'm a realist. I know how the world works."

"And how would you know what I was thinking? You didn't stick around long enough to find out. Hell, you would have walked out the night of the dinner dance if I hadn't pressed you for an explanation."

He leaned into her face, bringing his eyes and lips dangerously close. "You know," he said, his voice low, "you keep talking about me not trusting you, but I'm not the only one with trust issues. You were so certain you knew what I was thinking, you didn't give me the chance to give you the benefit of the doubt. Maybe, if you'd told me about your arrest. Let me in…"

"I let you in as much as I dared," she told him. "If I told you every lousy thing that's happened in my life, you'd…"

"What? Be disgusted. Throw you out?"

"Yes."

"Bull. You only let me in when circumstances pressured you. If Chablis hadn't crossed our paths, I'd never have found out about Feathers. Trust works both ways, babe." Taking a deep breath, he stepped away.

Patience hugged her midsection. Without Stuart's presence to warm it, the air became cold and empty feeling. "Big words coming from a guy who was still investigating me after we started sleeping together," she murmured.

Her words hit their mark, and he winced. A small

consolation. "That was a mistake," he said. "I meant to call Bob off."

"Of course, you did." He simply forgot, right? "Let me guess, the voice in your head telling you I wasn't good enough wouldn't let you. A woman with her background—no way she could be any good," she whispered, mimicking.

"That's bull."

"Is it?" She wondered. "Why else would a person 'forget' to stop an investigation?"

"Because I was distracted."

"By what? What could possibly be that distracting?" Why she was even bothering to push the issue she didn't know, other than that she needed to hear him admit the truth.

But his answer wasn't what she expected. "You," he said. "You distracted me."

"With what? My banging body."

"No, by being yourself. I forgot to call Bob because I was too busy falling in love with you."

Love? This had to be his idea of a cruel joke. He couldn't really be in love with her. Could he?

Slowly, she raised her eyes and looked into his. There was so much honesty in their blueness it hurt. "How can you love me? I'm—

"Sweet, wonderful, smart..."

"But the things I did. The life I led."

"Sweetheart, those are things you did. They aren't you, not the way you think," he told her. Suddenly, he was in her space again, his hands cradling her cheeks. "I'm in love with Patience Rush. The woman who was willing to do anything, including sacrifice herself, to keep her sister safe. Who survived despite all the hell life threw at her. The woman who was strong enough to pull her and her sister up from that world. That's the Patience I'm in love with."

A tear slipped down Patience's cheek. "When I think about all those years in the club…"

"Shh. Don't think about them. They're in the past." He kissed her. As gentle and sweet a kiss as she ever experienced. She wished she could hold on to the moment forever.

"Come home, Patience," he whispered.

Fighting not to cry, she broke away. "I can't…"

Stuart looked like she'd slapped him. Disappointed and hurt. His expression made the ache in her heart worse. "Can't or won't?" he challenged.

"Can't." Might as well be honest. The past was too much a part of her to let it go. What if a week from now he changed his mind when he'd had time to think? The rejection would be too much to bear.

"I think you should go," she told him.

"Patience…"

She shook him off before her resolve could crumble. "Please. If you respect me at all…"

They were the magic words. Stuart took back his touch. "Fine."

He stopped when he got to the door. Patience didn't turn around, but she heard the pause in his step. "Just remember, all my anger and mistrust was because you were keeping secrets. I never once judged you for your past. If anything, I have nothing but respect for how you survived. Too bad you can't cut yourself the same deal."

CHAPTER ELEVEN

THE TUBE IN the neon *e* was burned out, turning the sign into "Fathers." Patience grimaced at the unintentional creepiness.

She wasn't sure what she was doing here. After Stuart left, she'd tried to call Piper back, but her sister didn't pick up, so she'd spent the day sitting on the edge of the bed, replaying Stuart's accusations in her head. She'd spent the night lying in bed doing the same. At first she was angry. How dare he accuse her of having trust issues? Talk about the pot calling the kettle black. Eventually, however, her emotions turned to the important statements. *I love you*. His declaration scared her to death. How could he love her? *Her*. What did the two of them see in her that she didn't see?

When she finally got out of bed, her thoughts led her here. She stared at the broken neon sign wondering if inside held the answers she was looking for.

The front door of Feathers hadn't changed in her absence. The faded black door was still covered with stains, the source of which she never wanted to know, and the beer stench, so strong it seeped through the bricks to reach outside, still made her gag. Familiar as it was, however, she felt as if she was standing in someone else's memory, as if she'd stumbled across an old photograph in a thrift store. Could it be that she'd changed that much in less than a year?

Back when she started at Feathers, she'd had one dream and one dream only: to give Piper a better life. She'd succeeded, too. In fact, she'd go so far as to say she'd done a damn good job. Not only had she given Piper access to a better life, but all of her sister's dreams were coming true.

Did she dare dream a dream for herself now?

Don't let anyone tell you you're not as good as anyone else. How often had she drilled those words into her sister's head? Maybe she'd have done better to drill them into her own.

Stuart loved her. She loved him. She'd probably loved him from the moment he walked through the emergency room doors. Could she trust their love would last?

Then again, two months ago, she hadn't thought love was possible. Not for her, at any rate. She'd started the relationship with Stuart adamant she wouldn't risk her heart and look what happened: she'd fallen in love, anyway. Being with him had made her feel special. And if she could feel that good while believing their relationship to be a fantasy, how good might she feel if she opened her heart to it completely?

"Well, will you look who's come back." Like a miniskirt-wearing gift that kept on giving, Chablis ambled around the corner. She had a cigarette in her hand. Smoke break. Patience always did find it laughable that taking their clothes off was okay but smoking inside was against the law.

The dancer tapped ash onto the sidewalk. "What's the matter? Boyfriend dump your stuck-up behind?"

she asked, before taking a long drag. Smoke filtered through her magenta-lined lips. Guess you ain't better than us, after all?"

"You know what, Chablis…?" Patience paused. A week ago—even a day ago—Patience might have thrown Chablis's smack talk back in her face. She no longer felt the need. Chablis was stuck in a world Patience no longer belonged in.

"You're right. I'm not better than you. I'm not better than anybody." She smiled. "But I'm no worse, either."

Since Patience didn't expect the dancer to understand what she was saying, it wasn't a surprise when Chablis's face wrinkled in confusion. "Whatever." She reached for the door handle.

Through the gap, Patience saw the dimly lit scenery from a lifetime ago. Once again, it was like looking at someone else's photograph. Stuart was right—Feathers was in her past. The future was what she dared to make of it. That was something else she used to tell Piper. *Don't be afraid to go for your dreams.* High time she took her own advice.

And this time, she was going to do without lying or hiding from who she was. Stuart said he loved the real her? Well, the real her was who he was going to get.

"Excuse me, miss?"

The male voice startled her. Stiffening, she turned, expecting to find a customer. Instead, she came face-to-face with a young police officer.

He gave her an apologetic smile. "Is everything all right? You look lost."

If he only knew. "I was," she told him, "but I think I know where I'm going now."

"Do you need directions? Trust me, you don't want to go in there. It's no place for a lady."

Patience looked at the closed door of her past. "You're right," she agreed. "I think I'd much rather go home."

"You can't manage without a housekeeper," Stuart told Ana. They were having a lousy excuse for breakfast—his version of scrambled eggs and coffee—in the kitchen. Or rather he was. Pieces of Ana's eggs somehow kept landing on the floor for Nigel to eat. She'd been protesting his cooking the past three days. "What will you do when I move out?"

"You could stay."

"Sure." They'd had this argument before, too. "How about I adopt a cat and name her Patience, too. People won't talk."

He knew why his aunt was dragging her feet. She was hoping Patience would change her mind and come back. Stuart hoped she'd come home, too, but he was a realist. It'd been three days since he poured his heart out in Patience's motel room. Three days since he said he loved her. And they hadn't heard a word. Whether he wanted it to or not, life had to go on.

The doorbell rang. "That's the candidate from the employment agency. I'll go get her. Try to keep an open mind," he said.

"If an open mind means telling her no, then fine, I'll keep an open mind."

Rolling his eyes, Stuart left the kitchen, Nigel chasing after him. "I hope you're planning on being cooperative," he told the cat. Otherwise, this was going to be a long morning. He opened the front door...

And froze in place.

On the threshold stood Patience, dressed for work in her blue work shirt and capris. In her hands, she held a feather duster. "Rumor has it you need a housekeeper."

She was back. The hopefulness behind her smile made him want to pull her into his arms then and there, but he resisted. This was her decision; he needed to let her play it out her way.

He settled then for smiling. "Did the employment agency send you over."

"No. I'm just a woman who's made a lot of mistakes looking to start over. I don't suppose there's a place for someone like me here?"

"Oh, there is." He pushed the front door wide. "Come on in. There's a little old lady in the kitchen who's going to be thrilled to meet you."

"Just her?"

"Me, too."

"Good." She smiled. "Although I should warn you in advance. I'm very much in love with this lawyer I know."

Stuart's heart gave a tiny victory cheer. "Sounds like a lucky guy."

"I'm the lucky one. Like I said, I made a lot of mistakes, and am hoping he—you—will give me a second chance."

Now he gave in and pulled her close, kissing her with everything in his heart. "You don't have to ask twice," he told her.

Patience wrapped her arms around his waist. To Stuart it felt that she was afraid he'd disappear. "I'm sorry I didn't trust you," she said into his chest.

"Same here. This time we'll trust each other."

"That's a new thing for me—to trust someone. I

might stumble a little bit." She looked up, her eyes as bright as the brightest chocolate diamond in the world. "Will you be patient with me?"

"Patient with Patience?" Grinning at his lame joke, he kissed the top of her head. "I don't think that's going to be a problem. Both of us are going to screw up, sweetheart. But as far as I'm concerned we've got all the time in the world to teach each other. Forever even."

Her arms squeezed tighter. The word *forever* was scaring her, he knew. Someday it wouldn't, though. Someday she'd realize she was so loved that forever was the only possible time frame.

"Forever sounds like a good goal," she said finally, her bravery increasing the admiration he held for her. "I love you, Stuart Duchenko."

He'd never believed three words more. They'd get to forever. He knew they would. "I love you too. Now…" Giving her a reluctant last kiss, he shut the door. "How about we go make an old lady's day?"

A meow sounded at his feet. "You, too, Nigel."

Together, the three walked toward the future.

Two weeks later

"Why is the phone ringing in the middle of the night?" Stuart groaned. "Don't they realize we're tired?"

"Poor baby. They probably don't realize how hard furniture shopping was for you." Patience grinned at the pout she spied before he covered his head with his pillow. The two of them and Ana had spent the day shopping for Stuart's new condominium. He was scheduled to move out at the end of the week. Ana was disappointed, until she learned Patience would be staying put. For now. As madly as they loved each other, both she and Stuart decided they should take their relationship one step at a time. Eventually, Patience would move in, but for now, there was no need to rush. Like Stuart said. They had forever.

Forever was such a nice-sounding word. Patience believed in it a little more every day. Turned out Prince Charming not only walked through the door, but he stuck around, as well.

"Whoever it is, tell them they're insane," Stuart muttered from beneath his pillow. "Then get under these covers so I can do unspeakable things to you."

"I thought you were sleepy?" she whispered, snatching the phone off the end table.

A hand snaked around to splay against her bare abdomen. "I'm awake now."

She answered without bothering to suppress her giggle. There was only one person who'd call at this hour and she wouldn't care. "Piper?"

"Greetings from England." There was a pause. "I'm not interrupting something, am I?"

"Not yet." She slapped Stuart's roaming hand. "What are you doing in England?"

"Helping your boyfriend, of course. And I have good news, and more good news. Which one do you want first?"

"Start with the good news."

"We found Ana's painting."

"You did!" She sat up. "That's wonderful."

"That's why we're in England. The gallery in Paris gave us a lead on a collector here who purchased one of Nigel's paintings. Turns out, the painting is of Ana.

Almost identical to the one in the background of the picture Stuart emailed."

Seemed silly to be moved to tears over a nude painting, but Patience's eyes started to water. After all these years, Ana was finally getting a piece of her Nigel back. "Ana is going to be so thrilled when she hears the news."

Hearing his aunt's name, Stuart immediately sat up, too, and mouthed the word *painting*? Patience nodded. He pressed a kiss to her cheek.

"Even better, the owner is willing to sell. Tell Stuart I'll email him the name and contact information."

"Thank you so much for doing this, Piper." Ana meant so much to her and Stuart. That they could finally reclaim this piece of her past was but small repayment. "Thank Frederic, as well."

"I will. Now, do you want the other good news?"

Patience looked at the man sitting next to her, feeling overwhelmed with good fortune. She didn't think it was possible for life to get better. However, Piper certainly sounded happy, so she was definitely curious. "Yes. What's the other good news?"

"Well…" There was a long dramatic pause before her sister finally replied.

"I got married."

She nearly dropped the phone. "Did you say married?" How? When? *Who?*

"It's a long story," Piper said. "Do you have time?"

Was she kidding? For news like this, Patience had all the time in the world. "I couldn't hang up now if I tried." She settled back to hear what her baby sister had to say.

By the end of Piper's story, Patience had tears in her eyes. Stuart was right there, his strong arms ready to provide solace. "You going to be okay?" he asked, when she hung up the phone.

"She did it," Patience whispered. "Everything I ever dreamed for her. She did it." Her heart felt so full she thought it might burst.

One of her tears escaped. Stuart brushed the moisture from her cheek and she smiled, thinking about their first night on the roof. "I was so certain Piper would be the only one of us to find love and have a happy ending."

"And now?"

She shifted in his arms, so she could look into the eyes of the man who'd captured her heart the moment he walked through the hospital door. "Now, it looks like I was wrong. Because I can't imagine a happier ending than being with you."

* * * * *